Five Points
Akropolis

ξ

S. Dorman

By the author of

The God's Cycle
ξ

and

Fantastic Travelogue:

Mark Twain and C.S. Lewis
Talk Things over in The Hereafter

Five Points Akropolis

S. Dorman

~ ~

S. Dorman

Five Points Akropolis

© 2010, 2016 by Susan C. Dorman
Hardcover ISBN: 978-0-578-08536-4
Softcover ISBN: 978-0-578-09852-4
Digital ISBN: 978-1-4659-5990-4

S. Dorman
P.O. Box 172
Greenwood, ME 04255
USA

In Loving Memory of

Protective Lion and *Little Fairy*

S. Dorman

We have our forefathers and great-grandames all
before us . . . their general characters are still
remaining in mankind . . . for mankind is ever
the same, and nothing lost out of nature, tho'
everything is alter'd.

PREFACE TO FABLES, ANCIENT AND MODERN
John Dryden

S. Dorman

Anno Domine 1769

ξ

Five Points Akropolis

Heirolynn Out of the Gorge

The year was *Anno Domine* 1769, but the girl did not know it.

In the spring night at the stone-age encampment she fed sticks to the cook fire, one at a time. (The sticks had been gathered in woods along the river.) The fire caught well, flames stepping up the pile, shining into her eyes. She crept back beneath the deep-hanging rock-ledge, again to grind dried kernels into cornmeal with the grinding stone. But for reflecting fire it was dark night. It was A.D. 1769 but she did not know about Time. She did not know of time past. She did not know of time ahead.

Kneeling on cold hard rock she ground fine the maize she had planted, tended and dried—down by the rapids of the gorge where soil was rich and deep. There had been squash and beans, and a store of acorns, beechnuts, and dried berries she would yet be grinding for meal, with which to make cakes and pemmican. And there would be other provender for carrying away, roasted and dried. But she did not think of it. She used both her small hands and ground diligently upon the kernals with a cobblestone from the river. She was nine years old but she did not know it.

Her hands were different in hue from that of her captors, the *True People*. Her skin was the hue of the interlopers who must be kept away, lest there come too many for use by True People. As the girl herself was of use. She understood, rarely, that she was kept, in part, to keep the others away. Often this was forgotten. Hardly anything was remembered.

The Cat-people had been destroyed not far from here, not long ago—to the last child—but she did not know it. She did not know of the Cat-people, though she had heard mention of *People-from-the-Big-Hill* and *People-of-the-Great-Swamp*. Both were of that league of the Longhouse, *Haudenosaunee*. Those two peoples had utterly annihilated the *Lost Nation*, as the Cat-people would be known by interlopers in some future time. She did not know of future time.

11

S. Dorman

She bent to the maize-meal, sifting it, sniffing it. She liked the meal scent. It reminded her of something good and kind. Good and kind were but elusive feelings without any words for them. She had been told nothing of the interlopers but that they be repelled. This was remembered sometimes. Sometimes she saw interlopers again, unexpectedly. She saw them in the same way as seeing what the medicine man or storyteller placed in her mind's eye. These speakers made things visible that had not been there a moment before. The newly visible people and things would be familiar in look by their recurrence in the story or telling. Interlopers looked different and the storytellers did not put them there for her to see. But they came of their own... and she loved them, yet also she was afraid.

The interlopers were cruelly treated, smote, laughed at for cowardice shining in their eyes. They were slain there before her gaze. Again and again. Stoned and cut and stomped. This had happened also to her, but she had not cried. So they kept her. But mostly she did not know this last part, this reason. She had forgotten it. But she saw the bleak turmoil of the slaughter again, heard again the shrieks and cries, seeing their tears shining, falling, before they went down around and on top of her, slain. The heavy bodies covered her and she looked up suddenly, gasping—

There was the fire now, ready with coals for the roasting, and baking of cakes.

True People were themselves dispossessed from the coastal plain by the interlopers. From there they had come away to the deep forest. Now, sparsely, they filled the place of the Cat-people in these wooded hills and valleys. Some of them, too, fringed their buckskin cloaks, as had the others, in cat's tails—the lynx, as the Fronche would call them. These were not now so numerous. The tails were harder to achieve. The girl had one of her own. She had taken this when no one noticed and kept it hidden in a crevice under the ledge. Sometimes she took it out and felt it all over, rubbed its softness gently along her cheek and the backs of her small thin hands. It reminded her.... She could almost see the face of the interloper it tried telling her of.... But not quite. No. She could not see. But sometimes, when she was sleeping, she saw the face bending over her, smiling and light. It did not look like the faces around her on waking. And she could never remember it after.

She looked over at Crowfeather sitting there in coal-light, crosslegged, sewing doeskin with sinew. No, the face would not look like that. Not high with bones, high with looks, not so dark as that. Not those black eyes, pulled straight at their corners.

They were talking now, as she laid cakes on hot stone

12

prepared with oil of the green nut husks. Things seen came into her head as they spoke. These were men's voices but she did not think of that, she did not think which men's voices; though if she had they would turn out to be Clovenfoot and Eaglebeak. The pictures showed True People talking to the *Haudenosaunee* whose language-stock was different. *Haudenosaunee are not to do with True People as they did to the Cat-people*—said the Haudenosaunee with the hair that stood high on their heads, stiff like the crests of birds. They want to smoke the pipe and treat with True People to make war, joining together against interlopers. *So that is good,* say the things seen, full of sunlight and clouds, the top of the hill, the scent of the pipe. The interlopers will be destroyed and we will live and keep on in this place. We will not be driven from here as from that other place far away nigh the sea. And we will have weapons, the long slender sticks that flash and roar.

The slender sticks came into her mind. They were in hands held out, arms stretched and level, left arm crooked, covered in coat sleeves she had not seen before. But she had seen them before: She just did not remember. She did not remember the three-corner hats they wore, but she saw them. She gazed at the cakes among the coals without seeing the cakes.

These things are what I saw before, she thought now. But not in these words, not in words. *I have seen these men with tails under their hats. I have seen the sticks flaming.*

And they turned to her like that, smiling, and they called *Heirolynn,* and they ran after fallen game. But she could not see what game. She could not remember it. Their faces were pale, they went away.

Intently she lay studying the pattern above her, white stars snared amid high branches and crisscrossed twigs. Every-which-way, fascinating. She studied and found the precise weave of the pattern, warp and weft, and how each small bright white star so rightly fit in its twig-sewn space. The next time she looked, the stars had moved places, but that meant it was right to study again. Her bed was spruce covered in patched deerskin she herself had sewn of leftovers Crowfeather permitted by leaving them there for the girl to find. She fitted the feel of the spruce twigs beneath her into the pattern.

The rapids below sounded rough and white. True People were talking about her. It did not often happen. She was stupid and clumsy. One not far away in the woodland had said this against her. Said another beneath the pattern of stars and twigs, *But she did not cry.* Voices trading words in the dark and among white rough rapids sounding.

She can grind maize without stopping until done. See how

13

she sets the twigs to make the fire?   Just so. No one does that.
And with great concentration. She stares but not in a good trance
like the *meteu*. She doesn't look went I speak. She is an interloper.
We can do some but not all to make her True People.

The talk fitted into the pattern she saw. Here it was: sounds
in the surrounding, above-looking and below-feeling. It all aligned
this way, that way: Just so. There. It was right now. All were
perfectly fitted together. The girl fell down into sleep. She did not
think it. It was part of a pattern, too, that she did not know she fell
down into sleep.

In the next day's pattern she ground maize, and wandered
away. The river was here, flowing on her left hand hanging loose by
her side. Sometimes as she walked the hand flew up, the thin arm.
She saw it from the corner of her eye. If she tried to do it, to see it
fly up by looking directly, it went away. The flying part went away.
She kept following downstream, away from the rapids. More Rapids
would show, it was part of a pattern.

Not True People. Clumsy. Stupid.

The pattern picked up the song, sing-song. The girl's
chanting continued, gathering bits and pieces of words, of syllables,
sounds; the chippings of birds, the clickings of squirrels. If anyone
came—the fixed look of the fawn. Everything went into the pattern
of everything, and she passed by True People river bathers and kept
on. They were calling to her and laughing, it fitted the pattern: The
sing-song ceased before the calling started, it ceased at the fixed look
of the fawn.

The girl drifted on going deeper and deeper, the gorge growing
greater, the stream longer. On kept the girl, her arms sometimes
flapping. Once she stopped to examine the rock. She climbed onto
it, weathered and worn. Not smooth, not rough. Some texture
between. Dark. It sloped. She sat down, her feet and legs dangling
over the edge. Her palms were flat on the rock, either side of her.
She looked at the grim rock, not at the view with twig patterns
etching, surrounding brown hillsides. The rock grew older and
older. She sensed this because the rock made her older and older.
There was a long time ago, she saw briefly now. There was a very
long time ago filled with strange things. There was ice, she heard
the envoy saying; saw the great ice told him by the crest-headed
people. Long, long ago. Long. Long. Long, long. Long-long ago-
ago, long long ago. Before the interlopers, long long ago. Almost
now she was the rock. The girl was the rock of long long ago.

The afternoon shone into the river ahead where the river stopped,
walled with deep forest. She kept on toward it: over freshets falling,
over deadfall, over springs gurgling, over rocks large and small,

sometimes the arm flapping, sometimes it was still. There ahead the bright sunfall sheeted the river. On she kept, walls of the gorge parting. Yellow-golden light—pouring through there ahead—made the girl forget herself, the singsong of herself. Forget she was clumsy, stupid, not True People. Golden light lit with dust fetched her deep into a pattern, yellow-light-shaft ending the river ahead.

But now. As she went, abruptly the pattern changed. The sing-song stopping, quiet light pouring onto the river ... but the river was changed. It did *not* end. The river did not stop but kept going, looping, amid low green patches; there were oxbows. It turned a different way. She did not recollect names of the six directions so much as the pattern, new pattern itself speaking the old True People word. *South.* The river turned south around the lowering hillside.

" '*The ice!* " She sang it then, seeing it. " 'We will be as the great ice growing and pushing. We will push, together, interlopers away.' " Her thin voice, in the words of True People, sang upwards without thought out of the departing gorge.

The steep wooded hillside of the bend lowered away southward on the river's far side. Many times the clumsy girl had fallen on the journey down river.

It was dark before she stopped to lay down for the pattern. She lay on the hillside gazing into trees, gazing beyond to the moon-brightened dimming of stars. She did not see the moon directly. It was there in the hill behind, casting brightness. She did not see the clan planning the-getting-back-of-her to them, nor hear their words spoken in trees by the cook-fire beneath the great overhanging rock. Nor did she have pictures for her mind's eye that this would have conjured had she heard.

She studied the pattern, such as it was: There was the wider sky above the river, there the steep hillside, the river sinuous long sometimes looping beneath it. There, straight above, were the branches and small few faint stars. There the sounds of the wind—not down here with her. —The faint jolting beat almost dead center of her. She shivered and chattered and burrowed deeper. The leaves began covering her by her hands plucking them. The chattering stopped, the shivering. If she had but known it: She'd gone to sleep again in the pattern of life. A pattern of life's captivity.

Something woke her. She did not know what, nor care; did not think of it. The moon shone on her now, great calm white eye not in a pattern but in the sky. She jumped up, the leaves falling from her. She stood still. The sounds were none but an owl hooting, one remote over there, one up there; and of softly flowing river, down where the moon lapped in it. It shone there also, she saw, further down-river's length. She went low to the sandbar in its long curve and stood looking. Then she stooped and brought damp sand up, rubbed it on her arms, on her legs. She shivered and jumped. She knelt in the wet sand, leaned to the water, stuck in her face, waggled and washed it. She drank then the water, stood and walked down the stream in moonlight, going on. Going on.

Going on, going on. She did not now drift, not wander so much as look about at all things there for her gaze, moon showing shadows and twisting of roots and leafless bushes, deadfall and sandbars and curves. She liked the feel of the sand in her feet, the arches and soles, the gripping toes. She liked deep woodland soil with its blanket of leaves.

When she walked into dawn there joined the river with another making it more. Two Rivers, she saw, and the flight of geese overhead going back the way she had come. Dawn showed the tips of nearby twigs, swollen and reddish, where alders and willows tangled and hung in the flood two streams were making. She waded in and walked, she swam to the upstream out of the confluence and climbed out, dripping—as befitted the pattern—on the right hand side. Not the sun's side—the other side, the west, given the movements of light. Time was unknown. It was the movement of light on the work she did—work she'd stepped out of, stepped out of that pattern and into the river's pattern. Rivers moved different from light, but not from rain, not from snow, nor snow's several kinds. River was a fullness of these moving over the earth and in troughs, and hollows; quicker here, slower there. Rain fell most in sheets, but sometimes in pieces. So too did snow. But all fell. Light she did not perceive as falling except when it sometimes looked like a wall coming down from clouds, in broad strokes and very still.

The girl was walking upstream. One side of the ravine, on her left hand, was spread broad, not narrow as in the gorge where were the rapids, and the cooking cave that was high wide and cold. Above her it steepened on her right hand.

She did not fit the scouts in a pattern, coming downstream from the gorge in vessels, canoes. Not True People, not Cat-people, interlopers, bird-crest-people, swamp, hill—people, the kind she had had pictured for her in the mind's eye. People did not fit well the pattern. Most times they were beings unaccounted for, intruding, unwanted, requiring. The maize made sense, the grinding stone, the awl to poke holes for the pattern in deerskin. Now they were nought—the people were nought, even the familiar True People. She did not fit the scouts, coming after her, into the pattern.

The river's pattern she was working, her trail aligning, the leavings of her feet, their imprint stitching behind her. She looked back and saw them in a curve of the sandbar, following her. The other rivers were now behind, traveling northward while she traveled south. While the moon had shone the way, the first river had turned and twisted across and through a pattern, and the hills had seemed to agree with this because they were shaped so. She looked back again and saw her track aligned with the river—but against the way of its movement, as though in contrary or complement, she knew not. She did not know these words in any language. She knew patterns, rhythms, sensations, mind pictures, scarcely any emotion, no philosophy, right-nor-wrong doing. Simple words. Pain. She knew pain, simple words. Pain came with people. Pain came with mishappening things—stones falling, feet slipping on stone, a mishandling of the awl. Pain could not be recalled, was forgotten. Was not except when it lingered or came again in a pattern.

Late in the day... the stream she now felt to follow the sun's invisible trail.

She had eaten little all day, small curled emerging fern heads in flat moist places streamside, and a bit of the pemmican she almost always had in her pouch. That was most sustaining, tasty with fat and dried roast meal, nutmeat and dried berries, several kinds. But it would not last. She did not think of it. It was to hand or not when needed. That was *all*.

The girl had followed the sinuous day-long stream valley until its tributary crossings, hitherto small, met with a larger. She stood looking upstream there, at both streams. She followed the smaller. It felt right.

The hills went lower, the sky in its leaving light closer. She came to another stream, joining, also smaller than this, the latest sinew of drawing forth through a pattern. She went upstream, it narrowed and laughed with her, bubbling. She looked around suddenly, stood as a stock, stopped looking. She was the fawn again.

They did not care if she perceived them. Young scouts of True People, but very few, had come after her, for the joy and because it must be. The tracking of youths, mere boys, was good practice but she was not tolerable quarry, they thought; not even as deer to be watchful and careful. Though she could stand invisible were she so moved, they knew it of her. The scout boys came on, playing the day long, down the river and up the creek, tracking her. Stopping at vines hanging down through the trees, swinging and dropping; stopping at rocks jutting, jumping to the swimming hole; stopping to tickle the river trout—always half-mindfully following the girl.

Brown with faint moony glimmers, between gray-seeming gently greening slopes, the stream now was small, scarcely wide

enough for her length athwart. Still she followed. It was thickly
wooded country, small slopes. She followed not far before finding
the black shadow on her left hand. Feet dripping, she climbed out
toward it and sat down against the shadowy rock-ledge. Here it was
very dark, almost black. She lay curled against it, facing the hard
bosom. She reached round and over the rough surfaces, her hand
seeking the crevice where the cattail lay. But found it not. She had
forgotten the place, had never known it. This was not where the
cattail was hidden, but some other rock, some otherwhere in another
pattern. She had been like the stars to move places in the warp and
weft while she slept, but she had moved out of her own familiar
pattern and now had not the cattail to fondle, had not the kind pale
face to recall in the dream.

The boy-voices, speaking True People (led by Red Fox), had
ceased distant murmuring. There were no canoe deeps on the little
stream. But she was not thinking of it. She was sleeping. The
pattern was set to change again. There would be a newer, stranger
way.

August 1900 A.D.

ξ

Willie

The girl knew nothing of dwarf-wanderer Pluto's completion of his
steeply inclined and eccentric orbit around the sun—beginning in
Anno Domine 1769. Sensitive to the orbit of Neptune, sensitive as
well to minutiae in the solar system, the dwarf planet was worked
upon by the chaos in his own orbit ... and was perhaps a chaotic
worker among the millions of bodies or objects orbiting earth's sun.
His orbit begun in 1769 would end—that is, begin again—in 248.09
years. But the girl knew nothing of planets, orbits, dates or years,
she knew nothing of Pluto. 1900 A.D. knew little or nothing of Pluto
as well.

Distantly bore the storm-sound to the girl's sleeping ears, waking
ears. Not like storm coming in winter—first above and beyond the
gorge from northward, humbling. Not the remote then swooping
gusts of summer that upended leaves. But she thought not of these
more familiar storm sounds when she heard it.

It opened her eyes in the dark and she saw very fine green
light, very few and fine—lines regular, intersecting, long. The girl lay
against rock in the dark, staring at the new pattern of light. There
were smells here, earthy and moldy and like mushrooms. And some
kind of smell she had not before. She did not decide the light
familiar. But it was. She had seen something like it before. She lay
watching it. Perpendicular line of green light in the dark before
her—with slim light sills at top and bottom either side, regularly
intersecting. The light faded away in the dark from its centerline of
bright lengthy green. She lay lit in the dark, studying the peculiar
perpendicular and horizontal lengths of light.

She did not remember the boy-voices calling her. She did not
remember the recent travels. She thought not of the gorge, camp-
cooking, grinding, white rapids, moonlight, wandering night and day.
Not the streamlet she had followed. She looked at the geometric
light-lines splitting her darkness. She stood and went to these, still

staring. She reached out to touch the light, desiring intently to feel of it.

Its edges were rough. She ran small, thin, lit fingers along one edge, snagging a splinter or two. She sucked unconsciously on the fingers, staring at the big green light. Big because it was close. She put her eye up to it, looked out into the light. Her one-eyed gaze was taken complete out of the dark, and looked on things green: shorn grass, high leafy trees. Stones stood there. More regular in placement and shape than any she'd seen. Staring outward with one eye, she leaned on the light.

It burst opened wide. Her balance self-correcting, there she stood outside the dark in the green summer. And the storm-sound had grown great.

She stood listening. It was full of voices, full of rumbling low thunder, lit with shrieks like flashes of lightning—but sounds. The sound-storm was big here, big with sunlight strewing through leafy limbs and shedding on shorn grass. She'd never seen grass like it—except.

She saw the cow eating, in her mind's eye. She did not say *cow*, did not think cow. She saw cow and shorn grass beneath it. She smelled the sharpish rich scent that made her retch. She did not see it, but the kind face was near. The cat's tail was not in the crevice.

"You can't sleep in the tool crib! You vagrant, you urchin!" He grabbed for her, expecting she'd run—he'd let her run, he wanted her to.

But she stood there: She was the fawn but he saw her anyway. He was taller, gave her a shove. "Go on!"

She fell and he reached down, sorry, pulled her up on her feet still staring. He looked at her, he looked at her staring place, a slate marker in the memorial yard. One of the Beckley Post markers for the Civil War veterans. He squatted, not too close, looking in her eyes, searching—and saw not a glimmer of return.

He stood then, looking at her all over, noting the patched garment of soft... mud-colored—chamois it was. He was tempted to touch it but thought better of this. One of her pockets looked greasy, and the pouch, thong-hanging around her neck, seemed empty and flat. Her long hair was the wildest tangle he'd ever seen. Looked like it had briars in it. A squirrel's nest his mother would call it. But worse. Her face was not filthy, but it and the skin of her arms were red with rash, or maybe scratches.... "I'm Willie, who are you?" He said it low, as though to himself, expecting no answer. He stood thoughtful, aloof, thumbs running up and down the insides of his suspenders. "Ain't you gunna move?" He saw no recognition in her.

He looked then at the vault out of which she'd come, heavy oak framed slate doors ajar. Inside were shovels for digging graves, and other grounds-keeping tools. He knew the vault. Liked to kid his pals about it. It was his work area when he wasn't out on the grounds of the *Akropolis Rural Cemetery*, mowing, picking up fallen branches, or digging a grave. It was the oldest structure in the cemetery (as he called the grounds—though to his pals, the Five Points Gang, it was the graveyard). The vault had been intended for tools from the beginning, but it had also been a showpiece to let refined clientele know what to expect in the way of shelter for themselves, for their dead. His mother had joshed: These tombs were finer than an apartment house for Five Points—Five Points, where immigrant tenant families were stacked together with less room than the dead required for their stone cold rest. Sometimes he sat in there looking out, smoking a fresh rolled cigarette, surveying his peaceable realm.

But those clothes. He'd never seen anything like them except in the minstrel entertainments, or the church or school play. Nobody wore that. Again he was tempted to touch the soft garment, thought she might take no notice if he did—but again decided against it. Her standing there, staring, began to tell in him. His flesh creeped—a little—and he backed off a bit more. At first he was affronted that she'd take no notice of his speaking, but now he wondered how it would do if she did.

He turned and walked slowly, thoughtfully, over the lawn toward the memorial, pretending to see to the gate in the picket fence surrounding it. When he looked up from unlatching, relatching, unlatching it (the hinge he was wanting to check squealed), he felt her near and stopped, flesh a'creep. He looked back over his shoulder. She stood by, staring at Lt. Beecher's slate marker.

He trimmed his voice to a curt matter-of-factness (it wanted to quaver), saying, "You should not have been in the vault nor yet the grand cemetery. Go on home.... You live around—somewhere...." The spoken word died. She took no notice. Standing near, staring.

Something familiar.... He remembered the minstrel entertainments from last spring. The ghoul had been featured in it, one of the living dead like is spoke of in the Bible. Also the Arabian grave walker who plundered and fed off the unsuspecting living in the vaudeville. *That had a look of one walking and dead. So did this.*

Stepping backward, shoulders hunching, he turned, looked wildly about. Hoping to see someone, a mourner, his boss Mr. Sneed; or maybe one of his pals come sneaking in to distract him from work, beg a chew or the makings, tobacco. But there was no one. The sun shone, early and golden, into the green lawn surrounded and scattered with elegant tall elms and monuments, mausoleums, markers, neo-Gothic tombs. Here and there gold shone off a marble vase trimmed to catch and reflect back the light.

He edged past the picket fence and began to run along the cinder path down toward the gravel lane, intersecting on its way to the gatehouse. As he pounded along he passed over the tile culvert laid in long ago to carry off the old streamlet which poured in the basin between knolls shouldering either side of the cemetery. This place of rest between downtown and Five Points.

It was the same stream the girl had followed but the night before; True People boys following to bring her back along the bending rivers to the camp stone-kitchen, to her job of grinding the meal. Only the night before.

The girl stood looking at the green-shining memorial yard nubbled and darkened by upright narrow stones with their strange regular etchings. She had never seen anything so regular. Not that she tried to remember, it did not occur to her to try. They but called to her, "Come put your fingers here, even with splinters, see what we feel like to your fingers."

So she walked through the squeaking gate. This squeak stopped her and she swung the gate to and fro, making the gate squeal, this way and that. There was something not quite unfamiliar in it. She kept after the gate, making it move this way and that. The mind pictures showed her another, not too unlike it, but there the ground was packed black beneath it, and the trees were high, thick and dim. Yet it was not the same sound. There had been no such sound. Only the swinging back and forth. This was the difference between the leathern and steel hinges, between Rovmorian mission pioneer housekeeping and the industrialized New World. But this time-pattern, with its long scope, impinged not on the girl. She walked over the shorn lawn to a marker stone with its regular carving. She had seen carving before, in wood, but all those carvings were faces, totems—were animals and birds. Some looked like Crowfeather, like Clovenfoot, like Eaglesbeak, almost like True People.

The new person did not look like True People as much as an interloper. He was an interloper—not quite True People. Not quite not True People. He was a difference in the pattern of people. She was different, too. Almost she understood the pattern of his speaking.... If not the thought it held, then the sounds it was sounding.

The etchings stayed still under her moving fingers. They spoke only of stone and strangeness and regularity. Her fingers found no more of understanding. She felt the stone and thought of maize and meal and her grinding. But she remembered something.

Yes.

She was not True People. Clumsy. Stupid. That was what the grinding was for—clumsy. Stupid. An interloper: Fear shone in his eyes.

She stood listening. The storm was sounding, but not like a storm. The storm stood still about the edges, sounding above and beyond the shorn vale in its green-golden light. The storm was not remote, as though coming. The storm was there, and there, and there. She turned slowly, pointing with both arms extended, feeling, listening to this pattern. It clanked and rumbled, and gave off shouts, was lit with sudden sounds high-pitched, undergirt with rumbling. A horse neighed in the neighborhood above her and she saw a picture: Horses were in the hamlet and in the village and in the barn or were pulling the blade through soil.

As she turned—her arms thrown out—pointing upward, over, under (down past the falling stream); this way and that; to north to south to east to west and in between all these—she got a movement in the corner of her vision, and stopped. Stood still. Small, down that way, eastward (by the sun—she was not unconscious of it), they were coming.

She saw not who. She knew not who was coming.

It was the fearful groundskeeper, Willie, and Mr. Sneed, the former gesturing toward her and toward the vault. Along the quiet path a few other vaults were lined up, here and there, between evenly spaced and upstanding stones. Solid and impassive, arching; pillars and cornice stones, carved in a lacework, weathering to mellow darkness, various in shades. She stared at the great rubber-baron's vault, all marble and granite stone, stones freighted (had she known it) over land and sea.

The murmur of their voices grew, in its nest of storm sounds that did not tell of storm so much as living mysterious patterning. Unresolved, as were all her mysteries.

Mr. Sneed looked sternly at the ragamuffin girl, peppered her with words, with queries, comments and instructions, all scarcely before he came into articulate earshot. Insistent. His soundings came not like the other, the big boy's, but like a lengthening impenetrable thicket of brambles, rapid with thorns, with arrows, barbs. At length he stopped and took her by thin shoulders, either hand, not big hands, but one lit by a ring. He squatted and put his face beside hers, such as the boy had not dared to do, eye to eye, and tried to call her from her trance—for so he almost thought it.

Almost. He had a suspicion, fully formed the instant he laid eyes upon her sudden non-movement—after all that turning and pointing. Mr. Sneed thought perhaps it had not been silently done (it had been, and without her singsong). It had been some sort of

Five Points Akropolis

game: And she was having them on as well. He scoffed at Willie's tales of ghouls and minstrel fables and whatnot. The girl was simply playing—and ought not to be!—playing in the grand cemetery! This was the height of disrespect. What if someone came early to mourn their dead and found the unkempt thing playing on their loved one's grave? All these things he'd said to her and now his anger boiled to see such disrespectful unresponsiveness. He shook her very hard. Neck snapping, her hair waggling about her face, shadowing. She would not look at him. (She looked at the asymmetric scattering of freckles before her.)

"Here!"

He almost hollered in her face, red with rash, her rat's nest hair thick about her, head and shoulders, moving like shrubbery. Her eyes refused to look... and yet.... He hesitated, hands yet upon her.

Willie stood by watching. "That's all wrong. She is a queer ghoul or a foreigner, Mr. Sneed."

Mr. Sneed's voice was rapidfire, clipped. "She can't be a ghoul, Willie."

"Why not, Mr. Sneed?"

"Because I don't believe in ghouls and neither should you. This is the 20th-century now, young man. There are no ghouls. There is a rational explanation for what ails the girl and takes but a physician or a scientist to tell it."

"Oh," said Willie, feeling some relief. "That's right. The 20th-century.... Will she see a doctor, do you think?"

"You mean, will the doctor see her?"

Willie knew on the instant what that meant. She would have to pay the doctor: She would have no money for the doctor. Not even a chicken or some eggs to give him.

"Be that as it may, it is no concern of ours. Ours is to take care of the Cemetery and grounds, help the architect see to the building of houses for its dead, and maintain the dignity of their resting place." He stood, took up the girl's hand and led her somnambulant through the Civil War memorial yard, out its squeaking gate.

Robins chirped, each in its own separate territory among high branching elm bowers along the path. The trio passed under their song, and down to the white pea-gravel of the lower lane, contrasting crosswise at the intersection. The girl saw the crux of black-and-white paths crisscrossing with also their contrasting textures—the black finer particles, the white coarser—and kept on, her hand high as they walked: His own hand, beringed, was higher than hers, leading.

"She is not hurt, not sickly otherwise, and no great concern

25

as she is—despite her peculiarity." Mr. Sneed was engaging his rational part to inure him to her condition, but Willie felt himself—if relieved of responsibility—still at a loss. *What about the rash?*

Upon reaching the lane nearby the ornate neo-Gothic lodge, Mr. Sneed handed her to Willie—verily picking up the boy's hand, placing it around hers—and told him to lead her down into the way below.

There the street was elegant in shade and something of a main thoroughfare itself; leading indirectly toward downtown, a boulevard split with grassy lawn down its midst, intersecting Market Avenue, leading to downtown. The young man looked perplexed at his boss, who was not much taller than his own adolescent gangling frame.

"But what'll we do with her?" *Just leave her stand?*

Mr. Sneed did a quick calculation for time lost to lawn-mowing on the errand. He said, "Take her up the hill to the church. The big one." In this he meant the darkening massive pile of St. Invincible. Before the boy had asked Sneed had given it no thought, supposing her best disposed for his own purpose on Market Avenue. But seeing Willie's face, he decided instantly on the other course. It suited. The religious would better be able to find exactly where she belonged, and it occurred to him, perhaps through Willie's troubled look alone, that she should really go somewhere particular.

Willie stood with her while Mr. Sneed turned again toward the grand picturesque lodge, as the gatehouse was known. Yet more uneasy, Willie watched his boss disappear, dapper in three-piece finely woven suit, but without his bowler, slipping under the Etalianate portico into the lodge. He dropped the girl's hand and gazed up toward the street slightly above the quiet boulevard. On his right the boulevard itself led to a knoll topped with grand mansions and carriage houses. It was said that the man who invented the electric light bulb was married up there in a mansion. On the left went the boulevard out to the busy street. He was to go that way up the hill to the big dark church on Market Avenue. Scarcely looking at her he started off that way.

He stopped, looked back, gestured, said *C'mon*, but she stood there. He came back, reluctantly, gingerly picked up her hand and led her. He did not want to be seen on this wretched errand, but what could he do? Also, he still felt her something of a ghoul, and could not quite gather the 20th-century into himself as quickly as did Mr. Sneed.

This part of the street was paved with steamrolled layers of cinder, sand, and gravel. Its sidewalks were wooden planks. Main Street, up the opposite hill, was all brick-paving, recently replacing wooden blocks that used to pop out after frost. They went up the opposite way, up Market Avenue toward the church, Willie before her, as far ahead as he could walk, the length of their two arms between them. His demeanor was purposeful and yet with a gloss of nonchalance, an expression of hope that no one of the many passersby would take notice. The effect was confusing, neither one nor the other of his poses sufficing to cover acute embarrassment.

There went the omnibus passing before shop windows opposite, its iron-bound spoked wheels rumbling along, its stogie-smoking driver teetering, perched high above the coach behind two small sturdy chestnut draft horses with blinders. The driver looked down on them. Willie watched the coachload bitterly, every face turned, eight or a dozen, staring out the windows at them as though in some trance akin to the ragamuffin girl's. He looked back to see if she noticed them or even the whole of the lumbering coach, *The Republic Omnibus*, squeaking, rumbling, swaying. She stared at nothing, led by his hand, unable to keep his pace. How could she be staring at nothing, he thought, as he turned back, climbing the hill over the sidewalk, feet clumping on its planks.

All the crowded avenue opposite, shopkeepers setting out crates of fruits and vegetables, janitors sweeping, window-washing; playing children weaving in and out, pointing: But her look was decidedly inward, seeing nothing at all. The eyes were her watch holes—but people, interlopers, might see into them, too. Instead, without concentration, the girl was immersed in the rest of the pattern, the sounds, smells, touches, light flashes, shadows passing along: the play of the experience upon all her senses. She was held down in the storm. Whether she might rise up out of it was not in her thought. She was in the storm and it covered her, sensory, and there were multitudes—interlopers—in the pattern. Too many people and they made most the pattern, pushing her under them. She waited and followed, unthinking, until she should be uncovered again.

Willie left the girl, burning wax smell in her nostrils, gazing at flaming votary candles in their red glasses. High stained-glass reared above with its passionate procession, pouring forth lights of its own down through heights, and also onto the darker opposite leaded glass panes. Candle smell mingled with the overarching dankness, keeping it at bay.

When he came back with the religious he found her still standing as though she had not stared wonderous at the color-filled patterns surrounding the great church.

"May I go, ma'am?" He asked, his adolescent voice squeaking and cracking. His voice had not finished changing and he was ashamed at its treble-and-tenor breaking—sounding at once small

and too large in the cavernous place. Of course he could not
address the nun as sister. That would be outlandish, as his mother
might say. His mother had come to the great stirring stinking town
from the country, the country girl, farm girl knowing a farm girl's
hardship and isolation. The town itself had seemed to her
outlandish, as she recollected it to him, now and again.

This bespeckled black-wrapped, wimple wearing religious,
peered at the girl's rashes, scrutinized her ragtag garment and bare
feet, saying, "And you told all—haven't left anything out?" Carefully
she inspected the girl for fleas and lice.

"No," he said, desiring escape but careful to show patience of
body. He would tell her of the job that was waiting and how
important it was, but only if necessary. "I mean, yeah, I said all as I
found it—we found it."

"Very well then. Yes. You may go. Slowly, quietly, if you
please." She said this with a touch of asperity as though she knew
every vice and subterfuge within the young bosom of humanity; and
would not suffer in the slightest its continuance if she might restrain
it.

Willie was relieved; happy to give a nice display of decorum
since it meant parting in good conscience with the small ghoul.

He whistled all the way back downhill, occasionally throwing
a bit of hop-skip into his footfalls, soft-shoeing over the planking.
On his right hand he passed a great mansion already drowning in
overgrown hedges of cedar and juniper and fir. That was the Old
Churman's mansion, the one who had designed all the rubber-
making machinery and then up and died, leaving all to his daughter
and the church to care for her. Wrought-iron palings with leafy
speared tips scarcely contained the growth of prickly evergreen. He
had picked up a discarded barrel stave on his way downhill and held
it level, rat-tating the bars as he passed downhill. *There are no
ghouls in the 20th-century*, he thought, determining to forget all about
it, whistling.

But, when he saw the tool crib again after stopping by Mr.
Sneed's office, he grew thoughtful. Coming toward it over the cinder
path he slowed, looking the vault over carefully.

It was not so grand as what had come after its (showpiece)
construction. For the first time he studied the great stone behind it.
Ledge outcrop of rough unhewn sandstone—wingéd rock—extending
on either side behind the vault's walls and its faux Gothic front. He
pulled the doors wide, propping them, and went inside with as much
sunlight as possible. There were his grave-digging pickaxes and
shovels lining the left-hand wall. (Sometimes he called for help from
one of his chums, with Mr. Sneed's permission; especially if more
than one grave was called for that day.) On the right were push

mowers, in the rear a wheelbarrow, and in the front corners, either side the doorway, some old copper urns. On a shelf above the barrow were oilcans and rags, imparting the smell, with must, coming at him on propping the doors. The shelving was detached. Nothing was attached to the great outcropping rear wall (much greater than the vault itself). He knelt not far from the barrow and examined the packed earth in the gloom. Packed earth was all it was.... Now what was the ghoul doing in here? He stood up, gazing around again. He walked out, puzzling, onto the lawn. He turned and looked back into the vault. Indirect late morning light shone onto its floor, diffusing over the iron implements against the wall of man-hewn stone.

He turned, looking up above the grand cemetery toward Bechtel Avenue, the noise of the busy street coming down muted through shrubbery and trees. She might have come that way, through bushes and over the low stone wall, crept over the lawn, entered the vault that he seldom locked, and so slept the night away.... But still; where had she come from dressed outlandish, so uncombed, and slow-headed? *Like a groundhog.*

He reentered and drew out the lawnmower, squealing and clucking, went back in to the shelf and got down the oil can. Willie got to work on the grounds and kept at it all day, mowing. Late in the afternoon Mr. Sneed did not wait for his return but went to him in a distant sector, where Willie was mowing next the stone wall near the Stock Exchange Street entrance.

"Willie, we've got another grave for you to get started on before leaving today. It's small, so you'll have time enough to finish digging in the morning well before the procession gets here with the Ripley child's coffin."

Willie nodded and turned over the mower handle, starting back easily with it beside the man beneath leafy trees on one of the white gravel lanes. He got the dimensions by heart, and was shown where the plot lay. It was for a child and would not take so long digging as that for a grown man.

The day's work had put the strange girl from his mind, except at odd moments when his mind wasn't wanted for its other pleasures, such as invention, picturing the minstrelsy, working on sums, or recollecting *The First Men In The Moon*—which Parry had been steadily reading to him from the Harper's Weekly. On account of his labors and preoccupations, Willie was seldom in trouble like some others of the Five Points Gang. But when she came to mind again at some odd moment, such as when he sat down for a bite of bread and cheese or for a smoke, there she was again. Until somehow he succeeded in banishing her—usually with the thought that she'd be gone for a nun, or taken back to the asylum from which she had slipped out by accident. Slipped out by not thinking of it, he was sure. But Mr. Sneed had, after his own surmise, convinced Willie that she was no ghoul but an escapee. Probably insane.

Probably insane. This conjecture had opened up all sorts of ideas in Willie's brain about what can go wrong with people and what might or might not be done about it if so. The thought that it might happen so to him did not enter his thought, but he did recollect stories he had read or heard, one in particular full of traveler's tales, about one crazed—held in a dark stone pit underground until cured. He had heard of an asylum in A'ndian Falls, the town just north of Akropolis, where the crazed were kept in chains and fed on bread and water, but he was afraid to credit this last. In the 20th-century crazed people would be studied and experimented upon, not made into prisoners like beasts in cages.

He laid out the small plot before the upright family marker, dug in and flung a shovelful of sod and dirt, and another and another. The smell of earth filled his nostrils and, as always, he thought of earthworms feeding. He spied a few dark-red wet ends wriggling, sticking out in quest of what was going on. He was glad of coffins whenever he saw them. And there were other things underground, he knew, meant to feed on bodies and help break them down to make more earth and nourishment. It helped to think, sometimes, how everything was put together—but he never talked about it with his chums—except for Aneas, maybe Johan. Willie liked to read of scientific things and machine marvels.

Five Points Akropolis

Among the Wilusas

After work at 7 p.m. he went home, not through the lower gate down by the lodge, but through the Stock Exchange Street entrance where the more common, not so elegant, graves slept beneath their overshadowing and younger trees: elms, maples, butternuts. Messy butternuts: Each fall his job now was to clean up all those nuts. Good thing Ma liked them. They were part of his pay.

Ignoring the tall wrought iron gate, he climbed over the stonewall onto the plank walk below and shoved toward Five Points where he lived with his mother above the clasp-locker hospital. Traffic at Five Points, with its shops and intersecting streets, had quieted down but would start up again after suppertime, when bars would regain all their custom after sparser trade most of the day.

The smell of chicken stew floating down to him, Willie trudged upstairs and turned the rattling doorknob. "I'm home!" The voice raised in grateful relief for supper stopped short. For there she was again—the ghoul!

The hackles on his nape rose, his mouth open, and he *himself* staring at *her*. The only thing about her different was the scarf she wore over her bramble patch. That was new. She'd not had the scarf. He wondered over that in a distant way, but mostly he just stared. At first. Then he poured his gaze on Ma cooking at the gas ring beside the coal-burning range. His little brother Parry stood beside her, watching the girl. The girl standing in soft brown tatters by the old deal table set for four.

Staring.

Willie did not at first notice that she stared at the place settings—tin knives and forks on pointed napkins, with white crockery plates between. In the midst of this design stood a great circular pot of cornbread, like the yellow head of the daisy amid its napkin-and-tinware petals. Late summer sunlight yet fell onto the kitchen table from the row of open windows above Sharon Road. It was hot up here, from both the day and Ma's cooking.

He croaked. "What's—what's that doing here?"

She threw a look back at him over her shoulder. "You've seen her before, have you?"

31

Ma's voice was ever husky—she said from childhood—from calling home the pigs and cows, horses, farmhands to supper. Her brown hair was piled in layers atop her head, blouse with long sleeves not too poofy, her collar tight and high and brown—she said, to show less soil. Sweat stood on her brow and soaked her armpits. All the other ladies had white collars no matter what they worked at. Ma was the clasp-locker repair woman. The hospital downstairs was hers alone now that Pop's body was in the *Akropolis Rural Cemetery*, and Pop had gone to heaven to be with THE LORD. Willie had buried his boxed, scorched and mangled, body. Mr. Priam, the rubber baron, as people pleased themselves to call him, promised Ma could keep the hospital and pay him, bit by bit, the sum outstanding.

Parry said, "She doesn't talk or look at us, you see." With a toss of his head he flung his blond bang from his eyes.

"I know. I found her in the vault this morning. That is, I was about to enter when she fell out.... —Didn't just walk out like normal."

Ma nodded to him to bring the plates and he looked at Parry. "Help your brother, Parry, he's been working hard all day."

With evident reluctance Parry picked up a plate. Ma ladled out the fat-rich stew, all yellow and with bits of brown meat, and onions carrots potato celery peas swimming in the broth.

"But how'd she —"

"I saw her in the street just standing, staring. Some of your scalawag friends were playing rudely, pelting her with bits of this and that, garbage from the street. I shooed'em long and asked her what the matter was. I guess you know the answer."

He nodded. "Nothing."

"It's peculiar," she agreed.

Willie mumbled, pulling out his chair. "Thought I got rid of her." He raised his voice: "She was supposed to be in the church. The big one.... Peculiar isn't quite the right word, Ma. Mr. Sneed says insane."

"What do you think?"

The three of them were seated. The girl had moved toward her full plate but stood there, sniffing, hardly looking.

Willie was too embarrassed to say. He had hoped quoting Mr. Sneed would do. "Maybe what Mr. Sneed said. He thinks she escaped from the asylum at A'ndian Falls.

"I've heard of that place. I wouldn't want to be there, either."

"She's a ghoul," said Parry, watching. A bit thrilled. "She can't even eat. Ghouls can't eat regular, you see."

They looked at her, head down, her face almost bathing itself in stew steam. She stood up more and put in her hand, came out with a greasy handful, dripping, and put it in her mouth. Chewing, slobbering it down her chin.

Parry laughed. Ma looked amazed. Willie got the creeps.
"Ma," he said.

Ma stood and grabbed her apron corner, wiping the little
mouth. "Here," she said, "sit down." She pulled out the ladderback
chair, scraping on the wooden floor. The girl stood staring at the
stew. Her lips smacked. Ma took her hand and drew her gently
down, repeating, but distinctly, "Sit down."

She picked up the big soup spoon and ladled up, bringing
near her mouth. The girl opened it, the soup went in, she chewed
some more. This commenced a short succession of ladling in the
stew, and Ma then put the spoon handle directly in her hand,
making it to clasp. "Put—put in the spoon, and get out the stew,"
she said and repeated thrice. The spoon scraped in the plate, the
spoon went in her mouth. It dribbled at the edges of mouth and
spoon. She chewed.

"I guess that's no ghoul," muttered Willie beneath his breath,
looking under his brows at Parry.

"We ought to wash her," said Parry, who was always as
dapper as a working man's son had wherewithal to be. Parry was
ten years old, blond, wearing short pants, and a pale blouse with
dark blue string necktie, castoffs from James Priam's wardrobe. He
used his napkin at table: which Willie, four years his senior, always
neglected as sissified. Willie prided himself on saving Ma the
washing. He was the same with his clothes, wearing no more
changes than necessary. Laundry day was hard enough on her.

"We ought to get her treated for the rash," said Ma, also
letting her napkin stay folded.

Willie thought a moment, chewing. "Maybe the rash will
need washing to help it." But he was being theoretical. He thought
she must go back to the church.

The girl stood, her chair falling over backwards. The broad
plate was empty, but she bent to lick it. Then she, still as one
entranced, stared at rows of corn-on-the-cob laid out to dry on the
sideboard. She ghosted over to these. That was how Willie framed it
to himself, withstanding what he's said to Parry, still quite
unconvinced by the mere fact of her eating. Her back was then to
them, where they sat, heads turned, watching.

In the midst of the supper table was a dark old dutch-oven
with cornbread, of which they'd been eating, thickly buttered.
Without looking at the cornbread, Willie watched her as he helped
himself to more.

Her hands reached out and, lickety-split, she began to
rearrange the yellow ears on the sideboard—although they'd been in
orderly rows (that he could see) before.

"Isn't that peculiar," said Ma when the girl stopped. She continued with her back to them, standing slight between them and the work of her hands. Then, lickety, she changed the order of arrangement once more. None of the three could see much of the design made; but that there was a design each time, and perhaps each time different.

Ma said, "I think..." and stood, careful of her approach so as not to startle the little girl. She stood quietly at first beside her but then picked up one corncob and felt it for moisture, finding the kernels hard and dry. She put it, small end downward, into the cast iron sheller mounted to the sideboard next the array of corn ears. Ma cranked the handle, watching the girl's face. The kernels fell plinking into the wooden box beside the sideboard. With its framing bush of hair beneath the scarf, the small scratched face seemed unchanged, it hadn't even looked. Gently, Ma picked up her small hand and clasped it firmly around the cob within her own larger hand. Down went the corn ear, just so, into the sheller's cob-shaped receptacle. She picked up the hand again and brought it to the crank, formed its clasp around the handle, and made it turn. The girl stared at the revolving whorled spokes of the sheller's wheel. Faster and faster Ma made it go. Faster and faster. The corn was quickly shelled. She put another ear into the little hand and made it to press in behind the first. Beside the wooden box for kernels stood a basketful of husks into which the empty cobs now fell.

This procedure happened very fast. Eating cornbread all the while, almost mesmerized themselves, the two boys watched, Parry careful where crumbs fell. When the thing had been performed by the girl alone, they smiled. Parry laughed, quite entertained. Willie dropped his gaze and grunted. *Maybe a ghoul wouldn't do that.*

She stood cranking, mechanical, shelling in rapid succession every yellow corn ear until the sideboard stood empty, the girl herself seeming quite empty with it. She merely stood as, perhaps, a mannequin seen in O'Shaughnessy's department store plateglass window downtown.

By that time they'd finished eating. Parry, picking up her hand, placed a piece of buttered cornbread in it and brought it to her mouth. He was quite happy with her work. The husking, shelling, and grain-milling were his jobs, and now all that remained for him to do was mill the kernels into meal. He had the idea she'd do that for him, too.

"That's for you, pretty girl. If you are crazed it's good to know you. I could use three more!" And he smiled at his joke, tossing back his bang. Then he washed his hands in the long shallow galvanized sink where Ma was working. "Let me draw water for her bath, Ma?"

Five Points Akropolis

"She should go back to the church," said Willie, standing above the box eyeing the white and yellow kernels, munching a summer apple from Miller's orchard.

"I don't know," said Ma, not quite decided. She was washing dishes, last of all the great dutch oven in the now greasy water.

"I think we should keep her," said Parry.

Ma opened the drain and water swirled down. She began mopping out the sink.

"Let me draw the water, Ma?"

"Parry, you make it sound like she's a puppy, some stray we can adopt." Ma frowned disapproval.

"What's wrong? We can get rid of her rash, cut down your old frock. She'll use your apron."

"Willie?" asked Ma, turning to the elder boy.

"She should go back to the church." He looked at the girl intently. She was just the same, gray eyes entranced, her deep abstraction clear upon the still face. But he was weakening. They both sensed it.

Ma, still doubtful, began. "... Suppose it won't hurt to fix her up, take her about wherever we go, one or the other of us. Maybe someone will see and claim her." She liked the idea of the big church only a little better than that of the asylum. By the time she finished speaking they could see her mind made up. Parry had not yet lifted up the hinged sink. He was gone around between the sink and sideboard and was pumping water into the tub in its wainscoted compartment hidden under the sink; even as Ma was finishing up. "Better get the kettle going, Willie," she said.

Willie moved the great full kettle onto, and lit, the ring. He wondered how he would sleep tonight with her on the parlor sofa not far from his door. Willie tried to think of the science of it. It would be easier to figure out if she were a machine, a pumping jack or a combustion engine. He looked over at Parry happily pumping away in the corner between the sideboard and the tub. Parry wasn't a bit perturbed. Not a bit. And not for the first time, nor the last, Willie wished he was like Parry in that. *Unperturbed.*

Parry, he thought, liked that word. Parry liked the word *perturbed*, too. Often Parry said new words picked up here and there, prizing them. Vagrant, urchin, unperturbed. Willie might use them after Parry picked them up, but it was Parry who liked to think of their meanings, match them up with others. Willie knew it: It was a gift not far different from the ghoul's corn-arranging gift. But Willie knew, as Parry did not, why bicyclists stop teetering, gained better balance, as they gather speed. Willie understood angular momentum, the concept. Parry just liked the feel of "angular momentum" moving about in his mouth. Willie was aware, intelligent, feeling, alive in his love of mechanical things. The girl seemed not alive yet. She was but partly formed.

Ma shooed them out, knelt before the waif and gently undressed her. She ran her rough working woman's hand over the thatch, and then picked her up, cradling the slight unresisting creature from another time. She seemed to weigh almost nothing. Like a newborn robin. Parry had raised the sink so that now Ma placed her in water made temperate by the kettleful Willie had poured.

Parry was in the parlor on the sofa beneath the Sharon Road window, reading "The Adventure of the Empty House," waiting for Ma to get done so as to inspect the outcome. He had placed one of his fresh nightshirts, upon the dresser just this side of the swinging kitchen door, ready for Ma's dressing of his prize. Every so often he looked up from the story to gaze at the roses-and-lilies wallpaper in dreaming abstraction over his new pet. He had taken possession of her in his imagination, if not his heart. He planned to take her by the hand and lead her everywhere, telling her to stop when she must stop and go when she must go.

Five Points Akropolis

The Five Points Gang

Willie had gone out to Five Points to meet his pals, on the corner three fronts down. He was now recounting to them, with some reservation, the adventure of the ghoul. He was embarrassed to call her that so he merely gave the highlights of the thing in a calm tone as matter-of-fact. He related her state as peculiar, but withheld Mr. Sneed's supposition of escape from the county asylum. The evening air was August balmy but stinking; cooling as the sun slid down behind Cake Eaters Hill (as it was known to the neighborhood). The wind had shifted more from the south, bringing with it the rotten egg smell of the sulfur curative process in rubber-making—located south and east of downtown. There three principal rubber-works turned out tires and other products for new industries rapidly building from the invention of the internal combustion engine. But the smell was also a sad one for Willie, reminding him of his father and the accident that took him away.

Here among Akropolis' expanding neighborhoods, of which Five Points was but one, lived Willie and his pals. Most of his friends were foreigners, immigrant offspring of one sort or another like Cheenie or Gregoff, either migratory from down south and especially North Regina, or from the recent descent of Etalios, Eriemen, Churman, or other R'opeans. One small section of the neighborhood was colored. Some of these were also from down south, or North Regina, but some were sons of long-lived residents with jobs in the rubber mills. There were few such jobs for them. Here coloreds and whites went to school together, though in other areas they were more segregated by prejudice and impecuniosity. The Five Points gang, of sometimes a half-dozen, sometimes a score, was mixed, and as such somewhat anomalous.

"What color is she?" asked the newsboy, colored Aneas, wearing neat long stockings, striped shirt and slouch hat. He had not been there earlier with the others throwing garbage. "You should give her back to the church. Why'd—how she be coming here? —I mean after she left St. Invincible's?"

37

"Don't know. Like I said, she don't talk."

"We seed that," said Glacas, the North Regina hillbilly, as people in Akropolis called them. "The kinnypiky Aneas weren't here then. At least she don't cry—we seed also." He was one of the ragged ones whose mother did not bother to patch his pants. He had no suspenders and the pants were held up with a piece of twine. There were holes at his elbows and his clothes were not very clean. Unawares, he descended from the nobility of Llywelyn ab Iorwerth.

They were standing on the corner by the communal pump and watering trough, not ten steps from the door of a corner saloon—Paddy's Saloon and Pool Parlor—where young men and those of middling age went in and out. It was Friday night and a few horses were tethered close by. Also, propped on kickstands, stood a couple motorbikes, motor-cycles they were called; the maker *Hedström*, and the gang, including Gregoff and the handsome Cheenie, had been admiring them.

Willie said, "Yeah, you found that out so you can leave off trying to make her. And let me know if you hear of anyone like that missing. I guess Ma thinks she'll be all right with us—for now."

Johan Zettler, tidy and clean in a porkpie cap, climbed onto one of the motor-cycles, straight-faced. Glacas grinned, revealing toothless gaps, wishing he could be so bold. His throat chocolate-brown against his white shirt, Aneas stood, dark eyes impassive, but, as always, wondering over the boldness of some white kids and their presumption. His mother had taught him that he was as good as the whites and ought to try to be better. He thought now he could sometimes just about see what was better. And, he also knew, White Man would be quick to stick his butt in jail if *he* sat on a motor-cycle.

"My mind's about made-up I might set on this here motor-cycle," said Glacas, flinging a leg over the saddle seat, his dirty white bony knees protruding.

Willie noticed how much the machine looked like the bicycle he wanted, but with a sleek little engine between the pedal sprocket-wheel and the seat. It gleamed some in twilight, scarcely bigger than the bike he'd seen in the Sears Roebuck catalog, the one he'd been saving for, the *Acme Jewel*. He tried to imagine the feel of ignition and power between his legs, the thrill of steering above the engine, keeping his mass centered over the wheels in dynamic forward motion. Leaning into the turn at motor-cycle speeds would keep him in the saddle, balancing (as he had read), with the wheel's roll-torque between centrifugal and gravitational forces. No matter his desire—all he might reasonably afford (in time) would be the $14.00 *Jewel*. Or, failing that, the Cincinnatus Bicycle, cheaper by two dollars.

Five Points Akropolis

"Better not let the owner catch a glimpse of you on that," he warned Glacas, knowing it no use to say anything to Zettler.

Glacas looked past him into the plateglass of the Pool Hall. It was already lit up in there, smoky. He saw the swell—the motor-cycle owner—stretched across the table with his cue, about to sink one of the colored balls into the end pocket. He grinned, revealing gaps, aware of his obscurity out here in the dark. "All they had in Backswitch Holler was a few nags like those there," he said, scarcely shooting a glance at the horses, one of which was lapping noisily with a long tongue at the trough. "This is my best chance."

Gaslight nearby on the corner ignited with a sudden soft explosion, and he scrambled off, the gang about him jeering.

"You're going to catch it hot, Johan," he said. "Them is cake eaters in there."

Johan Zettler sat his seat a while, knowing the other spoke true warning, but withholding every muscle fiber against being moved by words from the likes of Glacas—or anyone else for that matter.

"Let's have a smoke and play kick-the-can," said Willie, moving along toward the *Clasp-locker Hospital* (as said the sign above the front door of the repair shop). He did not look back to see if he were followed but began fumbling in the pockets of his knee britches for the makings. Of course the boys would come.

"The Churmans invented that, you'll know," said Zettler at his elbow. It was clipped speech, the first he had spoken since Willie came out from supper.

Daimler, thought Willie, too tired to speak.

"Daimler is a Churman," said Johan.

Willie sat down on the stoop, rolled his smoke and lit up, his pals standing by waiting their turn for a puff or two. Willie was not so generous with the makings tonight. And he was just sitting here. Now he leaned back against the corner frame of the entryway, smoking, silent.

In fact, Willie was exhausted and ready for sleep. They got bored waiting for him to move. Glacas picked up and emptied out a chew can. He moved off the boardwalk into the road. Across the street loomed the dark superstructure of the new grammar school—almost finished—on the corner of the intersection of Five Points: Sharon Road, Bechtel Ave., Stock Exchange Street, and Third (a short distance past the alleyway). Parry would go to the new school, Harkins Grammar School. Willie would go to Nor'west High School, on which the cemetery bordered—his first year there. The gang of—tonight—half a dozen stood around the can, horse-n-goggling for *It*. Aneas lost and Glacas, hamming it up, went down as far as he could, almost to the intersection free at the moment of

39

nonpedestrian traffic. (There was the rare cabby or horseman arriving at Paddy's.) Glacas now ran back to kick the can. The can flew into the dark beyond the gaslight and Aneas went to pick it up. Six or seven others had gone miscellaneous directions into the dark as well.

Willie, still leaning back, eyes virtually closed, heard Aneas counting toward 100. By time the Negro boy got through the count Willie was sleeping. The ghoul was before him, her rashy face eye-by-eye with his, its look inward. As though he did not exist. She's dead, he said to himself. He heard the can kicked again and roused. With one eye he made out boys running. Aneas, in the dark, was *It* again.

Impossible to win this game in the dark. He shut both eyes but did not doze again.

The ghoul would be sleeping in the parlor.

"You better go to bed," said Aneas out of the dark. Aneas could see him in the gaslight, cigarette clutched by his knee. "You be burning a hole in your pants with that." The street was empty but for Aneas and the saloon noise pouring from the front door near the corner.

"I should," agreed Willie to the dark. He stood and stretched, flicked the butt into the street. Aneas came into the light, checking to see if it had any smoke left in it.

Willie heard the tin can fly again across the tarred and cinder street.

"Beans," said Aneas. There was nothing left of the cigarette, either. He looked up the road, which led beyond Cake Eaters Hill toward the country town of Sharon, and saw the gasman with his long ignition stick moving from one lit lamp to the next lamppost. On into the dark. The gang members fled in and out of the lamplight on Sharon Road, calling to Aneas. His hair absorbed the light of the lamp, kinky black, sticking out beneath the slouch-cap.

"We'll be freshmen this year," said Willie stating a suppressed excitement, of which they were both aware. He turned to enter the door on the stoop next the shop door. But he stopped to look at Aneas, the whites of that one's eyes a-gleam. "She's white," he said. "The queer girl they used for target practice ain't colored."

He turned in to the landing and climbed slowly upstairs. He had a grave to finish digging in the morning. But when he reached the landing and door to their rooms, he bethought himself. There had been two robberies in the neighborhood lately. Here was another door that would open on stairs—leading to the third floor and the rooms of their neighbors Humboldt. He went in to Wilusa's rooms and shut the door, clicking with the skeleton key in its lock.

Willie, careful to avoid squeaking floorboards between

kitchen and parlor rug, kept well wide of the sofa in the dark, not daring to notice the ghoul. He knew she lay beneath the windows and feared to see her staring into nothing: Feared to think what deeps fell away in ghouls, who slept not. He hurried away from thoughts of what he did not know about the living dead.

He and Parry and Ma each had their rooms in back and the water closet was off the hall, sharing a wall with the kitchen. Did the ghoul, know how to use it? He decided not to look into that. It was all Ma's to do now. And Parry's ... as long as Parry did not lose interest. Willie was ashamed in light of Parry's fearlessness, but not in light of his sloth.

He undressed, got on his nightshirt and fell heavily onto the bed. Soon he'd be asleep... but he lay listening to the calls of his chums, remotely. Soon he was gone. Gone from his form into dream forms until he should be summoned once again to it by his Maker—whether God Almighty or the Progress of Natural Selection. Willie did not yet know.

Out on Sharon Road the gang played out their energy given them for the day. Then for the most part they dispersed, or went by twos or threes. Johan followed the track of light ignited by the gasman part way up the left side of Cake Eaters Hill. The road he lived on lay more left of Cake Eaters and out past the zoo, part within, part bordering, Harkins Woods. Beyond, were farm and wood lots. Aneas went home to the rooms on Third St. above the Leg Bone Diner. Glacas also lived on Third St. but he stuck with Mancheenie, the boy whose surname had been misspelled by officials as his family left Roanoak Island in New Amsterdam. He was an olive-skinned dimpled boy, handsome, smiling; in comparison to the serious younger, bulbous-nosed and skinny Greg.

A lot of R'opean names were so abused on landing stateside. Gregoff was another, a boy of recent Grak descent, who tagged along with them. Sometimes he palled with Parry, his own age, but really Parry was too young-seeming or too unmanly for Gregoff to be much seen with him—even though he really liked playing with the imaginative, immaculate boy. But tonight he was all for palling with the others, exploring the alleyways, peeking into windows, trying to find cast-off butts with just enough white paper and tobacco to hold onto and re-light. It would be Gregoff's job to climb the pole and get a light, if so. There was always some adventure or, if not, it felt adventurous even so. Life in Americle was for adventure. Life was for playing, rolling hoops with sticks; stickball, if you couldn't get a hoop, visiting the fun house and riding roller-coaster when you could afford it.

Or there was the adventure of stealing. Last night they stole a pair of roller skates some cake-eater left lying in a yard. Only trouble was there'd been no key. So now they kept their eyes open for a key, or whatever might be used instead to lock the skates to length. Not so easy as at first supposed.

They knew better than to invite Willie or his brother. Willie, had he known it, would have opined that theft does not require cunning. Cunning, for Willie, meant invention, meant putting mechanisms together, meant how things were made. He himself hoped to be an inventor one day. Imagining how things might work. Akropolis was where invention walked or sat, like some old thoughtful god. He told this once to Greg when he came for supper. Greg's mother and father came from Greice. He thought the boy might know about all that but he didn't. Mr. Priam said the Graks were as ignorant as Appalachians, and that he himself was almost Grak. Or would have been one. What was meant had been unclear to Willie. The man had laughed, showing fine white even teeth.

"Church'a key'd work," declared Cheenie as they prowled along the alley behind the pool hall. Cheenie—dressed in knickerbockers, homemade shirt and suspenders, easily the handsomest of the gang, glistening black hair and shiny white teeth. "What we want here—when inside some'a one leave'a de bar-key out?" He jerked his faintly glistening and curly head toward the open back door of the saloon. "Greg—he go in'a find one—maybe at'a de bar—bring it back."

"Swell idea," grinned Glacas, flourishing city slang.

Light streamed out into the alleyway, with the smell of kitchen slops. He peeked inside. "Only the dishwasher'n' she's set to get done. Get in there, Greg, I seed her to her armpits. Get in."

Gregoff, not liking to be seen shrinking, stepped inside, slightly, lifted a tin fork from the sideboard.

The dishwasher saw him and screeched. He ran out. Off they scrambled to the getaway. In a moment they were on Stock Exchange Street and heading for the graveyard. Just in case.

Once over the wall they peered out to see if the gasman was about. It was dark in the graveyard and they would not venture far inside. The cool dry-stone mossy wall was shade enough for them, should he appear. The gasman was also the Five Points night watchman for the city of Akropolis. Akropolis had police, of course, but the gasman had to make these rounds and was commissioned to do double duty in aid of law and order. And the gasmen were as likely, if not more so, to be about nights, than was the copper on the beat.

Five Points Akropolis

Mr. Priam and the Cake Eaters

The two were seated at right angles on separate brocaded couches in the long gleaming drawing room, complete with baroque golden harp and pianoforte. She glanced upward once or twice. At intervals, from cherub-painted ceilings, the great hall was hung with gold and silver electrified chandeliers. She had her notebook open on a low gilt table before her. He was drinking an iced glass of draft beer imported from Prussia. The grand room was scented with carelessly scattered abundance of roses in delicate floral-painted Oriental vases.

"Yes," said Mr. Priam with a twinkling eye. His voice was rich and gruff. "This was the Red A'ndian territory as you call it, and despite its denuded condition retains the legendary history. A picturesque background to our industrialism as the rubber-making capital of the world. For instance, we might walk from here a scant quarter mile to see the fabled boundary of the Americle frontier. If you stay with us, as we hope, I'm sure the children will be happy to show you the carriage road demarcating that famous portage. An ancient trail between the A'ndian River and the southern watershed—now split in canals and locks for use in the manufacture of rubber. We are planning to build a country club on the legendary boundary-site, west of here."

He had large mustaches of luxuriant brown tinged with gold and silver, a tanned pate surrounded by equally luxuriant hair of the same coloring, and dark eyes full of intelligent sparkle and lively interest in anything they might encounter—except when preoccupied with business. Then the eyes were serious and very intent. Mrs. Havard was pleased that Mr. Priam was not the duller sort of industrialist she had expected to find here in the manufacturers' midwestern Americle. She had anticipated an arrogant man, culturally obtuse, who knew nothing but machinery, blast furnaces, material charts and flowage, completely self-satisfied and complacent about the place of industrial progress in the world. She did, however, suspect that Priam's father was of this sort, though he had been a medical man before adapting Goody's process—or Hanock's—depending on one's view of the patent.

Her hair was softly piled and feminine, but she wore the tailored business jacket with poofy shoulders and soft skirt falling to just above the hightop white kid shoes. She smiled, more with her eyes than lips, and said, "But are there now Red A'ndians anymore? I know they remain in woodland east of here, or so I'm told—in Pensil'swood and New Amsterdam and New Angleland—if rather confined to distinct—what do you call them—enclaves? And of course they are but lately overtaken and subdued in the West."

"Reservations," he replied and gave her a verbal sketch of A'ndian Reservations in the Wild West.

Mrs. Edith Havard, lately off the train from New Amsterdam, and before that the steamship *Greenock*, was seated in the drawing room of the mighty Mr. Priam, one of the so-called rubber barons, and an object of her assignment as correspondent for *The Observer*. She had hoped to be a war correspondent and become immersed in the excitement on the Gold Coast. But the editor would not hear of it. So here she was in Akropolis, among other industrial cities with their various products, whether of steel or glass or leather, inquiring into the burgeoning business of rubber-making—necessary to everything from tires and inner tubes, boots, waterproof sou'westers, and mats, sports-balls, gaskets for machinery—. The vulcanized rubber would endure strain and retain its purpose and shape. Mrs. Havard, as the much-anticipated E. Havard of Londinium, already had one curtailed tour of the rubber works where she had been baptized to the experience of vulcanization and found the god's name apt for the process: Except she had seen it in Burningem, she could not have told beforehand the dense soul-destroying cacophony; the might of heat, stench, filth; the alternately glowing and dark turmoil of blast furnaces, of machinery with its awful din and mass of incessant making and remaking—turning raw materials of earth and sky into things for the everyday use of humankind.

Mr. Priam, in his turn, had been surprised to find his anticipated visitor, E. Havard, in the form of this lovely but distinguished women—stepping from the elevator into the hallway outside his office. On further acquaintance he was delighted. And now he was delighted to offer her a tour of *Stonehewn*. His children were fetched from their various pursuits of the evening, largely from the game room, but also from the aquarium and the library, to accompany them on the grand tour.

Stonehewn was that mansion seen at a distance from Five Points on the wooded knoll above the rest of Cake Eaters Hill. To the gang at Five Points it looked like a castle, and Cheenie, whose father worked here as gardener, had known real castles in Etalio and pronounced it good enough, if not better than those castles. For it had new elegance and appliance, convenience, electric lighting broadcast throughout, to couple with the old elegance of what had gone before on continental R'opea.

"But we like the elevators best!" This exclamation came from James Horatio, one of the middle children. Mrs. Havard had been introduced and taken round to all the ground-floor rooms. There were six siblings, vivacious, buoyant, seeming almost of an age until one considered only the youngest and the eldest together in order to distinguish the range. They were not yet distinct to her, and names also did not yet cling to each but young James Horatio was far from reticent, holding forth on particulars of every room (and there were more than she cared to count, far more). He was like a smoother, compact miniature of his industrialist father, and very affectionate. He was often holding hands with one or another of his sisters, as he pointed out the pieces of ebony and ivory chessmen, or the seascape of the USS Maine on her way to Havana Harbor. As always, in such variety, two siblings stood aloof as shy or quiet but without the least mannerism of it except for uttering hardly a word to her, and they, both Brant and Kate, were as keen about the eyes as any little Priam would be—being from birth in the entitled setting out of which they were forming. As they walked from great room to great room over polished parquet floors, she saw the children as uninhibited through force of privilege and abundance, not through lack of discipline. Mrs. Havard could not help but wonder if Mr. Priam, like some magnates, felt any duty to make good use of this ease—founded on capital, invention, and the labor of others—to plan or act for the common good.

"There are three, and one is for the servants." continued James Horatio. "Papa, let me show Mrs. Havard the elevator off the entrance hall. We can go to the second story. That's the first story in Angleland, Mrs. Havard," said the precocious boy with crisp precision.

She smiled at him, more with her eyes. "Yes, peculiar of you Americles to call it so."

"Oh we are great people for peculiar. You wait and see. We are going to fill the whole world with it, by and by."

"Shan't it cease to be peculiar then? Or particularly of Americle?—if it fills up the world?"

"Well, I hadn't thought of that," said he with a happy smile. "I will have to think up some invention to keep that from happening."

Delighted, Mr. Priam said, "See if you can't make it out of rubber, James," and all the children laughed. "But perhaps Mrs.

Havard would be pleased instead to see the swimming pool and aquarium, the billiards room downstairs."

James opened the paneled doors, then pressed the brass button, opening the brass gate. The elevator was not large enough to accommodate them all, so Ann Gladys, who was next to James Horatio in verbal command and regulation—and in age—apportioned each of two elevator loads among them, making sure to place Papa in the first with Mrs. Havard.

"You must allow me to pilot the first load," said her brother. Ann Gladys, brightly dressed in ruffles and long skirt and with a big bow in her golden hair, looked at Papa.

The Anglish correspondent now suspected that had it not been for the new visitor, the little girl would be speaking in forthright objection.

Mr. Priam said, "Be satisfied that we obey you in the arrangement, and wait your turn. James Horatio has proposed the ride and should be allowed some of the mastery."

Mrs. Havard was surprised to see that even the lift had its electric lights, and potted palm in the corner. She could not remember a single potted palm in any Londinium lifts—clubs' or hotels'. "What does it do for sunlight?"

"Oh, we swap them out," said big brother Brant. "We make sure they all get enough of that."

Later, Mr. Priam and Mrs. Havard stood on the urn-scattered terrace in rich moonlight, leaning on the ornamental parapet, and looking over grounds bespangled with flowering rosebushes and fruit trees in silvery variety. In shady places glimmered quiet pools, reflecting moonlight. Mr. Priam was saying how the goldfish in them had grown, that the children sometimes fed them, sometimes fished them out and threw them back. "But I think the sport's gone out of it. They haven't played at this since early July."

Mrs. Havard stood with him above the fragrant roses, sipping wine. She had declined to be a guest of the house. She wanted to get back in order to write an important letter; and to think about the work, look over her notes without distraction. Her things would stay where they were, downtown on the fifth floor of the Portage Park Hotel in her corner room overlooking the Akropolis Opera House on Market Ave.. From the other window she could also look straight up the canal, Main Street, and the rail lines—all paralleling one another, spaced by city blocks: barges, steel rails and brick blocks going straight away out of sight toward the gigantic lots where rubber factories turned out their products day and night amid the screeching din and fumes; enough to sicken mortals of lesser make than those mighty men—mechanics, wrights of all kinds, electricians

Five Points Akropolis

and gas pipe fitters, toolpath barrowmen, teams of workers in production.

"Show me a view of the neighborhood, might not you?" asked the correspondent.

"We can go out to the carriage house and use the balcony to oversee it, if you like."

"Your sister has her own apartments there, you have said. She will not mind?"

"No. And she has been out for the evening at the Women's City Club. I don't know if she's back yet." He led the way over gravel paths toward the stabling and carriage house roofed in thatch. Moonlight shone the way unmixed with gaslight, for such a walk had not been expected until time to have the lady driven back downtown. The sheen it spread was mysterious and enlivening, every flowering plant reflecting muted white or silver, the shadowy undersides deep and dark beneath each tree and shrub. Here all was quiet but for the faint rustling of her gown and crunch of gravel under foot.

"We drove past the *Akropolis Rural Cemetery* on our way up," said Mrs. Havard beside him. "It does not seem so aptly named, surrounded as it is by the west side commercial neighborhoods. The houses there are broken up into flats? And, above the five points, there are plenty of brownstones too, I notice, as in New Amsterdam."

Mr. Priam liked the cultured lilt of her voice. It was rich in precision, Anglish intonation, so unlike the hard swift and often indistinct syllables of the midwestern Americle speech.

"We've grown up around our dead and hemmed them in, I suppose you could say. We hardly know they're there... unless it's time to visit—or bestow someone new to the burial.... In fact we've been thinking of rechristening it. Something more poetic. Perhaps you can think of something." He turned and smiled but kept his hand beneath her elbow, and they walked on.

His smile was gentle and a bit sad, she noticed.

They walked on in silence. She could think of nothing to say. At last she ventured, "Your wife is buried there." The faint tonal lift at the end of her comment suggested a question. She was interested in all she was seeing, hearing, learning on this trip abroad, and knew she had to bring human interest to her pieces. But, still, she was reticent to delve. She thought the personal, fraught with emotion of whatever kind, did not belong to solid reportage. She liked her workmanship to be—not colorless—but not yellow, rose, or purple, either. She depended on *the real* for its coloring, as befit her modern not populist taste. Local coloring and Impressionism were well in novels... but Akropolis was no novel in the making for her. It was too dirty and real, too much so—for all she could see east and south of what the coach driver had called Cake Eaters Hill.

And then they were out on the balcony looking down on it in moonlight, this somewhat fabled neighborhood. She could not help but see the romantic beauty of The Hill, and wish it well... and that it may be founded on hopes apart from the ill-use of others. There were newer suburban roofs, surrounded by young trees and those of middling age; and all bathed in subtle light—the silver of disappeared sunlight, mediated by the moon. She knew that Mr. Priam, however great his power and his loved familial surroundings, was often lonely. She felt that kinship with him.... But it didn't matter. It was the work that mattered. And in whatever form she might have found this rich industrialist he would make good copy under the increasing power of her craft.

"But —!" She exclaimed. "Here's the rubber-making smell!" She almost gagged, surprised, on stepping beneath the arch of the upper portico. —That penetrating stench! It had been stealing on them as they walked and now its full force smote them.

He laughed. "Oh surely you've heard the saying...."

"—'Smells like money.' Yes. I've heard it. I heard it traveling through shoe factory country, papermaking, the steel country east of here in Pensil'wood. That name—. But should not that tell you something about money itself?" She was bold because she knew he liked her and because he seemed to have a sense of humor about himself and what was his. Had he been otherwise she knew she would have kept the question to herself. She needed him too much, in his position, for the work. As it was, she swiftly thought that perhaps whatever he might answer would make good reading.

He looked thoughtful, but slowly a smile developed. "I suppose it should." He looked around, back toward the grounds and then down upon the leafy tiers of Cake Eaters Hill. Slyly resisting his own thoughtfulness, he said, "Usually we don't smell it here. Why all this is up here, west of the city. Only when the wind is wrong. Then we smell it."

"The wind—wrong?" Mrs. Havard persisted. The smile, which usually hovered in her lovely eyes was momently absent. Then, as a light returning slowly, it came back.

He laughed, delighted. "It is the things money may buy us — these have a much more fragrant smell."

She let it pass, gazing out upon the nestled houses. "Who lives there?" Not a question couched complexly, but one that interested her chiefly in how he would answer.

"The professional class—yes we have one here, growing—as you see—and the mercantile community—who used to live above their shops and are now able to take good things, better than before; because of that smell you speak of. It all feeds the economy of Akropolis—this development of what comes raw from the earth, whether anthracite or iron-ore and the like; or from its growing things, the latex in the rubber trees for instance. It's progress, offering opportunity for all. It's why the foreigner, the immigrant comes here."

"Interesting word it is—progress. Does it signify toward what, toward where it is we go.... There are those who think of evolution as obtaining to a greater good. If Cake Eaters—"

Here her companion laughed at the colloquial use. "—We call it West Hill."

But she continued. "If this neighborhood is an example of a successful progress... might it be the end of progress? You have progressed until you reach your destination? Akropolis is come to be, will always be as West Hill is? Lives will continue ...as well-lived in shall we say 100 years, 200... as they are here now? And all will continue so upon the basis of rubber manufacturing?"

"Well, I don't think about that. It's a bit beyond my scope, the scope of my powers. I will leave that to Chronos." He saw she was pleased with his reference to Father Time. "My hands are full with life as I find it. Time: I'm not there, then; I'm here and now.... But yes, I would hope so."

But her first thought, before his clarification, was that he had spoken of the Titan, youngest of the elder gods; Kronos, the harvester, who was said to have castrated his father with a scythe. Now she said, "And that would include a similar place—since you call it progress and attainment—for the rubber-workers? The men we saw today who actually charge the furnaces, load machines with mixture, ply their tools and trade in making all the rubber products...?"

He ceased looking out with her, and glanced swiftly back to note her demeanor. Agitation was anathema to Mr. Priam. He had to know at once if he'd taken a rattler to his breast in allowing her such access to him.

She saw, and said, "No, I do not bait you, sir. Please do not mistake my question. I feel fairly certain that your concern over the current climate of union-making may be coloring your receptivity to my query. I've no intention of bestirring labor passions. Surely the question is put in the context of our conversation about the habitation of West Hill and evolution." She pronounced the word with a long *e* in the Anglish way.

He was silent, gazing at her. Then he said, "You will want to include the union question, and the opposition to collective bargaining in your correspondence. You shall do it." Decisive as it was, he felt a precarious position. He knew he could have no control except perhaps what his personal touch might bring to her stories. His person itself, his methods, philosophy of management and

49

manufacturing, might alone influence how she cast them. It might do. He might win well for his cause by simply being what he was without resort to false compelling, manipulation. *I must leave the thuggery to them.*

He saw it all in this glance exchanged. And he saw it in himself. In his aspiration. This was what he wanted, not the other. In being Priam alone was true command. Command of Priam. Only in this could the city be looked down on by the gods—by God... and be spared. No riots, no industrial "accidents", perhaps, even, no incitement. Just sense. Good sense. He made good products by good sense. Perhaps he could make good relations in the same way.

They heard the door opening at the far end of the balcony.

"Here you are, poor things," called out a coarse female voice. The pale figure came toward them. "Enjoying the vulcanic night air, are you?"

"Daphnes, come, I want you to meet Mrs. Havard, the Havard I mentioned to you yesterday."

"Yes," said Daphnes Priam, coming to them, her pale dressing-gown over pajamas billowing open below the waist as she crossed to them. "He turns out to be a she. Delighted." She held out her hand and, quite firm, shook that of the Anglish lady.

The upper sleeves and shoulders of her gown were fuller than the fashion of the day allowed. Those of Mrs. Havard's more fashionable dress were slimmer at the shoulder, sooner tapering to the wrist, than those of the older woman's gown now reflecting moonlight. Miss Priam's dark hair was down, freshly brushed out for the night's rest. Silver threads, not many, gleamed in it. Her smile was cordial, hawkish about the nose, a bit of no-nonsense in it. Immediately she saw the correspondent as also no-nonsense, but would watch nonetheless to make sure of her first impression. Handsome was the word for Mrs. Havard, though one would not ordinarily associate it with a woman younger than oneself. Daphnes would not fear the look of intelligence in her gaze. She thought perhaps Mrs. Havard wore a touch of makeup and wondered if her brother might find the fact alone attractive.

"I heard you through the open window just now." She gestured directly behind her at the darkened open casement. "Something about progress, survival of the fittest, unionization and all that."

"Naturally you have to come out and stick your oar in to tug the conversation along." Mr. Priam's smile was one of good nature, perhaps affectionate but not markedly so.

She laughed nasally, not attractive laughter, but self-aware. "Oh I do firmly believe the lesser brethren will have to go for help beyond the lumbering work of natural selection. If you see the world above you cosseting itself in eugenics you must do something to improve your lot. I would. I do."

A smile played in Mrs. Havard's gaze.

Encouraged, Daphnes continued. "Eugenics is making for itself the new aristocracy or nobility, or whatever you call it. The recent excuse for lording it over the new serfs, the workers. It thinks better of itself than of the old nobility now so full of degenerated numb-skulls." Her adenoidal laughter broke out.

Mr. Priam was surprised to see a smile break across their guest's face. She laughed—a delicious melodic contrast to the unattractive neighing of his sister. Mr. Priam thought his sister's lot far from hard and would have mentioned it with humor, had his guest been another man. Or a female friend. Both his ignorance and fledgling sense of Mrs. Havard checked him. The brother and sister had had bantering arguments enough upon the subject of female power or lack of it, over breakfasts. And—simply, he did not know enough about Edith Havard. Her background and associations were unknown to him. He wanted to change that. "Oh let's talk of something else," he said.

"Buildings, perhaps," said Mrs. Havard before he could put in his own oar.

The others looked at her a moment with amused bafflement.

"Buildings," queried Miss Daphnes Priam.

"Yes. I can't help noticing how like"—here she disliked to be rude in using the pejorative *imitative of*—"the old manor houses of the Anglish countryside is *Stonehewn*. Compare that fact, if you will, with factory architecture. I do sometimes find that noun almost a misnomer in conjunction with its modifier. —But that aside, even though we began historically in Mainchester, over there we've copied your industrial innovation as the best possible structure for adding light—sunlight—and space for workers and machinery. Nothing else could provide for such banks of windows needed to cast light on workstations."

"It's true," agreed Priam, appreciative of her observation and insightful coupling with cultural concerns. "And a revolution for industry—a real leap for progress, if you will. Take the arc of this portico." He swept his arm to show its shape in the angle below them where the carriage entrance arched. "And those buttresses for cathedrals such as they are making plans for in the Capitol District. The *last cathedral* they are calling it—because industry is changing even the very structure of public space. It is bestowing an aesthetic of simplicity and function. Look, even, at the painter's squaring tendency. The decorative neo-classic structural designs are the ideal of the past. They are no longer necessary now we have the I-beam, the structural steel." He paused. "And—James Horatio's favorite—

51

the elevator. The building is borne by its steel frame, whereas before it must be borne in the piling up of stone. You can't do as much with that. Bedelham, which you saw in Pensil'swood, has instead taken stone from the earth, melted, removed dross, and refused it to bear the weight of building. It has forged beams to carry phenomenal amounts of freight in locomotion: it has forged sheets, riveted together, to carry goods *en masse* across the sea. *That* is progress."

Mrs. Havard saw the glory of it shining in his gaze as he spoke.

Miss Priam said, "And still you go back to the Anglish Manor to find house for you and yours. Face it, you know very well those rubber works, no matter how much sunlight falls in, are ugly—like the smell you fill the air with. Progress moves, yes. Onward, leaving what is used up in its wake."

He frowned, yet his eyes sparkled the more. They went on talking a while, then Mrs. Havard said that she must go back downtown. Priam urged her to let him drive her back down in his motor-car, but she declined. He really wanted to show off his *Motorwagen*. But she was weary and did not like to bear the noise, the smell and shaking. She asked for the horse and driver, exclaiming her firm wish not to trouble him. The three parted formally there upon the balcony, and he took her down and stood by with her, chatting, while the man prepared a single horse and fly.

Then she was being driven out the large gated entrance. There in the moonlight as horse and driver drove along the carriage road, she saw a figure departing the estate through a small wrought-iron gate in the low dry-stone wall. The man started off in the road near them and she asked the driver to stop. There, in a pool of moonlight between dark shades of leafy trees, she asked if he might like a ride, as they were going downtown. The driver, whose name was Gilbert, glanced back at her, a startled look grading into pleasure. "It will mean a slightly different route." But she nodded, smiling.

"Come, Argus, get in at this lady's urging," he said to the Negro, dark of skin and hair, darkly dressed.

"Don't mind f'I do." He answered gladly but with a look of apology at Mrs. Havard. He flashed a shy white smile then looked quickly back at Gilbert, who moved over to let him lumber up, the buggy dipping, to sit the seat beside.

The pair talked quietly, easily together as friends, Mrs. Havard sitting behind listening, as they passed in and out of lustrous moonlight between the shades of trees. Also, lulled by the gentle clopping of the hooves, she watched the walls and gardens pass, the lawns; and then yards, and finally the frame houses and apartment dwellings, as they passed downhill and into Five Points.

The saloon was lit with gas, its patrons moving about at games, the smell of its tobacco in the intersection as they passed. Fiddle music drifted out. She saw Argus gesture at the motor-cycles and say something to Gilbert. Then they were stopping where Third came into Stock Exchange Street. Here Argus Griffin climbed down.

"Thank you kindly, ma'am." He said this nodding. And with a wave to Gilbert he passed into the darker sidestreet. And they drove on.

"Would Argus have walked all this way at this late hour, Gilbert?"

"Every night, Missus."

"What does he do for Mr. Priam?"

"He's in the scullery. And he gardens under direction from the gardener."

"Oh. It seems a long day for him."

"And that's not all. He also runs a little eating-place on Third St. with his wife, Mabel. They both work pretty hard."

S. Dorman

And Now the Unexpected Event!

Parry was up bright and early next morning. Bright and early, in this instance, the exact condition of his young soul as he rose quietly, dressed, and went into the parlor to check on his prize. There she sat, staring at the roses-and-lilies wallpaper with rays of sunlight reflecting off new windows across the street into the room. Shot onto the pattern, it illuminated all with golden reflected brilliance. She still wore his nightshirt.

He pulled the clothes off the dresser and went to her. This was a frock Mrs. Wilusa had placed there to be worked on in continuation of the start made on it last evening by gaslight. Someday soon they'd have some of Mr. Edison's electric lights installed, but that was of no consequence now. She would finish the dress down in the shop in odd moments. Now Parry was taking it up and draping across the girl's front, speculatively. The girl did not look down at it. She looked at the wallpaper, pattern and light.

"Don't you want to see it?" He knelt before her, flinging his blond bangs back, and further arranging the frock. "See? It's white with lavender checks. It's called ging-ham." He looked up in her eyes expectantly.

He was not disappointed in her lack of response. He had some vague idea that he would be teaching her things, but he did not dwell on the concept. Rather she was to be his living plaything. Something like a doll, something like an imaginary friend who would nonetheless be visible to everyone. Mother had told them they must be attentive to her when they were out together, not forget and leave her somewhere unattended.

Now he stood and smoothed her brown hair with his slim white fingers. Her rashy skin, he saw again, was also tanned by the sun. He went to the dresser, got the hairbrush Ma had used last night, and began brushing her long hair. Except for the movement of bristles tugging through the thick mass—pushing back on her head in rhythm with the brushing—she made no other bodily or ocular sign that she was aware of his touches upon her person. Even so, he sensed, not yet consciously, that it was not wanted.

54

Five Points Akropolis

He had been hearing Ma in the kitchen and now he left the girl and pushed through the swinging door, holding it open, leaning in, asking, "Can you dress her, Ma?"

Ma looked back from the range where she was frying eggs and corn pone with fat-back for breakfast, the heavy homey smells thickening. She had brought up the coal, started the fire pumped the sink full of water, and wanted Parry to set the table. She said, "Parry, I'm busy. Try to get her to dress and we can see how it looks. I hemmed it but—certain—it'll need more, some tucks, like as not.

Parry went back to the sofa and said, "Ma says put on the frock, you see.... Do you know what that means, Put on the frock?"

He pantomimed the movements necessary to the act of doffing the nightshirt with crossed arms, fingers gripping its hem. Then he acted out putting the dress over his head with the actual dress slipping down over his clothes. When he did this he saw it would be too big. Parry acted everything over again a few times, though she never looked at him. Then he left the room and went in to set the table. From the icebox he drew a carnival-glass pitcher of milk and poured it into tumblers—four—amid the clinking of glass on glass.

The while he chattered about how he'd shown her what to do, and how she took no notice, and what plans he had for the day. Ma interrupted to tell him what her plans were for him, and to say, "You can keep her by you while you do your chores, and if that works out, then you can take her round. Not before."

Ma's hair had been hastily coiled and some of its pins were loose. Her hair was piled and poofy. She was dressed in her shop clothes, consisting of shop-apron over long skirt, and blouse with long sleeves and waistcoat. She had on her high button shoes.

"I'll dress her when the meal's on the table. Call your brother. He should have been up. He's got that li'l grave to finish this morning in time for internment. Mr. Sneed would not want him late."

All this while the smell of pork and eggs and cornmeal frying filled the rooms, and the sounds of metal spatula scraping on the iron skillet mingled with those street sounds coming up from Five Points—the low thunder of iron-bound wooden wheels, the occasional whinnying of horses, the squealing window from Humboldt's apartment upstairs; the shout of the newsboy, Aneas, telling the headline...which Mrs. Wilusa could not quite make out.

Parry hurried through the swinging door, through the parlor corner, down the hall, and knocked on Willie's door. "Ma wants you," he said, and went back into the parlor.

He started. The girl was sitting as before but now wearing Ma's frock. The nightshirt lay on the floor.

He knelt to pick it up, wondering. Evidently she had changed clothes while he was in the kitchen, and he did not notice on coming through because she sat the same. He knelt and looked up into her eyes.

Nothing is there, he said to himself. Then he had a thought: *Maybe she is imaginary... to herself.* He thought: *No—we are imaginary.* She thinks we are imaginary.

Parry had used that word to himself a lot lately since Willie had called it to his attention. Normally Willie did not think of words as Parry did, and if Parry spoke of one he might let it pass. But not this one. They both liked it. It went with stories like *The Adventure of the Empty House*; and with words came to mind pictures... making *real.* But only in the mind. *The girl is only imagining us... like we are only in her mind.*

Now if anyone had looked, they would have seen Parry gazing inwardly like the girl—as he thought of all this—stopped like stone with the nightshirt in his hand, kneeling before the girl. He felt a small thrill through his live frame and began to be afraid, only a little. Parry was somewhat fearless, as his brother knew.

Parry did not know that his big brother was completely gripped by the hunch that, little as she was, the girl was a ghoul, a living creep. He himself had not long entertained it, but his own new idea was taking hold of him, with cosmic unease, though he did not couch it so. It was a bit of awe. He could not have told beyond the thought that her imagining troubled him. Vaguely he thought of something vast, unknowable, *beyond* imagining. *And did not understand.* He continued gazing at her.

"She's got to go back to the church," said Willie as, pulling up the suspenders of his britches, he passed quickly into the kitchen.

On entering and asking Ma what he should do, but half his mind was on the chores, the other part engaged in a (more and more) pre-dominating insight (as he felt it), that a church was where ghouls could get help. However, he sensed that Ma did not much like it. Or maybe the family, the community of Five Points might be helped by the ghoul *going to the church.* And now he thought of it as Church, with a capital C. However, later in the morning Mr. Sneed would once more get him thinking about the 20th-century. He would again listen to the idea that medical science and the asylum might be the way through this problem. Mr. Sneed was involved in the 20th-century. He liked to think of the epoch separating all those in the graves, as being far off now from all ongoing.

Ma, putting the great skillet in the middle of the table, with her usual warning that it was hot, next said, "I think the doctor ought to come round today and see those rashes."

ζ

Five Points Akropolis

Ma worked most of the day in the *Clasp-Locker Hospital*, as the sign read hanging above the shop's plate glass window. Five Points, being modern, was noted for its plate glass. Light flooded in from the street and sky, though, in winter coming, it would be occluded earlier in the day because of the new grammar school across the street at the foot of Cake Eaters Hill. Parry had done his straightening- washing and-carrying chores, and was now in the shop with Ma and the girl—who had remained with Ma when she was discovered a distraction to him as he worked. His idea was that corn-shelling had proved her adaptable to what ever needed doing, but he was mistaken.

The shop had a clerk's counter where Ma greeted customers, looked over what needed doing, whether repairs of clasp lockers, or heavy industrial sewing—mending of items like leather or sailcloth. Ma would write down the name and ticket the item. Sometimes Parry did this. Ma didn't think it right to keep him constant at labor, so he was freer than either she or Willie to be out and about in the neighborhood. He knew Five Points well and was in and out of shops and also ran errands for Ma—which he found to be no work at all but possible openings into adventure. Behind the counter were workstations, each with its own equipment, and Ma moved back and forth: three work benches and one industrial treadle sewing-machine. The big draw was clasp repair which was not easily done at home. Metallic clasp-lockers lock and unlock a series of clasps in one continuous motion by the pull of a large brass ring. The teeth of the lockers may become bent or broken off and need repair. Ma did this at the bench with small hand tools, pliers and drivers and rivets of various sizes—these being used in the main. Clasp-lockers are used to open and close many things, but the main use is on hightop boots, shoes, and bags. It was the latest invention for opening and closing, in a snug manner, the items that might normally require dozens of buttons lined close on one another. As yet these openers were too big and coarse for delicate dresses.

The girl had stood like a statue as Ma completed tightening the frock's seams and tucks. Ma was quick, as she sensed its being disliked. The bell jangled and Dr. Zettler came in with his bag, having been fetched by Parry as he was come up from Stock Exchange Street—after a call at a house with typhus. The doctor called it *jail fever* so folks could understand. He had been on his way to order a legal quarantine when Parry had stopped him.

"Yes, the order is stuck to the door. It is definitely typhus, this case. The Parkers on Third St. Do you know them, Wilma?"

"Their nephew, Glacas, plays with Willie. He doesn't live in the house does he?"

"No. No, he lives three doors down, I believe. The

57

neighborhood is thick with Parkers and Setterlings. They are starting to call it Little North Regina, hmmm? Is this the girl you want me to see?"

He set his black bag on the stool by the counter. The doctor was careful never to set the bag on the countertop or table where germs of disease might the more easily be communicated. People were apt to set food there... or anything that might be used in hand. His worn leather bag had a clasp-locker Mrs. Wilusa had once or twice repaired for him.

"Come here, little maid," he said with Churman intonation. He coaxed, toward the small lavender- and white-clad back standing, face toward the rear. "Let me take a look at you." He studied her particularly. Parry had chatted a little of her, enough to let him know 'twas peculiar.

She did not obey. She had not looked at the doctor who was tall, rugged, and a bit stooped, wearing dark clothing and dark hat. In fact, he looked vaguely menacing to anyone on first sight, but after more familiar intercourse, he was pleasant to know. He had a big hook nose and bristling dark brows and teeth stained by coffee. Her back was turned, her face toward the dark interior, where walls to either side and rear were a warren of shelves and cubbyholes full of materials and supplies. The pattern upon a tranced eye was as honeycomb without the honey. As yet, Ma had not lit the illuminating gas back there. The girl stood with her back to him surrounded by the dim pattern, flecked here and there with reflected light from bits of metallic stock, though for the most part there were tools of iron and wood, and spools and bolts of heavy cloth. It was the warren the girl was caught in. Nothing else existed but the pattern and maybe a twittering of talk as creatures plucking at the pattern with voices, animal and bird voices; and once or twice there was a *ting-ling-aling.*

Dr. Zettler saw her standing virtually surrounded by what he scarcely saw.

"She can't hear us," said Ma. "I don't think."

"Yes, Ma, she can. —But don't know what to make of it, you see." Parry flung back his bang.

"Doesn't," said Ma. "Doesn't know."

The doctor went through the small swinging gate, at the counter separating custom space from shop space, and knelt beside her. She did not turn. He beheld her profile, a dark shrubbery or nest about the small shoulders and dark face besplotched with rash. *Does not like to be handled.* Gently he lifted her small hand, making small comforting sounds, not dispensing words so much as tone; and turned her, gently pulling her back toward the light.

ζ

Five Points Akropolis

"We want to be careful of this till I have given it thought, and looked at it under the microscope." He had taken a scraping off her skin. "She does not have the fever or other sign of illness such as accompanies the typhus—the jail fever—now in the neighborhood. It has a rash with it, too. Whatever this is I don't think it's contagious but you might keep her clothes and bedclothes separate from yours, hmmm? It may be impetigo. You will have to keep up a hygienic regimen, handwashing, etc. Send Parry around to my office for a wash you can use on her."

Ma was back of the counter as he stood at the open door facing her. Her hands were busy sorting tickets, bills of receipt, the accounts; and small tools such as tape measure and needles, pins. She had a constant habit of straightening. "Now what about the other?" She asked it, looking at him with attention.

"Yes," he said. "Quite peculiar. And of course he was thinking, *Very interesting indeed.* "I will let you know what I think when I've had a chance to study it. There are treatises on *this and that* I will read. And I will keep my eye on her, of that you can be sure." He looked at Parry solemnly, with thoughtfulness. "I think you may keep items on her for me. Even write them down if you get a chance, hmmm?"

Parry, quite happily, said from under his pale bang, looking up at him, "It will be my pleasure." Parry liked saying that. He said it often to the adults, less often to the neighborhood kids, who usually laughed. "First I will write that she makes designs with corn. Second, that she dressed after I showed her."

"Exactly so," said the doctor, and smiled.

Holding the girl's hand, he drew her out after Dr. Zettler onto the boardwalk along Sharon Road. The street was busy with custom, pedestrians, bicyclists, those on horseback or in omnibus or carriage. Aneas was on the corner selling papers. The doctor turned with Parry from the shop as he led his plaything down toward the intersection. Parry had spied his sometime playmate Gregoff kneeling on the boardwalk. The doctor continued from there on his way to the police station with the order of quarantine for that house on Third St..

"Hi, Greg," said Parry, leading the girl, coming up to big-nosed small-faced Gregoff. (He was sensing she did not much like hand-holding, but Ma said it was all right.) He said nothing about his charge though he was longing to tell them about her and the corn sheller. He wanted to say, You should see how fast she gets the corn off the cob and does not stop at it till the last kernal is gone. But he said, instead, "Where'd you get the skates?" Gregoff played less with him of late.

Gregoff was twirling the ball-bearing wheels with his fingers, making a metallic spinning sound.

"Read about it in the *Akropolis Lamppost*!!" yelled Aneas. "Read all about the minstrel entertainments at the Opera House!!" Now happy in this mandate to yell, normally Aneas said very little, and that in a low voice, always respectful. A strawberry blonde woman—in saucily plumed straw hat, a short bodice jacket with ruffles showing at buttons and sleeve—trotted along the sidewalk and stopped.

"I'll have one of those," she said crisply, handing him a penny, then swiftly perusing the front page with avid eyes.

Aneas saw a man in plaid suit and bowler coming toward him on Stock Exchange, and hollered, "Latest patent medicine for constipation and diarrhea tested in court!"

The man looked away as he came near, but then he sidestepped up to Aneas and bought the paper.

The colored boy was tickled at his cunning prowess but gave no sign. To Parry he contradicted Gregoff's reply, but in a way swiftly calculated not to offend. For Greg had told Parry that the skates came from Glacas and Cheenie. "You mean they went partners to buy' em...."

Parry said, "How can they belong to both Glacas and Cheenie? Their folks don't hardly know each other, you see."

Gregoff said, "They assigned me to find how I fix the skates. May be your Ma have the tools, Parry?"

"You can check if you want," said Parry, losing interest. He looked at the girl. "She looks prettier today. Ma got her this dress fixed."

"What's wrong with her?"

"Nothing," said Parry. Then, boldly he said, "She's just imagining us."

"What that? She what—us?" Greg asked this, looking her over speculatively.

Parry could not have said his motivation in confiding this broadly on the neighborhood sidewalk at one of the busiest corners in Akropolis. He didn't think of it. He said his thought without regret. If he had been paying attention to himself he would have noticed a small amount of relief in having uttered it. But now a certain amount of anxiety transferred into first Aneas, and then Gregoff, as Parry said further, "*We aren't really here. She's imagining us. Thinking us up.*"

Neither boy, the colored adolescent with short dark kinky hair, nor the small swart Grak, with boy-sized bulbous nose and scraggly brown hair, answered this. They looked at Parry and then the girl. Quietly; but with an uncertain feeling of creep.

At last Aneas could not bear it without objection. "I be

scared to axe you what that mean."

But Parry was now staring up Bechtel Avenue and did not answer. The other two turned their heads that way. Up there stood the high school Willie and Aneas were to attend. Backing that—Church and Cemetery with low stone wall overhung with trees. Having moved down from there on Bechtel Avenue, and now standing in the midst of the intersection!—

—There moved an array of half naked salvages, with heads half-shaven, marks on their fierce faces, and bright feathers hanging down. They had stopped all traffic, and stood poised, knees bent; having quivers to their backs, full of arrows. And each had an arrow nocked, ready to spring off the bow. And the traffic itself stood still. And passersby now stood, poised, watching. Beaded with sweat, the A'ndian scouts did a little dance movement, clockwise and then counterclockwise, each with fierce eyes, deep radiant flesh; toes clutching the hot and dusty pavement, some with moccasins to their ankles and feet.

Parry, who had seen them almost before anyone, now loosed the girl's hand and began clapping, smiling very broad, flinging back his bangs and gesturing with extreme goodwill and happiness.

Slowly his mood overtook them, and the whole of the crowd at Five Points—with its intersecting streets and avenues choked with blinkered horses and buggies—began clapping and cheering and going wild.

"The minstrel entertainments!" squeaked Parry, delighted. "The minstrel show! The Wild West has come to Akropolis!"

Then, amid the glut of street vendors, carriages, wagons and horses, with drivers standing atop their conveyance; pedestrian watchers clapping, cheering, whistling shrill: Amid all this, in space cleared as though for an A'ndians' promotional, came toward them a lad of stunning self-possession. With his father's permission, James Horatio Priam had climbed down from the spacious landau, and made now to welcome the minstrels, after their manner and kind.

He was dressed in a suit of Ewing cashmere, and wearing sailor's blouse with wide collar and lapels, the sleeves of which were trimmed in red silk braid. Knee pants and long dark blue stockings completed his outfit. He came right into the circle of A'ndians, solemn-eyed, his hand extended. Yet, as an arrow was aimed almost point-blank at his throat, he withdrew his hand, bowed away but slightly and held his right hand up, palm outward.

"How!" said James Horatio Priam.

Many in the crowd recognized him as the son of the great man, and craned round to see how that one might be taking it. But his carriage was stopped in the traffic as it had been coming down from Cake Eaters Hill on Stock Exchange. It was not nearly so visible as his bold middle child (James sharing that privileged position with Ann Gladys).

The A'ndians drew together, tightening their circle, backing one another, in small dismay but making no sign, as befits true warriors. They looked out on the interlopers as fiercely as ever they might have looked upon interlopers. For at least one of these had been at the raid on the Rovmorian hamlet where the girl had been taken alive because she cried not. These were the True People, whose faces were trained, as well as their bodies, to show no emotion whatever to enemies. Save fierceness. In the midst of this strange welcome, and its fantastically alien surroundings (the mercantile cityscape), they kept their formation and posture, awaiting a signal from Red Fox to let arrow fly.

It happened that James Horatio Priam went straight to this leader as if by instinct, looked him in the eye, and said "How!" This was not the tradition of the *True People*. But James had studied these A'ndian cultures in popular magazines and western romances, enough to feel sure of his ground. Every participant in the drama at hand, with the exception of newly arrived immigrants (from northern, southern and eastern R'opea), was aware that these were indeed true Red A'ndians, as Mrs. Havard would call them. They would think them to be genuine Plains A'ndians, and a well-known part of the "Wild West" vaudeville acts. The audience would understand that this was the true manner in which to make acquaintance of profound and dignified salvages. And the audience, to the last, understood wrong.

And yet. Red Fox received the homage of the spectacle, the peopled, riveted attention; complete with fantastic, solemn and formalized attendance of the self-possessed boy. He respected James's intuitive recognition. The boy was surely the son of a great warrior and chief. After but few words, low spoken in the unknown tongue of *True People*, the ring of warriors relaxed and looked then to Red Fox. Red Fox had been old enough to take part in the raid into Pensil'swood as a youth-in-training—in the middle of the 18th-century, which designation had no meaning to him. With careless extravagance he had led this new expedition, began in the Gorge but two days before.

And from there Red Fox found the passage foreshortened through *Time*—in the land of True People's too brief inheritance. *This* land, dressed in its guise of 1900 A.D.. In the middle of stopped traffic at Five Points of Akropolis, heaped with anticipatory admiration, he nevertheless kept his commission in mind. To find and bring back the girl.

Five Points Akropolis

(Passage)
Scouting Five Points

Anno Domine 1769.

Red Fox pointed signs of the girl's passage as they went. First downstream to the turning of the watershed; then upstream toward what would be called Carnival Lake (or Acme Lake), in a future time. Sometimes he ceased pointing and let Quick Claws, Deereye, or one of the others find the telling spoor. They had sport in plenty, for it was easy to track the corn-girl—better called *following* than tracking, the latter word signifying craft. As yet Red Fox was looking to find her, without real labor, and return to the Gorge. But, upon reaching the great rock of her rest—on the morning after—they found no more sign.

"Spread out your ways," said Red Fox and sat down in moist duff by the shale ledge to meditate. The clan had had its encampment not far from here many many moons ago and the rock was familiar to him. Then he had been as young as Eaglestreak.

The other young scouts went wide of his rest, Quick Claws further up the small stream. Deereye, loving the tall trees, went deepest there. Dark Cloak and Walleye-stare went up, the west slope and east slope, respectively. They came out on opposite knolls and searched ground and leafless budding brush, amid robins' territorial singing. Here grew also poison oak, but as yet there were no leaves. Only the swelling had begun since winter. As ever in scouting, they betrayed no human sound when apart and abroad. Yesterday their search had been careless and sporting, altogether a bird-flight for them, but not today. The girl had vanished. They had failed.

Red Fox was considering. He sat wrapped in his cloak with its few cattails for fringes, his feet tucked inside his crossed legs. He wore loincloth, and buckskin leggings fringed at the seams. His eyes were closed, his look inward but yet hearing the robins. Seeing the girl as he had seen her before: at the grinding, at the sewing of buckskin, the squash- and corn-growing, and the falling beneath slaughtered bodies of her kind. She was there, there, and there, but she was not here. She had been here, but not now.

Quick Claws returned first.

"We should follow upstream," he said. His voice was breaking, as a young man's voice breaks, as the voice of Red Fox broke daily, momently, in the moons before these moons, but no more. He had learned then to speak less because it was undignified to betray what could not be controlled.

Quick Claws also sat down in the forest duff, but far off from Red Fox who dominated. After some short passage of the sun through swelling twigs in the east, Deereye returned and sat not far from Quick Claws. He also had found nothing of import. Came back, not long after, three others; then a fourth; and all waited on Red Fox for guidance. Quick Claws and Deereye and tall, lithe Dark Cloak were most inwardly impatient, but only one who knew them intimately or familially, could have told it.

Lastly, Red Fox stood, and they came toward him, as he said, "We will do as Quick Claws thinks likely for us. I, too, think that likely." He gestured toward the stream, and they followed the gesture. Last of all came Red Fox after them up the stream.

This is the stream that, in 1900 A.D. nearly 130 years downstream of time, would be partly hidden, flowing down toward them through culverts and yards and under small bridges from the heights of Harkins Woods. In the A'ndians' own time it followed much the same, but these structures—with tall houses and pavement—bridges of timber and iron—all are invisible to them. Are of the time out-flowing, as yet separate from their own. But the falling and rising of the land, its native covering (where remaining) in streams and twigs, in coming leaves, that is much the same.

They followed up through the woodland of maples, oaks, hickories and other hardwoods, girthy with twig-ends swollen; full of sap flow, glowing with red-colored life. Unlike the day before, full of revels, now they were silent and watchful. But their weapons, as then, were put away in quiver, pouch, and belt. A faint breeze billowed their cloaks as they climbed the slight rise through leafmould broken with opening heads of skunk cabbage, curled fern heads, the small stream falling back away between and behind them. Before long the land began climbing steeper, these scouts following and feeling its steepness; and some other, nebulous, change. And now the trees were not so girthy great.

Sensitive as ever they were to every nuance of nature's ways, they felt the strangeness of night's too quickly falling and, with it, the odd rapid increase in heat. Above, Red Fox spied an unusual glimmering in the dusk, and went toward it as though drawn by a deep, and gripping, curiosity. Strange glimmerings appeared out of nowhere, and a rush or *woosh* of sound almost like approaching storm. But the sweat was soaking them, heat—as it seemed—of summer drenching them, and they found themselves moving dreamily, slow, doffing cloaks. And there was a work of net, or weaving, *standing* before them. Somewhat gleaming, *stiff. Barbed like a hawthorn.* Something they had not seen before. "...*Tspat....*" said Red Fox.

Surely we move in the spirit-time, he thought. *And we have no meteu here to interpret.*

They had forgotten the corn-girl. The scouts stood face to the stiff woven-work, each one placing hands on it wondering, fingering barbs stronger than thorns. They had been murmuring in wonder aloud to themselves, and to each other.

In the dark, behind it, something big moved, and Quick Claws perceived that it was a buffalo. The great massive horned and bearded, humped, cloven-footed creature; giver of warmth, much meat; and its horns for the keeping of meal and other dry things in fine. This form is what the *Haudenosaunee* used to carry their powder for fire weapons. Almost he went eye to eye with it.

"How can it be?" said Quick Claws to its dark shape. "He stands and is unafraid."

"More," said Red Fox, "how do we get past this strange tangle of vines to see closer? So perfectly they are sewn together." He plucked at its strings. They were hard as flint. Harder, he judged.

So concentrated where they on the mystery that it was long before they were aware of lights changing behind them, of the swelling of the storm sound. Then distantly they heard a great gonging, a regular sounding unlike anything they knew in the clans save perhaps the regular drumbeat, the regular heartbeat, or stroking of raven wings through air overhead. It occurred to them all at the same moment. "*Tschuppinamen....*" And almost as one, they turned.

There, spread out below them and now illuminating their faces, was the great lake of fire told to their elders of the *Haudenosaunee* (the which had it of the Hesuits). And it sent, faintly, shrieks as of pent gas and groans as from invisible spirits of the natural realm in which, ordinarily, they walked. Thrilled, stunned, and amazed, by turns, the A'ndians of *Anno Domine* 1769 stared out on the city of Akropolis, 1900 A.D.. Below them stretched the neighborhood of Five Points, and beyond, far—upon the bow-hand—shone fitfully as lit from beneath, powerful smokes—the rubber manufactories; while, on the arrow-hand rose, not so remotely, Cake Eaters Hill. And the powerful spell of fulminating sulfur dioxide surrounded, invaded them. They had found this smell in water, brackish not far from their campsites in the past. *But different.*

They spoke no words, braves in training, only they wondered and were deeply moved. It behooved them, they knew, to stand still in silence and try, if possible, to master the sight with gaze and sense alone. For what use were weapons or skills of tracking, of campfire kindling or to be now with care lifting the innards of deer (so as not to taint its meat)? What use anything in their power to perform—in the fierce reach of such a mighty vision as this? They were swept, together, into the *Other World*, the world of the medicine man, the world sometimes prepared for him by the Wise hands of the herbalist, the Squau who might assist at the entrance to other worlds: The realm of spirits in which *anything might be*.

And now (in quest for the corn-girl scarcely remembered), unlooked for, un-worked toward, without herbal preparation, without incantation, without looking to the wind, or to any of the six directions with reverence, the realm had caught them up *of its own*. And this was most astonishing to the elder scouts, to those whose voices had changed. To Red Fox and Dark Cloak, whose voices were already manly. But, to the younger scouts, it was less of astonishment. For they were younger—Eaglestreak, Walleye-stare, Sharp-Quill: They knew that anything likely was beyond their control.

Can it have been she?

Can it have been she? thought Red Fox. *Has the girl opened the vision to us?* And, *Was it the corn-girl?* thought Dark Cloak. And Quick Claws wondered, *Has she carried us away to the spirits?*

These words do not give the true condition of the A'ndian scouts, but point to it. Who holds the book in hand will not feel their dread and awe, both shrinking of and at once enlarging their being. Has he or she fought hand-to-hand the black bear enraged—springing out of nowhere—from the tree roots—its slashing claws longer than anyone's face? Red Fox has. Red Fox knows the fight with nature, and survives it every day. Dark Cloak has been surrounded by the ravening pack with but his flint, gathering wounds but besting them, ending in the pack's going off. He can take his living from the woodland every day, days unnumbered, and he survives. But we, who read, need these gates of hell, such as he now looks out toward, for survival. We take it as given these places exist.

Many in the family and clan believed the girl no bridge between the natural and spiritual. Not as was the medicine man. She was scarcely teachable to become *True People*. The elders, mostly, thought her too stupid. But not now Red Fox—as he would soon be able to confirm. And some of the others he dominated thought her maybe covert to the spirit realm. But not all.

In this even these would differ from Red Fox, who, with decision, would soon proclaim her one with the six directions, and worthy to be revered: Through the Pass of altered Time, a messenger, unintelligible to full understanding. Nevertheless, she was not to be obeyed as were the other Wise. (She never gave assignments, did not hunt medicinals, did not share of any visions of other worlds, rarely spoke). She would be separate from all, meant but to be observed, but considered, maybe even meditated upon: like The Wind, the Ways of the Water, the Paths of Sun-Moon-Stars. She would teach you without looking, without speaking, without, if it might be, your knowledge. Red Fox would be one of the rare ones she taught. This he would say to himself after the passage: For Red Fox she could not become True People. She could become only more. This would be his interpretation of the girl.... *Now that she would show him this vision.*

The A'ndian youths stood gazing out, not refusing of their senses but encountering what was to them at that moment unknown, spiritual in its reach. Fearsome as loneliness, as the *unknowable beyond*; beyond, even, the furthest reach of light or sound. We who read might say it went down into the subatomic abyss eternal, plunging through the dark matter of our material existence and forms. That young Walleye-stare should tremble was to be expected. Red Fox saw that trembling from the corner of his eye. Red Fox now passed gaze back and forth from his companions to the Akropolis night spread out below them. But that he himself should be also trembling!—it but added to the supernatural awe rough-shaking him.

And she had done it. The stupid clumsy *girl.*

But Akropolis will not, on the heels of primitive existence, much daunt them after its initial revelation. After some hours and especially days in it, they may even join the benighted denizens who naturally feel, through use, that they understand how it got here.

The vision did not depart. After some time they sat down on the hillside gazing round about them, scarcely trembling, maybe now and yet again. The ground was August dry, yet the air was moist with sweat and diffuse fumes of the city. They sat and watched, acute senses trying these elements to wrestle forth their meaning. For the older scouts knew this territory, south of the Gorge thence rising toward the high small lake southward. And all its river courses they knew. They had hunted deer here and elk. And now its trees were small trees, not tall and great, making small *True People.* Always, trees made them small. However the landform itself was most unchanged.

The big breathing of the buffalo behind them—with occasional snorts and deep smell of musk—is small comfort, calming: inside its strange bower, as Red Fox now conceives it (based on the enclosures seen in the lands south of *Haudenosaunee* out of which she came from the dwellings of interlopers). And the generalized reflected glow above the cityscape blotted out the stars— with light! Below them, in a strange regularity (of streets if they had known it), they began descrying movement, recognizably their fellow creatures. Tiny made by distance—a few folk and animals, horses, dogs. The dogs, distantly barking, were a comfort.

Suddenly on their bow-hand, through trees below, a light flared and stayed. Perhaps a campfire brought to blaze. But then another blazed up not far from it. And they, looking out, now distinguished many lit about the city they had not attended to till now. These showed the strange regularity of places animated by the scattered moving creatures. Another light flared, but it was lower, as though making a new trail of light in that direction, downward. For long they sat watching, and their trembling ceased.

Then Red Fox made up his mind. He said, "They are the interlopers. She is showing us they have overcome. They will overcome us and we will be as not."

This is why she did not cry, why she was brave. The other interlopers, fallen over her, were the arrowheads. One small quiverful of many quivers: the spirit realm is hurling at us. And, at unawares, she chose us; and we are here watching.

And tears ran down his solemn face. Not tears of fear such as he saw in that first quiver-full, not of cowardice, as he had supposed of them. But his tears were of infinite sadness, and from the pit of sorrow and of loneliness, and the longing for a friend of like mind.

He stood. And they all stood. They had already taken off their cloaks, but now they removed all save the loincloths, and stood almost naked and very beautiful, if one should look. Their muscled forms sweat-glistening, lithe and various in height; and Dark Cloak was tallest, and Walleye-stare would one day have more of power in his form. Their hair was pulled back in tails or braids with thongs of buckskin, and they carried all their weapons. Dark Cloak and Red Fox had spears.

Red Fox felt his confidence return as they went stealthy among the trees, leafy trees but thin and thickly growing on the hillside. "Stay with the stream," he said. It was now deep-ditched below them. It would lead them back toward where the girl last slept, and *where she had slept* may be something to show the way. He wondered if the interlopers' makings would hide it.

They were headed toward the strange campfire. Here the path was broad and pat. Smoother than anything they had ever known. Toward the one below it, too, they went. He thought there'd be the stream. For, watching, he thought it seemed to disappear, and the strange broad way was pat there.

But *hush*!

They stopped still in the shade. His fingers splayed by his thigh, Red Fox made them quiet. No one moved among the trees where the scouts were hid and sparsely scattered.

An interloper moved there, on the pat way. They saw him walking, saw the place: It was not unlike the hut of interlopers, seen scorched in *Haudenosaunee* woods. Red Fox saw this from where he stood nigh the maple tree. But it was bigger, strangely made in ways he could not tell. Smoother, more regular. The tall house-face was cut here and there with regular lights.

Had they known him: Johan Zettler, the doctor's son, was going home after playing kick-the-can. He ran up its few straight steps, not unlike stones, and entered.

The A'ndians stood. After a bit the light in the bottom of the house was gone.

Red Fox had studied all. The roadway, the corner where the tall house stood with few others, the street lamps leading along the hillside, and those leading down the way he judged the stream had vanished. Somehow it was gone underground. He had known another under-earth moving stream in 1769, the which had put itself there. This, he thought, was put that way by interlopers. Seeing all was still, he moved out.

They started down with attention to the way's smoothness, to its regularity and patness they had observed throughout the vision. Less and less they thought it dreamlike. True and yet more true they found it, as among the girl's thoughts they trod, searching for the sound of water.

Below them structure increased, was densely fashioned, became a landscape—fixed. They spied the gasman ahead; far ahead, along the length of lights he lit. They did not like the lights. The placement was bad for sight. Lights shut the upward gaze, gave it not to see the guiding stars. Red Fox said, "Do not look there. There are no stories in it. Look away." He gestured how to do so. In this way they discovered once again the use of fire for those who wished to be hidden. Firelight makes deeper darker shadows outside its scope. So the scouts feinted in and out of shadow, as they should when human beings showed. They scouted parts of Five Points within reach of their slow passage along the intermittent water. For they found the stream again as it passed through neighborhood backyards (with increasing foul smell), under bridges, and under buildings. They found gardens in configuration different from their plantings by the river where they grew crops in little hills. They saw cats, made friends with dogs, heard the fiddle-playing somewhere higher; and there were doves—most marvelous in wired cages. They remembered the buffalo seen in its woodland cage above.

At last they came to the brightest way. It blazed and spoke compactly of tall structure, with some few lights above in building faces. But they kept to the stream, and it had vanished once more. It was under Stock Exchange Street. They waited in the shadows of the walls, seeing but few of interlopers. And the gasman had stopped igniting lamps, he talked with someone. They two talked and smoked tobacco, had no clay pipes, but small sticks of fire. The A'ndians waited. Here they were bunched together in shadows, thick shadows of the pat and cindered alleyway between the buildings. Weapons ready, knives and spears. The stench of running sewage filled their noses. A horse and rider passed.

Two interlopers walked the boards toward the place where broad ways met, as these scouts watched. Twas lit on every corner, and one little street almost met with them, but not quite. This was Third Street, the extra way-meet which made the name, Five Points. The two men went round the corner inside Paddy's (which the A'ndians did not see for the door opened on Sharon Road).

Now they gave attention to the darkness behind the wall across the way in which was a tall gate with iron pickets. The stream was over there. In the relative silence of the gaslit night they heard it murmuring. Quickly they crossed, and vaulted the dry-stone wall. The wall, mossy with years, felt good and strong beneath their hands and skin. Red Fox marveled briefly over wall and gate. He would speak with the others of this surprising construction later.

They had gone over, as had three of the Five Points' gang earlier, in almost the same place. Those boys were gone home now to rooms in buildings not far from where Sharon, Bechtel, Third, and Stock Exchange had their intersection. The A'ndians, long-legged, free at last from stealth's constraint, loped down across the lawn, among strangely regular standing stones, and some trees; and down to the stream but faintly redolent of sewage (as they had not so remembered it). But they lay in it, apart from one another along its night- and tree-shadowed flowing narrows, refreshing themselves despite its smell.

After long-lying in the water they sat up and, moving not much closer to one another, began to talk in low tones of what they'd seen. Carefully they showed to one another each thing to amaze, and carefully thought what it might mean. Of these were spoken particularly how the lamps blazed to life without tinder, without wooden sticks; and how some had at base a flame bluer than they had known. And one thing Red Fox in particular thought on was the mossy stonework fronting the place. And he talked of mold growing on standing stones.

Five Points Akropolis

He said, "The stones have been set so evenly and piled in long line—but it was long ago. At least this stone pile is older than are we, older than our fathers and mothers. She is showing us important seeing. All is true here, as true as formerly—two suns ago—we saw our encampment beside the rapids. This is not what shaman sees or shows of spirit-world and then it vanishes: If we eat its food it too will nourish us as surely as the deer Quick Claws slew not long ago." He looked at Quick Claws, whose face had that straight white scar from when he fought the mountain lion in the east among the little mountains below the great ones.

"But where is she?" asked that one. He did not look then at Red Fox, nor did the others but they looked about them. They saw the landform, noting features seen before in their reconnoiter of her last resting place. But the light of the city glowed atop the landforms, its strange sources out of sight.

"She was not far from here when last she slept... if she has not slept since...." And he stopped; for thinking of that, thinking of the strangeness of Time, would bring them away from what was now needful.

He stood in the stream then followed down its course. As he went he saw higher the little stone hut—as he thought these mausoleums standing here and there. This one was more peculiar. He came out of the water, up toward it and stood a moment, then began to walk about on either side. He recognized the rock behind it, shale ledge extending on both sides. He did not like to touch the stone house itself. He touched the ledge.

"Here she slept."

He turned to Dark Cloak who was with him at the corner. The other scouts were scattered, looking closely all around it, Walleye-stare on the ledge above (about three hand-lengths of man higher than the hut itself).

"And now interlopers have put the stone hut here. Is it like the house of the *Haudenosaunee*?"

"It is smaller, stone made, not their long-log houses."

"It's openings are shut," said Eaglestreak, the youngest, coming around the corner.

"Did you go within?" asked Red Fox.

"No." Eaglestreak did not like to admit his cowardice. He lowered his gaze.

The scouts were lit by ghastly light escaping down through trees from high edges of the graveyard. They did not yet know its purpose as dwelling place of the dead, but they were no doubt attuned to the grave spirit of the stone houses, stone markers, stone bones beneath the close-cropped surface. Red Fox said, "I, too, would not go in there.... Yet, sometime, I think we must. But not

71

tonight. I do not think the girl is in there.... She may be. But I do not think it. I think she is abroad somewhere. She has been showing us what she sees."

All the others had gathered close to them. Now together they moved from the rock ledge behind, toward the entrance. They stood down a bit below on the cinder path. They were familiar with this paving from the alleyways encountered as they followed hard the streamlet through the neighborhood of Five Points. Its doors were in shadow, the shadow of the backlit knolls and trees, the ledges of the park. But the small wrought iron bolt shone a bit from light above the graveyard on the opposite knoll. Up there, behind them as they glanced westward, the great monolithic bulk of the church cut off light to the east side.

"Tonight, in twos, we scout the land round about this place, and meet here in the light of dawn, as he approaches; but above, upon the knoll in trees there." He gestured higher, with his spear of thongéd flint, to where the knoll rose a bit above the mausoleum's backing ledge.

"Then shall we discover what this place is, and its purpose and this great village made of stones compressed, and soils, and clays, and shaven timbers. We may learn what lives in these little houses set here apart from them. But we will scout in secret, remain in hiding, learning all we might about the over-comers. The girl's spoor is lost and may not yet be found.... Though I doubt not she is showing all to us, if at unawares. She cannot remain hidden. For she is not herself in hiding. She hides not, but wanders as the spirit leads her. She may be one of the great ones, but at unawares. In that *other world*, wherein she has a long home, she is not at unawares. But when she is in this world, whether in our time or that of interlopers, she is unaware.... This is as I think," said Red Fox. "As I think."

By this they knew that nothing here was certain. Not like the ways of sun and moon and stars, and water flowing *down* the stream. More like the waywards of wind and weather, of creatures yet unstudied, plants encountered the first time.

Time encountered in a different, it may be truer, aspect. For they did not know Time except as day-and-night following, and as the seasons changing to reveal their good and evil.

With profound and unexpected suddenness the great deep sound shook them, making itself in their forms, reverberant; then leaving them a'tremble as it dissipated echoing in the night. Trembling they looked to one another. "It is a sound we heard from afar many times on the night air. But it came from below as above we waited in the peculiar woods, first encountering, seeing the vision." This was said by tall lean Dark Cloak.

Five Points Akropolis

"And now it is here with us," answered Quick Claws who was drenched in sudden sweat. His voice was always higher, of thin timbre and therefore odd in comparison to his stature. But now it was even more shrill.

"It is mighty to slay." The voice of Eaglestreak quavered and quitted. The last word was a whisper.

Two others spoke humbly of it, also hushed, inarticulate, reverent.

Only Red Fox did not acknowledge with speaking. He alone perhaps distinguished its direction of force, coming, he felt certain, out of the great dark featureless bulk, backlit, on the hillside above the Civil War Veterans monument and its fenced yard. Featureless but for a tower, something he had never seen.

The monolith of the massive stone church above the graveyard had given out the deep resonant *BONG* that ran through them still. He shuddered and gestured, lifting of his spear toward it slowly, but then, as though to attack, he flung spear into the air carrying the athletic force of a Grecian javelin. A missile of impersonal vehemence and verve. It pierced through the air with a swift straight sound and stuck fast to the great pin-oak, branching below the knoll inside the pickets of the memorial yard. The thrust lifted Red Fox, releasing him from terror. He became voluble and let loose his voice with the sudden confidence that had *thrust* toward the core of the oak.

"It is a token of Passage," he said. "Have you not heard—as Dark Cloak said—how it spoke at whiles throughout the night since our coming here among interlopers? They have done this! With soundings from the deep, the depths of the earth and heat. They have contrived further to divide the day and night, the circuit of sunrise and moonrise and sunset and rising again. They have marked out its passages in ways unfamiliar ... and perhaps unwise. For it shakes the very bones and loosens them. 'Tis dearly paid to have the seasonal circles and moons so divided. Too finely they cut them, their days and their nights. It will take all rest from them and give it to dogs to eat, to tear at, worry over, growling. The interlopers devour everything good with this. They have made yonder mountainside." He gestured up toward the church with his unstrung bow.

But they had already lifted their eyes to that shape-shadow. And, shadow as 'twas, these True People appreciate without drawing near its mass and crystallinity of form.

Red Fox loped up around the fenced plot to retrieve his spear, and the others followed him, quickened.

S. Dorman

The Grandmaster in Akropolis

Through tall wrought-iron palings of the cemetery gate, Willie saw the passing Priam carriage—full of A'ndians—as he came beneath tall August-green trees toward Stock Exchange Street. A'ndians?? The Ripley child's grave was dug and, having heard the cheering followed by unnatural quiet in the neighborhood (on a Saturday morning market day), he left the hole awaiting its small occupant and went to see what was the matter. But now chaotic horse-and-buggy traffic had started again, moving according to its seeming haphazard purposes. And there was James Priam seated among some A'ndians, like a monarch with his protectorate tribesmen. Willie stepped out the gate, staring after as they passed, spears and bows like spines on a thistle sticking every which way from the open carriage. It was stuffed with *True People*, though he did not know that name. He was sorry to have missed the recent spectacle—whatever it was—at Five Points.

He knew James though, something of a friend, and a favorite source for the contents of Parry's wardrobe. Sometimes James came down the hill to play with the Five Points gang. He was good at kick-the-can and seemed to relish being *It*. Which no one else could stand. It's not that easy locating your pals in hiding. There were too many doorways, alleys full of garbage cans, backyard sheds, climbing trees, pigeon coops....

And now he had A'ndians! Willie shook his head, flinging sweat off his sun-browned brow. He should not be surprised. It was James Priam after all.

They were with the careening traffic moving up Stock Exchange Street toward the city center with its railyards, cattle and other impoundments—stock coming from the countryside to the local butcheries or for freighting to markets elsewhere. The sewage running under the boardwalk was from the cattle pound up toward the railroad stockyard. Akropolis, of 1900 A.D, was working to correct the passage of raw sewage, falling into the A'ndian River north of the city. It would be a temporary fix. A permanent aqueduct was planned to bring it all out to a plant on the edge of town, within wind drift of the (formerly) A'ndian encampment (*Anno Domine 1769*). Of which camp Willie knew nothing but local historians did.

Willie wondered briefly on their destination—James Priam and the plains A'ndians.

Absently he dusted off his old knickerbockers, shined the tops of his worn leather high button boots on his long dark stockings, and closed the gate with a clang. Ma might have dinner, and he could come back to fill in the hole—if the Ripley child was in it—later. There was always groundskeeping, but now he wanted a break, and to find out about the A'ndians if he could. He doubted not they were part of the minstrel entertainments at the Opera House. The latest troupe must be in town. This was not the usual thing. Blackface, banjos, tableaux, the gorgeously dressed pale Opera singer, the juggler, bantering comedians and the like; the playlets with strange goings-on. All these were familiar—when they could afford to see them. But though Wilusas had heard and read of the Wild West, they had never seen those shows in which it featured. He had not so much as glimpsed an A'ndian in real life before.

He ran down the boardwalk alongside the stinking gutter, jumped it, and dodged between passing bicyclists, horsemen, carts and carriages, and so down to the corner where a few of the gang still loitered, talking.

Meanwhile, young James Priam sat trying to face the scouts, turning this way and that in impossible conversation... a monologue, of course. They were crammed on two bench seats in back. The A'ndians merely looked stoically on him in front, or out at the passing scene: the cemetery on the left, followed by tea parlors, bars and shops. The carriage roof was folded down, accordion like, behind the scouts, and Mr. Priam had also moved up in front with Gilbert, who was driving. Every so often the handsome portly rubber baron glanced back at them all; or eyed, with a twinkle, his delighted chattering son. Mr. Priam's pate of thinning brown hair was parted down the middle and he had two brown mustaches. He looked very dapper. But, with care, he scrutinized the redskins.

It must be part of the attraction, the silent look, this nonspeaking. Yes, he thought. *This is the way to give the real feel for these folk and get us to the show.*

Wearing the three-piece suit with glinting watch-chain draped on his vest, he was not much looking at their own costume. It was to be expected. He'd seen the Wild West Show before at the Groverland Opera. But never, in society, had the A'ndians failed to oblige with talk and smiles, if seeming sometimes forced and unnatural, at other times merely silly. This is the way to make us see and feel what it must be to live in hot drylands and be treaty-bound to certain places. Of course, they would not be happy, but silent, stern, like this. The A'ndians, he noted, were young, very young a couple of them. Were their parents traveling with them?

"Father, let Gilbert and I drop you off at the Works, all right? I want to deliver them to the grandmaster myself, if I may."

"Don't forget, son, the grandmaster has them out here to gather for the attraction. ...But no doubt you'll do best in the matter, James. That will do, eh, Gilbert," he said to the driver. Mr. Priam trusted Gilbert to take care of it... and of James.

"Right, Mr. Priam. Right," said Gilbert with a nod of his capped head. The hair stuck out on either side, but beneath it Gilbert was as bald as a billiard ball, as James Horatio and all the Priam children liked to say.

As one, the A'ndians turned suddenly toward the North. Only for an instant Priam was puzzled by their sudden movement in unison. Then he saw it was the Tower Clock, striking the hour. *They are not so used to the traveling entertainments as yet, for surely they'd know all about the tolling hours of the city neighborhoods.* All across Americle magnates like him had donated the sounding clocks, mainly to churches, but sometimes to the town hall.

Mr. Priam had donated two, this of the Catholic Church on the knoll above the Cemetery, and the other one downtown for the city. There was one also, of course, at the factory. This is what he could do to help his workers arrive on time for their 12-hour shifts. Most had no clocks of their own, and few if any had pocket watches.

Gilbert sped them on South Main Street, the great wheels of the carriage reeling them along, giant paired horses wearing dark blinders, weaving in and out traffic with chaotic turns and twists.

True People scouts wore a taut self-control. Piled up on either side, passing factories did not block the welter in the air, the fuming of the blast furnaces, and heat of the rubber works, at that south end of town where, also, the ironworks stood. Modern-day industry stood over the land monolithic as the hills, as the mountains Red Fox had seen in Pensil'swood. The heat and fuming increased, with cacophony, and, as they drew near Priam's Works, they glimpsed inward lights among many openings, and heard horrific screeching as though the earth itself were in torment. The dirty industrial August sweat stood out on their brows. But their eyes betrayed nothing except a careful watch.

Mr. Priam climbed down and bid James goodbye. They watched him walk along the short flagged path, well-tended with evergreen shrubbery. He disappeared among its quaint turnings. Near above stood a tall (to their eyes) brick office building twined about with thin clinging trees, dwarfed by the works surrounding it on nearly three sides. These giants had the look of glacier-washed hills. Except these had specially cut holes at regular intervals. They fumed and shrieked, boomed and gave off gigantic hissings. The A'ndians clutched tight their weapons—knives and tomahawks girt in the belts of their loincloths. All other garments, leggings, cloaks and leathern shirts were bundled in Harkins Woods not far from the Zoo. Hidden among rocks and trees and brush as only an A'ndian scout might hide his good.

Already Gilbert was driving the team around the curved gravel path lined with flowering roses, back out onto the street. Gratefully the A'ndians smelled the heavy scent of the blossoms despite the rubber-making smell. He turned them along the way they had come, toward the newly paved and elegant portion of Akropolis, elegant with tall globed lamps ornately wrought, the square clock tower sending its solemn quarter-hour knell out above the factories. As they crossed rumbling over the bridge above the materials barges, James Priam fell silent.

James Priam. Silent... alternately gazing at them, and looking away with discomfort. He did not understand why the A'ndians could not come toward his friendliness.

Usually my overtures work wonders.

He almost gave up to sit silently waiting out the chaotic drive up Main Street... but that was not his way either: It was so queer. So beyond his experience. Everyone yields to James's charm. Everyone. So much was their quiet unnatural to him ... it piqued him, not with pride (he had heard of the ego of course, but was not exactly sure what that was)—but with disquiet converging on alien fear.

To quiet his internal disturbance he began a verbal tour of Main Street, the one he generally gave to visiting dignitaries or to Mr. Priam's business associates. "These great tall elegant round glass things are our new electric street lamps. See those long tall poles with rows of glass insulators and wires strung all the way down the street? The whole of downtown is being electrified, as you will see while we travel along toward the Opera House. And oh yes, that you are staring at is the tallest, most massive, clock tower in the city. It calls everyone to their job. And here is Latham's Apothecary with all the latest remedies on hand, no need to patronize the traveling medicine show. And here is a whole block devoted to our first department store, rival (or could be) to Macy's in New Amsterdam City! Oh and Hannibal's lunch counter! The most spacious soda fountain you can imagine, with sixteen kinds of sundaes." On fluttered his monologue telling the sights.

The A'ndians sat out this tour, gazing with silent care on

everything, and looking where he gestured as though listening to his spiel. The dominant quality of their demeanor, and as though one man, was attention; coupled with inward wonder suppressed. They were amazed, sorting the chaos without sign. As noted by Mr. Priam, they carried themselves (without knowing whither they were headed or anything about Wild West Shows) as though in character for the Wild West act of the minstrelsy.

Nevertheless James felt something—indefinable to him—of their inward watch. His verbose tour increased in speed and pitch until finally Gilbert looked down upon him to reassure himself of James's confidence with the salvages, before flicking rein to get up the horses around an oncoming omnibus. The look in the boy's blue eyes beneath the brown bang was not afraid, but a bit strained. Gilbert decided it would be all right. Young James Priam could do with a dose of subtle rebuff. Gilbert removed his chauffeur's cap and mopped his brow on a shirt sleeve. He had removed his coat after Mr. Priam had stepped out of sight beyond the shrubbery on S. Main St..

Gilbert drew the horse and carriage up alongside the Akropolis Opera House at the corner of Main and Market Avenue. From beneath the square portcullis across the street, James saw Mrs. Havard coming out of the grand Portage Park Hotel. He waved happily, turning his gesture to a come-hither wave. Very commanding and sophisticated.

She had just emerged through the glass revolving door onto the brick pavement between red-clay potted ornamental trees with dark August-drooping leaves. She looked very elegant, wearing a pale green blouse with long sleeves and ravishing long dark green skirt, very trim and altogether womanly, he thought. Fortunately there was a policeman to manage the traffic, and she skipped ably and elegantly across Main to join him. Oh how he wanted to share the A'ndians with her! And she was bound to know ever so much about them and may have known a few, even, personally. Perhaps she had been on hand to see some presented to the Queen! Lovely Mrs. Havard. The great Londinium journalist!

With a few words to the uncomprehending A'ndians about her, he had climbed down, and now hurried to meet Mrs. Havard as she stepped over the gutter of the red brick pavement up onto the brick-and-mortar sidewalk. The tall Victorian opera house with its neoGothic cornices, brick and buff limestone construction, towered over them. The A'ndians stayed in the conveyance gazing about, moveless. James spoke quickly of his latest adventure and she glanced at the carriage with six or seven A'ndians and Gilbert—a suppressed smile in her lovely hazel eyes beneath her uplifted softly coiled hair.

Five Points Akropolis

Instantly she saw that the best course was to let James take the lead in introducing her to his exotica. She was prepared to be very quiet and demure. This would give James a check, she was sure, but it would certainly do him no harm. *My but they're magnificent!*

With gestures accommodating to their nonspeaking roles, James bade them alight from the carriage, bringing Mrs. Havard forward with careful introduction. She looked in each fierce face, with its high cheekbones and tattooed coloration; she nodding, but not speaking. Two of them had white scars across their darkened features. The A'ndians looked at her.

"Aren't you going to speak to them? They're in character, I reckon. But you must make them feel appreciated."

"How am I to do that, I should like to know," she said, thinking; *This is the real thing.* "James, I'm afraid I must leave you to your charge as I have an appointment with your father. If you mean to go in there with them, I shall be very much obliged, if I may have Gilbert and carriage. They shall be back directly, I promise. I shall be staying the day, I shouldn't wonder, at the rubber works."

"Of course, you may. But I had hoped you'd be with us all speaking to the grandmaster! I want to invite everyone to *Stonehewn* for a lawn fête."

The woman from Londinium was surprised and couldn't help wondering if Mr. Priam knew anything about it. She glanced at Gilbert past the statuesque young red men, scarcely clothed. But Gilbert was in the box merely mopping his forehead and watching traffic while his betters conversed.

"I'm sure you can manage that on your own. Now be a dear and let me go. They'll be back directly," she said again, and climbed up without aid of man or boy.

James was momently cast down. The aspect of his A'ndians was daunting. They merely stood in the sun appearing not to watch the gathering spectators all around the brick paved corner beneath the tall opera house. James watched Gilbert pull out into the careering traffic. He looked around then, wondering which entrance to try. He was sweating his short belted jacket. His knee pants gave some relief from the heat but his feet itched in stockings and high button shoes. The entrance he loved and generally used was on Market Avenue—slightly uphill, arched and lined on either side with rows of tall windows, shorter arcing windows ranged in rows above the entrance. The roof, high overhead, was mansard with shallow Venetian Gothic dormers. But the stairs leading up to the great double oaken doors were wide and tall. That's what inspired him as the crowd gathered, staring and murmuring among themselves. Here was something!

He mounted the hewn granite steps of the great central entrance way, and motioned the A'ndians after. They looked to one of their number in particular, the one whom James had first approached at Five Points with his forthright, "HOW!" James stood speaking and gesturing to the crowd, formally, and was not quite prepared for the informal response.

"Where'd ja get th' Injuns!"

"They gonna get that sleek scalp of yours, kid?"

"They powwowing in the opree house 'nite? Watch it don't burn down!"

The R'opean immigrants in the crowd only looked on.

Red Fox understood the tone and tenor, having witnessed and then partaken of jeering and jesting when testing the courage of enemies. With inward reluctance and outward alacrity he climbed the hewn steps (still well below the entrance), spear in hand, bow and arrows slung on his brown back. He stood above James, his scouts with him, staring out across the crowded Main Street with parallel rail lines above and canal traffic below it. He did not deign to look at anyone, but at the distance. His fellows did likewise, ranged about him but slightly lower. And there they stood beautiful, poised beyond anything admirable in Akropolis, receiving the jeers they thought were their due. Yet without loss of dignity.

The crowd, while enamored, stood shouting and heckling, some praising, applauding and back-slapping their approval. For the most part its women and children stood merely gawking with the quieter immigrants.

James gave up trying to speak to them and looked about for a way in. Somehow, he doubted the great doors above would be open at this time of day.

"Ah! My new act has arrived!" said this particular Grandmaster. Massively, he stepped out the small door inset from the great oaken entrance. His voice was unexpectedly loud. The custom of his particular circuit had always been aware that it was deep, but few had thought he might speak like this outside the theater. From its stage his great voice carried to the furthest reach amid the audience's hushed expectation. Its boxes, main floor and galleries had no problem hearing him when he spoke. But, that he should sound so powerful, mellow and inviting, the instant he sprang from the doorway—this was colossal and galvanizing to the crowd on the street below. He came down the steps deliberately but was not dressed in his entertainment clothes, no! He was dressed like one of the workmen who set up the stage for its acts. Yet all there in the crowd knew who he was, both by his capacious size (seeming almost as if it were possible to fill the great stone stair with his bulk)—and by his rich outsized voice. It was distinctive, unique! Seeming to compass every timbre, from low to high, earthy deep and stargazing heavenly. There could be no mistaking him when he came to town. One found no comparison to other grandmasters on the vaudeville circuit.

The whole street, with its chaos of careering or lumbering traffic, was, if not absolutely stopped, at least checked by this unusual sight of Grandmaster, the A'ndians, and the boy (seeming self-assured—was that the rubber baron's son?)—all ranged upon the square stone massive staircase beneath the showplace; which in itself was an architectural marvel. They'd been getting used to the newest House since its erection by a consortium of business associates, of which Mr. Priam was one. Naturally, seeing a crowd gathered there, yet more crowding was bound to accrete.

"My friends!" boomed the Grandmaster, swaying lightly on his prodigious legs, his massive arms outspread. "I'm delighted you've gathered to get a peep at our newest act on the circuit. Yes!! *Absolutely delighted!* Happily, Akropolis is in for a treat denied other stages, other ages, even, of humankind!" The Grandmaster was given to hyperbole. He relished it. One could almost see him lick his full lips over it, yet there was nothing of greed, sneering or maliciousness in his expressions. For he was a great man in other respects than his size. One almost feels like writing his pronoun in capitals, so great, kind, and courteous a man was HE. He seemed, when speaking to one, or to many at once, to have all the time in the world somewhere about him. And he was so very light on his feet! Some in the crowd began to fancy he might lift off the hewn stone stairs any moment and float lightly away with a fanciful smile and confiding twinkle in his gray eyes. Oh! He was a great man. Anyone might see it! Even in his workaday clothes, paint-stained. Patched—by some struggling hand no doubt. It would take a mighty effort to keep this man in clothes!

"My friends!" said the colossus. "My friends! What you all have been waiting for...!"

The crowd of men, women and children, some from every country in R'opea, Akrika, even Osiia, stood absolutely still to listen. The traffic had slowed and was even now stopping, that its passengers might gape in wonder. The ringing and clanging of iron-shod hooves on the pavement, the thundering of delivery drays—all ceased. The dew of morning had long disappeared except it had moved into the crowd; for all were perspiring. The horse traffic choked the intersection, its horses' tails and ears twitching flies away. It is most unexpected to see the great man out here, and displayed with part of his retinue. Though a teaser now and then in the form of some lone jugglers, at any of the four corners, tossing ten pins was to be expected.

To see the Grandmaster was not merely curious, not curiosity at all. To see the Grandmaster was instantly to love him. To trust, if not your self to his hands, then your soul. So charismatic! You would from the moment he appeared, eyes joyfully twinkling or gravely eloquent, trust to his handling. He was sure to rivet your attention and capably see to your entertainment. Except your heart were desperately hard and exceeding corrupt, you would not want even to question, consider; but would fully appreciate and enjoy his show. The grandmaster would have cleared all else, any concerns whatsoever, from your mind with his grand entertainments and presence.

Even young James Priam was instantly reframed in his certainty. The A'ndians, however, naked but for their loincloths and weapons, looked backward and up in wonder at him. They had never seen so large, so rotund, a man. Nor had they seen such lightness of expression; and mingled with such command. His was not at all like the silence commanded of the *meteu*—of the shaman whose anticipation was of a different sort (more of reverent waiting upon the spirit-message). No. But here they most, of all the assembled, were amazed by such a girthy great man seeming to turn on a toe. And apparently possessed of the ability to float off, hovering above the City of Akropolis, spread as it was over the shoulders of these supporting hills—its downtown jutting and bristling with structures alien to the A'ndians. (These were the hills they had known covered with deep, earthy, high woodland; cleft here and there with ravines and river vales.) The grey eyes of the grandmaster welcomed them, but it was an alien welcome, of a kind they had not seen before. He looked into the eyes of each familiarly, as the crowd quieted, awaiting his speech.

"My friends," he said at last, his look now on the crowd. "This is our latest act! These are your best visitors, to this great city of Akropolis, so far. You will have heard of the *Ghosts Leaping* which true natives of Americle have been performing out on the vast plains. You will have read of it in the *Lamppost*, no doubt! Now, for the first time, you will have opportunity to see, firsthand, its true and most worthy practitioners. Make no mistake, my friends! They have come to turn your very lives, even the lives of your furthest descendents, upside down absolutely. Quite astonish and possibly even delight you!" He paused, beaming, and the crowd, galvanized speechless with pent energy, exploded into cheers. *Hurrah!* and *Huzz-AH!* its many members cried.

They had at the moment no recognition of hyperbole, but trusted the grandmaster so explicitly that his ebullience and goodwill, his massive abundance of energetic enthusiasm, lifted

Five Points Akropolis

them into a consciousness new to many of them gathered round. Some felt entirely sure of him and would believe, henceforth, in him and his sayings. Some started counting the pennies in their pockets and reticules to see if they might have enough for the evening's entertainments. Not one in the crowd, however, was knowledgeable enough on recent or past A'ndian lore to be certain what *Ghosts Leaping* was.

James wondered if possibly Mrs. Havard would have heard of it, but she was not there to ask. *Ghosts Leaping*—it seemed to the crowd—was a particular display of savagery and cunning, evoking of spirits ... in which few in the crowd now actually believed. Some of the immigrants from the east of R'opea and the Orient did, of course, believe in such things, but they had not been long enough in the rapidly industrializing and increasing modern and materialistic midwest to question it. The A'ndians did not question it because they did not know Anglish. They did not know what he was saying.

Yet Red Fox, Dark Cloak, Quick Claws, Eaglestreak and the others, more than any here, know what he is.

Stonehewn

The lawn of the Stonehewn estate sparkled with lightning bugs.
Spangling gaslit lanterns dotted the nooks of shrubbery and
flowering borders. Coal-oil lanterns were also strung above
walkways in colored glass: all very pretty in the warm night air.
Tents for refreshment were set in the midst of the great lawn, and at
opposite ends of the sweet evening expanse. At one far edge a low
dais, lit at each corner with foot-lanterns, glowed about a set of
string musicians ... wafting delightful music into the night, a night
filled with gay children and smiling grownups. The children flitted in
and out among the legs of their elders, or hopped about hiding and
giggling in the trees—only to pop out again, often with shrieks.
Sometimes their parents, or others of their elders, would step up to
hush them, making sure of their good behavior and decorum.

Among the most decorous of the children were members of
the Five Points gang, especially invited by James Priam and sister
Ann Gladys who, as the two middle children were more conversant
with these who lived at the bottom of Cake Eaters Hill. Their two
elders, Kate and Brant, were too mature (as they thought) to go
down to Five Points for games and rough doings. They desired
refinement (lofty fancies yearning for grownup pursuits and
accomplishments); while the two youngest children were too
immature to be out and about anywhere. They kept mostly to the
estate, inviting their friends; or going to grand houses roundabout
(these so dependent on the industry of Akropolis for their grandeur);
or they went to church, to Sunday School and children's activities
there. The church was a grand new Opiscapolion edifice, with great
pipe organ, situated in the slight vale between the more rural
Harkins Hill and Cake Eaters, formally called West Hill. The latter
itself was the most glorious and comfortable neighborhood of
Akropolis, slung as it was across the five principal hills.

James had a fine time giving all the children their
assignments in preparation for his lawn fête welcoming the Wild
West act of A'ndians, minus Cowboys. The Cowboys were in the
minstrel show, of course, but the entertainments had not come off
quite as intended or—better put—expected. As we shall see later

upon hearing James report of it to the Five Points gang in one corner of the grounds.

The A'ndians were also at the lawn fête, honored presence. The Grandmaster (disappointingly) had not come with them, and but few members of the troupe had been invited, those whose roles in the entertainments were cultured, or truly operatic, the harpist, the Shakespearean recitationists, and the like. The other entertainers were all at Five Points or in other neighborhoods—with pool halls and taverns—enjoying themselves in a lively and less refined manner; among workaday denizens who were naturally delighted to have them. But Red Fox, Eaglestreak, Dark Cloak and the others did not now group together as might have been expected from the entertainment of the previous night. Instead they wandered around singly, looking at everything, seeming to hearken, stopping now and then to gaze thoughtfully, pick up a bite of food, or stare curiously at the musicians.

All the ladies wore their long white dresses with long white sleeves and lace bodices. They moved like moths from group to group, as if from clustered flowering shrub to shrub, engaging. One of the stationary moths was Mrs. Havard, the journalist from Angleland come over to send correspondence home on the state of Americle's industry. She stood near the pale rhododendrons watching, and often had clustered about her two or three gentlemen, and their ladies, speaking a few pleasantries and then moving on. Mr. Priam was most often with her. His sister Daphnes, who lived above the carriage house near the road, was sometimes with them, too. To the right along the pathway played the chamber musicians, now the Piano Quintet in C Minor by Ralph Vaughn Williams. The air about these quaintly lit grounds was so August-evening mild, and almost indistinguishable from the distant music drifting through it. As though the grounds of *Stonehewn* were borne aloft in scent, spangling lights, and wordless song.

Young Ann Gladys and James Horatio came to them, the former inquiring, "Will you be interviewing the A'ndians, Mrs. Havard? James and I would like to be there if you do." She wore golden sausage curls, a big bow, and a bright smile.

Her brother said, "I have not heard them say one word yet! It's quite intriguing."

"I couldn't be so restrained, could you, Papa?" said Ann Gladys. All were looking off across the lawn toward the musicians' dais where a couple of the A'ndians stood watching, listening.

Mr. Priam laughed, smoothing his mustaches, and referred them to Aunt Daphnes. Who also laughed—that nasal grating industrial laugh of hers. Her brown hair, faintly threaded with gleams in the lantern light, was piled upon her head in the fashion of the day. Mrs. Havard's features were lovely and quiet, its smiles in her eyes, rarely on her lips, yet she was not one secretly to despise a loud talker full of gestures. Such was Daphnes Priam. Miss Priam's face was interesting in an unattractive way, as was her manner. She shouted, "James they don't talk period! Haven't you noticed?! They don't say a word!"

"Yes but that's part of the show. They must stay in character in order to drum up business. If Mrs. Havard interviews them it will be part of the drumming up, you see."

He turned with businesslike eagerness to that lady. "You can even sell this to the *Lamppost*—a sort of Anglish view of vaudeville. If you see what I mean. That way it will do them the most good."

Daphnes guffawed. "I'm so glad you added that last part," she said.

After a moment Mrs. Havard said, "James dear, I don't think they speak Anglish."

James Horatio blinked. "They don't? You mean really? They are like the immigrants? The foreigners who come here?"

"Yes. That's what I mean."

"Oh." James became thoughtful, then drifted away from them.

It was all coming together. He walked across the lawn already dewing itself in the evening air. Fireflies were showing, confusedly mingling among the lantern lights, dipping and turning. He thought, That's why they did not enact the *Ghosts Leaping*. — *That's why they had the tableau instead.*

He looked about for someone to share his discovery with and straightway saw the Five Points gang over by the goldfish pond, pointing out the pale gaping catfish and talking among themselves. Five Points were dressed in their own best among these their betters (as both sides felt). The goldfish pool was beneath the shade trees and shadows were deep here, though lantern-lit. Each member had his plateful and cup of punch from the great bowl in the midst of a serving table. One or two of the more daring, having gotten over their timidity of being on Mr. Priam's grounds, poked at the fish or prodded them deeper. Others were casting out bits of bread to them. The pale goldfish waggled confusedly in the dark water, lit here and there with lantern reflections. Mrs. Wilusa was with them. She first spoke to James as he approached.

"Will the fish be all right, James Horatio?"

"Oh yes, Mrs. Wilusa. They are used to it with us, don't you see. Though we haven't bothered them in ages."

She was relieved. Mrs. Wilusa wore her best pale frock and her hair was also piled fashionably high. She stayed with the children and didn't venture among the other guests except when taking a plate to dish up crackers and liverwurst, which is what some called pâté. She had not eaten much because she wanted to keep her eye on Heirolynn, otherwise known as "the girl." It had taken Mrs. Wilusa much gentle persistence and a dense patience to learn the girl's name. In fact, when it came out of her mouth it was quite a surprise, not to the girl herself for nothing surprised her. The repetition of the question, "What do I call you?" had not done it. Then the repair woman had changed the wording and kept repeating the phrase in odd moments, as when doing repairs, making supper, or cleaning the rooms they lived in: "What are you called?" Then, while working and the woman had all but forgotten—out came the word just as the treadling of the Sanger machine had stopped.

"Oh here is Parry's girl," said James Priam. "I have been meaning to get to know her. She is a curious thing. Do you think she understands us?"

"I don't know. Sometimes," said Mrs. Wilusa.

"Do you know the A'ndians here?" He gestured toward those at the dais across the lawn. They had been joined by two others and seemed intent on the piano player's brief solo. The A'ndians had on their cloaks now. They always carried their weapons. "They don't speak Anglish. They can't understand what we say. In one way they are like Parry's girl here. She does not speak, huh."

Parry came over to them, dressed something like James in sailor blouse and short pants. The girl stood like a statue by the pool. If they had but known, she was caught in the goldfish-lights and lantern gleamings. She had on one of Ma's cutdown frocks, also pale. But her hair was long and bushy as ever. She did not much like to be combed or touched.

"They are? Like that too?" Parry said.

"In a particular way."

"Maybe they are both from *the country of the blind*," said Parry.

"What do you mean?" said James. "They're not blind."

"Well, that's just the name of this story, but —"

"—yes, I see it—"

"—but couldn't it just as easily be the *country of the dumb*?"

"Exactly," said James. "Well, they wouldn't like it here in that case. And they seem to, at least the A'ndians. It's hard to tell with your girl."

Parry, who'd had that mysterious thrill when first contemplating the girl, said, "Would we want to live in their world?"

"Could we?"

So serious were they that the idea of just having fun in some strange world did not occur to them. James said, "The answer to both questions is *no*."

Mrs. Wilusa looked on them wonderingly. Often it happened so, this kind of talk when James Priam was near them. She was used to it in Parry but it always surprised her when James could do it too, right along with Parry as though it were the most natural thing instead of otherwise. In fact, the two boys looked almost identical except that Parry's bang was blond and James Horatio's brown. And they were dressed nearly alike tonight, too.

James had had to be more circumspect than was his wont when inviting the Five Points gang to *Stonehewn*. He issued the invitation as general to Willie, trusting him to pick the right kids. Willie had sometimes dropped hints about who was trusty ... but seldom said anything about who was not. James relied on his discretion.... There'd been that time the light globes in the entry were smashed by one the Priam boy's poorly chosen guests. After that he spoke to Willie when Five Points was to be included. Thus, his audience by the fish pool included Parry, the girl, Mrs. Wilusa, Aneas, Gregoff, who tonight was without his prime instigators; Johan, Phileas, and Gwendolyn were here. The last was the best girl in the neighborhood as far as Willie was concerned. She had to be included.

James held forth on the A'ndians' tableau of the night before.

"They stood onstage as the curtain rose and did not move the whole time. At first it was peculiarly disappointing."

The Five Points kids stood around him in a semicircle, Mrs. Wilusa nearby to James, holding the girl's hand. Moonlight struck into shadows illuminating the top of James Horatio's head. The pool was behind him. Gregoff, sometimes standing to the side, poked at the fish. The eyes of Aneas searched the servants dressed in white moving to and fro, with bowls and platters or drinks trays, to see if he might get a glimpse of his father Argus or mother Mabel, the latter hired on especially for tonight. With Argus helping there too, she was the proprietess of the *Leg Bone Diner* on Third St.. Argus also worked two other jobs, one at Stonehewn in the scullery.

James said, "The audience had been expecting something called *Ghosts Leaping*, a type of dance performed in the East and South Lakotas and other Prairies in the West. Mrs. Havard said we were lucky they were in the entertainments at all, and opined that there must have been some mistake, and perhaps the wrong act showed up for the show; and that the Grandmaster just had to make do."

He paused to make sure of his listeners, one leg in knee socks propped upon a shapely copper-and-concrete planter with pale flowering shrub. Willie turned to eye Gregoff, who then began to attend.

"But I think, *I think* the Grandmaster knew what he was

doing and intended the tableau as a sort of appetite whetter, don't-you-see. For tomorrow night's entertainments. The A'ndians stood as though in ready ambush, perfectly still, as though they had been in the woods. And bushes and trees were set in pots carefully about the stage, everything shining in beautiful silver and gold lights. The A'ndians stood by these trees apparently carelessly spaced to give an impression of them in hiding. And some had their weaponry aimed at us, the audience. Offstage tom-toms were beat and chants made, but the A'ndians stood perfectly still. It was quite beautiful and made a most moving effect. It was even, after a bit, quite unsettling."

"And then what happened?" asked Parry.

"And then the curtain fell and we were left wondering."

We had to be there, is that it? Willie thought.

"You had to be there," said James after a moment, seeing no one responded much to his account.

"I think I'd rather see them leaping," said Gwendolyn honestly and with skepticism. Her dark hair was pulled back and bunched in dangling sausage curls that waggled as she spoke.

"We can see people standing around anytime," said Johan with precision.

"But have you ever seen a loaded pistol pointing at you by someone just standing there looking at you fiercely?"

Johan frowned. "Pistols?"

"Well, weapons. Knives, spears, arrows."

"But yes, I see," said Gwendolyn nodding. She was one who had no absolute need to stick with her first opinion. "How long was it they held those positions? I'd be afraid to go see one now, though I did want to till I heard that." She looked across the lawn toward Red Fox, Quick Claws, and Eaglestreak standing by the piano quintet. They did not seem that much older than herself. The music was more joyous now, and yet the A'ndians stood unmoving, watching. Maybe even rapt.

"Oh, but you must let me introduce you," said James gallantly.

But he turned away, first desiring to see if he could try his winning ways upon the girl and find out what she was.

James was short of stature, thin, and what some called delicate. He was but slightly taller than the girl. Yet he squatted before her as she stood gazing at nothing, almost like a statue. Ma did not like to interfere with James Horatio (seeing she felt herself a debtor to his father) but gently pulled the girl back a bit as James began his coaxing to get her to unfold; to recognize him, and her surroundings.

"Hello, my name is James Horatio." He offered his hand.

She did not take it. She did not ignore him, either. She was there. Barely. James was fascinated and disturbed: A bit like the A'ndians on the ride to the Opera House. But they had been alert, observing everything closely. Much as some of them were doing now, over by the dais.

"Is she pretending, playing, d'you think?" He turned to Parry.

"No. She is imagining us. We aren't really here."

At this James did a double-take, such as he had seen acted in vaudeville—but had never before done a real one himself. This silenced him, momently, like lightning from a sun-blue heaven. He put the coaxing back in its friendly velvet-lined box and stood talking to Parry about that possibility.

"Wouldn't it be rather that we are imagining her?" He tapped his head.

"But I'm holding her hand, you see?" Parry took up the girl's hand.

Ma, still holding her other hand, said, "You boys talk the strangest things." She knew they probably did this because of the stories they read. Stories she sometimes read aloud to Parry—things he particularly liked.

"If I was imagining her I wouldn't feel her hand.... My imagination's not that good. If I were imagining her I'd only pretend I held her hand.... To myself."

The boys around them, with Gwendolyn, began to edge away. They drifted toward the fish-pool, some still to think and listen, and some went over toward the dais to look, with a short space between, at the A'ndians.

Dr. Zettler came along a moon-whitened path toward them, bringing back his son Johan. Johan had on his best short pants, jacket and shined shoes. Dr. Zettler's slightly stooped rugged frame was all dressed up. He wore a circular stiff straw hat, waistcoat, dark pants (probably blue) and white spats. The colors were washed out except when near the lantern or gaslight. "How is our little girl today, hmmm?" He was looking first at the girl but speaking to Mrs. Wilusa. Then he looked at the woman.

"Her rashes are better since the treatment."

The doctor looked her over carefully, as he gently brought her forth from shadow.

"Ah, yes, much improved," he said in his slight Churman accent. "What's this I hear about her imagining us? Johan has told me your little joke, Parry." He smiled with good humor on the boy.

James Horatio said, "That's quite—well, apart from being scary—isn't it also something absurd?"

"She may not be thinking of us at all," returned the doctor.

"She may be almost completely unaware of us."

Ma wanted to interrupt to learn if he had found out something of her condition from his books.

"What *is* she aware of then?" asked James. I'm afraid someone might—I reckon—hurt her."

"Yes. That would be an evil person or one under an evil impetus surely, hmmm? But it will not be her fault if it happened." To himself he thought, We may as well fault that part we are not yet evolving. He said, "I'm not sure she would be able to save herself if it did."

"Well," said Parry, "We hold her hand, and I think she's perfect. Why do we have to say something is wrong?"

Meanwhile the A'ndian scouts moved away from the dais as the musicians stepped down, leaving their instruments behind in the stands or sitting upon chairs. Eaglestreak stayed a moment to scrutinize each one. The tinkling piano was especially interesting, tinkling in comparison with the grand pipe organ they had seen at the Akropolis Opera House. That had lifted him almost off his feet and captivated him entire. He was younger, shorter, more wiry than the others. His facial scars distinguished him. Others had scars but not like this, white and crisscrossed.

Red Fox signaled the braves and they sat together in a circle around one of the low path-lights fueled by gas. Of course he and the other scouts had been aware of the Five Points gang ever since they spied the girl. The path was ignored in respect of their pipe circle and the flame. It was turned low and showed blue at its base. When the partygoers saw them they converged, allowing a ring of space on the grey lawn between their own circle and that of the braves. The encircling space was an intuitive barrier which Red Fox apprehended before calling the scouts to the deliberation. The audience, dressed in finery, with drinks and plates for nibbling dainties, murmured among themselves about this ritualistic *piawaw*, but were otherwise respectful. When Red Fox began to speak, their murmurs ceased.

He spoke openly, frankly, to the *True People* scouts—each seated, feet tucked inside crossed legs—in the language of True People. He said,

"These people may listen to us and catch of our speaking, but I think it no trouble to us. They can but hardly, if at all, understand. Therefore, since it has pleased them to display us in our country—which is our land by adoption as the elders have said—and not our land only but it is their country in their passage: *The Passage of Interlopers*: Therefore speak freely in turn, each, when I say." He looked at each in turn.

"They have displayed us with great curiosity and refreshment to themselves, but they cannot understand us. Not when we speak, nor how we live. We understand too little of their speech and how they live, but are learning. How they live is of more importance to us than what they say. Therefore I, Red Fox, declare my purpose in this PASSAGE OF INTERLOPERS: We will scout the place-things they have made in our place and see what it means. It shall be displayed for us, and they shall be for our understanding. I perceive they have no purpose in displaying *True People* beyond curiosity and refreshment and that they will disapprove us once they are filled. We will become stupid to them. Thus we will now not return to the stage in Grandmaster's longhouse. Once is enough to understand. Instead we must search out this place, in this Passage. How say the brothers True People to this?"

The audience about them murmured again among themselves as he finished. He had taken a twig and lit his long-stemmed clay pipe, from the flame that showed all their faces staring at him roundabout. He began puffing, the light catching also in his pipe smoke. The A'ndians' faces, in the smoke-lit center, were far more illumined. Faces barbaric, unreadable. Full of a primitive logic and force. Yet the audience were unable to acknowledge the logic and could admit only the primal, the inscrutable, a dramatic force.

Even portly Mr. Priam was arrested. He tried to visualize the conception of harnessing such primitives in Brazil to work the rubber plantations. Looking now on these faces he saw not a diversion, not actors in a Wild West Show but an obstacle to such a plan: There could be no peaceful working colony, no hopeful leap for natural selection in helping such as these to build an industrial complex based on the tapping of orderly and industrially produced rubber trees. He stood mulling this.

Mrs. Havard and Daphnes stood by him marveling, watchful, reveling in the distinct, mysterious and alien beauty before them. To the two women these now also were no showpieces, no sad lowering of native Americles for the purpose of entertainment. And there was no personal element, no trace of guessing how to capture and use such primeval beauty to endow their own small individual lives with vain meaning. The romance was in the mere seeing of something not made in the advertisements, not shaped by machinery, not made by human hands or devising. It was uncapturable by any manipulation.

But the purest experience was with the children. James Horatio stood with his brothers and sisters, next to Ann Gladys holding her hand. Gwendolyn from Five Points also was there. He was thrilled speechless, as were all the children, who said not a word but would remember this night on their beautiful estate almost perfectly for the rest of their lives.

One reason for the perfection of memory in this, even among the grownups, was verbal incomprehension. There were no words to misremember, only a setting and scene, an atmosphere over and above, and altogether surrounding them. One of its striking elements was aural, of course, but their minds could make nothing of the guttural yet strangely melodic speaking, except what it makes of such *music*. Calm. Calm and quiet. In this it made part of the night's limpid, yet faintly smoking, atmosphere of subtly powerful—but to them disjointed—beauty. For these two worlds—meeting here—might not do anything meaningful with one another. They might but destroy each other, but what is meaningful in that? Individuals can only befriend as one soul to another. It would not happen this night.

The scouts assented to Red Fox's proposal in one low, powerful voice—thrilling to James Horatio, to Parry Wilusa and others, coming as it did after a pause on the heels of the leader's long-speaking: As, each A'ndian, puffing, the pipe went round the circle of braves, smoke lifting gently, streaming up through the gaslight.

Deereye now said, "And what of the corn-girl? When will we take her?"

"Will she indeed bring us back again to our place?" This was Dark Cloak speaking, tallest of scouts. Thinking of it now, he had no conception as that of Red Fox concerning her. He did believe they were *perhaps* present in this world by her own presence in it, but he felt it *completely unwitting*. Red Fox had said almost as much—in his speech three days before about the spirit realm of which she had come—but her form was not complete and so—Dark Cloak believed in somewhat dismissive way—*she could do nothing in aid of their predicament*. Yet he was not troubled, so great was his curiosity about 1900 A.D. Akropolis, and his slight but increasing thirst for adventure here.

"That is yet to be seen," admitted Red Fox in a tone of decision. "She is the sinew holding the skin of these Two Passages together. If once she is pulled loose through the holes of these skins, the garment of togetherness will part. We must be on one side or the other, then, I think. This is as I, Red Fox, think."

Dark Cloak then reiterated his assent to scouting the place of Akropolis. He had great interest; but only those intimate with him might tell. Most but not all of the scouts knew him well enough for that.

Now Walleye-stare, puffing then handing the pipe off to Quick Claws, said, "I would like to return to the rapids and our Gorge encampment. I would see whether or no 'tis truly gone in the way of flood. If, as we see, the landform is yet the same, we will quickly find it and understand." And he was hopeful, without speaking of it, that he would find still his canoe on the shore of the tributary where he left it but four days ago.

In the midst of the outer circle, round the lit and smoking circle, stood the Wilusas, with the girl and others of Five Points, watching. (Though the girl did not watch as the others.) Red Fox, Deereye, and Quick Claws were aware of her without now looking. She was there, her hand held by the boy who always held it, and the woman, supposed his mother, and the crowd of reverent watchers. The guests, Red Fox knew, would not long be held attentive. But some in the gathering, beneath the moon, would even be entranced. But he said,

"We cannot long hold them. And who knows if by some strange chance one here knows our tongue. Only let one or two become restless and it breaks the enchantment. We will keep her in our thought and leave one to keep watch."

The girl herself, meanwhile, was of course of those so mesmerized, but without concepts of romance to support her observation. She saw the patterns embedded in the *Stonehewn* night, the circle within the circle within the circle of grounds: lit by fireflies and lanterns and the mist breathing with smoke and gaslight; the moon's light afar, casting its circle. She even felt the hands holding her hands. The True People were always part of the circles. She was not yet True People, stupid, clumsy, corn-grinding circle patterns of grain on the stone. In the gathering right now she saw them again. It changed, became diffuse, but for the anchor of handholding, corn-grinding. Now it was more what it had been, though she did not remember it, think it, it was a part of her glance at a pattern.

Red Fox said, "I deem she is best bestowed with her watchers at the present moment. Those who hold her hands will keep her, and we will leave one of our number to stay, not far, watching as well. So we will depart this place, all but that one watcher, having seen what is here, without intermeddling. That is best to keep in mind: Do not intermeddle, watcher, with them." He was looking at Dark Cloak. "Watch only. Keep that in mind."

He drew the last of the smoke himself as befits the dominant one, exhaled into the lit darkness and, without haste, stood. The others did, as well. Then, Red Fox leading, they filed through the crowd as close to the girl as her watch permitted. Each scout looked her full on, a gleam of amazement or awe or curiosity in his otherwise solemn eye. They saw her friends watching about her, and her strange clothing.

Five Points Akropolis

The crowd parted for them in great admiration ... except those few who looked on with horror or disdain.

S. Dorman

Violence in Akropolis

They went back to camp in Harkins Woods. Here they determined to subsist while in Akropolis 1900 A.D. They had no such conception—1900 A.D., no *Anno Domine* 1769. They had *Timebefore* and *Aftertime*. Harkins Woods was between the old first settler's mansion-house on Cake Eaters Hill and the Akropolis zoo. The zoo and woods were an extension of the undesignated historic site. Undesignated in part because it was still in the family. The mansion there was almost 100 years old and would be called antebellum in style. Also on the site was a ramshackle dwelling called the Johnny Green Home—where abolitionists, father and son, once dwelt as near neighbor to the first successful settler and founding family of Akropolis. The area entire was known as Harkins Woods. The zoo was to be the next place explored.

But Dark Cloak, at a distance from the girl, stayed in *Stonehewn* grounds till the lawn fête was ended and the last horse-and-carriage, also the horseless carriage with occupants, bid farewell. Then he started down the hill in the train of pedestrian revelers on their way to Five Points. He was not quite with the company, but not far off from them either. Here were the neighborhoods, soon descending from elegant decorum through the indifferent, to the poor—the last because of its mercantile quality. There were many lanes, then alleys, on the way, interspersed with paths and drives, dense with frame houses; becoming denser in the descent. That August smell of sweat and heavy blossom-scent, then sweat and garbage, then sweat and sewage followed, respectively, downhill with them to Five Points. Few were unaware of Dark Cloak's presence behind them, and some of the bolder alternately tried speaking with him, kindly, or in raillery, or looking suspicion. Johan, turning, watched him, sometimes directly, sometimes from the corner of his eye. But Dark Cloak made no sign, only looked at them. He did not approach toward the corn-girl. As the several groups trailed noisily downward, they lost many members going into their own several houses. The girl was now with the boy, now with the woman, now with another girl, as the gang and others of Five

96

Five Points Akropolis

Points neighbors straggled downhill.

Just as it was deemed not good to cut the day and night so fine—
with the bonging of clock towers and church bells—so they thought
it not good to plan without understanding; to go ahead of what is
known, to what is to be done. Therefore Red Fox took thought to
hide camp, cloaks, provisions, and all but their weapons; and go
throughout the city seeing of its ways until the dawn should come.
They would know then what next to do. They would go stealthy
roundabout toward the center of industry in Akropolis; by way of the
High Lake they had known in that former time, the one who's stream
would lead back as tributary toward the great river where the rapids
fell in force.

The A'ndians first overtook the enclosure that had so puzzled
them that first night in Akropolis when the buffalo was seen trapped
amid the strange metallic vines. Here is what Red Fox, Quick Claws,
Deereye, and the others discovered at the zoo: pathways and cages
and stone huts roofed over in ferns and vines with all manner of
animals. The scout leader had determined that they would not
intermeddle with anything in this strange time to which the corn-girl
had brought them. But it was a wonder and emotional hardship to
see elk, buffalo, whitetail deer, woodchucks, raccoon, fox, bear and
other fellow creatures *kept*. Held. Stopped of all natural life, yet
alive. It daunted them, making low the spirit of man that yearned to
see all things free to live as they will. The hardest to endure were
the lynx, or bobcat, so prized in the hunt; always with thanks; not
for meat, but for their sleek pelts and beautiful tails. It seemed to
Quick Claws that the lynx stood looking accusation at him in the
moonlight, its handsome head staring as ever, with tall pointed ears,
down-curving markings and tufts beneath its dark slant-eyes. Its
usual tawny and spotted fur was patched and scraped bare, as with
mange. It was a shame so to captivate and compel the prowling
creatures, put on display before the audience. For the scouts
weren't long in understanding that this was the sole purpose of the
cruel captivity. This was the baseness they found in Akropolis, and
it was a wonder, and cruelty almost beyond enduring.

Once past the zoo they stopped to sample apples from an
orderly orchard, the scouts smitten by the largeness and beauty and
the apple-crisp sour-sweet taste. Never had they seen apples of this
quality, never tasted in one piece of fruit enough to slake hunger.
Nevertheless they gorged on their plenty as they walked with
purpose beneath the tall trees in moonlight, in and out the shade of
the ordered early-bearing not wholly ripened fruit trees. They could
but praise whatever working had so produced such fruit. For they
understood that the interlopers had somehow changed the wild fruit

trees of the scouts' own before-time.

"I thought she was with you, though, Ma," said Parry.

"Well, Parry, she was but then she was with Gwen. Gwen was going to hand her to you." Ma turned to her lad of all work. "Willie, will you go up to Gwendolyn's and see if the girl's with her? I don't think we should wait till morning." As the churchtower clock struck eleven Ma apologized to Willie where they stood outside the clasp-locker hospital by the stoop leading to stairs that reached to their apartment above the shop.

Below and opposite were three great arched brick tunnels pouring out filth in the moonlight. Upstream the scouts had seen the intake tunnels: clean water was there flowing in for the process, but here below, and in the shade of these tall tenements, the stench and filth flowed forth in huge discoloration. In these waters the moon ceased its pure reflecting. And fish stopped leaping as was their wont. They saw what had become of their river's watercourses and tributaries; how these had been funneled and dammed for canals and power generation, used as dumps for chemicals and sewage.

Spying their shades creeping along the river, the policemen chased after them. Shrilly the officers blew on their whistles, calling their fellows on both sides of the river to give chase.

The A'ndians scattered in their pursuit, but Red Fox called out in their guttural tongue to meet at the Opera House, on eluding the strange men (all darkly dressed alike). Two of the A'ndians slipped into the canal hard by great Priam's Works, bleakly lit. The screaming of machinery high above them pierced through the night. Two crossed the bridge and went into shadows of storefronts north of the Works; two others disappeared into railyards laid with lines of iron; crammed with boxcars, some moving slowly, jolting through the filthy miasma of the sweltering August night. Smoke now mingled with fog, hiding the moonlight. Here Red Fox and Eagle-streak moved warily, hearing the shouts of pursuers, now near, now remote, now again near. Here the clanging of railway signals, the Works' tower-clock striking, unnerved them. The explosive hissing of monster iron steam-engines, screeching of mechanical brakes.

"We will lose limbs under those," said Red Fox to Eaglestreak, pointing to the huge steel wheels rolling, monstrous, mighty but unearthly, near their taut frames. "Watch," he cautioned, "we stay together, watch we step not blindly away ... from one lumbering giant into the path of another."

Eaglestreak said nothing except he grunted, and stayed as nigh Red Fox as he could (always within reach). The policemen had left the chase in this fearful netherworld. The two A'ndians heard

them no more, but kept moving as intended, northward, keeping in
mind the trend of the tracks, running parallel as they did now
through a small canyon prepared for it through the city. They had
recalled in great detail everything pointed out to them by young
James Priam, as they were conveyed down Main Street that day
toward the Opera House.

Trembling hand on the banister, Gwendolyn's mother called up the
darkened staircase for her daughter, seeming not to care if she woke
the whole house. She screeched and stank of alcohol.

Willie stepped back toward the gaslight streaming in from the
street behind him, repressing a shudder, gagging.

Gwendolyn, he thought, as she came down the stairs. She
yet wore the dress clothes, tied behind with a wide bow, in which
he'd seen her at *Stonehewn.* Her hair was tumbling down, its dark
ringlets fallen about her small pale shoulders. Her feet were bare on
the filthy stair. Immediately he saw her withdraw the look of
defiance toward his finding her mother so.

Quickly Willie said, "Have you seen the girl?"

"Seen—? I walked with her partway down.... I don't know.
She just dropped my hand." She stopped and looked down at the
dust and grit on the stairs. *It was when I saw Pa.*

This was the gasman going his rounds on the lamps of the
lower Cake Eaters Hill and Five Points. Sometimes he was drunk,
like tonight. But not like Ma—not making himself sick, not killing
himself and his family with him—*killing them in another way*—but
not that.

Gwendolyn was a bit older than Parry, younger than Willie,
smart enough for a good conversation with James Priam. She
always looked ladylike for a poor girl. No one knew the amount of
effort put into that.

"I'm sorry, Willie." She looked up with regret, maybe even
sadness, straight into his eyes.

He turned away, muttering, "It'll be all right."

"What girl?" he heard Mrs. Partum say as he stepped off the
stoop. An aureole of mist-light seemed to express itself from the
street lamp. And everywhere, up- and down-street, was in darkness
but for that orderly chain of light moving off into the night-mist, left
hand and right hand along the street. He walked off, thinking of it.

The grand opera house stood in the dark moving mist like a
monolith, shadows and light dimly casting upward over its heavy
ornate façade. Not made like the rubber factory, squat and square
and regularly lighted, booming and screeching and hissing: The
opera house stood as though lone. And it was quiet now. The horse

traffic of the weekday-busy streets was missing. The place looked
mysterious—waiting—as Deereye and Walleye-stare approached
then stood in one of its arched great window niches where Market
Avenue climbed eastward.

After a while they heard Red Fox faintly hooting as does the
barred owl. They stepped out. He and Eaglestreak came through
the shadows, evading the lamplight, to greet them.

"It is still Quick Claws and Sharp-quill to meet us." said Red
Fox. There was a pause.

Suddenly, from above, a voice light and firm quietly spoke. It
spoke in the tongue of True People. It was the voice of Grandmaster.
This was one of the words they had learned, obliquely, from James
Priam.

The voice drew their eyes thither, and they saw him, or rather
his great mass, spread darkly on the hewn stone stairs above them.
The soles of his shoes looked largest of all, so immense were they
jutting from the hewn stair, in the mist-light. He peered down on
them from between those soles, his eyes bright as blossoms of
moonshine.

Here let it be said that the A'ndians did not fault the
grandmaster for putting them on display. The appetite for display
they faulted, not him. They were at first surprised the night before
when he spoke in their tongue, telling them how to dispose
themselves for the vaudeville act. The native Americle tableau, he
called it, carefully explaining all these unfamiliar names and nouns
for them. They had never heard of Americle. They knew lands of
Haudenosaunee, the Cat People, and others, but this land Americle
was new to them. "This Americle is what displaces *True People* and
Haudenosaunee in their passage," he had said.

"What is it, Willie?" asked Dr. Zettler who stood on the stoop of his
house at the corner two blocks from Sharon Road—toward farm
country on Harkins Woods Road. Sharon Road divided Cake Eaters'
from Harkins Woods' hills.

The doctor had been looking up past his neighbors, across
the Harkins Farm Road where the woods marched up the hillside. A
few frame houses stood there. Beyond, through thick woods above
stood the old abolitionists' homestead and across from that, on
Sharon Road, was the old mansion of Simeon Harkins. The doctor
was simply taking in the night air. He did not smoke nor did he
drink, but he loved his coffee; a cup of tea, the habit acquired from
his Anglish wife, now dead. He saw Willie round the corner on his
way up from Five Points.

"Have you seen the girl?"

"No, but I may roust Johan to ask him if you like. He came

down with the gang as I stayed talking with Miss Priam." The doctor stepped in and called up the stairs. He stepped out again and said, "When was the last time you saw her?"

"She was with Gwendolyn but then got separated on the way down Cake Eaters on Stock Exchange."

Dark Cloak, while himself a keen observer, had never been certain of the corn-girl's awareness. Many thought her stupid, and he thought this might be so. She had been with them a while and he had not seen her betray intelligence beyond the sphere of concern she was given. She could grow and grind corn. But she was clumsy withal. Red Fox, he knew, believed in her powers much as they all believed in the assists of the squau toward the visionary shaman. Red Fox believed they were in this place by her assist alone. That is, had it not been for her they'd not found it, but itself would be in the Passage even so. Dark Cloak watched the corn-girl wander off from the groups descending the house-choked hill. It happened as another girl, loosing her hand, spoke low and with feeling to the man who lit flames without kindling and twigs. The corn-girl drifted, as was her wont, through a neighborhood like that of the five way-meets below. As Red Fox required of him, Dark Cloak followed at a distance.

Lanes dark and light she wandered, turning this way and that but never uphill. Her course, he saw, tended downward. People were in windows with lights like those he'd seen the flame-man ignite. At first, when there were many on stoops, and yards or on porches (the names of these things he knew not), they might call out to either of them in manifold spirit, some laughing with kindness, some with jeering; some merely quiet, solemn or smiling. The corn-girl did not look when they called to her; she did not look when Dark Cloak was called. Later more and more windows were dark, less and less people left in the ways. Those there merely watched as first the girl and then Dark Cloak himself walked past.

The grandmaster spoke in the tongue of True People from the great weighty height of the Akropolis Opera House hewn staircase. He himself seemed weightier, then denser and more monolithic than the granite ornate house itself. He told them, in good grace, where their fellows might be found, for he had told them how to go. And it was even after the fashion of Red Fox's authority and Walleye-stare's desire, directing in a manner to honor both the contours of the land and the paved ways of the built portion these contours supported.

"One thing you desire to know of me, Red Fox?" he then

asked in their tongue. A short speech but full of the sounds of the sea their elders saw and told stories of.

Red Fox looked keenly up at the grandmaster's moon-flower bright eyes, shining silver on him between Grandmaster's great soles. His own voice drifted up through the night air toward those eyes. "I would know, not how these things were done. For I understand the full quiver and power. But I would know *why*. For I perceive that Americle is not as it is for these reasons, nor the interlopers and invaders come to displace us. The reason is other than numbers and power, though these are the means of its accomplishment."

The great eyes overhead grew more than silver-bright. Just a bit, their silver-brightness was now tinged with gold.

"The question you ask is of breadth and depth and height beyond your capacity to receive it... yet some understanding is indeed figured in your stories and may be meditated upon there. It will be felt, if not fully known." He stopped speaking and seemed to spread out more over the hewn stone stairs—while seeming, as well, to grow lighter; that is, more cloudlike and not, no not nearly, so heavy.

His voice seemed also much more like vapor, more distant and spreading; his speaking seeming almost to take on the sheen of the eyes, now spreading out like great flowers in moonlight on water, like water-lilies reflecting moonshine on Cat People's lakes. "But one thing you may know, for it tells of itself in the stories: It is to prove what will be done by Americle. For *True People*. And for others; who will serve her."

And then, to Deereye and to Walleye-stare, it seemed that ponderously he stood and heaved his great bulk back up the stairs and through the small door set in the greater theatrical doors. But to Red Fox and Eaglestreak it seemed he spread himself out on the night air: volumes of Grandmaster drifting upward in the cloudy seething industrious Akropolis air—as smoky mist lit by the blast furnaces they had seen: Thence disappearing into the night.

The man wanted something from her. She couldn't tell what it was. And it was dark. She did not look at him talking to her. He was there talking to her, she didn't look at him. In the labyrinth of rhythm and association he was part of light and dark, darkness and light, the man. A man. Talking at her. She did not look at him. He did not desire a response. He wanted no response, he was looking for something, observing, testing, covering everything in talk. She knew this, barely, dimly. No interest. She did not look at him.

He led her up into the woods not far from the camp, talking, holding her hand without caring, leading her up into the woods where were only few stars above. He was talking, covering her in talk. He threw her to the ground and, unprotesting, she hurt now. Gigantic PAIN permeating all being. Turning everything inside out with great violence and force. Inside came out. He was hurting her, she looked at him, dark, blotting the light, showing the light, hurting her rhythmically hurting, his breathing a rhythm, his grunting and groaning; and stopping and fleeing. And she had big hurt, and hurting and stood and went down through darkness, many dark boles, wandered along the street and it was dark and the man had gone off and was not making the light.

Clumsy, stupid. She was walking on the dirt road lined with great trees, dusty road, and she was hurting and walking hurt along the road. Here were some houses.

The doctor came out of his house in dressing gown and stood on the stoop a moment, smelling the night. Earlier he had been reading *Henry Von Ofterdingen* to Johan in Anglish. Johan had no Churman. Dr. Zettler wanted complete assimilation in his son. Now Dr. Zettler saw the girl walking, glimmering, and saw she was naked, hurting, and went down to her in the road and took her hand and brought her into his house. He saw she was dirty, her dress torn off her; and he talked gentle and gave water from the pitcher on the hall table, and led her into and through his office and gently, into the next room, and covered her. He had lit the gas and also now held up the candle to her features. With curious but caring attention—he saw tear streaks in the dirt on her face—but otherwise she seemed as before: no looking, a gaze inward.

He laid her on the table and examined her in the gaslight. He went into the hall and called upstairs for Johan, and Johan came out of his room and leaned over the banister. He had no candlelight and it was dark. The doctor could not see him distinctly up there.

"What is it, father?"

"Go get Mrs. Wilusa and tell her the girl is found. She is hurt. Tell her bring clothes."

He heard Johan go back to his room. Johan would soon be down, dressed, with candlelight. Dr. Zettler had gone back into his examining room and the girl had stood up but was naked. Gently he laid her back down and spoke comfortingly, laying the thin white cotton blanket on her again. The gaslight was low. She had no tears now. Her eyes seemed to look at the ghastly ceiling of wavering shadows. He doubted she saw it as he wiped her dirty face.

Johan had gone out the front door from the hall, the candlelight still lit on the hall table next the wall telephone, its light shining into the office. (The examining room was beyond in its own light.) The cake eaters always called him by 'phone. The Wilusas had no telephone.

S. Dorman

Having gone out, to put on the wash water in the kitchen, Dr. Zettler went back through the hall and blew out the candle flame. The scent of hot wax followed him through the office, past the desk and consultation chairs, and into the examining room, where she lay, bloodied, under the blanket.

Dark Cloak sits up in a tree in the yard across the street from Dr. Zettler's tall house, meditating. All houses of the interlopers seemed tall to the True People. Dark Cloak had seen the rape of the corn-girl, did not intermeddle as Red Fox commanded, did nothing to stop it. The girl was herself a spoil of violence—the rape, destruction of the village in Penns'ilwood. She had not cried; valiant, and True People took her. But in the Akropolis gaslight he had seen, then, tears falling. This was not like the repulsion of invaders, this act upon the corn-girl. Repulsion with violence was in the way of his people, whom they themselves called *True People*. Yet this was not why he did not interfere but because Red Fox commanded. Dark Cloak knew it had something to do with the non-time in which they now are.

Dark Cloak is tallest and, like Red Fox, carries the spear. His features are sharpest and he is most lithe, like a panther. Dark Cloak, unlike Red Fox who in fact fought the bear, thinks now (while sitting on the limb of the walnut tree) of the eldest of stories, the *Bear Without Hair*. It had but one small growth of hair on its back— all white, that hair—and smelled everything but did not well see. It had the smallest heart of all animals and so was hardest to kill. The *Arrow of Passage*, even, would have difficulty finding that target.

Two city blocks beyond the Opera House jutted the edge of the hill on which the city central was perched. There, across a gulf, was the North Hill called by that name and surrounded by valleys with streams and river waters. On the far side of this north hill had stood the former encampment where the corn-girl worked for her keep, and the scouts were taught of their elders according to custom. But now, in 1900 A.D., the scouts descended this central city hill and saw many houses in the stream vale (some of its waters ran now in tunnels) and saw houses rising up the opposite slope ... vale and slopes, everywhere, choked with houses. Even so, were streams here to follow and they followed one from the base of North Hill till it joined with the stream and then the river which the corn-girl had led them along in *Anno Domine 1769*. Dawn was yet forming among the low hills, most houses still in slumber, when they came upon the two scouts who had escaped the police by hiding in shop-fronts and alleyway shadows: Quick Claws and Sharp-quill. These they sat down with in cool water—remote from one another—and thought now to meditate upon their stories. And this in the midst of intersecting streams—now polluted with sewage; where they were nonetheless cool.

Each sat in silent meditation, stoical regardless of stench, looking up and contemplatively revisiting their stories. Here they were surrounded by low mountains (called North Hill and West Hill), sloping in woodland, *with houses on top*. They had passed now that place of refuse, great hills of it, stinking to heaven. The valley itself, on its way to the gorge, was in that place a great, nay monolithic, heap of refuse—the city's outpouring of garbage and trash. In their own time-country they had no refuse—where everything was used and reused. There was no dunghill. But the land surrounding the encampment, when it became foul, saw the encampment move away to the new place unspoiled.

Eaglestreak was younger and more obedient than Dark Cloak. He was not much older than the corn-girl (of whose sun-age they knew not.) He too thought of the naked bear, not in complexity as had Dark Cloak after the rape of the corn-girl, but as the scare-story of his mother and aunts who used it to obtain obedience: No child wanted to be *eaten* by the naked bear, the threat of which discouraged rebellion. Eaglestreak had one finger missing from the hatchet stroke that went astray when, as an infant, he used it in secret without supervision. His thought now was of the interlopers, who worked in the open at what they little knew the end of.

Red Fox, having now surveyed all that became in the land of Akropolis, meditated upon the earth-turtle's submergence in the great flood wherein all land was lost from its back. The tree on its back was flooded as well, whose limbs sprouted *True People*, and the turtle then petitioned the red loon to fly out and dive, looking for land. But the loon found only the bottomless sea no matter what depth it sought toward. Only could it find that small bit of earth to repair all earth's future and.... Would it be enough? Now Red Fox went further back... to the Passage of Loneliness (before the origin of Time). To the coming of great fire to force the outcome of Place and Time from loneliness and no-thing.

As Monday's dawn was breaking, Melbourne the rooster in the backyard crowing, Mabel heard the hurried rapping on the lights of the door downstairs. The Leg Bone Diner fronted the street beneath her window. She had been about to dress, next to go down and ready the fire and pump water and brew the coffee for the new day. She looked out the window at Cherisha below and saw fear, on her young neighbor's face, looking up at her.

"Oh laws, hurry and get Argus out de house, Mabel, de gwone get him, kill him sure!"

Mabel did not ever like to wake Argus, so hard he worked and at many jobs. But last night he came down the hill well after her, so this threw the fright into her. However, Argus had heard it, all the fear and concern drifting up past Mabel to the bed by the wall opposite. Choco the infant was still asleep beneath the bosom of Mabel, where she leaned over him as he lay under the window on blankets.

Aneas, in the next room with his little brothers and sisters, jumped up and stuck out his head to see Cherisha down there. He felt his hackles rise and fear tremble along his backbone. He bound to the door and flung it wide to see his father standing, blinking, in the hall. Thoughtfully working his way into his clothes, his wiry hair not yet tucked into its bandanna. Argus was thinking what he should do.

Mabel clippity-clopped downstairs, past the kitchen and tiny dining room to let Cherisha in.

Cherisha had on her pale night clothes and white rags tied in her hair, pupils surrounded in the white wide-open circles of her frightened eyes. Breathless she said, "They think he done hurt the new li'l gull-don't-talk! Hurry, git him out de house!"

"But he ain't. He be asleepin' wit me de night long since we see her at Priam's. So's de don't be taking it so."

"Donne matter. They gone kill him sure!"

They heard shouts in the street and stuck out their two dark faces to see the police coming. There was a jumbled excited crowd of white men with them. The mob was just rounding the corner onto Third St. from the direction of the Stock Exchange station house (out of sight four blocks up on the corner of Haven Street and Exchange, toward downtown from Five Points).

Argus came behind Mabel and sat on the stool at the counter next the kitchen door, his hands trembling so hard he held them together. Aneas then moved between his mother and father, eyes wide, shaking like the omnibus on a log-cobbled street. He had a confused idea he was shielding his father, that somehow the Lord would make Argus invisible just by Aneas standing in the way. "Lordy Lordy," and "Jesus Lordy!" He cried (though all unaware). All the small children of Argus and Mabel crowded in among the few wooden tables and chairs. Crying.

Choco hung heavy and low in the arms of his big sister—Li'l Mabel—howling. Like Cherisha, the girl wore her white nightdress with hair tied in bits of white rag. Sometimes Choco stopped howling and looked about at the crying others, his big eyes staring solemnly, as if to say, "What be all this?"

ς

Five Points Akropolis

The police came slowly along Haven to Third St., where lately the only trouble was in checking the jail fever quarantine at the Ripley's. For the most part there was nothing to that. Folks were scared to go in, but the children inside, still alive and kicking, all wanted out to play. And there were a few petty thefts in the neighborhood toward Cake Eaters. Maybe immigrant foreigners, maybe not. There were three police officers coming toward the Leg Bone, two with good hearts, meaning sound if not sentimental; dressed in blue uniforms of officialdom. Officer Sgt. Phillips was determined that, if he had to stop a runaway thief or riotous rubber workers, he'd shoot for the legs. Better a cripple, he thought, then a dead man. Officer Sgt. Levinson was cooler, his pace more deliberate while coming over the cobbled pavement where doors open direct on the street. Many doors were opening now, folks sticking their heads out, still in their nightclothes, more men coming out, following. Levinson was the so-called smart one, the intellectual who kept his head no matter what. But Phillips had been a good friend to Wilum Wilusa, Willie's Pa, and had sat by—but sometimes helping his boy dig the grave of his father—sometimes silent, sometimes talking what a good man Wilum was.

The third officer of the law, unofficial, was the gasman; whose job it was to keep this part of Akropolis lit during the night. His name was Partum. He was not small, not large, but usually grizzled with a day's growth of beard. He did not like to shave. The straight razor was never steady in his hands. Sometimes he cut himself just stropping it on the leather hanging below the bathroom mirror next the basin. It was his job to help with the keeping of law and order in Five Points because he was always about on his rounds at night. He was not well-liked among families there, but he had cronies enough, and his job of illumination was essential to the neighborhood. His own family generally feared him, in a covert way. Gwendolyn tried to keep out of his line of sight, and her mother kept her head down as best she could, soaked in the taps of the Bill Boones Bar on the corner of Third and Haven where she worked for her brew. That was hiding at its best for Ma, as Gwen called her; Nag, as she was called by Partum—though he it was who did most of the nagging.

When Partum saw the two nagger-women (as he was pleased to call them) stick their heads out the Leg Bone Diner, he yelled and ran ahead of the crowd and police. Till then the officers had kept the crowd back with a calm yet determined demeanor. But now it surged ahead with Partum. The Officers Phillips and Levinson had no choice but to loose their billy-clubs and begin bellowing for order. This was helped along with a few blows to the backs of those ahead of them. They caught up with Partum just as he moved shoulder against the oaken door with its small high divided panes.

"Open, in the name of the law!" said Phillips, as he laid his ham-hand on Partum's shoulder. He said, "Give'em a chance to come peaceable, Partum."

Partum stepped behind the officers, his slouch hat knocked askew. Giving his cronies the eye, he indicated to some of them: *Go back of the house.* There were narrow paths between buildings on either side of the place which housed the eating-house. Houses and shops were chockablock, but there were alleys and paths. Four or five of Partum's friends went back along these paths, to left and right. There they found Aneas standing, arms crossed. And Argus, climbing metal ash cans, next the chicken and pigeon coops, for a boost to the shed—hoping to drop over the tall picket fencing into the leaf-shaded yard behind. Here, this side of the fence beneath high neighboring maples, tall spindly sunflowers shone in early light, many with great black-and-yellow heads a-droop.

In front on Third St., Phillips, Partum, and Levinson stood outside as Mabel opened and peered out, cautiously, fear lighting her eyes like great lamps.

"We've come to see Argus, Mabel," said Phillips. "We've at least got to take him for questioning."

"Don't look so scared," said Levinson, morning sun agleam off his spectacles. "You know he didn't do it. It'll come out right."

But, as Mabel stepped back and they went inside, came shouts through the open windows and the kitchen behind. Phillips pushed past crying children through the tables and chairs into the kitchen, then out the back door, Partum with him. Meanwhile, Levinson stood talking to Mabel about the night just past.

Her voice was helped in its willed calm by his reasonable manner. But it was soft in speaking, and the children gathered close; the big baby, Choco (in diapers), hanging lower and lower in Li'l Mabel's arms. At last she sat him on the floor, and, sitting, he looked up big-eyed roundabout on the giants talking so far above. His lower lip stuck out further and further until a howl of such magnitude escaped him that everyone stepped back. Mabel picked him up and jounced him in her arms until he stopped, talking all the while in answer to Levinson's questions.

In the back yard Phillips found the cronies of Partum beating on Argus with pickets. One of them held tight to Aneas, backing against the fowl coops and knocking them open. Partum, not with them in violence, was standing by. The fencing had been torn loose, sunflowers broken and crushed, the two tabby cats scrambling up maple trees overhanging from the neighboring yard; chickens scattering, pigeons flying. And Argus had ceased protecting himself with his hands. He lay in a heap among the debris of ash cans, fence, and flowers in the yard, the vigilantes delighting themselves—amid their own grunts, pants, and curses—with kicking and thrashing the breath out of him.

Phillips loosed the gun from its holster and fired into the maple-tops.

The blast stopped them. His words, "Stop in the name of the law," would have been ineffectual without that. He doubted they would have heard him. So much of ruckus and violence had consumed their persons. Only like violence against them in the form of explosion could outspread their own violence to overtake them, he thought. Poor Argus was practically invisible, so small was he lying inert among the debris. The youngest crony of the gasman, who wrestled with struggling panting Aneas, was a member of the Five Points gang—Glacas. They had been fiercely fighting until the blast put an end to it.

Phillips went toward Argus, ignoring fast-talking Dreiser, the newspaper man who had come out of the alleyway along the path to ask—What was the upshot?

"Stand back! Or you'll all be cripples before lunchtime," said Phillips, snarling; but shoving the revolver back into its holster without a thought, as a matter of course. The air smelled of strewn garbage, cat urine, chicken dung, broken sunflowers, gunpowder and violence.

The cronies stood back from the work they'd been doing, gasping, panting, hungry-eyed, ready for more. Everyone of them was a white man, several with no jobs to speak of. And they were young, not older than thirty. A few were known for loitering overlong on the shady side of the law.

Phillips also was breathing hard, sweat soaking his dark blue uniform, not from exertion, but from the power of violence coursing through him at top speed. How he held his tongue then was a mystery to him afterward. In the night he would wonder to himself over it, and, at last, determined that somehow it was God. God had kept his tongue quiet.

A bowler shoved back on Dreiser's balding head, shirtsleeves rolled up, and his checkered jacket flung on a shoulder: this newsman moved into the group to peer down at bloody Argus, cold out among the trash. Already his pencil stub was working over the page of the small black notebook in his left hand.

Partum stepped close to see the results of these jabs to the paper. He said, "Doc Zettler says Argus fuked the dumb girl. —The can't-talk girl who lives with Wilusas."

Phillips looked up at him, considering; then back down at Argus, gently lifting him, setting his knee behind. "Go get the doctor, Partum," he said.

Partum stood a moment to see again what was written, then he turned and took the path between buildings and houses to the alleyway.

Mabel came out ringing her hands, Li'l Mabel coming, bringing a glass of water. Mabel had thrown an apron over her night clothes and tied her hair up in one of Argus's bandannas. She said, "He be the night long wid me. The night long wid me," she said audible, but soft.

"Write the doctor said the girl was violated. He did not say that Argus—or anyone specific—did the deed." —This from bespeckled Levinson who had tried to dissuade Mabel and the children from coming in back to see Argus brutalized. "It was Partum," he continued, "who said Argus did it."

The cronies of Partum began talking at once, watching as Mabel handed the water to Phillips, her great wet gaze set on Argus.

Her dear husband's head hung forward, then it lolled back and she saw his dark face cut and bleeding, one eye already swelling closed. His arm hung limp, his good eye opened, closed. She worried he would go blind.

Amid the roaring, Argus tried to stop the coming-round. The roaring unconscious full of ease and peace and rest. But no, no— here were the angry voices outside Eden, clambering and complaining; harrowing their souls and others'. He could not escape them but must join in the harrowing of his ground, be it ever so good or evil.

"*Argus Argus,*" said Mabel softly from a distant world.

"Argus drink this water," said another voice, gruff, not so remote.

...The voice, he thought, somehow connected with the arm upholding. His one good eye looked at him.

The police.

Midafternoon the two uniformed detectives were in the bare wooden interior of Five Points station house. Even the tall filing cabinet was wooden. The room smelled of tobacco smoke and gun oil, leather holsters. At nearly bare wooden desks, on folding wooden chairs, Phillips and Levinson were filling out their reports. At the other desk sat the lieutenant, thinking over what they had reported. The tall nearly naked A'ndian was still standing mutely against the wall, between the chair assigned him and the door.

The police lieutenant got up from his desk nearby to take the telephone call, standing at the wall, and saying into the 'phone, with receiver at his ear, "Lt. Baker."

The others scribbled on their sheets.

"Yeah. I'll tell'em."

Five Points Akropolis

He hung up and leaned against the open windowsill. The sounds of Stock Exchange Street traffic, along with the usual sewage smell and newsboys cries came in on the August breeze. The crying voice was not that of Aneas. This was not his corner but he probably would not be working anyhow. Someone even younger was out shouting the headline (which was printed in bold with red ink).

"They've got it done. He's well on his way to Groverland city prison. He'll be safe there till arraignment."

Phillips looked up from his desk across the aisle between the desks, one for the lieutenant and one each for the officers on duty. He said, "And that means no mob action tonight."

Levinson was silent except for the scratching of his pencil. Then he paused and, still looking over his report, said, "Except if word doesn't get out."

The lieutenant scratched a match on the window frame. There were uncounted match scratch-marks on the wooden frame. He lit a big cigar and kept puffing, but he said between puffs, and through yellow teeth, "I don't see it."

Levinson was always making sense—but still he didn't like it. Baker could not help resisting the Ju's sense.

Levinson said, "A few rabble rousers ought to get the word, and go see if it's so."

"I don't see it. What do you think, Phillips?"

Phillips stopped scratching his pencil, chewed the end. He picked up the gum eraser, played finger-fiddling with it, back and forth across his knuckles. "I guess I don't see it either."

Levinson went back to the report to dot his i's. *You will*, he thought. But he said nothing. Would that do? He wondered.

Neither man showed signs of movement. If they thought about it there was no sign. Levinson waited for a half hour. Then he brought it up again.

Phillips and Baker were on their way out the door, guns and holsters, batons, helmets and badges. All this stuff went home with them.

"I think we ought to spread the word."

"Let it be," said Baker.

The A'ndian was still standing stoically against the wall, practically naked except for his weapons. *Suspect or potential witness?* Levinson decided to wait for the Grandmaster and his interpretive skill—who was, it seemed, taking his time. Levinson was just curious about the Grandmaster. That's why he stayed past his shift.

Baker and Phillips parted on the boardwalk below, the streetcar just going by. The early supper was waiting. And their fellow officers were already on second-shift beat.

All day long the other word, fomenting—of Argus and the crime
alleged—rumbled through the town. Not just in Five Points, but
spreading with contempt and violent verbiage throughout the city.
Akropolis was humming, its furnaces blasting, and streetcars
rattling, horse wagons rumbling. All factories buzzed with more
than shouting and screeching machinery; machinery melting,
molding, hissing, steaming. —Shouts and whispers about what was
to be done for "the nagger that raped a helpless little girl."

The big men in Akropolis had prepared, the city officials hired
to keep the peace and see the law was respected, carried forward to
its full and correct penalties. Downtown—the County Jail, the City
Building and the Courthouse had made their preparations. Small
doings, to see that all would come off civilized, and with due process.
The rumor was that the crowd would come from every corner after
second shift and demand the prisoner that he might well and swiftly
hang. So what did these wise officials do, but well and swiftly get
the prisoner out of town? It was a fair stroke and prudent. The
accused was not there, so folks—by reason—would disperse, go
home—to houses, family, cronies, lovers; there to stew and simmer.
Let the rumored foment wither in the cooling off of Akropolis, as
night fell. So Argus the accused was taken off to Groverland prison.
Let the mob go sixty miles and there soak itself in the Great Lake
beside the port city.

Would the mob, so strangely extrapolating itself out of
individual soulish entities, have achieved its mass and weight and
heft, its energetic force—had it been discouraged *early* by the *known*
fact of Argus's absence?

Dreiser's newspaper account was later clear. The officials did
wisely... up to a point.... One point, one jot, one particle of the plan
was missing. Just one.

The mob assembled, it accreted, gained spectators, traffic,
mass; and stones and bricks and, later, other kinds of ammunition;
gained energy, gained force. And *then*, wrote Dreiser later, *then* it
was told the prisoner was gone. *Then*, the announcement was made
from the steps of the County Jail. Then. When it was too late.

Now they were at the confluence where they had tracked the corn-
girl—in the scheme of uninterrupted time but five days before. Here
the greater river of the encampment joined with smaller tributaries,
gathered from the High Lake southward, to this meeting north of
Akropolis. And all now fell toward the Great Lake in the north,
many leagues away by the flight of the crow. They had seen many
wonders of the new world (in which guise it presented itself so fully
to these scouts), and now were more than curious, and a bit fearful,

to see what the encampment had become in this selfsame new world.

The low wooded slopes and hills among which the river snaked were above on one side, crowded with tall houses of the interlopers; but opposite were works in preliminary stages to bring sewage from the town to the place appointed north of Cake Eaters Hill on this selfsame river. They saw but little of these workings and some strange small sticks, bits and pieces meant to help with surveying, of which they did not understand. Here were few workmen. But the A'ndians went on upstream, sometimes wading, sometimes swimming, for the river was low but had, here and there, swimming holes. Fish did not abound as Red Fox, Sharp-quill, Deereye and the others had known on their way in *Anno Domine* 1769, those few days ago.

On they followed upstream, and after some few leagues rounded the last bend but one before they should reach the encampment above the stretch nigh the rapids where fish leapt following out of the Great Lake up to the spawning. The scouts' bodies glistened with sweat, and the foul odor of sewage clung to them. Now they saw tall houses crowded on hills and ledges high above, beneath which their home should soon show itself in great activity. With dogs playing, and seed ready for planting, corn, squash, tomato vines and other, in the earth by the rapids; with smoke streaming up, handily to preserve their venison and other stores for the next winter to come.

But, rounding the last bend, en route from Akropolis with its Opera House, downtown, and rubber works; they saw a great work building (for power generation), the water falling mightily, not as rapids where fish might leap, but from a great height all at once, with roaring. It would be long moments before they turned to look on the opposite slope homeward.

Men, minute in the distance, climbed about on piers and planking, signaling and waving—as beams hauled up by horses with aid of block-and-tackle rigging were lifted, great timbers, swinging, swaying. A great steaming monster with boiler, water tank, main engine, winch, bucket and pivoting boom, stood above the works wresting rocks from the side of the hill. All this, on the side opposite their encampment met and arrested their gaze. They looked back and forth from seeing first the falls, and then the works, and back to the falls again. And back again.

As one the scouts stood shoulder deep in water, abreast, watching the Great Fall high and pouring forth, foaming, silvering as water flew upward, shivering to droplets and heaving mist. It poured from beneath side openings on the south side. And above the main fall, they saw other falls behind.

After long staring, they looked then across to see how fared the place of their encampment. The A'ndian gardens were now covered over in buildings and works. All that remained was the great and powerful ledge, towering; beneath which the corn-girl and other squaus had had their kitchens (as these were now known to the local historians of Akropolis 1900 and A'ndian Falls). They recognized the steep powerful sandstone of its overhanging cliff, and the shale undergirding its massive and ancient support. Had they but climbed to look, had they but known how to read in the style of the interlopers, they would have encountered this plaque, embossed in bronze lettering:

TO MEMORIALIZE HEIROLYNN HAMPBELL

Who, as a child, was kidnapped circa 1765
From a Pensil'swood Rovmorian Mission
And made to work beneath this ledge
in A'ndian kitchens.

Heirolynn Hampbell
Thus was the first white person
To live in the Western Stock Reserve.
This plaque is set in dedication by the
Children of the Americle Revolt.

The water fell. The works and men made it fall from heights they had contrived—cutting back the gradual fall that made the rapids of *Coppacow*. With dynamite they'd done it, though this was not evident or even known to the scouts. Nothing in all Akropolis compared with this part of the corn-girl's vision. For them no gradual change had overtaken this place as it had for generations of interlopers. A'stew in waters only slightly more refreshing than those pouring below-stream at the way-meet of waters from Akropolis and A'ndian Falls: Now the scouts were shaken as by nothing else in the great seeing of which they were a part. For this had been wilderness, nought but trees and hills and waters—yet days ago. Their home as few places along the river, above or below these rapids, had been home to them before.

Red Fox looked from the falls, to the works, to the ledge of their former encampment. All roaring of the Falls and of the screech and bellowing, the clank of great machinery an aural atmosphere, an immersion of his being. He thought proudly looking up at it: *The ledge alone stands. They cannot take it away.*

But then he looked again to see what they had done to the hillside. And knew. He knew that if they wanted, they could take the A'ndians' ledge away as well. They could level, flattened out the Gorge, and steep it up with houses. If they but wanted.

On either side of him, shoulder to shoulder glistening with water beads and August sweat, his companions looked back and forth on all these things. Already Eaglestreak was thinking of a story to explain all this. Quick Claws was dancing round the fire telling all the might and unreason of the interlopers in his form, moving in and out the light and shadow; and among his family and clan, telling what these interlopers are and do. A howl escaped him and he knew it not at first. Then he saw that all his brother braves have thrown back their heads to howl. And not a sound escaped but what was mingled with the mighty pandemonium already loosed upon the world and working. ...Changing all the face of all the many lands....

Red Fox thought, *Have they done this everywhere? All wheres? Every place in earth, earth being the midst of all directions?* He thought: Have they done this to the moon? The stars? (To him the sun was the light, and a very great unthinkable unknowable fire). And it came then in his mind that the sun alone might put a stop to this. The sun alone. And then—it would itself destroy both all the works and Nature—. Nature herself could not escape the sun's destruction. If it so choose to come.

But what of that? Whatever story said the sun would come?

Pulling berries off the brambles by the Riverside, garnering scratches, gorging on plumpness—sweet dark blackberries, purple juice a'dribble down chins and chests: alternately dozing and swimming or water-wrestling; the scouts spent the day in the river on its banks, trolling the leagues away on their playful travels back toward Akropolis city center, the cemetery, and Five Points.

"I will tell you...." said Red Fox as he lay back dripping on a great weather-darkened sandstone. Red Fox recollected this rock just as it had stood in their scouting, anciently, to this time and place. Eddies of waters swirled up and slipped back around his sun-warmed sloping couch. He had stopped speaking and closed his eyes. Then he said, "No. You will tell me." He looked at Eaglestreak, the youngest. "You, *tschutti*, what do these things mean?"

Walleye-stare especially waited to see what would be said, for his disappointment was great that their canoes were not found. He sat in the waterhole, greasy mud squishing through his fingers as he played. Eaglestreak was soaking in the brown water below Red Fox, also leaning against the sandstone, but mostly submerged. He sat up straight, preparing. And other scouts were by them in the water. Quick Claws, his face engraved with special scars, had before handed handfuls of berries across to them from the lowering bank of the river. He brought now a pouch full, holding high above his head, wading. All were here but Dark Cloak. The sun was in the sweltering smaze of the rubber city making its own medium— thoughtless outpouring of industrial breath for the lungs of the town. They smelled it sulfurous stinking, mingling with that of the sewage, stoically supping on blackberries, sometimes quiet.

Eaglestreak chanted low. He made everything they'd done and seen on the previous night, and this day long, into an epic worthy of all primitive verse. From the music and musicians at *Stonehewn*, where they had covert *piawaw* (displaying their tradition for the audience)... to the exploration of zoo, apple orchard, carnival works at the High Lake, all land forms and industry—where police chased two of them into the murderous railyard. The Grandmaster speaking. And on to the current day's work and observation. Also of how the canoes were not found. A song in gutturals, not untraceable to that of other-creaturely utterance. It was long-chanting, and much regrouping, recouping, to get all things into it. And when he got done there was a deep resonant silence... except for the distant humming of the neighboring hillside, and the nearby swirling of waters. In the meditative silence the meaning became clear to them. Red Fox said it was enough, and pronounced it satisfying.

"We will have it again tonight at the campfire. And Dark Cloak will meet us and have more to report."

Yet Red Fox used the word for Dark Cloak's *story*, which in this context meant much the same. It is beginning to grow in Red Fox that some way must *soon* be found to regain the girl ... in a questing but splendid hope that she might somehow return them to their own *Passage*. He saw again the small ledge-shale as it had been when she lay down to sleep but a few days before. Again, he saw in his mind's eye the fearsome stone hut it had become on her waking. When she had practically started the vision for their experience. He marveled again over the vision's great life—the inner feel of it, outer smell-touch-look-sound of true life.

Meanwhile, Dark Cloak had stood the day on Sharon Road watching the storefront of the clasp-locker hospital and open windows above it. Dust rose around him with the traffic. People went in and out the shop. The corn-girl was up there. The dirty atmosphere developed through sunshine as he stood long, watching. The blue

men had come and gone, the doctor came and went, and came
again, and stayed a while and went away again. The woman who
watched the corn-girl had gone, briefly, below. At first going in and
out the grammar school, great monolithic structure behind him, the
workers stopped early to stand talking; as messengers and newsboys
went about speaking loudly and with great indignation.

Filthy sweat rolled slowly down Dark Cloak's almost naked,
tall, lithe, muscled form. He stood, wearing but loincloth, with
spear, bow and arrows, flint knife in its sheath at his torso. Waiting,
watching. He wanted to go about and see what was wrong—or
right—or just what caused the change in the city. But he had his
duty to perform. He denied himself the search for food, the necessity
of his body (till it would not be denied and he must step into the way
behind Sharon Road businesses, gazing yet on the rear upper
windows above the alley, relieving himself).

And then Dark Cloak came back to find the blue men
coming, stopping, conferring, then stepping up to him as he came
unto the boardwalk below the school. Two of them.

They spoke to him. But he did not understand. He looked at
them, talking at him. They wore clothes alike, as do the A'ndians
(not Akropolites); but these were dark blue and had a bit of
shimmering what looked like mica on their breasts. *They are of a
tribe or a peculiar clan*, he thought. He looked at their speaking
interloper faces. Their speech was more angular sounding than True
People's speech. He looked eye to eye with them. One slowly
unbuttoned his holster, but kept his hand there. Here was
weaponry. He wondered. There were such weapons as these in the
Wild West entertainments with cowboys and lariats. But they only
seemed to kill people with these. Carrying fire in them, and smoking
abruptly with terrible ignition. Yet, if true weapons, these were the
things reported that True People hoped to get from *Haudenosaunee.*

That one was about to reach and take hold on Dark Cloak's
wrist, where the scout would reach for his flint knife. But the other
one stopped him. They spoke one to another. Dark Cloak did not
take his knife from its sheath in his loincloth thong. He remembered
the A'ndians were in *the vision*—whatever its source—and to do
nothing.

The other one seemed to speak to the scout with his hands.
The hands gestured in "follow after" manner, and Dark Cloak
withheld a moment. He looked to the windows with shadows
sometimes moving above the clasp-locker repair shop. Briefly the
girl stared out the open window, a small white face unseeing.

Then he followed the blue men and thought in himself, *This
will teach me, and I will not break my part of the vision.* (By this he

meant greatly change it.) For he understood that to fight now would do it damage.

Dark Cloak did not so much follow as walk between them, his moccasins quiet on the boardwalks while their shod feet beat hard on the boards. He followed across Sharon Road to the crossroad with Stock Exchange Street, on past its intersection with Third, past shops and apartments and other streets and lanes meeting, to the corner of Haven and the small brick block housing the police station with two tall lamp-stands projecting from either side of its door. He did not yet know they were for light, but thought it likely. Up stone steps they went into shadow where a few people moved, then turning to climb—as he thought—some tall, very tall and narrow, confined stairs. What Parry Wilusa would call a *flight*, and rejoice in the word.

He entered the bare wooden room where interlopers looked up at him from what he knew were called, in their tongue, *table*. They sat on wooden chairs at wooden tables, a few, and looked at him. The blue men went back into the hall and down the stairs, he felt and heard, rather than saw. He did not take his gaze from the men looking at him, but passed it from one to another and back to the one whose look seemed most trusty. He could not be sure. He could but say to himself, *His look is more savory than that of the others.* There were degrees of spirit and expression in their eyes. And there had been derision in those who went back down the stairs. How would they talk to him? Would they ask him to smoke?

He had noticed smoke going out the window. Big brown leaves wrapped smoking in a small bowl on the table. He looked at it, lowering his eyes. Quickly he put his gaze back up again to the trusty-seeming one. He had seen the show folk use it in small white papers, and people using this at *Stonehewn*.

He happened to be looking at Phillips.

"So he doesn't know the language," said the lieutenant, Lt. Baker, scraping back his chair. He moved to the window to look out briefly and drag on his cigarette.

This is what the boys in blue had said on leaving Dark Cloak with them. There had been laughter but the A'ndian showed no sign. He was young, haughty, tattooed, scarred. Full of weapons like a porcupine with his back up. And he had been seen following the girl.

Detective Sgt. Levinson thought he had the look of a formidable and primitive barbarism. It would take a lot of men and hardware to subdue him. There was plenty of that, of course. He said, "Try the Grandmaster, maybe. He might know how to talk with them." It was a suggestion. He knew better than to sound declarative.

The lieutenant stood stolid a moment then called down to the officers stepping onto the boardwalk from the front. "Bart! Go get the Grandmaster at the Opera House. Be sure to make nice and tell them what it's for. And —if you see Dreiser or anybody don't say anything. They can wait for a story."

Bart looked up at him, blue helmet on the back of his head. His face looked oval and reddened except for that white spot where his visor shielded his forehead from sunburn. He had a ginger colored mustache and sideburns. Bart called back, "To interpret, you mean."

"Yeah. That." The voice of the lieutenant was a growl. He blew a gust of smoke into the breathless smaze of Akropolis. He turned back into the room, muttering. "Someone who speaks gibberish and knows what it means."

Phillips stood and gestured to Dark Cloak.

Here is a sitting-place for you, he seemed to say. Dark Cloak went to stand by the wooden chair against the wall. He would not sit there. He would stand and wait for what they would do. He still had his weapons. He had been standing since before dawn. At that time he had dozed off and on, against the workmen's monolith. The sun struck his eyelids just as they were coming with wagons and tools. Dark Cloak had well eaten at *Stonehewn* the night before. So he could wait meat, perhaps as much as half a moon. But he would've smoked with them, on its offering. He had smoked with the show folk's offering. In his pipe. His own tobacco was gone. It had been spring on their coming here and the curings of his pouch were by then depleted.

The girl had been busy fitting the A'ndian scout against the grammar school into a pattern. She did not know she was busy. It was all in a pattern—from what she had seen. The A'ndians were part of the pattern of Akropolis that she had seen in the light-spangled-peopled dark at *Stonehewn*. The rhythmic pain and heavy weight and gas smell were all fitted into a pattern. On the close side of that. And hands were always fitted into the pattern. She admitted the hands in the pattern, the feel of her hand in other hands, the peculiar way each hand felt, some lumpy and hard, one bony and fragile, one small and smooth. They handed her hand around. The kind one in long skirts, another the size of the girl with soft hair on his forehead. Almost like the cattail, the rabbit foot, but she did not much touch it. It was attached to him.

Later, Bart and Fletcher, the blue uniforms, came walking brick blocks and past canal boats unloading beside Main Street; toward the intersection looming with tall stone buildings, the Portage Park Hotel and Opera House on either side. They were craning their necks, as others were, gathering to watch the spectacle of the great man they had come to fetch for the interpretation. As usual when the vaudeville was in town, there was a parti-colored juggler during the day on the corner. Just to whet appetite for the minstrel entertainments of the evening. But this was different. Never had they seen the Grandmaster so-doing. He wore his working-man's clothes, juggling.

The Grandmaster, great and physically adept (as was now seen), stood on the corner of Main Street and Market Avenue, where the brick paving was broadest, tossing tenpins and balls high in the air. It appeared to all watching that his hands were several, and that the balls and bowling-pins were as numerous as flies. To the two officers approaching through the gathering these things seemed gnats, swarming high in the air above the Grandmaster. Nearby traffic was stopped along with unloading of barges at the canal alongside Main Street. Seeming flies buzzed above the crowd parting to let these officers pass. Then the men in blue saw: The Spectacle Himself most often content but to direct the spectacle—was now seen to be its *greatest attraction*.

Huge, ponderous massive, planted like a squat giant with legs thick as old-growth tree trunks; his arms like a multitude of limbs thrashing on a tremendous gale, bits of everything from his thick fingers flying in the air like leaves going up in whirlwind. But as they watched, the debris flying with almost mathematical precision up through and surrounding the vortex, they forgot about him in the frightening beauty and rhythm of the display. They thought they saw bits of everything, in miniature, whirling and thickening, expanding into the air above the boardwalk, beneath the monumental ornate façade of the Opera House: bicycles and horseless-carriages, elevator cars and canvas-covered biplanes, wringer-washers, pearl-handle jack knives and celluloid-handled straight razors. Breech-loading shotguns, telegraph instruments, Edgeware sewing machines, and forged steel-beamed pony plows. The whole contents of households and farm-holds and manufactuaries seen blowing sky-high past the heavy Gothic crenulated-roof dormers of the building. If some chanced to see his expression they might have seen its look of concentrated delight.

The crowd gathered, it seemed, from every corner of the city, flowing and flooding, surging toward the massive focal-point in human form that was the Grandmaster—juggling his *thingamajigs* like so many toys in a cyclone of expanding proportions. Great arms, too many arms to keep track of, tossing and spewing and spiking things mile-high. As the cloud of things expanded and expanded and expanded, it seemed to fill the whole sky above, far out over the dense industrial city of Akropolis, a town hunkered on five hills beneath the full stinky-sticky smaze of its industry and accomplishment. A great storm cloud, ominously dark, about to rain all this at any moment down on them.

And still he threw up this stuff. Where it came from, and how it got into his many-seeming hands to fly upwards, no one could tell. Certainly not the police officers sent to fetch him for the interrogation of the A'ndian.

It seemed much of this stuff must have fallen back into his great ham-hands only to fly up again as something different and new—and brightening. Gadgets of every conceivable size shape color and mysterious whirling purpose, now much of it shining with strange metallic lights and coruscations. Still-standing: His many hands seemed to be up-floating and flying, whirling and scattering the universe into being from out of nowhere ... nowhere but those great hands.

To Bart and Fletcher, the two officers in blue, it now seemed that all this highflying blizzard of making and remaking was inches away from their foreheads. Each could not now even recognize the other for the intolerable whirlwind of matter energetically moving before his gaze. As if he could skip off into this great mathematical flux, these astounding formulas and ... in fact each momently felt himself to *be* bits sailing into this world-pool of numerical harmonies. Gazing was become but the nextness of everything, but the pretense of each officer's own extinguishable being in the fleet eye of the Grandmaster—whose great very face seemed to winnow the officer's thought, and to wink at him from moon-flashing curious eyes.

The station house was deserted. Second shift detectives had left— hectic within, batons at the ready, running down the stairs and into the street. Even Levinson was gone.

Dark Cloak yet stood by the wall, invisible (almost) as a shadow; listening to the silence of the building, the increasing distant roar of the city. He went to the window and looked out. The industrial atmosphere was strangely lit. It was not yet night, level sunlight still imbuing the swelter. He looked back at the old stub stogie left, earlier, by Lt. Baker, picked it up, sniffed it. Cold. Dark Cloak carried it out and down the narrow stairway. Outside the station house he looked for the street lamp to light it on, but the lamps were not lit. Dark Cloak loped off, long lean legs carrying swiftly silently through the filthy street, crossing into the alleyway toward the cattle impoundments; heading him off toward the sounds of the city—that way. Northeast, he told by the sun behind him.

Meanwhile his fellow scouts had been dozing the day away in the deep river valley ... until night should come. They woke intermittently on the river bank, then dozing back down into sleep. Later, in the dark, it came to them, waking.

They sat up listening, looking, almost as a man. No one spoke but the gleaming of their eyes told it: there were lit streets and houses on the steep hillside above. And beyond it the tumult and wavering glow of the hidden city center. Its north hill hid it, but the sky above and beyond shone with the unexpected light of the forest fire. This came first to mind as they gazed. Even the roaring was like the forest fire... but yet... somehow... No! This was roaring of the many-voiced. The storm that might only be made of *The People*! *People*, then, were making the storm, people setting fire, making the earth to shake; light ascending through darkness torrid as the sun. Or—had the sun indeed come after all?

Red Fox stood. The others jumped up, scratching themselves on bramble canes. But he stood still. They followed his lead. Then he walked into the warmish water and started to swim for the city. Walleye-stare and Quick Claws and Eaglestreak and the others went into the river-water carrying its load of filth and stench, flooding now behind them. They swam until the stream, diverted, was walkable. Soon they would reach the Akropolis Rural Cemetery and go into its peaceful vale.

Red Fox was fervent to see the ledge-stone with its hut in front—where initially the girl disclosed the vision. Having now finished the showing, would she be there?

Dark Cloak had left his post of corn-girl watcher. He was gone to see what was the matter with the city. But the scouts did not know this yet. Red Fox was unaware of it, but he did wonder if the other brave had, in obedience, restrained his curiosity about Akropolis. For Red Fox knew Dark Cloak was curious in ways that might overcome and thwart his duty.

On arriving at the graveyard, Eaglestreak, smallest of stature, cast himself down in the stream below the tomb, supine. He lay still. The others spread out to watch. Red Fox went up toward the small ledge-backed stone hut. So neatly piled together was it. Again he scrutinized it, marveling over its regular stone construction and ornamentation. How had men cut the stones and so stuck them smack together? That was no matter as easy as shaping chert or flint. He peered within, scarcely moving the oaken door. City-glow fell through, slightly. He had touched the door, breaking his own taboo. He stepped back and walked around it one more time, climbing even above onto the turf-covered ledge and back down the other side where it sloped. There was no corn-girl.

Five Points Akropolis

He looked down toward the youngest, Eaglestreak lying in the stream. Something was amiss. He walked down and looked. On first seeing him lie down in the waters, he had thought the young brave quite still. But it was not so. Eaglestreak, bright-eyed, was trembling violently. Red Fox stood staring at him in the ambient glow from Five Points Akropolis, surrounding the vale of the dark graveyard. He felt for his buckskin pouch, slung on his back with his weaponry, and pulled it round. He knelt by the young brave, in this small running stream, and opened its folds. Here were the healing herbs, *tschuppik*, and talisman needed to help his charge.

Red Fox was very sorry. So sorrowful. Red Fox was mourning. Their life was gone. And the corn-girl was not here.

S. Dorman

Willie Gets the Willies

Akropolis delivered its mail to each house twice a day, morning and afternoon. *The Akropolis Lamppost* gave out the city's news daily in two editions, *early* and *late*. The town's denizens were chronically news hungry, thought Dreiser the newsman. News was more frequent, and almost as entertaining as the minstrel show—and *could be* far more palpitating, maddening, rejuvenating. It played upon its receivers, not with frothy escapism nor with historic and dramatic or orchestral excitements and delights, but with the press of *the actual*. *The actual* was the most genuine of levers employed in the great imponderable movements of the world. The actual of the past, he thought, was now no more real than the minstrelsy whether in history books or old documents, legends, and myths. Even Uncle Llewellyn's accident in the mines of Woles one generation ago was almost no more than a fable. You might hear of it again with cringing or affectionate diversion but it had no bearing, was not the accident of Uncle MacDonald, who lost some limbs to the scorching in Priams. You might quibble over the emigré descent of one or the other, trifle over this or that scandalous intermarriage of one's more recent forebears—scandalous even among the various nationalities of the Calts. (Everyone knows that the Scoach are superior to the Wilsh, who are notorious wilchers.) But that was then, thought Dreiser. Last week. This is now. Today is the thing that matters.

"And what this colored man did to that poor little white girl is unspeakable." This, and other such phrases more blatantly derogatory, flew along the telephone lines, and went in envelopes at the rate of a penny, and were coded in the headlines of *The Lamppost*. Now downtown Akropolis was burning, as he'd seen for himself, and some of its folks were hurrying away from the city center, and some rushed toward it with cudgels, ball bats and other weaponry. The police and the Mayor and City Council were going to answer for it now! Right this minute! Give the colored miscreant to the mob and be done with it!

On Third St., the newspaper man sat in the establishment of Argus and Mabel, talking quietly to the newsboy Aneas and his mother—the proprietress of the Leg Bone eating-house. Notebook open on the checkered oilcloth-covered table beside him, in the light

of a coaloil lamp, Dreiser eyed them. A riot downtown outside the
County Courthouse and Jail was exciting stuff to cover, but there
might be more to the story, and Dreiser was going to find out.
Levinson and Phillips had been quiet, taciturn with the official
account. After the first two editions-full of burning, Dreiser thought
it would be well to tackle new angles. Of course he was late getting
back to Mabel on this. But this was going to be Big, Drawnout, and
Full for the next several days. There has to be more poured into the
telling or it just would not continue to sell as it should. Besides, it
was dangerous up there.

"Now, you've said that Argus was with you in the house here
all last night. And that you all knew nothing until this a.m. when
the detectives came to your door."

He tipped back in the ladderback chair then came forward
with sudden intention to look Mabel directly in her dark troublous
eyes. Some of her hair stuck out lightless and kinky through the
gap in her bandanna above these eyes. Dreiser still wore his blue-
and-white outrageously checkered suit, but the jacket was slung on
the back of the chair. The establishment did not smell as usual, not
with the cooking of fatback and collard greens. No chickens had
been slaughtered and fried. Now Dreiser shoved his black bowler
forward to add more menace to his gaze. A little intimidation never
hurt in getting the facts out of some people. These people.

Aneas stepped from among the children, huddled round him,
to be close to his mother. He said, "That right Mr. Dreiser, and
before that he be at Priam's do. Big do. Everybody see him up there
helping out."

Shadows in the corners as backdrop, the children were silent
and solemn, big-eyed. Even the baby at Li'l Mabel's feet. Looking up
into lamplight, he alternately sucked the fingers of one tiny hand
and a messy-looking rag in the other. Sometimes he gummed a bit
of apple Li'l Mabel reached down to him. Aneas spoke with unusual
confidence and authority to the newsman. *We be in the same
business*, he thought. He also thought, *Better not boss my mama.*

His dark eyes in his crisp dark face shone firmness. A slouch
cap sat atop his cropped head of dark kinked hair. His shoulders
had begun to broaden some, just a bit. Dreiser guessed his form
would soon be athletic. He smiled. *That's right*, he thought. *Brave it
out.*

He looked around—just for a moment. Shadows and
lamplight. The walls of the eating-house were whitewashed lath-
and-plaster, the floor wooden planks. Its front windows—the only
windows—were hung with fresh washed gingham puckered, that is
gathered, at the top over the curtain rod and tied back prettily with
gingham strips of the same color, probably peach. All the chairs but

these two were upside down on the tabletops. There was just a bit
more room than usual to walk around in here.

Dreiser tipped his bowler back and smiled at Mabel. His
dark eyes gleamed, his face pasty white and sweaty. The part
showed down the middle of his dark thinning hair. He looked a bit
clownish this way, with that smile but, as with the circus clown, no
one felt lightened or relieved. Yet he meant it to inspire confidence.

"Just tell me then. —Why do you think they're picking on ol'
Argus? He's not particularly mean. Got no reputation as a ladies
man—."

Here Aneas frowned and Mabel cast uneasy gaze at the
children.

"—No rep for abusing folks, women, girls. That sort of thing.
That's what I mean. I do know what goes on in this town. That's
not *one* thing."

Mabel looked back at him. "Be right," she said quietly,
emphatically.

"So?"

"Mr. Dreiser, sir," said Aneas. "It's the skin, sir." He
refrained from saying, *I be's reckoning.*

Dreiser paused, looking at him.

"...You mean someone's put the job on him to save their own
skin, that it?" Mr. Dreiser's smile broadened, his teeth showing like
fangs in the coaloil light.

There was silence. Then, "Yes. Sir."

"Any idea who?"

There was another pause, Aneas looking at him. He lowered
his eyes. "No, sir."

Dreiser was going to prod. Then, he thought of it. He closed
up his little leather notebook and stood. He thought about it going
out the door.

*Someone in Five Points... Who has a rep for that kind of
thing.... Only hearsay. Only once. But...—I know where to go next.*

The night on Third St. took him. Li'l Mabel turned the big
skeleton key, locking the door. Aneas put his arm around Mabel.
Until Dreiser had come with news, they had not known: Argus was
safe in Groverland.

Both the Mayor and County Sheriff thought it a joke. *Won't they feel
foolish when we tell them? The prisoner is not here! We've outwitted
you, now go home.* The County Sheriff painted a picture for the
mayor, and said that the latter may as well go on home to dinner.
Just stay out of it. Nothing will come of this but embarrassment. I
don't mind being the one to shed it. He had tipped back his broad
sheriff's hat, smiled. The mayor picked up his straw hat and went

out the back way. He saw down the alleyway out to the street in late afternoon light. Yes, it was all true. They were gathering. *The mob.* He went the other way down to the new garage. He was a young mayor, barely forty, and one of the first in city government to own a private electric horseless carriage. Sometimes he rejoiced in the salient fact.

But at dark the scene was ignited. Up Market Avenue East— not more than three blocks above the Opera House—first bricks were flying and then bottles with rags soaked in gasoline. The City Building was afire and police shooting down into the mob. One of those shots struck into a close-knit handful of rubber workers. But another volley went into a crowd of spectators just up the crowd- and building-choked hill.

Two of these uphill spectators were young James Priam and his brother Brandt. They had prevailed upon Gilbert to get them to the latest and best of shows, the breathlessly proposed riot not far from the Opera House—and better than anything showing there. This was to be an actual riot with real stones and bricks and broken windows, and attacks on official buildings and everything. Of course Gilbert knew better than to let himself be derailed by James Horatio. He'd been deceived into thinking (without direct lying) that this was *solely* an errand from Mr. Priam himself—the delivery of papers to the city building; strictly official. But the boys knew what was up from the Five Points grapevine, and their father—too occupied with his distinguished visitor, the Londinium journalist—was virtually ignorant of any rumors from either downhill or downtown. The papers were in need of delivery anyway, but Gilbert was for going back directly he saw the mobbed bodies of men in the electric light of the elegant downtown lampposts.

"But we must see it, Gilbert! This is extraordinary! Essential!" cried young James. "Father will want the story firsthand! Just keep the horses to one side, on the uphill. We shall be perfectly fine."

Brandt, who was tall, lean and freckled (those freckled bequeathed from his late mother) pretended an ease he did not feel. His normally serious gaze began showing alarm as it became evident no one could move on the crowded street. Brant's speech, unlike that of his little brother's, was unaffected by their foreign visitor's. He shouted—. "Out, Gilbert! Out!"

But no one was escaping the chaos—compact of fright, horse-muck stench, cries of men, females, animals. The mob, the traffic— wild-eyed horses and carriages choking the street—and now the fire department had blocked their nearest likely lane of retreat from above: The red polished hook-and-ladder, with well-trained horses urging its passage through the dense chaotic roaring sea—at the same moment Gilbert was wrestling reign and horse to courageous egress.

Then the gunshots flew.

But two city blocks below the mob, yet of a height with it, Dark Cloak surveyed the fray.

If some had chanced to look that way, they might have seen level across to the monumental Opera House with its Gothic embellishments... and noted something new: In appearance like a strangely weaponed gargoyle, burnished in reflected fire; motionless and as enduring with the ages. This sculpture of primitive man jutted next the stolid Victorian dormer; staring stern-eyed at the conflagration just now swelling out, now flowing back, toward its center. From this vantage, the keen-eyed gargoyle saw the strange recurring swirls of movement—as though a spirit, invisible, playing round and through the crowd, and overhead, underfoot—to make it move, and to breathe with fire.

Dark Cloak watched. At first the young A'ndian scout was too taken with its violence and tumult, its likeness to the warpath's end, to think much of its cause. He merely watched, involved, intent. He was amazed but showing nothing save his own fierce gaze enthralled. His breathing was steady, his lean taut form as reddish stone; shining as though bronzed from sweat and reflected glow of flickering flames—all combining to give hue and sheen to the strange, statuesque form.

Shots exploded from the great brick building now involved in flame a-thrust from many windows, as though eyes of fire blazing forth in fierce and pointed anger. The spirit of the mob moved yet more swift, frenzied; its shrieks and cries and bellows suddenly swollen with great madness and blame. Then he heard the deep-throated wonder—the great deep howling increase of spirit maddened—and saw its body red and gleaming. But yet the more the monster's color lessened, became as one with reflection of the fire, as—horses leading—it slowly pushed away the mob to either side. —The mob which once more flooded back to close its pathway should it decide to turn.

This was the way of war in the vision-time they'd entered. The way of war for interlopers when once they turned on one another... and, he thought, even as had the *Cat Folk* and *Haudenosaunee* when they fought with one another and the latter overcame. And still he did not know the meaning, nor the reasoning of these combatants. For he understood enough to know there was a reason even among interlopers who were yet such a mystery to *True People*. (Had it to do with the corn-girl where the bluemen came?) It was not just about the spirit come to join the fighting as they battled—though they might have not such strength and frenzy without it. For surely they had called it on the warpath: "Come!! Join us!! Come to our War!!"

The doctor might have said that it was glands above the kidneys, secreting chemicals, suffusing all those bodies enacting the scene with such violence and verve. Triggered by human psychological imbalance—the indignation and prejudice excreted of human bigotry. Dr. Zettler had been called up to *Stonehewn* to remove a bullet from one of the Priams. Just which Priam had not been established, but that the injury had been caused by the riot downtown was understood. The hospital further uphill from the City Building (its reputation not yet firmly established) was rumored loaded with casualty. Some of the funeral parlors would be doing a little business this week also. It was well after midnight and on toward the darkest hours as the doctor left his house and, Barouche springs protesting just a bit, climbed up beside Gilbert; who seemed fit not even to look him in the eye. Word had come originally by telephone of course, as had the news of the riot from other sources (it was still ongoing); but it was the non-look from the chauffeur that told him here was the reluctant eyewitness. One who would perhaps know more than he cared to.

As Gilbert got up the horse between its shafts and pulled out of the lamplight, rubber-lined wheels whooshing almost soundless through the dust of Harkins Farm Road, each man had his gaze taken off by a shadowy group, moving. It went with hurried but crippled stealth out of the alleyway and through the house-shades of the neighborhood where Dark Cloak, the night before, had seen the corn-girl rescued from her naked wandering by the doctor. Silent, Gilbert guessed what these shadows were. The doctor said, "Looks like others of the neighborhood have been injured." For certainly one was carried in the arms of another and two others seemed scarcely to keep up.

With their sick brothers, the A'ndians were on their way to the encampment hidden in Harkins Woods. Two others beside Eaglestreak were now ill. Gravely ill.

Gilbert thought morosely, *I missed seeing them A'ndians in the riot.* He even thought to wonder why, possibly, they had been there. The doctor, for his part, had gone on in thought, mainly to what awaited him at *Stonehewn*, but also he was wondering over the blazing lamplight. Apparently Partum, who had been such a force in the movement of mobs about the City, had been able, nonetheless, to do his job on the lamps. The doctor mused briefly on that peculiarity, but then turned his attention to Gilbert. Here was the man to talk to about what had happened.

"Who is injured, Gilbert? How extensive the wounding?" Dr.
Zettler had his bag with him and antiseptics with bandaging,
instruments for the removal of the bullets. He listened with quick
attention, at least with the analytical part of his mind. But he had
also an empathetic part, and it was tethered to his imagination: He
would have to seek out the injured others he saw passing in the
dark back there. A long night. A long day tomorrow. He would
rouse Johan to help him.

They passed above the nearly deserted Five Points, Dr. Zettler
glancing down Sharon Road toward its intersection with Stock
Exchange Street. Yes, the lamplight shone at intervals, steady
sparks atop still pools of light. Too, light gleamed out a patch upon
the pavement before Paddy's Pool Hall & Saloon. Down there, just a
few doors up this way, slept—if she slept—the mute little injured
thing—ostensibly the cause of everything. The doctor thought about
this. How can such enduring innocence be the cause? That's all
mixed up and wrongheaded. How many rioters truly care for her
injury? Care for her, the girl with her strange inadvertent
fascination, her lack of longing to be normal or even protected? And
yet there *were* those who cared. The Wilusas for instance. And
himself.

Gilbert got the horses up the hill past the mansion of
Akropolis' first settler. It was in fine shape still, a Georgian beauty
with tall columns, spacious veranda, and still home to the county's
First Family. The Simeon Harkins family, who had once a tenant
farmer, named Johnny Green, since hung at Hopper's Ferry, crying
for a war between the states. There, at least, one state was quite
literally sundered in two. And still, even here on West Hill, with its
newer and lavish mansions, the riot echoed distantly from the city
center across the intervening knolls, and the dark vale where the
Akropolis Rural Cemetery lay. Its many lawns gray and dewy,
peaceful. Hidden in the quiet dark below.

In the misty twilight of next morning three figures—two here and one
there—wove various ways through tall black boles. This world was
breathing out green exhalations, long and deep, of world's slow
breathing on world's way through space. No one could have guessed
that these poetic yet scientific thoughts came to taciturn young
Johan Zettler, as he stepped quiet through tall trunks of trees in
Harkins Woods, on his mission to find the wounded A'ndian scouts
for his father.

"Gilbert says they are A'ndians," his father had said at
breakfast. "Those we saw at the lawn fête the other night. They
were in the show downtown, hmmm?"

Five Points Akropolis

Gregoff's mother, a thin woman dressed in black, who came very early to cook, and would then be cleaning, had set down the hearty Prussian fare the Zettlers liked. Of course including cabbage, pickled beets and white sausage. She was learning to like the food she had to cook for them, but it had not been easy at the start. She loved the light Medioceanic fare she had been raised on in pitiful but very beautiful islands where olive trees grew in such abundance. Where was an olive tree in Akropolis—paah! She stepped quickly round the two Zettler's pouring out coffee.

"Yes," said Johan

"Can you take me to them?"

Johan was silent, eating. He stared at the gas stove where Marianna stood dishing up more sausage. The flame was almost always blue. He thought he knew why.

"I think so," he had said at last.

And so they were climbing up through early morning mist, the dim beginnings of another stifling day in Akropolis. It breathed out early, thought Johan. Then it got its breath and held it all day long. It was quiet down below at Five Points, and almost too far away to hear the rumor of the manufactuary southward, but he wondered. The city northward was quiet. Would it begin again its convulsions when night came? Convulsions. Parry Wilusa would like that word. Johan had learned it from his father. He decided he would use it sometime in conversation with the boy and see what would be the result.

Another figure made its way uphill, aware of them—as they were not of him. Dark Cloak's nature made sure of that. He was of the woodland. Mrs. Havard, the Anglish journalist, might have said he *was* the woodland. He was the deep, extensive, mysterious forest clothing all east Americle, torso, head; and foot—where it projected in warm Baribean waters. He was woodland in human form.

As were the A'ndians all. And so, in spite of how they searched the woods that morning, the A'ndians encampment was not found by the Zettlers.

Parry lounged on the sofa beneath the open upstairs Sharon Road window, sweat soaking his sailor suit, his blond bang sticking to his forehead. Intently, he was reading aloud to the listening roses-and-lilies wallpaper, from a chapter entitled, "At the House in Great Portland Street". He had thought, perhaps, of reading to the girl where she sat lax at the other end of the sofa staring, but now he was reading aloud to himself, engulfed in the story of *The Invisible Man*.

"And you processed her?"

*"I processed her. But doing it to a cat is no joke, Kemp!
And the process failed in some measure. She was bandaged
and clamped, of course, —so I had her safe; but she woke
while she was still misty, and* miaowled *dismally."*

"How long did it take?"

*"Three or four hours—for the cat. It was night outside
long before the business was over, and I stopped the gas
engine, and then, being tired, went to bed. But I lay awake
thinking aimless stuff, going over the experiment over and over
again, or dreaming feverishly of things growing misty and
vanishing about me, until everything, the ground I stood on,
vanished, and so I came to that sickly falling nightmare one
gets.*

"About two in the morning, the cat began miaowling
*about the room. I tried to hush it by talking to it, then decided
to turn it out. I remember the shock I had when striking a
light—there where just the round eyes shining green—and
nothing round them. The back part of the eye, tough iridescent
stuff, wouldn't go at all. I tried to catch it but it wouldn't be
caught, and vanished. Then it began* miaowling *in different
parts of the room. At last I opened the window and made a
bustle. I suppose it went out at last. I never saw any more of
it."*

*"You don't mean to say there's an invisible cat at-
large!"* said Kemp.

*"If it hasn't been killed, said the Invisible Man. "Why
not?"*

Parry kept reading, mesmerized. Ostensibly he was
entertaining the girl, in her seclusion from the turmoil and its
aftermath—as Akropolis was waking to the knowledge that Argus
really was gone and secure in the city, north of here. A city, some
thought, that would not be roused to any pitch of indignation by the
bigotry of largely Caucasian Akropolis. Groverland was shipping and
steel country. The men there were all iron men and looked down,
just a bit, on any doings in what was predominantly rubberland.
Also, the darkest of men were working there in foundries.

Parry stopped reading, and—again ostensibly—he was
explaining the story to her; but more as a way of understanding it
himself.

"You see, he's telling Kemp just how it all came about that he
was made invisible. First he treated the cat. It's all a work of
science, you see." He let the book fall as lax as the girl was, sitting
there against the soles of his bare feet. He combed back the sweaty
hair off his forehead with clean but sweaty fingers. For him, it was

not always as though the girl were attentive—nor even *there* with him. And then again sometimes she was; as either his audience or a field of study. But sometimes she was herself, and her real person, to him.

"Science is how you really find things out... Willie tells me this all the time. But I think he forgets, because he knows some mechanics and some formulas, that it's more based on fancy—what people can imagine—. At least that's how everything can be understood, you see."

The girl did not grasp it. She was working it into a pattern. The invisible man's story was in the pattern. He was not invisible and the boy was sometimes invisible. The teller was not in the story, nor was he the story. Parry said he was in Angleland and not Visible. Kemp was not the story's teller, he was its reader.

"I'm invisible, you see, but this sailor suit is not."

The boy thought he was going in the straight way he perceived. He had been sucked up by everything and thought he was going straight, whatever he did. But his makings were perceived in *every-which-way* from all the *mass-energy-momentum*, with all its internal pressure and tension—of which he was a part. He was the story he was reading, she was invisible. She was working it all in.

The great pattern's big pain was here. And it was there. It made an intersection with her body, there. And her being, here. The scents from the kitchen of cornbread and corn chowder were in her nostrils, going in her nose with other invisibles: the air she breathed, expanding, the air then depleting, going out, as her small chest alternately swelled and sank back. Dust motes filled the sunshine pouring in straight beams through the open windows, brightening roses-and-lilies and the whorls of her fingertips where they lay in view—the crevices of the whorls deep as ravines in the woodland and as full of minute things growing; the growing things themselves as full of limbs and joints, with feathery things and more crevices. There were no end of crevices and divisions, of minute lives or life stuffs, no end to keeping them all in order, as lesser kept giving way to lesser and lesser and lesser, and there was no least. She did not think of this in words, she experienced it as part of a pattern; her sitting here with the impress and stickiness of Parry's feet—skin adhering and combining with the molecules of her small thigh through its thin muslin covering. She was (as some sort of sometimes visible whole) one in an infinite stream of lesser things falling like snowflakes through the air of existence, part of the big piling on of the Big Ice the Haudenosaunee had told True People of. The stars at night were some great blizzard of neighborhoods falling around the lamplight and campfire in ever increasing and accreting endless multitudes. Snowing, falling through the experience.

The other was there, breaking the boy's voice reading *The Invisible Man*, breath on-cycling but ceasing to carry the storyteller's pattern in sounds and syllables. The crevice opened, widened to a crevasse, and the girl fell into the blizzard of Milky Way stars falling and falling and falling beneath the night horizon of bare open ledge and forest under her feet where she stood above the *Captive Maid's Kitchen*.

In dirty knee britches, shirt and suspenders, Willie had come through the swinging door from the Wilusa kitchen, quietly. On meeting his silence, Parry started up reading again.

Willie had come home for lunch, not the usual thing. He liked sitting, chewing a sandwich, just inside the door of the tomb-cum tool-crib when it was August sweltering and the earth there gave up its cool. But he was concerned, now the town was up-heaving its violence and bigotry, and he thought more of the girl than of anything, except maybe Aneas. And there was nothing he could do for Aneas at this time, he thought ... except maybe stand next to him when they met again. For some reason he thought also of Gwendolyn. But Willie was to go back to the cemetery immediately after eating to dig two graves out of the earth ... for joining up with the freshly made-earth—as he was now thinking of these waiting bodies. With a bit of thrill and wonder.

But Willie was unobtrusive, would not even be asking about the girl. It was enough just to see her sitting there with his brother, being read to.

Heirolynn had fallen into the gaze where everything was falling, cycling without ceasing, no *where* nor *when* not steeped in glory; whether greater or lesser in relative size or position: humanly-uncounted everything. Her own star among the blizzard of stars, hidden behind the earth... though now its light fell in waves and particles across her fingertips lying not quite uncurled on the arm of the sofa. All these familial interactions happening in a moment, one cohesion of action and thought—

Willie waving Parry to a stop and come into the kitchen, as he said over his shoulder, "I heard James Priam got shot last night—in the riot. Parry took the girl's hand and led her into the kitchen to the table set amid the great black range and gas ring, sideboard, sink and corn-sheller. Parry noticed in passing that she didn't seem as averse to hand-holding as formerly. Mrs. Wilusa, still wearing her shop apron, her piled brown hair limp and straggling, had set the table with bowls already ladled in corn chowder. There was the big cast-iron dutch-oven in the midst, slightly domed with yellow cornbread. She stood by the girl's chair, ready to push her up close once seated. Her worn hands on the spindles of the ladderback chair, Ma said, "It was Brant. Not James," but Parry astonished had already squealed, "Really? James—" "No, Brant," said Ma in her harsh-sounding voice, and moved the girl close to the table. The warm scent of the chowder she imbibed thoroughly, as sniffing, sniffing, her nostrils handled it.

"Brant. Dr. Zettler came by to see the girl and hear if I knew of anyone injured. He told me it."

"Really!" Reiterated the younger boy. He sat on the edge of his chair. He did not reach as usual for the cornbread. He said, "I think we should pray. Say grace, you see."

Mrs. Wilusa faintly smiled, a bit surprised. "Well, if you want to, Parry."

"First—is he all right?"

"Yes. Doing well's can be expected. Not blind but won't be able to eat for a while. James's hysterical, though. He got paregoric, too." Just as she didn't say what happened, exactly, to the girl, Ma did not like to say anything whatever about the shooting. But Willie's news was wrong and it had to be brought out.

"Dear God," said Parry, with a quiver. "We thank you for Brant and the cornbread. That Brant's going to be better, you see. We thank you," he remembered to say, "for Argus being safe in Groverland. And for the corn chowder and cornbread. ...And for the corn seed. The kernels themselves, the seeds. The seeds that go into the ground one by one."

Ma was again slightly smiling, her eyes closed, hands folded in her aproned lap, and remembering being little and hungry, and one to plant kernels, from corn dried overwinter—in the fields of her upbringing in Hoccoshton, south of here.

"Thanks for the farmers' hands—who work hard to put it there," said Parry. "Thanks for the water, the rain and sunshine where it warmed everything and the farmers, and actually is making it too hot. And for the night when it stays hot so it grows in the fat leaves and stalks that come first and keep growing and gets so tall and thick and like a forest with walls, and for the hands that come to pick it or drive horse and harvester and they gather it all huge, huge, heaping and cut it and drive it to the siding to get it to Akropolis and the hands that load it and peel it to look at it... and the engineer and coal man and—"

"Parry..." said Ma softly.

"—the foundry workers who forged the engine, the miners getting out the coal, with faces all dirty, and thank you, Lord, for the wagoneers and drays getting it to market and the bushel-basket makers and store clerks and..."

Parry went on and Willie's stomach was grumbling, his fists on either side of his chowder bowl itching to open, and take the big soup spoon, grab some of that cornbread... and he heard Parry saying,

"—and for pol-y-mers and doppel-gan-gers, mi-crobes and amino acids, nuc-leic acids and crystals—all minerals and bac-ter-i-a, and for super-conductors, super-collider—"

"Parry, what are you talking about?" demanded Willie.

"I don't know, Willie. I like the way these words feel in my mouth. Don't you like them?"

He closed his eyes again. "And hydrogen atoms, am-mon-ia, phos-phor-ic salts—"

"But you never—"

"Zip-pers, Vel-cro, quanta and quarks, and tril-o-bites, Lu-cerne Switzerland—"

"Parry, that's enough now," said Mrs. Wilusa. "Food's getting cold. Stop that now so's we can eat."

"Parry I've never heard of half that stuff," said Willie, frowning, reaching for cornbread. "Where'd you get all that?"

"It just came to me," said the younger boy, placing a carefully cut piece of yellow cornbread on the girl's small plate beside her chowder. She picked up her spoon and dipped it in the thick white-and-yellow soup speckled black with pepper grown in the Orient, picked by hand, dried and sent shipboard to the railroad; sniffing, nostrils handling it. Parry began buttering her crumbling cake-like piece. "Like in conversation. You see. When we're talking. Like this. It just comes to me to say this stuff. Like, ' How's everything at the clasp-locker hospital today, Ma?'" But he did not look at her. He glanced, but then was looking alternately at Willie and his own crumbling cornbread as he buttered it.

A thrill walked slowly up his big brother's backbone. Quickly he said, "Parry, it's not the same at all. We know what the clasp-locker hospital is. We know why it's there. ...If you wrote this stuff down I could go to the new lending library halfway up cake-eaters and ask the ma'am to look it up in books, maybe the dictionary."

"But I don't know how to spell them. Besides, they're gone now."

Another tingle along the backbone: Willie stared at Parry. Then, slowly his gaze shifted toward the staring ghoul. The ghoul was back. He had thought he was getting used to her. He was wrong.

For a half second Parry closed his eyes and amended, "In Jesus' name, as Pa used to say, amen."

They did not look at Ma till later.

It was late afternoon when Willie, Gregoff, and Aneas finished grave-digging. Aneas had not been selling papers from the start of the

136

Five Points Akropolis

Griffins' troubles and this was Willie's way of helping without much notice. There had also been another grave; this one for the typhoid. Dr. Zettler had said they could do nothing about typhoid except make the sewer, the aqueduct by the river; and quarantine. There was a vaccine but they didn't have it yet. The other boys had left and now Willie walked up toward the tomb, backed by the outcropping of ancient shale, serving as tool shed, original showpiece of the Akropolis Rural Cemetery. But it was 1900 A.D. and there were plans to change the name of the cemetery because the city had since grown up around it. Sounds of late afternoon delivery, horse-and-wagon traffic, filtered into the green park-like setting on all sides. Long green shadows thrown from the west contrasted with more golden light there. Lugging his shovels, the young gravedigger went past scrollworked pilasters of the arched keystone doorway into the cool dark of the tool crib, not noticing the smell of must and dank. He lined them neatly with the grounds-keeping tools ranged about the mortared stone walls just inside. He saw by new grass caked on the mower that Mr. Sneed had been doing some trimming of sites. Exhausted, he was glad of it. Then Willie stood thoughtfully eyeing the back wall of the tomb. It was not made with hands, not the work of masons. It was native rock ledge, had been there forever, long before the graveyard, the farming center, canal town, the O&B Railroad, rubber-works and foundry— the City in permutation.

Since the little girl had come he looked at it every time he put away his tools or got them back out again, puzzled. Outside, the ledge stood out on either side of the tool-tomb—stern wings of fern-tufted shale. Above it the lawn was shorn, mown by Willie Wilusa. In August as now the ledge was dry rock. In spring and autumn it glistened with moisture. The girl had come from inside this crib.

Creepy.

Willie was unaware that the young A'ndian scouts—no older than himself—had tracked the girl to this rock one spring almost 130 years before, and there lost her spoor for a time. But, for Willie, A'ndians were part of the vaudeauville show. One came to town occasionally in summertime and played the Opera House on Main Street. He thought of A'ndians as redskins that lived out west and traveled in the shows.

He went back out and closed the doors, this time latching, and shot the bolt with its short wrought-iron bar. He looked at the stonework and carven mausoleum he'd taken for granted before he had found the creep. That's what the little girl was to Willie's mind. She had come out of the tool-tomb—fell out actually—right on this spot, when the sun gleamed golden on the green lawn. She gave him the creeps but he felt for her; he had thought he was used to her but he was not. And she was always with his brother Parry, like a mascot, or ventriloquist's dummy in the minstrel show. The other kids in the Five Points gang either made fun or had various considered ideas of her condition, but to Willie she was always "the creep"—though he never said the word aloud. Now she was the wounded creep. But Aneas, his best pal, whose father was accused—Aneas thought she was an angel.

He walked up through the long shadows toward the gate, but then turned right and went up a little way on the grassy slope and threw himself down on top of Pop's grave. If he were assigned the right room (above him there in the pale brick high school come September), he'd be able to look out from the window down past the stone wall, more lawn and some graves, onto this particular grave. He was exhausted, but also afraid. He believed his father was in heaven now, and that this underneath was the made-earth of him, what was left. Because there'd been no oaken casket inside a mahogany casket inside a lead casket: The body was disposed in wood and was being made earth.

2017 CE Appears

S. Dorman

It was the next day, the day after Parry's reading the story, prayer of thanksgiving, and the girl fitting myriad things into a pattern. Aneas had started hawking his papers again.

Two days before, Argus had been arrested, the riot had started. Three days ago was Sunday and the lawn fête at *Stonehewn*; the girl had been raped after. Four days before this the A'ndians had appeared at the intersection of Five Points. Five days ago they had translated to 1900 A.D. Six days ago the corn-girl had traveled the watershed south to the rock in *Anno Domine* 1769. And eight days ago had come messengers of True People, telling of truce, fire weapons, the pact against interlopers from the *piawaw* with *Haudenosaunee* in the mountains east of here.

In 1900 A.D. the dwarf planet Pluto was yet to be discovered. At that time He was just past His ascent, losing angular momentum to Neptune. But this was unknown. In Akropolis, 1900 A.D., Willie knew only that the solar system had eight planets and a few asteroids and moons. He was one of the Five Points gang who knew about planets. Aneas Griffin was another. Johan Zettler a third. But they weren't thinking of planets when—with dapper blond Parry holding the little girl's hand and walking along Stock Exchange Street—they as one heard a strange rumbling high in the sky. Glacas, Gregoff, Cheenie and others of the Five Points gang were with them, Glacas keeping well out of Aneas' way and vice versa. Looking up the whole gang followed, at gaze, seeking to lay hold on the terror with their eyes.

What they saw made them stand still in thrilling wonder. Directly overhead they saw it, soaring straight up. Like a slow blolt of lightning in a pale sky. To Willie, at first it was as some tiny glowing insect. *What bug*, he wondered, *would make such a wake in the sky? What has such an echoing rumbling voice?*

Aneas thought, *This is an Angel, made out of light. I'm seeing an Angel like the prophet Ezekiel*; and he looked around swiftly to see if others saw it before shifting gaze upward to bless it, in awe, once more.

The gang members had heard, felt, seen the wonder, perhaps

140

all but the girl. No one would expect the girl to see anything except ordinary everyday things they did not much notice themselves, being used to them. And no comment would she make. Ever.

Willie's little brother Parry, in his favorite castoffs from James Priam—short pants and blouse with sailor's collar—tipped back his head and saw a tiny sleek cross-shape soaring straight into the blue high above. He was instantly struck by thoughts of *men in the moon.* Still holding her fingers with one hand, he tilted her chin toward the remote shining object. He liked her curious habit of staring at things. *She'd like to see it, I think.* And he was right.

The girl, wearing Ma's cut-down yellow frock and a scarf (from nuns at the church), over her bushy long hair, stared at the vapor trail of the jet soaring straight above Five Points—into the blue. She became captive of the split made in the sky, a division unlike any she'd seen in daylight, including the smooth doming of lenticular cloud, the light-mediating curve of a rainbow, and the lightning discharging and recharging the earth. But she did not think of these things nor of the sun pillar which also she'd seen in her child's life with True People in *Anno Domine* 1769 (these dates she knew not, nor would care). The division made by the jet fascinated her gaze.

"Look-a the teamsters!" For, crying, waving his hands, the Etalio kid Cheenie had seen the effort of the driver to hold his team to the street. It looked to Cheenie as though the great horses, with load, would sheer off through the dust into the plate-glass of *Paddy's Saloon and Pool Hall.*

The strange dreadful rumbling faded like thunder, its vaporous wake lingering, but its source out of sight. They heard its echo down the sky. Passing, it released grip on their senses, dropping them back toward each other ... but refusing to loose the imagination. Everyone spoke at once.

"—Did you see that!?"

"—You hear that!?"

"—What was that?!"

"It made a growing cloud!—See it?!"

Parry was the first to communicate his understanding. "It's the men in the moon. They are going just as Mr. Wills has predicted, and will see creatures we can't imagine. Telegrams will be sent from the spaceship telling the newspapers of it in Morse code." But his more taciturn and mechanically minded brother was thinking of Orville and Wilbur Wright: *The Wright brothers have succeeded in flying!*

"Willie!" Ma, wearing her leathern shop apron, was standing, waving; calling to him from the western corner of Five Points next to Paddy's across from the tall new brick grammar school.

"Willie! Parry!" She called and waved them to her. The other gang members, including the hill-country Glacas, the medical man's son Johan, and Gregoff the Grak kid, all followed; hopeful of some grown-up explanation of what they'd seen. Some idea of what made this thrust and thrill through the soul. Even the body was lifted to it, so strong did they feel the pull of the creature-thing-*super-nature*—hearts thudding—bodily sensations quickening.

But— "Willie!" she cried, "What's happening? What was that?" She had come out of the clasp-locker shop on Sharon Road in time to see the wagoneer's team brought under control in a cloud of street dust; but also she had heard the rumbling, felt the plateglass shaking a bit and looked up to see the jet in 2017 CE soaring after its takeoff from Pittsbury.

(Just seven years prior to this takeoff, one of its current passengers had discovered the changing appearance of Pluto's surface in comparison of Bubble telescopic space images: He oversaw the Projected Horizons robotic spacecraft, en route from the dwarf planet in a flyby to study both Pluto and its moons. The advent of the Projected Horizons venture revealed yet more of Pluto's estate to the world.)

When the young A'ndian scouts were tracking the girl in 1769, neither the stone nor yet the modern ages were aware of dwarf-wanderer Pluto's completion of His eccentric orbit around the sun— beginning *Anno Domine* 1769. The orbit ended, that is began again, in 2017 CE.

Red Fox, Dark Cloak, Eaglestreak, Quick Claws and two other scouts looked up from their hidden bivouac in Harkins Woods above Five Points. They heard the growling, and greatly wondered. These scouts, having come after the girl into 1900 A.D., did not think it just another industrial work meant to supplant them. Even though they were sickened in this passage. Now three of them had just fattened upon their meal of spitted rabbits and roasted roots and would not plan on eating again for two days, maybe more. The others had been either too sick to eat, tossing, turning, raving, or able to sup but little on steeped herbs; and maybe—as with Walleye-stare, sup drippings. Red Fox had found a bit of crockery from the trash heap in an alleyway for the steepings.

Hearing the growling in its wake, they saw the jet's streak of white expanding beyond the woven pattern of branches overhead.

Nearly naked in the August heat, each lay back in wonder, intently watching the pattern expanding its backdrop of cloudy white in the wake of the swift Arrow. For each young scout had glimpsed the wingéd Arrow—pure and clean, opaquely white yet ghostly pale— and knew it for a sign from the world of their ancestors, the world of

142

spirit and long life. But what the sign meant was at first unintelligible. Each lay, glistening with sweat, in silent meditation on the duff of the hillside. Each lay on top of his cloak looking up and contemplatively, or restively, revisiting their deep pouchful of stories: the naked bear that smelled everything but did not see well, the earth-turtle's submergence in the great flood, the tree whose limbs sprouted *True People*. Of the loneliness before the origin of Time, and the coming of great fire to force the outcome of Place and Time from no-thing.

At last Red Fox spoke.

"It is a sign from her."

The Gorge with rapids north of here, in which the clan of True People had had their 1769 encampment, was *Timebefore*. But, since A.D. 1900, the scouts had been exploring to the former A'ndian encampment, and saw the works building for power generation, little (nay never) understanding its purpose. But of its *influence* upon the land they possessed profound recognition. The valley itself, on its way to the gorge, was in one place a mountainous heap of refuse. And Dark Cloak had reported all his observation of the corn-girl's experience and of the battle in Akropolis: Red Fox was confirming all to himself: The silent corn-girl, in drifting from True People, had brought the scouts into her vision of the *Aftertime*... in which the interlopers she reveals as True People's conquerors. *True People* had the victory in her earlier capture and destruction of the missionary hamlet in *Haudenosaunee* woods—but the interlopers succeeded them anyway. And in this *Aftertime* they had tried to put the True People's scouts on display for the audience.

"It is the Arrow of Passage, which the seasons do follow, and has signified unto us the *Aftertime*," said Red Fox to his fellow scouts where they lay. "The corn-girl has carried us too far into Time. This swift growling arrow above is in token of this. And too, it means that we should go back now we have found her. We must take hold of her body from the grasp, if need be, of the interloper who lets not go her corn-grinding hand. We must take her to the gorge and instruct her to take us to the *Foretime* wherein we belong. It is for our descendents to live; and, if possible, know and fight these interlopers. NOT FOR US." And his last words had the slow solemn force of a decree.

CE 2017 Appears with Gamers.

He sat on the stone wall with the others. A doom-saying electronic voice emanated portentously from the gamescape in Fabian's hand:

"THE GOD OF UNDERWORLD HAS REACHED HIS ASCENDANCY OVER THE GOD OF UNDERSEA. HIS SURFACE, IN ROTATION, IS AGAIN DISTURBED IN TERRAFORMING HIMSELF TO MAKE READY THE INVADERS."

The first thing the FivePoints gang of 2017 noticed was the cessation of wireless service. This was after a jet had vanished (glimpsed from their place on the wall, not far from the old wrought-iron gates of the Glimmerdale Cemetery). Vanished, traceless. Some of the gang had not noticed it. The library across the street was also gone but they were unaware of it as yet. So keyed were they to their online pursuits that they did not at first notice the alien noises.

"Just took my eyes off it—poof! The Jet. The thing vanished. Just. Like. That." Fabian's eyes widened for emphasis. He had long blond hair—except for the buzz cut down the middle—tucked behind his ears, tattooed cheeks and earrings. This great-great-grandson of Glacas the so-called hillbilly was speaking. He had heard the joke, of course, about Akropolis once being the capital of neighboring North Regina. But Fabian had only a small idea that his ancestors had come from those mountains to look for work in the rubber factories. The rubber factories themselves were part of the dim past he'd heard of, maybe in school, maybe his grandmother had told him.

"Contrail and all—just like the Prez." This was HBBBAH speaking. "Look what he done, and now gone out, leaving behind...." He trailed off, puzzling. He was very dark with a big broom-cut, the sides of which were shaved bald. HBBBAH tilted back, seeking it—both his bald head and the broom-cut suddenly glistened.

Five Points Akropolis

"That doesn't mean it makes sense though," murmured Pomala, gazing upward out of a blue face. "Seriously, I feel weird. It's way too much like *CitiesUnderground*. This is real life. It doesn't happen. Things don't vanish here, big things like that." She was trembling, glancing back at them, and fell silent.

No one heard her apprehension. Tu, head bent, straight black hair hanging over his brow, had not even bothered to look up from the paper he had downloaded on Quantum Teleportation. Tu had his own little study going on the side that he didn't tell his friends about—too much mathematical geekery for them. Pomala sank back against the rocks, and noticed the library was gone. She stopped trembling and stared at the old shop in its place. Her gaze flicked back to Quadri's thumbs obsessively swiping his 7qz.phone screen. At the moment he was playing *Twinkle-in-Time*. Quadri, with rich almost olive-hued complexion, was the youngest; and usually the most oblivious.

All lounging here, in front of the GlimmerDale Cemetery, were born after the year 2000 CE. They were the communal descendents of Five Points. Three only were biological descendents of the original Five Points gang. The rest were immigrants from "the old country," as they were used to joking—places like Salia, Indonia, Tapi. Their parents were either refugees of poverty or fleeing régimes of brutality. Another neighborhood descendent (of Gregoff the Grak) was tattooed Pomala, who had been tested for gene variation and infused with the "immortality gene" to control aging. She wasn't alone in the experiment, though some kids were in a control group. Every kid in school had—through a grant from CossycSystems— been genetically tested, and the information given their parents on what will be ailing them as they age. All this the fruit of stem cell research in the 21st-century, more than 100 years after the birth of the original 1900 Five Points gang.

They knew about Pluto, of course. Once it was a planet but now only a dwarf-planet. Fabian knew more about that than his own heritage, but he called it Hades because, in the *Hadesthon* (pronounced HAD-s-thon) which he'd just been playing with HBBBAH, Pluto was Hades. *His Big Black Brother Arcturus Hipster*, a.k.a. HBBBAH, was the nickname and gaming ID of Blake Griffin, descendent of Argus, father of Aneas Griffin the angel watcher.

"The Z-pod stopped," HB said. "The game stalled. You note we was whumpin' yo butts," referencing Beri in LA and juanBoy in Rantano, their partners-in-game. He flashed a grin like a strobe at Fabian.

"Maybe—but the game ain't over. We're just about to destroy you. *Elevation 11, ThirdTier* yet to do."

"It's CyberWars," said Jayrai, who had just been reviewing

her feeds. "Wireless, and the whole net's down, but its temporary. The Gov's got it covered." She was guessing of course. Her hair was dark with white streaks, her complexion rich and smooth like Quadri's, but her eyes were rounder.

"Yeah," echoed HBBBAH.

"The home folk are sick of us," said Jayrai, referring to Tapi, over the sea from where such attacks were commonly launched.

"Can you blame'em," HBBBAH Griffin shot back. He thought Jayrai should be more loyal to the land he'd never see where her people—not his—came from.

"Uh..." said Jayrai, "don't know the place. This is the place." Fingers splayed, she waggled her bionic hand. All its works were exposed—tiny motors, electronics, metallic finger joints, and wires. She knew she should wear the sheer polychloroprene covering from fingertips to the shoulder beneath her jacket; but she loved the attention and triumph of the works. A donation from CossycSystems after her accident. Jayrai began to sweat beneath her jacket.

"This?!" screeched Pomala, spreading her arms. "This is the place?!" Her voice quavered.

They looked up at their surroundings.

Puzzled. Mouths agape, eyes shining questions.

FivePoints was gone. Here's what they saw.

People in movie costumes of the old days—long drab clothing—blinkered horses, and buggies of whatever style for which they had no names. There went a shiny three-wheel motorcar of some sort, putt-putting. And a couple of motorized old-fashioned bicycles. Pedestrians crossing any which way through traffic, like planets spiraling out of control. All traffic a chaos of movement seeming without law or rules of any kind; where the moment before were orderly streams of mostly solar-powered cars, and a few old junkers with fuel injection engines, ruled by the traffic lights at FivePoints. The pavement was gone. And right beneath their feet— those who weren't on the wall—was a low sidewalk of boards above a gutter running with what smelled like raw sewage. (Sewage from neighborhood outhouses and the cattle pound up toward the railroad stockyard.)

The City of Akropolis, 1900 A.D, was working on correcting the problem of raw sewage passing into the river north of Five Points. An aqueduct was planned to bring it all out to a plant on the edge of town, within wind drift of the (formerly) A'ndian encampment, *Anno Domine* 1769.

Directly across from them, where the FivePoints Library (one of many branches throughout the city) had stood a minute ago, was a music shop complete with hanging violins, horns on stands, woodwinds on display, an old upright—all in the window with a hanging shingle in the shape of a bass viola: *Gustav's Music.*

Huh?

What?

Sht!

Yikes!

A mass internal exclamation.

They looked at one another. "Pinch us!" squeaked Pomala. As always, her blue hair stood in spikes as though growing blue out of her blue tattooed face. She was albino underneath it all, greatly evidenced in her pink eyes with white lashes. She could not see well in the glare, keeping blue contacts in her pocket for when it was bad.

Jayrai obliged, with bionic fingers. Smiling through white-streaked hair somewhat veiling her dark mischievous round eyes. Pomala's eyes watered.

"We daid," said HBBBAH.

"What's happening?" said Fabian.

"Superstrings," said Tu, blinking stoically.

"Don't you mean super-stench?" Jayrai gagged and scrambled back up on the wall. "It smells like the park down in the river valley!" Then, "Look at this wall!"

They looked. It was moss-grown and moldy beneath the leafy shade trees. Wait. The leaves had been down a couple weeks. But a moment before the wall had been blasted hewn limestone, clean as a whistle. They looked at the trees, many of which were far younger, less girthy than they remembered—a moment ago? —The leaves are back! And there behind, in the cemetery where a large stump stood a moment ago (clean of all but the sawdust), rose a shapely spreading elm, high and overarching the wall.

It had been November. Now— they were sweating.

"This is... really... quite scary," said Fabian to the hazardous horse traffic.

"Guys! Guys! I'm so glad you're here!" squeaked Pomala. "I'd have to get me some new genes, otherwise. I mean a whole kitful, you know?"

"It's sick, really sick," whimpered young brown Quadri, voice trembling, almost inaudible.

Wondering, Fabian gazed off toward the intersection where, above the clattering, thundering chaos of the horse-drawn traffic, soared the old school that had been demolished two years ago to make room for the new medical laboratory and clinic. Jayrai glanced after his gaze. There stood the old school they remembered. It had been their decrepit gradeschool and now it was in a pristine state of near completion, clean crisp brick-work with pale stucco cornices above arched windows.

"Look at'em!" said Fabian with a gesture. "There, on the corner. All that dark clothing. ...Looks like a newsboy is selling papers! the Afrikan-Americle kid."

The others glanced from the monumental gradeschool toward the knot of kids on the corner across from it. An omnibus, drawn by a couple of huge horses with blinders—great hairy hooves ringing, wheels thunderous—pulled between them and the kids on the corner.

They looked around again. The street of shops, with the exception of the library (built in the 1990s when times were good), looked in better shape than what 2017 had for buildings. But two of the older kids, Fabian and HBBBAH, saw that these buildings were but the fresh version of their older decrepit structures: the building on the corner, for instance, they saw when the omnibus went past. For them it was the revivalist's deteriorating storefront. But now it looked—like a handsome old-time saloon! Golden curlicues on plateglass.

"You're right," said Fabian to Tu. "Don't know much about superstrings, if that's what it is—but you're right about Time.... We're here—"

"—But we're not," said Tu. His Southeast Osiian symmetrical features were blank but hiding an internal shivering.

"Really? Maybe it's the reverse," Jayrai said. "Gravity's been doing a number on this place. Everything's different but us."

"Yeah," said Pomala, "and we're sick, Bro. Majorly sick."

"Sick or not," said Jayrai, "I'm going exploring." She slid off the wall and stood on the low boardwalk. "C'mon." She waved them off the wall, Pomala and Tu reluctantly. "This is some serious sht we got here—like I said before." Jayrai smiled. Her EastA'ndian features were lit up like those of Columbo when he landed in the Islands and saw the beautiful Americle natives.

Tu sniffed at Jayrai's pun. He was all theoretical and did not really like the turn his senses were giving him. But Jayrai had already gone skipping ahead, her Z-pod stashed in the leg pocket of her purple cargo pants. Her bionic arm was about to have a few new admirers.

"Hey!" yelled Quadri, the youngest. "What about *WarsOfWorldCraft*?!! He'd been playing it simultaneous with T-i-T— with Jayrai, who had been simultaneously surfing Groverland via OoHHahEarth, looking for her new SlurpeeezPalz RL house. Quadri was a bit apprehensive about what they'd been saying, but also could not get his head around the fact that *WorldCraft* and *Twinkle* were just gone. WoWC—The best game going! The entire *City* was the Monster. It had to be defeated or they were toast!

Passing the brick fronts with plate glass (some of its lettering in goldleaf), Fabian was remembering... and coming up with the amazing insight that comes from seeing something backward—as in reflection: When he was little.... He'd seen one or two of these same places in the old family album when his uncle was digitizing a batch of old photos, probably circa 1920s or 30's—from FivePoints a hundred years ago. There were people in them, posing together, and no one now had any idea who, except that they must be old ancestors. The backs of the black-and-white photos weren't notated.

The thought made him stop, arms out to hold them all back as he considered this startling conception. His hand chafed his buzz cut fleetingly. *But maybe it's not a fact*, he thought. *Is this a fact?*

He said, "Maybe... —the newspaper he's selling would have the date on it! There are still newspapers!"

Jayrai had gone ahead, unaware of her friends' hesitation, unconcerned that she was about to make real contact with 1900 A.D. in human form—on her own. She had crossed over behind the slow-moving omnibus with driver perched atop it staring down at her; and was almost to the corner where *Paddy's* stood, plateglass on either side. In 2017 it should be Pastor Zettler's *Revival House and Soup Kitchen.* She saw straight through its gloom to the new gradeschool across Sharon Road. But that was in passing. She aimed for the clutch of kids standing around the aproned woman with old-fashioned poofy hair.—All talking at once, excited.

Here goes....

And, pumped on female bravado, she walked straight into their midst, turning sideways a bit to pass between Parry and Gregoff the Grak. Straight to Willie who had stood silent while others still peppered the air with exclamations over the jet.

Back down the block on Stock Exchange, the 2017 FivePoints gang stood watching, arrested, holding a breath. Slowly Fabian said, "You know... this could be tricky. Are we in the old days? Is it some alternate universe? Is it real?"

"Am I dreaming?—you mean," said Pomala. "Look guys, I'm sweating! The leaves are back on the trees. A minute ago it was November. It was just Halloween!" Pomala was majorly freaked.

HBBBAH jerked his jacket off. The others had already done so while on the wall or crossing the street. "She's done it," he said jabbing the air in the direction of Jayrai. "Maybe that's my great granddad down there with the newspapers. God knows what will happen. I might disappear at any moment. Maybe, yo!—you never gone heard a'me!"

"Have you got the old version loaded?" asked Quadri of anybody. He kept his gaze flashing over the screen. "The battery works. Maybe we don't need to stream it."

Tu put up his thin arm around HBBBAH's much broader

shoulders. Not something Tu would do.

"I don't think we need the game now," said Pomala to Quadri with a quiver, smiling, distracted. I think we *are* the game.—You know?"

They saw the group at the intersection spreading, leaving colorful bionic Jayrai a bit apart but still in their midst. A passing wind devil stirred the August dust around them. Jayrai's arms akimbo, she no doubt was talking large sht.

"C'mon, HB. You won't disappear," said Tu bravely, at last breaking his speculative half-fearful silence. "Hold my hand if you like, girl."

HBBBAH had been on a tangent lately trying to get his friends to call everyone girl, instead of guy. He wanted to change the dynamic of the language. ("The good thing is we all be girls now, not guys.")

Right off HBBBAH suspected sarcasm but thought better— sarcasm not something of Tu's really. Nor was the arm around his shoulders. Of course he did not take him up on the offer to hold hands. But he did laugh, a shrill giggle they'd never heard from HBBBAH before. And boldly he yelled at the corner in general, "Don't pay that extreme dude any mind, girls!! She's a freaking freak-show from the future. She's got no weapons, no nothing but a fuking two-year-old Z-pod, and a bionic arm! No fear!"

The group on the corner turned, saw them coming and fragmented. Scattering. It ran off like particles in all directions through traffic. Only to stand, reconfigured here and there, on every corner of Five Points, palpably, but distantly, curious.

From a few doors past Paddy's up Sharon Road—in the doorway of the clasp-locker hospital—Parry took hold of the girl's hand. He glanced back. He saw that Ma was still on the corner with Willie—with the *being from the moon*! and now the other moonmen were there! And—it was the first time he'd been scared that he'd noticed. It passed through his mind that he'd felt this way before. He looked at the girl who was staring, as usual, into space, into nothing. Yes. He *had* felt this way before—on meeting her.

Not meeting her. You couldn't really meet her. She is the thing that made him think of it ALL and how impossible it all is and how the universe is too big, too frightening. Almost!—but he did not drop her hand. Instead, he clutched tighter. And tighter; watching the group down there, the girl staring into space beside him. And she did not seem to notice he touched her at all.

Parry thought, *Ma's talking to the men from the moon.*

Willie, fearful-brave, stood the corner boardwalk by the horse trough in front of Paddy's; unwilling to move away from Ma, who also watched as 2017 FivePoints in human form approached. Here's what they saw:

Shapes not so unlike themselves, not well-clothed, moving toward them, each with arms and legs, one head each, but. ...Ma saw multifarious differences but hardly to be distinguished apart from a general sense of the alien. Not as foreignness, of which Ma, the former farm girl, had seen and gotten to know in the incoming waves of immigrants (having largely forgotten the immigration of her ancestors). But, never anything so *wildly* outlandish as was this swift approach. This one before them now had round distended eyes. In place, where the Wilusas had their ears, were green and purple strings hanging from great purple scars. Its hair—if that was hair—was half white, hanging before its brown bony shoulders, one of which was wires and things. All its clothing was purple or white— eerie, shining, glistering, light as paper. Its jacket hung tied round its waist by the sleeves (which was not the way jackets were worn in 1900 A.D.). The thing in semi-human form was sweating and speaking strange words in accents unknown, and very fast.

Willie, fearful, watched it speaking, and took Ma's hand; which he had not done since Pop died in the machinery at Priam's rubber works. Willie was the one of Ma's two sons who'd had to be brave because he *was* so apprehensive, always hiding it behind a stoic manner: the gravedigger at the Akropolis Rural Cemetery who'd dug his father's grave.

Seeing the other shapes moving down the boardwalk toward them, his grip on her tightened. Ma had stayed, the others gone off, and he'd no choice but to keep by her, see her safe from this alien threat. And it fled across his mind: Was Parry right? *Were these men from the moon?* Almost involuntarily he glanced back toward the shop at his little brother who'd always been the fearless one. It was the first time he'd seen him run from anything—dapper, light, almost feminine boy as he was. The creepy girl was there, completely unaware, staring off into space.

"How!" said Jayrai, seeing that her talk was going nowhere. She raised her bionic hand like in the old Westerns she sometimes downloaded for a giggle, and because she liked the innocent exaggerated take on Native Americles seen from old-timey Anglo eyes and memory. It was a word and gesture Willie recognized from the minstrel show. Slowly, a corner of his eye on the other approaching alien forms, he raised his human hand.

"How."

And here's what the FivePoints gang saw as they came strolling, talking, toward Willie and Ma:

A straight-backed woman of middle-age and height, slight, in old-fashioned blouse with long sleek sleeves except where gathered

151

at the shoulder; long dark skirt beneath the leather apron. Slim high button shoes. Her brown hair was in a pile atop her head, her face lined and seeming without emotion. The boy, of an age perhaps with Fabian and HBBBAH, wore knee pants, homemade shirt and suspenders, his shoes were high button workboots, the dust of his morning's labor still on them. The youth also was solemn, without emotion.

Turning, Jayrai said in a rush to 2017, "I told them the truth—had to—that we are from the planet Gliese 581d! Don't try to scare'em with anything else. They wouldn't understand."

"Neither do we, *Jay*," said Fabian, part amused, part embarrassed bemusement. To Ma and Willie he said simply, "We aren't from around here—you know?"

The words *you know*, while an afterthought, even a non-thought of Fabian's pushed a terrifying thrill through Willie, who hadn't heard this colloquialism for "I reckon." He looked back for Parry, thinking he could use his brother's careless almost reckless interjection now.

Parry was coming toward them, drawn by his love of things strange, and not so frightened since he had taken strong hold on his talisman, the girl in Ma's cutdown frock.

Slowly they gathered, the Five Points gang of 1900 A.D., straggling back to the corner. Drawing near, the sons of immigrants from the Medioceanic and Northern R'opea, their clothing similar to Willie's, if more or less patched: wearing slouch caps but otherwise their looks were telling of the "Old World", with the warm olive skins of the Medioceanic, the lighter coloring of the northern countries.

"I... don't," said Willie. "We don't know what you're talking about." His expression was earnest, his brow frowning.

"Are they from the moon?" said Parry, ignoring them at first.

"We are from the planet GlieseFiveEightOneSmallD," said Jayrai. "Yes," Jayrai herself confirmed. "That's the best way to understand it. There's no atmosphere on the—on your moon, not enough gravity there to keep the kids from bouncing off the walls. They're only mining it for stuff, minerals and stuff—Chino."

"Chino?" said Parry, for the first time addressing the people from outer space. He eyed her bionic arm in fascination. Willie's eyes had already taken to studying it in fear and awe. He was the gadget man of the gang, but fear restrained his questions.

"Oh yeah," she answered. "They've taken over the whole franchise."

The younger Pomala had been stroking the horses' great bony snouts. "They're gigantic!" Small Quadri stepped back, brown eyes unbelieving and big. Now Pomala, whose blue tattooed face and neck seemed leaching up into her tall blue hair, said, "What's wrong with her?" looking at the vacant girl. "Is she autistic? Does she talk? My cousin's baby might be going to be Asperger's and they're gonna try gene therapy before it gets past the zygote stage."

Stupefying incredulity, incomprehension, filled the three Wilusas. And also filled the look in the eyes of FivePoints 2017. The 1900 A.D. gang had filtered back through traffic to see and hear it.

Fabian saw the fear in Willie's eyes, contemplating the bionic hand. He said to him, "Don't mind these guys. They're scared, too."

HBBBAH interjected, "We've never been—uh—don't know how to get back—uh." He stopped. HBBBAH had never been at a loss for words before. He thought, *I been here all my life!!*

Aneas, his great-great-granduncle had come up to them from the corner of Bechtel and Stock Exchange Streets to sit down on the edge of the water trough, his pouch now empty of newspapers. (Of which Fabian took note.) It being August the water level was low— the trough's edge quite dry but cooling. Aneas watched the colored moon-boy, half amazed at his boldness, half bemused by his black-shining textilite jumpsuit, for which he had no name. The moon-boy, too, had green and purple strings hanging from knobby ears, like the moon-girl—and the youngest one in the bunch, who kept pushing his thumbs together over something small in his hand. Aneas took off his slouch cap and played with it nervously. He licked his full lips, listening intently.

"That makes no sense," said Mrs. Wilusa tersely to Pomala. "What on earth does that mean?" She grabbed hold of the girl's other hand tightly.

"They talk funny," said Glacas. "We seed that right off. Bad as a wop-ee-o."

Cheenie, eyes angry, whopped him alongside the head, swearing. "Ow!" said Glacas.

Parry said, "It's how moon-men talk. Are you a girl?"

The boys from 2017 eyed Pomala's tiny blue bosoms beneath the shimmering tank top and smiled. HBBBAH laughed out loud. He said, "We've got both genders on *Gliese 581d*. And there's two other kinds, too."

This made no sense either but no one said anything.

Glacas the hill-country boy exclaimed, "The minstrels!" A light was on in his eyes. "The minstrel show man outdone hisself. The grandmaster's got the best gol'danged show—he got rid of the A'ndians! That's what! Don't you see? I seed it right off! It's a whole shake better'n blackface, 'tis."

Aneas looked away. Pointedly.

Glacas boldly thumped Pomala on her back, but jerked back as he looked—grinning, gap-toothed—and saw Jayrai glaring at him, her bionic hand waggling impatiently by her thigh. He did not know

153

but what there was abnormal power in that trick hand. (He did not know that it was sensitive enough to lift the fragile newborn's arm between index finger and thumb, but able, too, of crushing a man's hand if need be.)

Meanwhile Quadri was still studying the 1900 CE girl speculatively... waking up to the fact of this new reality, this how-many-year-old reality—? But still he can't stop with the buttons on the 7qz: *Is she a botched droid?*

Aneas, twirling his cap, licking his lips, is granted one stupendous thought—again. He stops, but still listening to them all, thinking: *Maybe they be good as fallen angels ... some kind of messengers, warning.*

But most of the others were almost wet with relief, really wet. *Minstrels.* It was August and humid. The clattering Five Points traffic did stop and go—pedestrians and riders, on horse, omnibus and buggy—staring in passing at 2017; at Glacas pointing, exclaiming, "The minstrel show got a fresh act! The vaudeville!!" He could not stop grinning, rejoicing in the limelight just a bit himself, his hand smacking his ragged britches, his black stockings fallen down. He wore the stockings even though today was not his turn to wear the shoes he shared with his bigger brother.

Just then the puttering, hiccuping motorcar, driven by Gilbert, carried James Horatio and the Priam family lawyer, on its way along Stock Exchange Street to the law office. James Priam climbed out just past the intersection, and walked, head down with gaze on the ground, toward them. The car, bearing the lawyer drove on. The Five Points gang ... his favorite group of kids after his brothers and sisters. —And now his best brother Brant was injured, maybe desperately, *And it was all on account of me.*

Quadri continued considering "the girl," and now, still also distracted in the game, said softly to Jayrai, "In my family we called them ghouls. That's a zombie."

Jayrai, standing beside him, said aside, "I don't think so. That's gaming, fiction."

Pomala overhearing said, "She's autistic—gotta be."

James Priam, having skipped up past the gutter and coming along the boardwalk heard this. Of course his eyes were completely taken by the queer representatives of *Gliese 581d*, the moon-men, the minstrel act, or whatever they might prove to be. (He had heard Glacas as Gilbert drove him past.) James Priam was precocious, the boldest of the Five Points gang—he liked to think himself a member, and who would disavow that? Not these kids. Once or thrice he even came to play kick-the-can with them at night, rode down from gaslit Cake Eaters Hill on Brant's motorbike. Immediately he bestowed what insight he had on the girl to the newest act playing at the Opera House.

He said, "She is feeble-minded. Willie's boss, Mr. Sneed, told him she belongs in a lunatic asylum in A'ndian Falls. But Mrs. Havard, the journalist from London, says eugenists in Angleland want to criminalize feeble-mindedness, and that is bad. I think so too sometimes, don't you? They want to do scientific experiments on people and that is disturbing. My father is undecided. He thinks we may or may not be evolving and if we are we ought to help it along— but is that the best way? And if we aren't there's not much we can do." And thinking of his brother's slim escape from the malady, he said, "It would be good if we could help blind people to see again, don't you think?" This was said with great seriousness but also with as much fair mindedness as he could put into it. He did not want to talk rubbish, as Mrs. Havard would call it.

He watched as Fabian and HBBBAH held up their Z-pod's, capturing images of everything that passed. This was a great curiosity. He drew near Willie. "Are they the A'ndian replacement act of the grandmaster's? I can't imagine why they quit, but I think this may be even better. Willie! You will have to see the show as my guest. You and your mother and Parry and the girl." He took in the Wilusa family with his firm somewhat desolate gaze. Then he held out his hand for the leather-thin gadget. "May I see what you have? What is that you're doing?"

A rider pulled near and swung off his mount, stirring up pale dust. The horse pushed Aneas with his great dark snout and the boy moved off the trough. Aneas too came close in hopes of seeing what was in their hands.

"What's that awful smell?" said Jayrai looking around.

"The horse just did something, of course," said Parry

"That's no horse smell," said Jayrai. "Smells like rotten eggs."

"What does rotten egg smell like?" asked Pomala. "Our infrastructure is rotting, it's gonna be as bad smelling as this before you know it."

"Vulcanization," said James Priam. "You have to add sulfur to the latex."

"It's just the rubber factory," said Parry. "Sometimes it does that. That's a neat word—infa-structure. What is it?"

To FivePoints 2017 Glacas said (grinning), "You talk funny."

James Horatio said, "Strange, yes. Differently inflected speech, I'd say."

"Only smells here when the wind is from the east," said Willie, moving with Aneas closer to the Z-pod James was holding. He had dropped Ma's hand. Not so tense now, he spoke normally— flatly as always—for the first time since the encounter with 2017.

His gaze was on the tiny image of Paddy's plateglass window with its curlicue goldleaf lettering. Fabian had taken Tu's picture standing there at the corner of the pool hall. A perfect miniature. Again, he had many questions, but would not speak them. All gathered round gazing at it, mystified.

"You gonna delete that one? —MeTastASis could find out everything about Tu from that face info," said Jayrai, reminding Fabian. She looked at Mrs. Wilusa and, by way of explanation, saying, "OOga was bought up by MeTastASis—and we all know it's controlled by Alaeske. Totalitarian state—since the secession after the antiTrusting. We always thought it was gonna be Taxuse but—surprise."

Ma had only glanced at it, through the little clutch of kids, and now stared at her, wondering. Then she turned and said in her rough-sounding voice, "I'm going back now, Willie. You kids don't be too long. I've got to go up and get dinner. You come too, Aneas."

"We won't be," said Willie with distraction, taking his gaze off the alien. He recognized part of the word and knew *a little* about anti-trust. But the rest was outlandish gibberish!

Ma glanced again at Pomala who, ripping it, opened a slit in the leg of her pants pocket. Ma stopped a moment, scrutinizing it. She wanted to reach out and touch, manipulate. She didn't, of course.

"Velcra," said HBBBAH. "I don't suppose you have that yet?"

"What's the date?" asked Fabian, as nonchalantly as he could.

"And the time," said Tu, still standing by the plateglass, looking up from his own Z-pod. He stood as much apart as possible from the thundering chaos of the street, the seeming every-which-way-ed-ness, so disturbing to him. The horse so great and near was a monster. Big furred snout and huge black nostrils blowing.

"When the churchtower strikes the hour you'll know it!" said Glacas happily, with a touch of importance. He gestured up Bechtel Avenue where at its far end the church hunkered above the cemetery like a monolith, but on a slight bend, barely visible from here. The church was 2017, too, but without clockworks in its tower.

"But how accurate is that?" wondered Tu.

"Oh, it's calibrated as accurate as possible with Greenwich Mean Time," said James.

"That's not real calibration, James," put in Willie, meaning *infallible.* He was still looking at Fabian. "They can try, the clock-winders can, keeping them accurate."

"I'm sure they do," said James looking at Tu. "The telegraph office keeps track of all that."

"They know the moon is doable," said Jayrai to her friends.

Five Points Akropolis

"How can horse-n-buggy people not realize how far in the future real space travel is?"

Fabian was still looking at Willie, and Willie at Fabian. Fabian answered her without moving his gaze: "So, don't we think about aliens being smarter than us—able to come to us through a wormhole or whatever? To *Gliese 581d* we'd be savages, a slave resource." And still he looked his question at Willie, his nonchalance gone.

Perplexed, trying to understand with his small frown and steady look at Fabian: Willie said, "The 24th." And—tense—again waited.

"Twenty-fourth of... August?"

"Yeah." Willie waited.

"What year?"

"What year?" His frown deepened. He scowled. Willie did not like it.

"It's part of the show," said James Horatio Priam. To Fabian, he said, "It's 1900 Akropolis. What day is it where you come from?" He was seriously smiling, but not so much at play as he had been when he first saw the A'ndians at this intersection of Five Points less than a week ago. To 2017 in general he said, "The A'ndians seemed very fierce and pretended not to speak Anglish. But truly, Mrs. Havard said, they couldn't. So this makes it all quite intriguing."

"That's it!—we be minstrels." said HBBBAH and reached for his inadvertent great-great-granduncle's hand, pumping it and sending out a phrase or three of funkster rap.

Astounded, Aneas allowed the gesture, barely. He could not get over this boldness. And such talk that decency could not well tolerate. He shivered at the mention of the slave trade. This boldness belonged to the white man. Everything here did. He looked at Willie, his best friend, much as HBBBAH himself (in 2017 terms) was Fabian's best real friend, but also online. Willie now looked his frowning bemusement back at Aneas. A question passed between them. It had no verbal articulation ... but it was there, mutual.

And Tu, standing against the brick corner of Paddy's Saloon could not stop theorizing about Pluto and The Hadesthon, with this conjunction of PlaceAndTime, amidst this disturbing chaos. He saw that it was all there—analogous!—in the game! And that he could probably count on the UniversalTimeClock (so designated in 2017). All he had to do was work out a true calculation, a calibration, to get them back through the ripple in time perhaps made by the neighboring tug in the orbits of Neptune and Pluto. He had once proclaimed that the multiverse was made out of nothing and that once they got used to that fact they'd be all right. And sometimes he said, "We'll be able to comprehend everything before we can comprehend nothing." He was the one who planned to get out of FivePoints on scholarship to Carnegie Edison in Pittsbury. Begun as Ale Carnegie Technical School in 1900 by the steel baron. Willie, in his most hopeless dreams, might have wished to attend.

Five Points Akropolis

HB Gets an Idea, Mrs. Havard Would See Grandmaster

"I don't think they're in the show," said Willie to Aneas in a flat sullen tone, as they stood together in front of Paddy's after the midday meal. The vaudeville kids had crossed the street. The other kids were playing around on the corner and before the window, careful to keep out of the doorway. Sometimes folk went in and out the saloon even at this time of day.

Aneas nodded. He was watching Gwendolyn come downhill through heat waves toward them, clipping down on the boardwalk of Sharon Road, the road that ran toward Sharon between Harkins and Cake Eaters Hills. She did not look as fresh as she managed most days with regard to dress and deportment. Most days she seemed to shine, not with inner beauty or even outer beauty. She shone by some effort of will, as though she were built up of hard-won materials: long skirt and blouse, hightop black buttoned shoes showing; ribbons, bows, her hair just so, springy sausage curls. All put together by dint of effort, elaborate make-do craft. Not one of the boys, he knew, could really visualize or think of touching her. Also, she was impossible to make fun of. But today, in this heat, she seemed somehow *less* than usual. Not quite—not ever— bedraggled, but as if she *could* be—almost.

The invaders from outer space had all crossed through afternoon heat and traffic to the grammar school. For some reason they were excited to look over the new structure. Why the workmen let them in, no one considered. Anyone, seeing them, would stand aside staring. And James, the rich kid, was giving a tour. The 1900 Five Points gang had been excited earlier in the spring when Harkins Grammar had started building—it was so monumentally beautiful and so pleasing to the vanity in comparison to their outgrown schoolhouse with its lath-and-plaster rooms tacked on.

The other kids were also hanging around outside Paddy's, a bit listless—Gregoff, Cheenie, Glacas and others. Shooting craps for imaginary money, a penny a point or—the younger ones—playing

159

mumblety-peg with their pocket knives. Gwen came right down toward them on the corner.

Aneas heard Willie say, "They have stuff couldn't possibly be—from the most costly product line. Where'd it come from? That hand and arm with all its works!?"

Aneas looked back at him. He wished he could think about that now. But he couldn't. He just could not.

Gwendolyn came right up to the girl and went down on her knees. Willie had seen her, absently, coming down the boardwalk toward them. Now he did a double-take.

Gwen picked up Heirolynn's hand, almost tenderly. The little girl had just been standing there staring off as usual. She may have seen the pattern in the gang playing, heard the clicking of dice upon the boardwalk during a lull at the intersection; but if so gave no sign. Gwen looked up almost pleading into her far far distant gaze.

"Please forgive my letting go your hand the other night. I'm so so sorry I did that."

Surprisingly, Aneas said, "You be'nt blamed for that, Gwen."

Normally he would not have spoken to Gwendolyn in any case. But now he scarcely knew why he spoke or even how he was so able. He had expected a blazing gaze back from her, but she held the girl's hand and looked, looking looking, into her blank face. Then Gwen withdrew and stood.

She had the well-kept front again. She look coldly on Aneas and said, "I'm sorry."

Willie said, "He's right. We were supposed to do it. Not you. You can't be blamed."

She looked at him, and said, "Maybe and maybe not."

She went and stood over Gregoff and Parry playing mumblety-peg.

"I'm going back now," said Willie. "If you're done peddling papers you could come. I don't need help." This was a way of saying there'd be no pay in it from Mr. Sneed. Willie wanted to talk about the strangers, and what kind of strange or alien land they had come from, while he worked trimming shrubbery.

Wordless, mute, Aneas started off with him, head down. From beneath the brim of his slouch cap he glimpsed Gwen staring down on the kids throwing knives, trying to make the blades stick in the boardwalk. Staring. Without seeing, staring, at the play.

The two boys turned the corner past this listless gang at their lackadaisical play. Cheenie looked up as they stepped through. "They get-a your old-a man, sure."

Johan, kneeling with the dice, scraped them up and moved away, scowling.

Five Points Akropolis

When they reached Third St., Aneas said, "Guess I be gwine to help at the diner." He started away.

But the Leg Bone, Willie knew, was now closed. He said, "Maybe I'll try to be over tonight, Aneas," and crossed the street, weaving through traffic toward the cemetery gates.

Inside the fresh decorative monolith on the west corner of Stock Exchange and Sharon, James was showing the gang (2017) the new grammar school. Here was the smell of fresh paint and plaster. This was the building since razed to make room for the CossycSystems medical and biotech complex that was helping (somewhat) to revitalize the FivePoints of 2017. The district would fare better when it was shown that experiments on nearby residents (families including kids) proved successful. On this very site HB had received his contest prize of biodata transformation vis-à-vis his now part-artificial mind, integrated with infrared and other data imaging via the contact lens in his right eye.

The first thing the supposed show-kids noticed—and exclaimed over—was the absence, in the cavernous entrance hall, of the spanning, colorful mural, made from minute tiles, of A'ndian camp life. (Composed in the 1980s by individuals in an east coast A'ndian artists collective—in honor of the ancient portage.)

HBBBAH interrupted James Horatio's speech. "Where's the A'ndians, Bro!" He rapped out. "Bro, Bro, the A'ndians, Bro, the A'ndians."

James was perplexed on two counts. First, he'd never heard a Negro talk with such confidence. What was a *broh*? Second, he was surprised they'd think the Wild West A'ndians would be in the stately school. He simply stared up at HBBBAH, mouth agape, light-brown eyes wide beneath his brown bang.

The kids walked over to the wall with its painted turn-of-the-20th-century industrial mural, closely examining it, then stepping back again. A local Akropolis artist was still putting the finish to it, down at the far end near the stairs. Their conversation echoed along with the intermittent sounds of other laborers throughout the building.

Fabian said, "I think I remember seeing this at the CityHistory page online. There's old-timey everything there—even the stagecoach we saw on Exchange." By this he meant the omnibus, his terminology coming from (to his mind) ancient westerns available for free download—if you didn't mind the ads. (The ads were so entertaining you didn't much until they got old—generally by day two.)

"But what are you talking about?" asked James. They seemed immersed in the mural showing Priams and Yeargod and

161

Sibberline rubber factories with vast sweeps of dramatic smoke punctuated by tall stacks; flowing rivers and byways with canals and people at industrial work: toolpaths and windowlight and horse-drawn everything. "Don't you like the mural?"

"Like it?!" exclaimed the blue Pomala. "It's great! Love it! Awesome! So this is what Akropolis used to be? And this is where the clinic is—." She spun around, was about to say *now*, but stopped and looked blankly, then with trepidation, at the others.

"Yeah, but don't be thinking it was really like that," said HBBBAH. "That's the romantic view of it. Really it's full of sht."

James, while not quite understanding, was aghast. He was speechless, looking from one minstrel to the other: A collection of very strange, very alien—foreign was not the right word—. Foreigners were a motley sort in R'opean-recognizable clothing, maybe old women dressed in black from Greice or another eastern R'opean country. Their skins were a normal variety of shades, as was their hair. Or, foreigners were elegant Anglishmen with delicate shining exquisite flair, like Mrs. Havard. But here was freakish—nightmarish even—coloration, getup, gadgetry. Bizarre by any decent conventional standard. —Which was greatly respected, prized.

The fresco artist, first working on one section at the other end by the great stone stairs, came over to them, footfalls echoing. He wore a paint-spattered smock, now slightly inclining his head—a polite nod. But he could not refrain his gaze from studying the invaders. Tattoos, piercings, stiff sculpted hair. On Jayrai his look lingered longest. She turned just a bit so he might better see her arm and hand. A slow smile developed through his handsome olive-hued Medioceanic features. "Are you from outer space?" He asked with pleasant humor. But curious.

"From the show-folk at the Opera House, good man," said James.

"It outdoes everything so far," remarked the artist, his gaze complimentary upon them.

"Yes, quite. They can't mean it—about the mural, I'm sure," agreed the boy, half embarrassed, half high-toned.

The second-generation Etalio, still considering them with his peculiar artist's eye, said, "No. You're right. It's romantic, but you must get up on the far of Harkins Hill to see that it is quite ... as I do show here. You need the distance. Then it is beautiful. True, it is not shattered, cubic, not much textured, tortured, etc.... But I must follow my commission, eh?" His smile shone very white, appealing, his dimpled look quite charismatic. "I'm curious about the colorful tiles and its depictive use, you spoke of." Still he looked them up and down, very gracious and pleasant in his scrutinizing expression.

Five Points Akropolis

They talked on some moments, the conversation fragmenting, swift; as each varied interlocutor addressed either 1900 or 2017, in near-miraculous interweaving and shooting conversational threads. At the end it all made sense, and was possessed of a curious unity (as so the artist mused upon it by his jug of wine that evening).

Afterword he left them to their tour, and James took them down hallways—opening doors with frosted glass—and upstairs and round about what had been crumbling, old, familiar; but was now absorbingly, even inspirationally quaint and fresh in the thick, damp, clean smell of new plaster. Workers here and there stopped to eye them, curiously, remark or banter.

Quadri, unable to call home, had pocketed his 7qz in favor of holding tight to either Jay's or Pomala's hands. (In turn each girl dropped it while gesticulating, or in conversation.) Once he picked up Tu's hand, but that boy gently dropped it. Quadri was of a size with James Horatio, who was in fact a couple years older and many shades lighter in complexion. Of them all Quadri had been most fearfully perplexed, first by the mural-change, and now by the workmen with their trowels and screeds, lime-plastering, and decorative molding, making everything like it was new.

And all the while James was sinking, sinking down beneath his normal ebullience—which had been *his* till—. These kids frequently ignored him in their conversation. They reminisced with occasional sidelong looks at him about this room or that; the great gymnasium, the hushed theater-assembly hall. Often he thought it was a play put on for his benefit, especially on hearing their exclamations over the loss of crumbling decrepitude, or, say, the tattered upholstery of the theater seats: their bright acknowledgment of fine equipage for the stage. ...And, most, he was cast down in the knowledge of what awaited him on his return up the hill to *Stonehewn.* The sight of Brant, lying there in bandages, a weeping hole in his once firm healthy cheek.

"What's the matter," asked Pomala once or twice with curiosity. Even, as he prepared to take his leave (at least in his abstracted thought), she offered again—this time with seemly sympathy—to know the cause of his unhappy state.

"I must go home now," he said at last when they showed every sign of staying on, and his spirits were at their ebb.

Holding hands with Quadri, Pomala followed him through the little theater out and down the great stone stair. The artist was gone, leaving but the mural and fresh paint and plaster smell throughout the overarching hall.

At last her strange thoughtfulness released James's childish hold upon his pride, and he allowed that things might not be quite right with him.

They stood at the side entrance now. One with easy access down stone steps to the boardwalk, and that part of Stock Exchange leading up West Hill. To Pomala it was simply Exchange St.. The afternoon traffic was now going mostly that way, as the new professional class were driving home in horse and brougham or buggy to their new brick-and-stone comfortable nests up the hill.

"Don't you see.... It's the, well, the riot. You were there, you saw?"

"A riot? No. A riot?" Her eyes were wondering, wide.

He noticed then that they were pinkish in contrast to her blue skin and hair. Her lashes were white. "Last night," he said, his gaze now cast down.

"Ah —hmm. No. We weren't—. We weren't here last—*then*!"

Quadri looked up at them both, frowning slightly, dark brown eyes wide. He'd been quite still till now. He said it softly. "Where were we, Pom? Where were we last night?"

She looked at him and shook her head. She squeezed his hand.

James scarcely notice. He said, "It's all my fault, don't you see."

"The riot?! You started a riot?"

"—No. No not that. It was my fault Brant got shot —in it."

"Shot?" She tried to think. What would someone get shot with here in —1900? "You mean shotguns? Pistols? Who is he? Who shot him? Cowboys? Gangstas?"

Miserably he said, "My brother. Police."

She looked at Quadri and did not understand. She did not think she should ask more questions... although her curiosity was greatly piqued.

Her look was sympathetic. "Can you get home?"

"Yes," he said. "It's just up there. Someone will see me walking and give me a ride." Her talk and kindness had comforted James. He looked back at her as he went down toward the boardwalk leading up the hill. He never saw anything like it! Blue pointy hair, blue face. He would tell Brant.

...They'd never make it to the Opera House again. And now he'd always be there to tell Brant everything.

"Have you got the calculations worked out yet?"

"About 500 times. So far."

Fabian and Tu discussed it where the FivePoints gang sat on the stone steps of Harkins Grammar School (which they had always called Harkins Elementary).

"But how do you know? I mean about place-time coordinates. Specifically?"

Five Points Akropolis

"We can ask again about the clocks, I think. Maybe find someone who'd know. Some authority. They'd also know our exact location mathematically. The exact latitude and longitude of, say, FivePoints intersection; better, the cemetery entrance on Exchange Street."

Fabian looked at him.

Tu looked back. Flatly he said, "It's all I got."

The other sighed. He looked over toward the high school. "Too bad school's not on here yet. The library's gone."

It hasn't *been*. Tu had never had to know any of this RL precisely when playing—or even designing—a game. Real-place, RealLife had not been important ... except here or there in abstract or theoretical terms. "Another problem: they have not even heard of Hades—Pluto, that is. But it doesn't matter." He was thinking aloud. "If they did I'd still have to rely anyhow on OrbitalSync... with all the planets and other solar articles, galactic influence.

Little more than two days ago, Dark Cloak had stood just a bit below upon the tool-cluttered boardwalk. Standing watch upon the girl upstairs above the clasp-locker hospital. Now he was back again, again not far away, dividing his watch between the 1900 gang (the corn-girl with them)—in front of *Paddy's Saloon and Pool Hall*— and the gang of 2017, just off his bare left shoulder.

The girls were first to notice him. Quadri had let go of Pomala's hand and was playing a game he had on his 7qz, bought and paid for by his big brother (who worked at McRonald's) in 2017. No streaming or real-time required. He frowned intently, playing between the two girls next their legs.

"Absolutely. Gorgeous. Drop. Me. Off. The. Wall."

"Oh yeah," agreed Pomala, smiling toward Dark Cloak. "Any. Time. Drop. Me. Off. That Wall."

He was tall, muscled, hardly clothed, the sides of his tush revealed through slits in the scanty loincloth. Taller even than Fabian, or Blake—HBBBAH as he was called.

"Why don't they arrest his nakedness, I wonder?" Jayrai said it with gaze sweeping off toward the intersection and back again. Down there stood a quaint-looking policeman, risking life and limb directing traffic. "People here are just so... —So —you know."

"With their panties in a knot, you mean."

"Yeah," put in Fabian. "Uptight. As Granma would say." He wasn't saying what he thought of Dark Cloak's near-naked body. "Cool tattoos, though. Wonder what he's doing here? A'ndians in Akropolis 1900?"

Dark Cloak, partway up the block, was aware of their regard. He merely stood his post, absorbing all. But sometimes, as well, he considered. The Grandmaster had told them of the *Ghosts Leaping*.

He had said the audience was expecting it, but that they were not expected to perform it themselves. Just stand the tableau, he said. That was all. Yet, carefully he had both described and explained the dance, its purpose. *It is foreseeing*, he had said. *For in a time to come will its fulfillment be.*

HBBBAH said, "Didn't someone over there say something about them being in a show?" He looked at the 1900 kids, now quiet, on the corner.

"The real-life hillbilly said they were in vaudeville."

"Not PC, that, Fabe," said HB.

"I think Granma said we came from North Regina—way back. If you can say 'nigger,' I can say 'hillbilly.' "

HBBBAH grinned. "Good point. ... But I be stoppin' that soon." The bald sides of his broom-cut shone with sweat. Some of it dripped down past his eyes. He wiped it away. "Damn it's hot! That smell! We's all gwine be daid, girls." He looked around to see if anyone else was smelling, feeling it.

Pomala held her nose.

"Quite pungent," murmured Tu.

"Maybe if we took off our clothes?" It was Jay's suggestion. "The brave yonder gets a pass. We might, too."

"I don't think so." Fabian shook his head, swiftly letting sweat fly. "There's no precedent?"

"Get. Him." Jayrai said it with a roll of her round brown eyes. "I'll talk like a parrot when I grow up, too."

All, including Fabian, started saying, "*Awk*" and "*Arrgh*," and me-heartying each other.

"*PresiDent presiDent*." Jay repeated several times. They began falling over and knocking into each other. Next they were tussling on the boardwalk. The kids across the filthy street saw it and, heads popping up, stared.

1900 sat up with more attention, and Parry said it was part of the act. But he wondered. Like Willie, he had his doubts. He wasn't so new to Akropolis and city life. He was born to it. And he had his imaginative suspicions. They probably *were*, actually, from outer space. The way things looked—the tiny picture boxes, exposed electric-wiring on an arm. That shiver-making hand. Their accents, manners suggested everything alien to him. But the show-folk explanation was too reassuring to give up. 1900 had stopped their listless lounging before the pool hall to watch as the officer-of-the-law left Five Points traffic to itself and sauntered over to FivePoints 2017, jauntily swinging his nightstick. Stepping through the horse-drawn traffic. He wore a ginger-colored mustache and sideburns, a blue uniform and dark helmet. 2017 associated the helmet with Anglish bobbies in old movies.

Five Points Akropolis

2017 stopped tussling and jumped up, preparing to make his acquaintance. But he only stopped to inquire about the entertainments and go on toward the "salvage," as the officer called him. "And will the entertainments go on?" He smiled with good nature, going past.

"Oh yeah!" said Jayrai snappily. "The show always goes on!"

They watched him saunter toward the lone A'ndian brave. He stopped and spoke to Dark Cloak. They could not hear what was said for the clopping and jingling of horses, the rumbling of great, spoked wheels passing up hill and down. He stood the boardwalk thumping his palm with his baton. Abstractly thumping, thought Fabian. With menace, thought Tu. The A'ndian stood stolid in full panoply of weapons never moving, steady, still. The officer turned and came back down to them along the sidewalk.

"Do you speak that tongue? We tried to get the Grandmaster to speak with him but he's nowhere to be found—just yet I 'spect; since the riot and all. It about overtook the Opera House... as you're no doubt aware."

Now he did stop and look carefully at them. Then at Jayrai's arm and hand. She held it out, not shy, and waited for his reaction.

HBBBAH said, "We think that act got canceled."

"Before our time," said the ever quiet Tu.

Fabian glanced at Tu with sleek appreciation.

For the first time Tu registered with the officer—as the Oriental. Tu was not at all flamboyant in his dress. In fact, he wore long-sleeved shirt, arms rolled up, sweat soaked; and jeans. Canvas pants as the officer might say.

"That's quite the arm," said the officer. Care to shake?" He held out his hand. The nightstick was on his belt again. They shook hands, Jay careful to give him just enough pressure to signify superior strength.

"Impressive," said the policeman.

"What's with the riot?" asked Pomala.

He looked back a question into her pink eyes. He thought, *They're right. They do talk funny.* Then he was skeptical and just a bit wary. "You don't know?"

"So why'd you need us to talk to him?"

"It's not the riot but the speechless girl. Wanted for questioning, you might say." He did not go into it: how there was cause on account of Dark Cloak's evident surveillance here on Sharon Road—beneath the very gaze of her abode.

"The speechless—? Pomala looked across the street and noticed her with attention for the first time since remarking her. "The one with autism?"

"What? Don't tell me *she's* in the entainments?" He pulled on one of his ginger mustaches, thoughtfully. *What is autism?* Some new hypnosis? Another name for mesmerism? —*But.* Officer Bart decided to let that past.

"I guess you *did* just get off the boat," he said, thinking, *And your accent is very strange too.* "She was badly used—by the Negro. They say." He recollected not to be presuming on Argus before the trial.

"You mean rape? —So why don't they do tests. You know—DNA?" asked Jayrai.

"She needs counseling bad." Pomala was urging it.

The officer stopped at the word *rape*, amazed that it should have come from a girl—in company.... But they were show-folk after all, and very freakish. Again he eyed them.... *These are costumes meant to draw them. —How about that? The Negro wears an earring.* The officer also let mention of testing pass. It had no meaning in this situation. He pulled on his mustache, musingly. "Maybe you know where the Grandmaster is?" He looked at each in turn. "It's reckoned between one-and-another at the station house—they may have the wrong man." He glanced at the young brave standing uphill beneath the tall windows of the new building. "Not thinking it's the brave.... They just want to talk to him, so don't worry about his standing with the show."

"So," said Jayrai, ever more prone to mischievous display, or talk, than the others, "What if we told you he's hiding in a tiny box in one of these pockets?" She thrust her leg out, just a bit, full of lumpy pockets on her purple cargo pants.

This notion, of the Fantastical Fatman—along with his fantastical tricks—being held in a tiny box on her person was laughable. It would be like seeing the Milky Way swarming on the head of a dressmaker's pin. A thrill went along Bart's spine remembering that juggling outside the Opera House in the afternoon before the riot. But he gave no sign of it. Or of his laughter over that tiny box and purported contents, where some hereabouts might have shouted. Instead he smiled with good humor. "I'd say come along with me girlie—to the station house. We'll see if we can coax him out with a bit of cheese."

Jayrai's features glimmered, appreciatively.

"We might use that in the show," said Blake. "—But why's it always got to be the black man get his ass in jail? Why him? Have they got real evidence?" He glared at Jay, but still unsure if she had forgotten there was no DNA yet; or was just being the ultimate smart ass she was. Had it been Pomala he would have thought she'd forgotten. As it was Jayrai—he was not so sure.

The officer said, "We don't go noising the evidence. —You surely are bold. It might not be wise just now."

Now HBBBAH was thinking. He turned away, gazing toward Dark Cloak—distantly, not thinking of the scout.

"The Grandmaster, now," the officer persisted.

"No, actually," said Fabian, not good at dissembling nor distracting. " —We haven't seen him yet—today. We got off the train, not the boat, and started out in costume to get the trade in— as you might say? —and don't know yet. If—when we see him we'll let him know you're—they're—asking."

"We'll tell him why," said Pomala, smoothing everything over as best she could. "The wrong man—that's not good."

"Possibly the wrong man," the officer corrected. He glanced at Blake who was still gazing off, a frown between his dark brows ... beneath that radical broom-cut. That was definitely for show. No Negro would thus reveal the make of that hair. What is this evolution and all that talk, the policeman wondered. He started back toward the intersection. The heavy traffic hour was upon them.

HBBBAH shouted after him. "What's his name?!"

But the officer either did not hear, or chose to ignore him.

But Blake would not let it go. He ran thumping over the boardwalk to overtake the officer. Something, some intuition, perhaps, checked him. He did not reach out for the cop. He ran up alongside him, as his friends watched. The policeman stopped. Blake had lowered his eyes. He seemed to stare at something on the man's boot. Then he went past the officer and came back up toward them. Only Pomala and Fabian recognized his agitation.

"What's it, HB?" she said.

He sat down on the great stone steps. Staring. Staring at the hewn stone beneath his sneakers.

After a bit he said, "I've got the bullshtin'-est crazy idea."

They all stood there on the bottom steps, waiting.

"I think it's my—my something. Ancestor— granddad — something...." He looked at Fabian. "He said his name is *Griffin.* Argus Griffin."

They looked down as one. Each seemed to stare where Blake was staring.

That's when Pomala spied the horse-muck caking Quadri's sneakers.

Tu also saw and smelled it. *We can't take that back to the 21st-century with us.*

James was stopped on his way up the hill by Detective Phillips in a small, old, square brougham; driven by Fletcher and pulled by a couple of nags. It took two for getting up the hill because the nags, too, were old. The department had bought up a lot of these carriages, cheap, and had not bothered to refurbish them. Too much expense on the taxpayer's nickel—every one of which was a local merchant or landlord, homeowner.

"I'm on my way to *Stonehewn* to see how young Brant fares, and to speak with your father. Can I give you a ride, James Horatio?" Phillips said it kindly with just a touch of unconscious deference.

"Oh yes, thanks, Lt. Phillips," he said, climbing into the box with him. There was a driver upfront, Officer Fletcher. This was official, James could see, even in his depressed distracted state.

It did not bother Phillips in the least that he was not a lieutenant but a sergeant in the police force. This is the salutary way in which he thought of James's mistaken appellation. "Sergeant. I'm very sorry about what happened to your brother the other night, young man.... It was one of those things that ought not to happen." He stopped, wary of saying either too much or too little. He considered. Should he say more? The boy was very subdued.

At the gatehouse, beneath the arched entranceway between stables and garages, James got out and, seeing Mrs. Havard beneath its cooling shade, cast his look down, very woebegone under his bangs.

"Oh come, James," she said. "Stop blaming yourself. It shan't do either one of you any good. Your brother has every intention of living." And she smiled warmly. Even her lips smiled. She was so beautiful, hair piled just so, small shirtwaist, lace-edged collar, long gathered skirt, a lady. Somewhat tentative, James smiled back.

"But will you come up with me now?"

"Oh no. I'll wait here like everybody else." She smiled at the two men with her eyes.

He noticed Dreiser the newsman, whose beat included Five Points, standing off a bit to one side. Briefly he wondered, but, obedient to her injunction to go see his brother, went off immediately through the dim archway and along the flowering shrub-scattered drive to the great stone mansion beyond.

Sergeant Phillips had climbed out of the brougham and now spoke to Dreiser. Mrs. Havard stood looking briefly after the boy dwindling through the greenery. Then she joined the two men. The white horses stood still in their traces. Officer Fletcher secured the reins, and climbed down, went near the brick-paved street under the shade of a great acorn tree for a smoke. The tiny oak-corns, he noticed, were still up there, far, among the big dark oak leaves, ripening. Not a breath moved leaf or nuts upon their twigs. Across the street, among some trees, another new mansion was building. *For one of his cronies, or maybe a competitor*, Fletcher thought.

It seemed to Phillips that Dreiser and Mrs. Havard had been standing, talking together, a little before his arrival; as they waited to be summoned. Mrs. Havard's questions to both men were not what he would have expected—had Detective Phillips even been thinking in terms of a straight interview. But he did not know Mrs. Havard, and therefore did not know she was a journalist.

Dreiser, of course, knew what she was after and was more than willing to provide answers. Her beat, while for a time overlapping his with regard to gathering the news, was in no way competitive. Who in Londinium would be reading the *Akropolis Lamppost*, after all? On the other hand, once her series on the industry of Americle was complete, there might be interest over there for a refresher, an item now and then on industry in the heartland of the expanding nation. A nation soon, he well expected, to eclipse the Empire—however more or less the sun might or might not set upon it. Yet, as the dialogue between them progressed, Dreiser was fascinated by how her conversation seemed ... like conversation. She was evidently not one to pump. Or, if she was, he could not see the handle... at least not until Phillips should go away. In the meantime, it was pleasant enough and there were cigarettes. Daintily, Mrs. Havard accepted one from Dreiser's rather grubby case of black, stiff leather. She was not wearing gloves as other ladies might. Phillips, however, shook his head.

"Never use?" said Dreiser. He had forgotten that.

"Never."

The newsman asked him several questions about the case, few if any direct answers forthcoming.

"We don't know yet, do you?" Phillips had responded so, several times. The detective stepped over to smooth from shoulder to forearm of each horse.

How much he did or did not know was not easy for Dreiser to gauge, but the newspaper man decided to be forthcoming with his own answers—in hopes of getting anything at all from him. At last Phillips answered one. "What brings you up the hill?" said Dreiser. "I know it's not likely only to find out about the son—although that's part of why I'm here myself."

"Of course we want to know how young Priam gets on," answered the detective. He did not mention that he was to tender apologies as well.

"Your department being responsible and all," said Dreiser, his dark eyes in his white face gleaming. His black bowler, tilted back, revealed the equally white part of his black thinning hair, making for a flashing contrast.

171

"... It was *possibly* one of our bullets. Maybe you'd know more about that than we do? Have you heard of arms brought in, probably the single weapon—not specially obtained, most likely: the thing a man keeps in his factory-owned rooms down there near the canal where the squalor almost requires it?"

Mrs. Havard was listening, quietly standing, smoking. She did expect word momently from the house and thought it well to ask one thing more, by way of conversation. She stepped out of the shadow just a bit to see the servant, tiny, returning through distant rosebushes still shimmering among the heat waves.

"I wonder," she said, "how much this whole distressing case is affecting all the good things the city is trying to accomplish. I've heard so much about your plans to build the aqueduct, make safe electric transport, lay more and safer lines for gas, construct great bridges over some of the ravines that snake through the hills upon which Akropolis spreads."

It was pleasant, Phillips thought, to have Mr. Priam's high-toned well-spoken visitor interested in their burgeoning enterprise here in rubber land. Things in Angleland must be more flourishing and grand, certainly. So it was kind of her to ask. He smiled and was almost answering when Dreiser cut in.

"I wondered that myself and even asked the mayor. He's not the best-trimmed wick for giving light, but he says in no way will progress be stopped by a handful (as he put it) of rioters. Especially, he was careful to say, Luddites who might want to take the chaos elsewhere now the city center's burnt to stumps. By that he means the factories, of course. Those dammed unionizers." He winked.

Phillips looked away, disgusted.

The man came back to the carriage house to say Mr. Priam would be glad to see both Lt. Phillips and Mrs. Havard. "What about me?" said Dreiser, already in possession of the answer. "Apparently it counts for nothing that I walked up this hill on purpose to see the great man and inquire after his son."

"Guess so," said the carriage-house man, grinning.

Mrs. Havard's smile was nowhere to be seen but it was there nonetheless. She could not help comparing this attendant (as they were sometimes called here) to his counterpart in Angleland. There he would have declined his head and answered smoothly, deprecatingly: *Mr. Priam regrets that he cannot see you just now.*

Dreiser called to her as she was departing with Phillips. "Maybe we'll talk later, Mrs. Havard! Confidentially of course."

Mrs. Havard did not turn to respond as they moved along the curving drive toward the pathway that would lead through flowering rosebushes toward the great double oaken doors. (They would be using a smaller oaken door further along.)

From above, as they walked, came drifting out the coarse laughter of Miss Daphnes Priam.

"Damn," said Dreiser out loud below.

—But maybe Phillips would not be long and he could get a ride back down to Five Points. Suddenly he remembered another lead to follow on. He left the arched entranceway and hurried down the street.

Mrs. Havard, meanwhile, thought better of snubbing the coarse familiarity of Miss Priam. Threading along between low rosebushes, she turned, and lightly waved to her.

Tiny in the mullioned windows open to the lawn, that woman laughed once more, and returned her wave.

Dreiser had gone on, at a jog, angling diagonally down the hill toward Sharon Road, past the First Settler Family's Georgian Mansion on the corner of Sharon Road and Angle Street. And thence down diagonally once again toward the top of the Five Points neighborhood. Up there were the woods in which the girl had been raped, and now he hurried down into the squalid housescape where the Partums lived. By this time it was late afternoon. He scrutinized the house to see if he had it right, and went in. Dreiser knocked upon one of the doors leading from the dirty tiny foyer, with dust balls in its corners. Then he opened the door, knob rattling, and went up the stairs to the landing, for there were other rooms, other doors—this house having been partitioned from its original single-family form. He knocked again. It was long before an answer came. The groggy voice of Partum.

"Dreiser—with more questions for you."

"Go away," the voice croaked.

"C'mon. It'll only take a minute."

No answer came.

Dreiser knocked again, once. And was about to keep it up until it occurred to him that this was not the way. He had been meaning to follow up on this hunch ever since his talk with Mabel Griffin and her son in the Leg Bone the other night. But he had gotten sidetracked. ...Now he considered that Partum was not his man. Not his *source*, and he would have to seek it elsewhere.

He stood on the lackluster garbage-strewn street, full of filth and dust and heat, gutters running with sewage; dogs lying there listless, or raising up their snouts in bleak inquisition. He stared at nothing. Who should it be. Mrs. Partum. Or her daughter? The other kids—were there other kids?—might be too young... but he'd

173

give them a try if so, if he had to. Sometimes kids are the best source. They may yield a telling detail unawares.

Innocence. It was useful for something in the trade. Spill all kinds of family secrets showing off—still inadvertent after all. Just showing off without real thought of either exposé or harm. ...But not for now. He had to gather carefully, and a piece at a time. A bit here, a bit there, and after a while it all fits together. *Wall-lah!* Houdonio springs himself. Can't keep the truth—the story—locked up. It always outs.

After conveying the message of his superiors and gently pursuing the questioning of James in his father's presence, Lt. Phillips had gone. Then after a cheering visit upstairs to Brant's bedside (cheering for Brant), Mrs. Havard and Mr. Priam were seated on opposite settees, elegant but sturdy cane with upholstered cushions, in the family parlor. There were many more grander halls, parlors, chambers in this mansion house. Quietly wiping his wet face with his fingers, James Horatio stood nearby beneath the head of a white stag, as Mrs. Havard might call it. The room was white with vaulted half-timbered ceiling—fine dark walnut—from which was suspended a candelabra of complexly twiggy twining gilt. Colorful oil paintings of "the hunt" were to either side of the marbled hearth and chimney stone.

"James has been telling me about the grandmaster's newest act. He seems to think they are really from outer space. —Don't you James?" Mr. Priam smiled at them both, pleasantly with a twinkle in his brown eyes beneath his balding pate.

"Not me, father." James said this in rather a hurry it seemed to Mrs. Havard.

"Parry, *Parry Wilusa* thought." James felt a slight compunction. He said, "There really wasn't time for him to explain it so I may have misunderstood. The idea is that they've come from this planet outside our solar system, or on the very edge of it, Mrs. Havard. Did they know anything about that in Londinium besides—." He was about to say, What's in the *Magpie*. "I mean, maybe Mr. G. H. Wills has put it into the Grandmaster's head... or something."

More like the reverse, thought Mrs. Havard, having witnessed the Grandmaster giving his introductions to each act. His verbal overtures were a variety of the most elegant—yet conversely hyperbolic—extrapolations on the swiftly changing physical knowledge—that she had ever heard. And all spun out, like fine flying confection, in superb visionary splendor. She found his introductions almost always more riveting and charged than the acts they proposed to introduce. She had been greatly disappointed he had not been on hand at the recent lawn fête. She would have given a year off her career—off her life!—to meet and talk with him. Two years. Five... no make that three. But still, there was time for that, according to the bill.

James gave a brief description of the troupe with more detailing of their gadgetry than of their inflections, ethnicity, or costume. "Really quite various," he said, pleased with this speech.

Mrs. Havard was thoughtful. "Yes, it sounds quite alien...."

"Outlandish, certainly," declared Mr. Priam.

He then allowed his guest to continue.

"From what little I know of the matter," she said, "I can't think them meant to be from outer space. Would they need special suits in that case? With pumps and lines and strange gases for breathing in our atmosphere?"

"But Parry says it's what they said."

She nodded. "Perhaps they don't want to wear such cumbersome costuming in this weather. But it would take something like that to enhance verisimilitude, I should think."

"Yes," said James. He intended to look up that word just as soon as she left.... But really, he did not want her to leave. Most likely his father would send him away soon, anyway. The others were off playing in the game room in the cool downstairs, or swimming in the pool. All but poor Brant. After looking up that word, Brant's room was where James would have to go. —Or maybe they could look it up there together?

S. Dorman

The Leg Bone Diner

The FivePoints gang of 2017 now sat in the *Leg Bone Diner*, very hushed, whispering; not quite comfortable. They huddled close about the table, looking furtively for a sign of anyone else. The cemetery boy's friend was making noises in the kitchen back of the table cluttered room. How they came to be here will be seen by going back in time, just a bit....

There.

They had passed through traffic to the other side of Sharon Road opposite Dark Cloak—where he stood beneath the grammar cum grade cum elementary school, stoically watching halfway up the block. Some members of the 1900 gang had watched them go but it was too hot to consider following them. 2017's plan (hatched outside the school) had been to bypass the gathering on the corner and slip up, around, and then down. Through the 1900 A.D. cinder-paved alleyways with which they were (not now as) familiar, getting turned around—oh-ing and ah-ing over the changes, here a new street, there one cut off—toward Exchange Street, to the cemetery. Finally crossing that street at Gustav's musical instruments store where the library was supposed to be. This for purposes of talking together in the less crowded and virtually unnoticed arena of the dead.

Now they are seated in the grass behind the cemetery wall in 1900 A.D. after leaving the new grammar school where they had learned of Argus Griffin. All except Tu who stands before them working calculations, gravestones at his back. And they are going to have to come here again later tonight. They'll have to be in the exact place they were when it happened.... Tu calculates—*if* the others will follow through with him as agreed. About that he is in some doubt. *Time would tell.* He might smile but did not.

Five Points Akropolis

"So. Yeah," said Blake, a.k.a. HB. "That's my great grand somebody, that rapist. *Accused* rapist. I won't believe it till I find out for sure. Plus, I mean. I wish I could care about him. I don't know him. —But how am I gon get born? What if they kill him?"

Fabian laughed. He couldn't help it. "What do you mean, *how*? You're born, dude. You're here. —I mean you were in 2017...." He stopped, confused.

"He's right, HB," said Jayrai. She looked up into the elm limbs high above and arching, gracefully lowering their tips in elm leaves—late summer green, tired-looking green, she'd call it. "You were born. Your father's father and his father—if it goes back that far—was born, too. That means it doesn't matter if this Arcturus— was it? —gets um *whatever*."

HB was silent. Glum.

"She's right I think, Blake," said Tu. He had put the pod away to conserve energy. Battery symbol barely showing: No telling when it would give out, and they were going to be needing it. The afternoon traffic, horse-and-buggy traffic, passing this way and that without seeming order, shouts from the drivers—it all made his head spin. He sat down with them against the cooling wall. "What we don't want to do is go messing about with things. Just leave them as they are. There's no safe way of knowing without *a lot* of calculation and occult knowledge we just don't have—of how things we try might work. Good or bad—there's bound to be *something*.

"Occult knowledge?" asked Quadri. He was thinking of the game he and his big brother had been involved in last night. He shivered. Last night. Last night his bedroom had been up the hill among those houses. In a big brick apartment building not so old. Now there was a clump of treetops where that window should have been; up behind the library which was now an old Gothic music store. "Occult's what got people's heads cut off and burnt in StanaTerk in the Black Ages. IIRC." He turned a small brown face, scared, perplexed and frowning, up at them—one by one.

Tu said, "That's not what I mean, Quad. What I mean is *too much knowledge*—so much we can't know it all. Nothing can. No micromachine, calculations or software or anything."

The arms of their autumn jackets were tied in knots around their waists. They sat strung out in the shade of the wall, cooling mossy stones at their backs, the sun above and westering back toward Sharon in the countryside: If asked they would have said Sharon was not rural but suburban, crammed with megastores and malls and fancy restaurants, hotels and solar stations, the latter put in throughout the 1990s during the energy changeover to short-circuit the petroleum wars. Before they were born. Some of their relations and siblings took the ElectricBus to work there, tending bar, taking orders, selling clothes, theater tickets, cleaning rooms, nursing home orderlies, working the phone at the call center. Which was why their young siblings had the tech they did. That, and credit because of those jobs.

Suddenly HB sat up. There was that kid. The one who had exchanged a fierce look with Fabian when everybody was on the corner—before the gradeschool tour. He did not then think to wonder about Willie's clothes, how they got so dirty—seeing only that he was walking down through the golden dappled light through gravestones toward the gate, on the pathway leading to the drive. The Afrikan-Americle news-kid's friend.

Blake stood. He almost called out, almost waved him over, but thought better of involving the others. He considered that he might be more successful getting info if he were alone. The guy was awful defensive.

"Wait here," he growled; and went ahead.

They stayed. No use getting up in this heat, and it wasn't bad here. Jay and Quadri lay back against the stones. These mossy stones felt so good and cool on their heads and backs. Kinda soft, too. Pomala sat, her legs in cargo pants crossed before her. The ground was kind and cooling too. She watched Blake approach the guy.

"I hope he doesn't mess with things," murmured Tu.

"I think he got the message." Fabian was trying to give his friend some credit. "He's got maybe more to lose than we do anyway, so yeah—he'll be cool."

They watched Blake Griffin stand off with Willie on the drive leading to the gate facing on what they knew as Exchange St.. At first the body language of the 1900 kid told them he was wary. His stance—it was a stance. He wore knee pants, long stockings sagging near his hightop boots, suspenders apparently—for real—holding up his pants. The pants seemed loose around the top where his shirt was tucked in—all but the tail—they saw as he turned back to face HB: Either HB had gone behind him, apparently to make some point, or Willie had just tried to go on. But now the two stood still a moment. Then, 1900 turned and gestured toward Exchange St.. Then he went on that way himself, glancing at them sitting there— once—in passing distantly out the gate. But plainly they had seen him scowling.

She couldn't wait to know. "What happened? What'd you say?" cried Jay.

Pomala was more for examining HB to see how he was doing. A light of intention shone in his eye. He came up to them and knelt in the grass. His big broom-cut was full of sweat, especially at its roots, and his bald dark head glistened. So did his black textilite jumpsuit.

"There's this diner on Third St.. That's where he's from. He works there or something. And the news kid is a Griffin. I didn't think I'd get anything out of him at first. No, Tu, I didn't say anything about it. Except, like, *About that Afrikan-Americle man they say started the riot.* I'm proud 'myself—did not say the word rape. Somehow I figured it would annoy him. Anyway, I'm black, right?"

Pomala giggled. "*Yay*-ah."

"And that's why he told me. I'm sure of it. He said they're closed so it won't do me any good. Then—he glared and said, *Be careful with my friends!* How bout that? I'm surprised. If I hadn't been Afrikan-Americle—no way. That's it I'm sure.... Damn, I think he works here— *digging graves. With a shovel.*"

"Really?" This was fascinating to Jay. The 1900 guy's terse, somewhat severe manner was not without appeal.

"C'mon, girls," said Blake. "It's time to eat!"

So now they sat around the biggest table in the old-timey room, the room long and narrow, no windows on the walls shared with other shops; a bit dim but for evening light diffusing through windows with small divided-light panes. The ceiling above was of patterned stamped tin, painted white, and reflecting some brightness back down on the room. The guy who might be related to Blake was in back fixing supper for them—as he had called it. And was collard greens and chitlins good enough? Maybe some grits and gravy, biscuits?

"Good, all good," had said Jayrai, not quite certain what she was agreeing to but ready for anything. Really ready! She had not eaten since lunchtime. In the cafeteria. November 3rd. 2017.

The building seemed awfully quiet. They did not know that the guy's family was upstairs praying—all but Argus Griffin held in jail in Groverland. The church over on 11⅓ Street was full of people praying. Sometimes Li'l Mabel smiled, from the couch where she was holding the baby little Choco, for distantly she heard them shouting, praying, speaking in tongues, and singing deeply richly strongly to the Lord. The church-folk prayed for Argus and his family and for the little girl at the clasp-locker hospital, and for the pain and suffering and endurance of the whole world.

It was awful hot in the parlor upstairs where the family knelt or sat together, all the children, Mabel's sisters, cousins, and the babies. Sometimes they listened, careful, to the sounds of Aneas in the kitchen drifting up the back stairs. He had come back up to tell them, after answering at the Leg Bone Diner door, that the stranger-folk had been knocking. And he was going to feed them. So that was why they kept quiet upstairs in their prayers. And, he had said, that maybe they were some kind of messengers come at the Lord's behest. "Don't be afraid of them," he said. "Just pray, and pray I be not afraid of their faces." And that's in part what they—the children and Mabel—were praying for. That and the sweet, *sure* release of Argus with no smirch upon his name.

Meanwhile, downstairs, FivePoints 2017 were talking it over. Trying to figure it all out. Most of all they wanted back into 2017— with or without memory of this strange event. But Fabian knew—or thought he did—that if they might only get back and *possibly* remember, it would make them friends for-*evah*, friends for life. His family drama and its hurts had taught him this. For his hunch was, there were kinds of uncertainty and adversity that strengthened ties and did not break or sicken.

"Why can't we see them, though?" Jayrai was asking. "How do we know they're there?"

Tu was solemn. "We don't. Either they're too small or we can't penetrate our own brane."

"Our brain?" asked Quadri, getting scared. "What's penetrate? —Our brains?" His hand moved over the tabletop toward Pomala's and she clasped it.

"Not those brains," said Tu. "Branes are short for membranes.... In this theory," he was careful to add. They were talking about particles of particles; and dark matter; missing energy, and the possibility—or not—of sending off to other dimensions from what they knew of life in FivePoints; in Global 2017.

"The idea is—a particle leaves November 2017 and ends up in some other dimension where things are almost the same ... but not quite. Or maybe it's the same dimension, different time. That means these things—we don't exactly know what they *are*—can go back and forth in time. Like sending a message. Like in the true science of *The Hadesthon*."

"But we're too big for that," suggested Fabian, feeling himself out of his depth. The game he maybe understood, but this? A real understanding of such things was too high for him, he thought. *Or too far out—or maybe in the next dimension.* He grinned reflexively. "Unless... —*which* would we be then? Or come here *as*—particles or waves?" He shrugged shaking his long blond hair, then dusting the buzz cut down the middle with his hand. —*What is a fact?*

Quadri shivered. He remembered his brother saying they were nothing but some particles with a lot of space between. That we were like the stars with a lot of background radiation holding us altogether. It made Quadri wish his brother would go back to ghost stories, zombie stories.

Five Points Akropolis

Tu answered Fabian. "It's not as far-fetched as it seems. It's true The Collider has the acceleration to get something out of here and into there—but whether or not it's us—. They'd say no. But then again—they don't know. Maybe one of their collisions sent us here. Or sent lots of others, just like us—um—otherwheres."

"Please don't tell me that we're stuff that's even smaller," whispered HB with some little vehemence. "Next you'll be saying we are strings and then we're something smaller—I don't know what—boogers or something. I know everything is made out of smaller everything world-without-end! What's that got to do with *this*?"

Everyone was silent. What to say to him without making hard feelings? Fabian wondered. Tu thought him losing perspective. Pomala felt for him. Jayrai looked away to hide the rolling eyes. And Quadri was confused.

Then, greatly subdued, Tu reminded him of their mission. "The game can help us. *Calculus* might help us with this... and not messing much with," here Tu nodded in the direction of the kitchen, "—him. That's what we've got to do. Calculus, by helping us understand motion—changing position over time—might help me figure out the changes and get us in the right place at the right time to get back. Yes, there are a lot of *ifs* but ... well, we've got nothing else to try ... so why not this?"

Then he was quiet. In awe once more that right now, perhaps, Steinein was in R'opea working past Newman's calculus—a mathematical theory of the photoelectric effect! Tu could not let go his own conundrum, the dichotomy of his approach: Quanta or strings? It had to be one or the other, but which. Which laws and if he knew— ...well then he'd wonder why it was *these* laws and not some others. And on and on. It would go on. He almost smiled: Awesome. And now he was off again, and not in some old-fashioned restaurant in 1900 A.D.

There was awe of some variety among them at this speech, and Blake again began to consider.

But Aneas came into the room bearing white plates across his dark arms and in his hands, laden with food. He had on a white but stained apron. Jayrai admired his deftness in carrying everything for the feast, just so; and the way he slid plates-full onto the table before each of them. They sat back, making way for this crockery filled with dark grilled greens, the crisp intestines of pigs (which they did not recognize as such), and biscuits with gravy. He made small happy sounds as he did this, having fallen into the way of his mother, who always did so—at least until this happened to Argus. Then he went back with a promise of grits to come.

Meanwhile Blake had been scanning him diligently, and when Aneas came back, with white bowls full of grits (yellow with

butter), he started all over again. Using software implanted in the
back of his brain combined with its interface in his right contact
lens, HB was scanning the infrared DNA data off Aneas as he set
down the bowls. Aneas noticed his peculiar regard. It seemed to
him that the boy was looking not at him but through him, and yet —
he felt himself the object of intense scrutiny.

Be sure, he thought, *these are angels. They be messengers
from God. But what is their message?*

He stood back, watching them fill up, shoveling in the food
with the most glorious satisfying light in their eyes.

Oh mother and father, he thought. Oh-mammy-and-pappy,
these are eating angels, and we have done fed'em! His gaze fell
particularly on Pomala with her hair flowing up like a blue flame.
How it stood up so curling and stiff he could not tell. Her face and
neck and shoulders were blue, and her eyes were pink with white
lashes. In a blue upward flowing over detailed skin were designs of
the most splendid and original display.

HB, while also swiftly plying his laden fork from plate to
mouth, took note on his regard of the girl. He'd not yet integrated
the results of his scanning, but this was new and distracting. All at
once he put down his fork, an uneasy feeling disrupting HB's
multitasking. The thought coming to him was ridiculous and squee-
making, and he shook his head violently, glaring at Aneas.

Aneas, of course, noticed. He noticed that his worship was
kindling holy anger and he became afraid. He dropped gaze, and
backed away toward the kitchen, saying, "If you be's wanting
anymore, holler." Then he disappeared. It was silent back there,
Fabian noticed, and Tu did, and of course Blake Griffin. Then, along
with the guy's voice singing *Onward Christian Soldiers*, the sounds of
kitchen clatter, pots and pans rattling and clanging, shone out from
the doorway like a Sousa march. Like something they'd heard before
or seen clips of on *Yoube*.

> *At the sign of triumph Satan's host doth flee;*
> *on then, Christian soldiers, on to victory!*
> *Hell's foundations quiver at the shout of praise;*
> *brothers, lift your voices, loud your anthems raise.*
>
> *Like a mighty army moves the church of God;*
> *brothers, we are treading where the saints have trod.*
> *We are not divided, all one body we,*
> *one in hope and doctrine, one in charity!*

They recognized the rousing hymn. More than once or twice
it had issued from Zettler's Gospel Mission, a.k.a. revival house,

Five Points Akropolis

2017—where Paddy's 1900 now stood—along with the smell of soup. When they were sated they sat back, licking their lips and wiping their greasy mouths on shirt shoulders or tank tops, sighing.

"What was that stuff?" asked Jayrai, patting her belly. "Hoo—that was good!"

"Have you found out anything, HB?" asked Fabian. He was starting to get Tu's vibe mingling with HB's, and the combination caused him no little concern.

"In a minute." Blake lounged back, his eyes closed. His unconscious mind was doing all the work and he was literally resting. Full of good food, almost, not quite dozing, he murmured, "The guy is hard to believe."

They were quiet, sitting back, feeling so good, full of comfort, thinking no ill, not hurrying. Just resting, enjoying the moment.

HB said, "...And still ... I do. On the one hand...." He said it drowsily.

"So I think he's gorgeous?" said Jay. "And that 'fro of his is like wild. He's like from another world. A better one." She meant better than FivePoints, better than Americle, or the world—1900 or 2017.

"He is really really sweet," smiled Pomala, slouching back, her eyes closed, hands clasped on her tummy.

"Yeah, well, don't be thinkin'bout it, K? This is serious." Then HB frowned. "—Not. Sweet. *Slavish*."

She didn't bother answering, just laying back, shaking her head a bit, thinking, *Sweet*.

"We know what's not sweet." Jayrai growled, then she grinned at him.

HB grinned too.

"But listen to that song. It's like he means it," said HB seriously.

"Yeah, like he's got a sword. Like he's in *The Hadesthon*, battling away," said Fabian.

So look, Tu wanted to say. But he sat there, too full of something. Goodness. He did not try to analyze it. Quadri of course was most receptive to the good vibe. He was forward in his ladderback chair, legs dangling, plate pushed away; his small dark head on the table, an arm flung up in front of it, his chin on his palm. Almost as though curled in sleep, but listening to it all.

> *What the Saints established that I hold for true;*
> *What the Saints believe, that I believe too.*
> *Long as earth endureth, men the faith will hold;*
> *Kingdoms, nations, empires, in destruction rolled.*

S. Dorman

Onward, Christian soldiers, marching as to war,
With the cross of Jesus going on before.

At last HB sat forward, and clasped his hands on the table, seriously looking at the report, considering. He had code-blinked the report so that it appeared as on the wall opposite, projected by his right contact lens. No one else could see it. He said, "We are closely related... but this is not the one. I think his father is closer and must have another son—or is gonna have another—because the name is gonna pass, and not be like where the mom keeps her own name. I could be wrong. I just don't pay much attention to that stuff. My mom is the Griffin, however, but where she connects I don't know. She daid you recollect." He grinned evilly.

They knew he was hiding pain, and what the pain was, so they looked away; or faintly smiled in reflex of the grin, and then looked away.

"Tell you what." He stopped, still with his hands clasped before him: a serious expression somberly featured in his look and on his brow.

The sounds from the kitchen had stopped, including the clatter and song. In the silence they heard the murmuring of prayer upstairs. For the first time. They knew instantly what it was, having, each, come in contact with it at the SoupMission as they called it. Don't think they never resorted to the Mission's comforts from time to time, whether singly or with family members. But not often, if they could help it, not often.

Thinking of that, Jayrai started feeling her pockets dubiously, hoping there was enough cash for the meal.

The Griffins, and their female friends and children, up those back stairs were even now praying, both for their guests below and for Argus and the Griffin children—as they knew to be scriptural—unto the fourth generation. And the church people, 8 ⅓ streets cat-a-corner up the hill and a bit south toward the rubber factory, were praying along similar lines. But not of course for the divine messengers (as Aneas counted them) sitting in the Leg Bone. Angels, it would be reasoned, don't need prayers. The family had no knowledge of these beings' real mission.

"Tell you what," said Blake again after a bit. He eyed each one in turn, even Quadri, who looked at HB sidelong, head still on the table. (And HB never paid that much attention to Quadri.)

"I know yo'all worried. So stop it. I'm not gonna do nothin'. I'm stopping right here. You've made your case (and your faces)" here he looked at Jay, "and I think you are right about it. I'm born. Nothing is gonna take away my birth—no matter what. That's it. So...." He looked at Tu.

Five Points Akropolis

"So let's get going?" Tu said it tentatively, hiding his relief. There was so much to do *here* and *now*... in order that they might *be there then*. But getting these guys to go along ... on whatever...— faith in him? He was so full of doubt himself. He almost smiled, but that quickly passed. It was worse than herding cats. It was like trying to herd branes, like trying to locate and keep tabs on each kid as a universe ... mentally imaging branes here—trying to, and ... he was now off at a tangent: What did *parallel* mean in images anyway? What do parallel universes—the multiverse—what does it look like? Trying to think out a visual pattern made his head spin like the horse-traffic at FivePoints. He had to deal with the straight mathematical calculations or they were all—.

"Toast!" said Pomala. "The only thing missing from the meal is toast!"

Quadri's head popped up. "Water! Soda! Something to drink!"

"Yo, my man!" called HB toward the light now streaming from the kitchen. Outside twilight had fallen and the room was dim. It got dark fast inside around here! Doesn't anyone turn on the lights?

Aneas stepped into the doorway, backlit. Silently, he had been awaiting their call. The praying upstairs, he noticed, was a little bolder, louder. "Yes, sir?" he said.

"Have you got any water?"

"Right away, sir."

"Can the sir. I don't need it."

Aneas, nonplussed, disappeared, and they heard the squealing of an iron pump handle, and water splashing into a metal container. When he appeared with a brass bucket and ladle they looked at one another. He went to the sideboard for glasses, brought an armload and the bucket, set them on the next table and began to ladle.

"Wait!" said Fabian. "How'bout bottled water? I don't think we can drink that."

"The watertable's not that clean here—we noticed," said Jayrai.

"Bottled water, sir?" said Aneas, perplexed.

"You know—spring water. Vacuum-packed?" Pomala said this apologetically.

He looked at her bemused, entranced, his eyes happy and glowing.

HB said, "Kills the germs? My man, have you got beer?"

"We got no ID," said Jay, "but maybe you'd make an exception. We'd get sick drinking that." She pointed to the bucket with her bionic finger.

Aneas looked at the finger. *Lordy Lordy.*

Then he thought, *The messengers can eat but can't drink water.*

Slowly he said, "There's beer at Five Points—Paddy's beer is good, they say." *Do angels drink beer?*

"FivePoints!" said HB, smacking the tabletop. "FivePoints it is! How much do we owe you for that awesome meal? Wait!" He held up his hand. "We got to confer—make it fair." He motioned the others close around the table and they all leaned forward, whispering. "Anybody got cash money? Can you imagine using a credit card even if we had one? We could pool, but it's my fault we here—"

"Fault! Nothing but genius!" exclaimed Jay.

"I'll give all I got anyway," said HB.

They agreed, and dug into their pockets, drawing out a five, some ones and change. HB did have a grubby ten he'd been holding and was sorry to see go. They piled it up in front of Blake, hopeful. "How much?" he said again.

Aneas looked at the pile in bewilderment. "Sixty-cents," he said slowly.

"Sixty-cents!!" HB made a face like he'd eaten something sour and incredible. "Sixty-cents?"

"Well, fifty-five, then," said Aneas Griffin, ashamed. It was going to cost in legal fees for Argus after all. He would've fed the angels for free otherwise. You supposed to do that for angels. But he hoped they'd understand just this time. They had to know about Pappy. That's got to be—part—why they're here. In this exact eating-house. They *must* know.

"My man!" exclaimed Blake Griffin, smiling.

Everyone reached for their cash before the guy had time to change his mind.

They push back their chairs and stood. HB stuck out his hand. Slowly, just a bit afraid and hardly acknowledging it to himself, Aneas stuck out his hand. HB grabbed it, then clasped his arm, knuckled his fist, and kissed it. HB was also about to hug him. Aneas, sensing it, backed off so fast he fell over the chair, scrambled up, bowed and said, "Y-You be welcome here any time, sirs. Welcome anytime."

They walked out into the night, having left eight bits shining on the table, for which they had taken only a dime and one nickel in change.

Aneas looked at the shining quarters lying on the tabletop in the light of the kitchen, streaming out. He was awestruck. They shone surely as from heaven. Slowly he pick them up, one at a time. They were light-feeling, as though from heaven, too. Carefully, each laid out separate in his pale palm, Aneas brought them to the lamplight in the kitchen.

He laid them in a pool of yellow light on the sideboard where meals were prepared. Then, one by one, he examined them. *Lordy Lordy.* "2011" said one lightweight shining 25-cent piece. And *Americle*, and there were different pictures on each. "2000," "2003," "2011." What does it mean? Got to be part of the message. Got to. He went upstairs to show them the pieces.

Like First and Second Streets, Third St. angled into Stock Exchange. They followed both it and, distantly, the gasman who lit a lamp—distantly—as they walked toward the intersection. In the summer-hazy dimness, he looked like some sort of mathematical magician with a wand, regularly starting the gas flow and its ignition into light. They talked over their impressions as they went.

"There's only some near Exchange St.. They don't light Third St. hardly at all."

"The infrastructure's primitive, but at least it's not falling apart like ours. —Theirs is just getting started!"

"Yeah, pretty soon we'll have it almost as bad, we don't watch out."

"Who's watching out?"

"The bosses, that's who!"

"When they ain't kicking it down the road."

As they went they heard the prayers of the upstairs Griffin household lighting up the street with shouts and praises of glory.

There is power power wonder working power
In the blood in the blood of the lamb....

Two Stories in Paddy's

The night was bright with distant shouting jubilation, thus the darkness of the neighborhood was mitigated. Even down here they heard it as they stepped onto the boardwalk of Stock Exchange Street. There had been little in the way of boardwalks on Third, apparently each landlord made or did not make them in front of his or her place—and the pedestrian beware. They had already cleaned Quadri's shoes twice. Neighborhood water-pumps with long handles were on scattered corners and accessible to all.

Before reaching Exchange, still below the hillside chockablock with houses, they heard a faint new undersound steaming up. A low rumbling lit with bangs or crashes, telltale, vague, an undercurrent of chaos swelling and ebbing just a bit, then (maybe) swelling again. They couldn't see it, did not know what or *if* it was, but could not help speculating as they kept on toward Paddy's. Nearing the intersection Jayrai said, "It's the riot—gotta be."

"They're having some party at my whoever's expense," said HBBBAH with anger.

However, this night's riot, though precipitated by the energy of the Argus affair, was not so much about Argus but about conditions for workers at the rubber factory—at the opposite end of the main street from the Opera House and burnt out City Buildings, near South Main. As yet the folk and traffic at Five Points were oblivious.

Out on Exchange Street, 2017 passed by the gasman where he stood confrontationally with a man in bowler hat. And there, with them, was the pretty girl in bright dress with big bow, hair in ringlets. These three stood arguing, agitated and tense beneath the light of a lamp he had apparently just lit. The gang of the future, passing, rounded the corner onto Sharon Road where horses were

188

tied and motorbikes parked; and there was a gig or two. They went into Paddy's, not too too confident about the beer, but hopeful and willing to put on the chuff. Though it would turn out that the only ID needed was the change they had gotten from Aneas. Tu trailed after them, not so hopeful or bold in his design (such as it was) to herd cats.

Inside the gloaming of the saloon and pool-hall the night was stale, young, and smoky. Also its smelled not nearly as inviting as the *Leg Bone*. 2017 did not smoke. They knew better, were proud of it, and they grimaced and coughed through the haze. The place was full of mostly young men, in trousers and waistcoats, their shirtsleeves rolled up. Some of them stopped to gawk at the newcomers—before turning back to their games and cronies with talking and laughter over the received explanation abroad in the neighborhood: Well, how about that?! These are the odd show-folk—newest act. Ain't it right they'd be in the show right about now? One man pointed to the watch pocket in his friend's vest where a gold chain was tethered, asking him for the time. That pocketwatch, like motorbikes, was something special in this neighborhood.

Tu listened closely. 8:20 p.m.. *On August 24, 1900 A.D.*

Pomala considered briefly that the dark wooden bar was the exact same as the counter from which the soup was ladled in the Gospel Mission. Above it, in 1900, hung great mugs and cups which the dark arm of the bartender reached for. She went to the window facing Exchange Street, in part to escape the smoke, but also to watch the pretty-dressed girl and two men outside. She remembered seeing this girl on the corner with the FivePoints-kids-1900 earlier—when they were across the street outside the school. Maybe it was just her clothing and 'do that made her seem pretty? Small Quadri was with Pomala, holding her hand. Behind them talk—of the previous night's riot that had been interrupted by their entrance—surged back over the room.

"Won't be no vaudeville show if there's more rioting," said one man, answering the other as he stepped up to eye the cue ball against the others. He was chalking the tip of his stick.

"Better than the show, anyway," agreed another.

At the bar the FivePoints gang half-listened, backs to the bartender, all except Fabian, who was in charge of ordering. This despite HB's initial inclination to do it. "Better not chance that," Fabian had warned. HB was just, but just, smart enough to see it. Tu was relieved to see the universes running along orderly lines. Actually, he was thirsty and wanted to taste that beer. Yet he was prudent enough to see that his own cat needed herding now.

Pomala told Quadri to go ask for soda, and, wary but obedient, he threaded his way through the tall dark-clad strangers to the bar where Fabian stood near the spittoon, ordering. After seeing him safely with the others, she turned back, and looked out the window again. The gasman was angry and gesturing. He was mad at the bowler man. *What funny hats they wear. He's like Charlie Chaplin but—no mustache and his clothes are checkered.*

Suddenly the gasman stepped over and knocked at the window. He pounded on the plateglass, and Pomala, who was at its other end, stepped back just a bit. A couple men standing around, glass in hand, came over and stood a moment, saw the bowler man and girl, and the gasman motioning. They shook their heads at him and began to laugh. Then they stepped back to the pool table and, laughing, began a new conversation with the others there.

"Ol' Partum wants us to come rescue him from the rakemucker."

"He can't keep it up if the newspaper gets hold of it."

"They got no evidence—there's nothing they can do."

"It might help if Gwendolyn accuses him."

"She'd never do that. Would your daughter?"

"Shaddup. Keep others out of it. Some of us are actually decent folk. Partum's the one." The man poked the other with his cue stick, leaving a chalk mark on his waistcoat. "Watch that bringing good folks in with him."

"What's good about us?" said watch-chain man, brushing at the dust. "Are we doing good?"

And on the conversation went, Pomala listening, fascinated. Quadri came over with the pop and Pomala looked at the glass bottle curiously. "Look at that," she said, holding it out for him to see. "Is yours like this?"

Akropolis Pop.

"They've got their own soda-pop company. —I mean we did. They must bottle this here." She took a swig, cautiously. "Mmm. Sweet enough, fizzy. It's good," she declared.

"Here's the thing. Maybe just a suggestion *in the paper* will be enough to get ol' Argus off the hook. You know how it is when everyone reads the thing in black-and-white. Everyone. The whole town."

"Naw." The speaker deftly shot and, knocking, the balls ricocheted—red going off into the side pocket. He stood back grinning. "That'll just divide, and throw gas on the fire."

"Right," said another in rolled up shirtsleeves, tossing back clear liquid in a shot glass. He had a beer glass in the other hand, and now started on that. "Half the town wants a colored to be it, so there you are."

190

Five Points Akropolis

Pomala looked back out the window, frowning. Now the pretty girl was shaking her head vehemently at bowler man. Bowler man left. The gasman reached suddenly for the girl, but she eluded him, jerking away. She went after bowler, and Pomala, turning, saw them out the front window. It was darker here, but light shone dimly out from Paddy's Saloon. The gasman still had his job to do on Sharon Road. Quickly, holding fast to Quadri, Pomala threaded through to the doorway, now standing just inside.

"Don't do anything, Mr. Dreiser." The girl sounded pleading, even as though crying. "He can't have done it."

"But you told me he did."

"I'll saw nothing. There's no proof. I don't even know."

"And he'll just end up hurting you."

In lamplight from doorway and window Pomala thought she saw tears streaming. Pomala could not see that well in the glare.

Partum came around the corner, yelling. "You got no proof, you bag of sht! Get away from my little girl!"

At the bar Tu was watching HB. Alternately, Fabe and Jay watched HB and the pool players talking.

"We all know Argus didn't do it." The speaker finished off his beer and looked at the bar man. Turning, Pomala now, for the first time, registered the barman as Afrikan-Americle. He was tall, muscular, old, with graying kinky hair. The pool players looked over at him.

The rest of 2017 were standing at the bar, and they all heard the barman mutter. "Then why'd you say he did to the po-leese?" His hand on the bar with its rag was swiftly scrubbing scrubbing, scrubbing away.

As if reading it in his actions (not having heard the muttering), the drinker continued, "Ol' Partum had us bamboozled with the doctor's talk. Turns out the Doc said no such thing."

"An excuse," muttered the Negro, glaring, polishing away. "A lie, damn lie." It was all there under his breath ... but 2017 heard it. HB heard it, dawnlight in his eyes.

Before this, while 2017 was still in the *Leg Bone*, Mr. Priam and Mrs. Havard were having a conversation about the Grandmaster over dinner at *Stonehewn.* They sat in the vaulted but intimate parlor with the comfortable settees, white stag's head, and Anglish hunting pictures flanking the marble chimneypiece. But now they were at a table by the open window, tête-à-tête, intimate as Mr. Priam had hoped for. The heavy sweet rich odor of the summer garden mingled with that of the wine. It was too late in the season for nesting birdsong, and there was no breath of air here, but the garden, as always, was colorful and refreshing to gaze at through the open mullioned lattice. There were small ornamental trees, making yet more intimate in their flanking the open windows. The children, of course, were dining in one of the playrooms under big sister Kate's supervision. Later Mr. Priam and Mrs. Havard were to go up and see Brant.

For supper lamb and salad, all grown here at *Stonehewn*, followed by lavish desserts. The estate had a farm that reached down into the valley out toward Sharon and other farming communities west of here. Salad was unheard of in Five Points. Had Mrs. Havard been in a position to choose, she may well have sampled the fare at the *Leg Bone*, but she was not thinking of that now.

They were talking of the Grandmaster.

She had said, "I heard something quite intriguing about his juggling in the street."

You are so beautiful, thought Mr. Priam, looking at her finely featured face beneath stylishly piled hair. *You may talk of anything you like.* He himself was not so intrigued by the great man of the vaudeville circuit, although he did admire his showmanship. ...It was the best he had ever seen. Quite astonishing....

"Shall we?" Mrs. Havard was saying. "I wish we could get him to come to us sometime. I was disappointed he did not come the other night."

"Yes, quite the no-show," said the man smiling. "Too bad. Show people are fascinating."

She nodded, sipping from her longstemmed glass. "And how much more so—this gigantic man who seems as light as a feather when his oh-so-ponderous bulk moves about."

"Yes. Curious," said the rubber baron. He took a swallow for himself, swishing the dry, touched with sweet, wine over his tongue. This was how one got the fullness of wine... from its long-tasting.

"Don't you think we might?" she asked once more. "Perhaps someday soon for luncheon?"

Hers was a deliciously lovely gaze, smiling. Of herself toward him, this was bolder than anything hitherto. He thought about the request, but briefly. He recollected that he had felt a bit snubbed by the grandmaster's absence from the lawn fête. Usually showmen were all over themselves to mingle with the upper echelons of society. It was useful in the trade. *Yet surely, if specially asked—. I'm one of the few in Akropolis he would come to if summoned. That's why her appeal is to me, and to none other.*

"Well, Mrs. Havard, you may have your interview, if that's what it's to be.... I'll call for it myself."

She was hopeful and doubtful at once. "Oh, don't say it so," she said. "Let it be entirely social." But she knew she would write

up her impressions all the same. Mr. Priam, looking at her—
beautiful lady!—knew it as well.

He pushed out from the table, still dressed as it was with
four kinds of desert and the bottle of wine to hand. He went to the
small mahogany table near the arched doorway where sat an inkwell
with best writing paper, and the telephone standing tall and black.
He picked it up, lifted the receiver, clicked its cradle twice, and, in
his politest tones, asked kindly to be connected to the Opera House.
The grandmaster was bound to be there preparing the night's show.

He did not know that the Grandmaster was staying—not at
the best hotel, *The Portage Park*, across Main Street from the
showplace—but in the Opera House itself, on the top floor where its
neoGothic dormers looked out over the sometimes tumultuous but
thriving and industrious city. The show folk themselves stayed in
low class hotels down by the railroad, rubber-works, bars, and
canals; and, truth be told, they felt more at home there, though had
it been on offer—that is affordable—they'd have been charmed by a
stay in the grander hotel across the street.

To Mr. Priam's surprise, the grandmaster himself answered
the 'phone's call.

"Certainly," said he to the request, in his most quiet tones.
"With alacrity, if you wish it. I shall be delighted."

Mr. Priam hung up and came slowly back to her, gazing
thoughtfully past her out the window. "Strange," he said, seating
himself across from her again. "I'm not sure what I expected, but
certainly it wasn't that."

"What—may I ask?"

"He says he will come right away." His look was still
thoughtful, somewhat bemused. "And tonight, as you no doubt
reckon, is a show night,"

"Splendid!" She said it with delight. "And, only think, how
thrilled James will be. More so, I think, than when the A'ndians
came here."

"Perhaps he would stop in a moment for Brant to see him,"
said Mr. Priam, musing, half-doubtful.

But the Grandmaster was detained. The players were below,
getting ready for the show, but he stood high in the Opera House
filling one large Victorian dormers, looking out over the city
southward toward tall smokestacks pouring forth blackly. Puffing a
bit on his large cigar in his large fat dimpled hand. The light of its
ash shone red in the window, had one been looking up to see it.
Even though the sun was going down west of there, reflecting its
light off the panes. Still its glowing, in the midst of reflected
brightness there, told plainly, moving about. It was like a small fire,
like the sun itself in miniature, moving; as he stood, puffing and

lingering, looking out over the city toward the rubberworks, with the magic inherent in all things.

Mr. Priam strolled with his guest in the fragrant garden among flowering rosebushes and fading light, awaiting the conveyance of the grandmaster. The showman had declined Mr. Priam's kind offer to send for him. Priam even half-expected him to alight, for all his girth and density, from a cab-and-cob—were there one stout enough for the job. His was a surprising character. Perhaps that was where his charisma lay—in that surprise.

The butler came through the shrubbery to say that the plant manager was calling over the telephone.

"What does he want?" asked Mr. Priam, loath to leave the lady for business, or factory mishaps. Beef Bones, as he was called, usually knew better than to call for some trifle, however. For that Priam was grateful—

"There's another riot, sir. The unionizers—"

"Damn!" said the rubber baron. He turned to his guest. "I'm sorry, Mrs. Havard."

She watched him hurry away. Well? She wondered. Yes... she would miss the riot.... On the other hand, the great man was still coming.

Below in Five Points at Paddy's Saloon and Pool Hall, while watching the barman muttering and scrubbing the bar, it occurred to HB that he may well be looking at a former slave. *Maybe from Regina or one of those other idiot slave states.* But HB was not counting back the years. People don't count when enraged. Many things happened almost at once inside and out the dim smoky lamplit saloon and pool hall. To order them narratively, clearly, will be a feat for words.

Pomala had come up to Jayrai to whisper that she thought maybe the pretty girl they'd seen was the victim of sexual abuse by her father. Actually, she hoped Jayrai might scare the man off. Jayrai was already pumped on adrenaline listening to the barroom conversation, watching the hand of the barman furiously scrubbing over the wooden bar between beer mugs; seeing the anger and hearing the muttering; glimpsing the dawnlight in Blake Griffin's eye. Now Pomala came and said this to her. Jayrai then conceived that her adventure had brought her to an evil time, where but moments before she'd been happily larking—exploring this time of innocence and simplicity.

"Horrible *othering!*" She seethed. Her bionic hand flexed its fingers, it fisted.

But HB was already saying it all with much violence.

"This is a hate crime!" He bellowed, and turned round on the room. *"You fuking bastards are fuking hate criminals and your fuking po-lice are criminals with you!"*

The roomful of Paddy's clientele froze in swaying smoky lamplight. Shocked. *Scandalized.* All but Pomala who was dragging Jayrai by her inborn arm out onto the boardwalk. The gasman and the journalist stared at them. The pretty girl looked at them briefly, having heard the bellowing inside. Then she ran over the boardwalk toward Stock Exchange. She ran across through lamplight without looking. With relief Pomala saw the street deserted. The gasman started after her but Jayrai caught him. The strength in her hand grabbed hold so tight he could only lean away and not otherwise move. He looked back at her flashing eyes, a faint sneer mingled with hunger rising in him. He shouted. "You little bitch, let go'me!" Then he screamed, writhing in agony as this menace, ignorant whether or not he were guilty, squeezed his arm in a vise-grip of inhuman magnitude.

Inside the bar HB was bellowing, trying to fend off outraged attackers who howled racial epithets and piled on him—fists pummeling, feet kicking—tables and chairs knocking, lamps a'swing.

Tu stood rooted, gaping until someone began socking him. It was Glacas, one of Fabian's ancestors, but Tu did not know this. First punch to the arm, then to the stomach and groin—doubling, staggering him.

Fabian, blond hair flying, his tattoos more grotesque as he screamed; slap-punching, kicking on the perimeter of those beating and booting HB, called to the barman to help them. The man vaulted the bar in one sleek muscular move—glass mugs spilling and spinning—and began walloping the attackers before settling to wrestle one man into a painful hammerlock.

HB was on the filthy floor, gasping and grunting, the smells of old beer and tobacco juice and his own blood in his nostrils—still screaming with what might remained to him.

What was he screaming, his face beaten and bloody, a tooth hanging by a thread from his mouth?

"*Show-master! Show-master! Show-master!*" He had forgotten what they called the master, vaguely thinking *there* might be an ally if only someone would call him on the phone. They were supposed by Five Points 1900 to belong to the vaudeville, and that was the only help he could think of. "*Help me! God help me! Somebody call the show-master!!*"

At that moment, out on the crossroads of what was once a country hamlet with its quiet rural cemetery, rode the massive Grandmaster himself, astride a massive draft horse with shaggy fetlocks, one no doubt used in the hauling of freight by a local teamster. How he had procured the beast is a detail left unexplained, but the Grandmaster was riding past on the great Clydesdale just then—of that there can be no doubt. He might have gone up the partly parallel Market Avenue and through a different neighborhood toward his destination, *Stonehewn.* In fact, that street past St. Invincible's would have been the more direct route for him, especially had the horse come from a livery or stable nearby the opera house. In an alternate story he *did* go up that way, standing, one leg each on a brace of white stallions, their iron shoes ringing on brick-cobbled pavement.

"*The grandmaster! The grandmaster!*" went up the shout from inside the bar; from the pool hall habitués as they worked kicking and pounding. They knew what "the naggers" were about and mock-called on him themselves—quite unaware that he was in the road riding past.

Pomala saw the Great Man passing among gaslight and shadows on the great horse. Jayrai was busy. The gasman was too much in agony, down on his knees, and unable to summon any move to escape the immense pain he hardly endured. Dreiser stood aloof against the plateglass, watching everything; indeterminate, almost without presence of mind to retrieve the notebook he had dropped. The intersection, he saw, was empty of all but the Grandmaster, massively, imperturbably passing; and the tall lone A'ndian standing on the corner of the boardwalk; at the grammar school where Stock Exchange and Sharon met.

Also watching everything. Impassive.

The next moment everything changed. It was precisely at that moment that the gig, horse, and driver carrying Mr. Priam came charging down Cake Eaters Hill. The Grandmaster passed upward, the rubber baron passed downward ripping through the crossroads—Mr. Priam turning to watch him as they passed one another, balding head leaning out the buggy, his voice (however) urging Gilbert the driver onwards toward the Akropolis industrial section.

Meanwhile, inside Paddy's Saloon, the bartender was scrubbing the bar, muttering, "Damn lie. It's a damned lie."

And Pomala was at the window, having turned back to watch the girl, the reporter, and the gasman in conversation beneath the gaslight on Exchange St.. And Tu was at the bar fervently hoping the cats would come with him to the cemetery before 11 o'clock. Quadri, who had not even been present during the fracas— (experienced in all its violence by the others)—was standing by Pomala, looking at his pop bottle.

Akropolis Pop.

196

Five Points Akropolis

A-Krop-O-lis Pop? Quadri remembered being surprised last night on hearing from his brother that FivePoints was smaller than Akropolis. He had showed him on a map in the PopPad that Akropolis was smaller than EHio or PencilsWood. "It's *inside* EHio, see?" It had always seemed in reverse order to Quadri: things and places smaller—the further away from him they were.

At the dim bar, HB's gaze moved from the scrubbing hand to the roomful of natterers, jawing about Argus the innocent and Partum the guilty. The cue stick struck, knocking, spinning balls off one another. One fell into a side pocket, decisively. Standing there strangely, heart palpitating, HB looked out the doorway and saw a huge man on a great horse, hooves clopping and ringing up the street rising to Cake Eaters Hill. As though the fat man had all the time in the world. He noticed also a horse and gig thundering down Stock Exchange Street, passing huge horse and rider at breakneck speed.

The Clydesdale and its Great Rider then clopped into shadow past the grammar school, out of sight. HB, as with moonlight in his eyes, turned back to watch the barman still scrubbing.

Blake Griffin shook his head slowly. He held out his arms; looked at each, at his torso. His body remembered no pain, but his psyche its trauma. *Recollecting it all...but the pain.* He felt the dawnlight in him. He felt dawnlight swelling up in his being, then gently lifting away. He looked back at everybody, each seeming as before—everybody but Pomala and Quadri... who were not at the door... but—he saw now—at the window in the corner. Blake licked the beer foam off his lip, wondering, just a bit afraid. Amazed.

After a moment, he said, stepping closer to the barman: "Hard, huh. I heard it was hard, but I had no idea."

The barman looked up from the bar he was scrubbing, fuming over. He was about to say, *What cabbage patch you been living in?* But he said, "Yeah ... bet yo mama's life it is." Then he almost seemed to smile. "No," he said. "Don't do that."

Nodding and frowning, HB said, "Okay."

At which the barman gave him a quizzical look.

Dark Cloak was back up the road just a bit, again across the street from the *Clasp-locker Hospital.* He saw lampglow in the corn-girl's window above. No light in the rest of the windows at that level although there were lights higher on the third level. He knew others lived up there, workers in various shops. One man was a blacksmith. Fascinated, both Dark Cloak and the corn-girl had watched him from the alleyway when his dim shop was wide open, sparks flying from his hammer blows off red-hot iron. The girl, of course, had been with the boy in short pants with blond bang, holding hands. And Dark Cloak had crouched on a nearby shed and chicken house, watching, but not at all hidden.

Now he saw the boy, blond hair faintly gleaming, looking out from the upper window onto Sharon Road. The other children were gathering below.

Upstairs, in the parlor with roses-and-lilies wallpaper, Ma had fallen asleep on the sofa beside the little girl; while listening to Parry, at the other end of the sofa, reading *The Secret Garden*.

Why are children in stories so often without mothers or fathers? She had worried ... just on the edge of sleep. It was now so much that way in life—but did stories need it, too? She dropped off into that slumber of the just workers, and then Parry, looking over at her, quietly set down the book next the girl. He turned and knelt on the sofa to see what if anything was happening outside. They weren't shouting. Were they playing? And then he thought maybe a storm was coming. Was it another riot?

Back down on the boardwalk, at the corner hitching posts, some grownup slid from his horse and ran into Paddy's to announce that a riot was on at Priam's rubber-works. Not knowing the language Dark Cloak did not understand this. But he had known about this night's riot before anyone at Five Points, before even Jayrai and 2017 had speculated on it while walking down Third St. after eating at the Leg Bone Diner. Dark Cloak knew because he was an A'ndian scout trained in the ways of observation and tactical considerations. He had given his report on the previous riot (and on the stockyards he had passed through) to Red Fox, as together they tended the sick braves in hiding. Red Fox had then reported to him on the location and layout of the factory, as well as the refuse heap and dam, building by the river near the clan's encampment beneath the great shale ledge.

Now he watched as Paddy's emptied itself of about one third of its pool players and drunkards—just as the neighborhood kids stepped back in their approach to crowd around the doors for a listen. The grownups rode off on their various conveyance, leaving the Five Points gang in the dust. The short pants boy had come down and out onto the boardwalk—the corn-girl in hand—to join the others in a game. Dark Cloak did not at first know what it was but, after watching some moments, he gathered that it was a form of play. Then, watching more, he recognized it as a fair likeness to the game played among boy-and-girl braves, and among older boys in the aftermath of the *piawaws*. But the A'ndians used no can, nor even a pot. They kicked what the Upeast A'ndians called a *guffmoggin*. And it was made out of deerskin stuffed with closely bound grass. Dark Cloak loped off up the hill towards Harkins

Five Points Akropolis

Woods. His feet used the dust-and-cinder road, not the boardwalk.
It felt better, gripping well between his toes as he ran.

Up on Cake Eaters Hill, at *Stonehewn* mansion-house, the
conversation between Mrs. Havard and the Grandmaster was about
to begin. You will remember that very few people were aware of his
passing through the then deserted crossroads and up the hill, and
that although Blake Griffin noticed a huge man and huge horse
going up past the Harkins Grammar School, he did not exactly know
it was the Grandmaster of the minstrel show.

Mrs. Havard had lingered in the Garden after Mr. Priam
hurried off to see to his rubber-works. She was not a child but
neither had she mother or father. She had one child in school that
she wrote to every night in Nottinbright Angleland. She had no
husband to speak of. From time to time she reminded herself that
an adulterer was not a husband.

Anticipating her interview she was excited: but also excited
because there was so much in the air tonight. Life itself was
tremendously exciting just at the moment, but, as always, you could
not tell from her outward demeanor.

Alone, she knelt in the dewy grass beside a thorny flowering
shrub, and buried her nose in the fragrant great blossom of a moon-
pale rose. The fragrance went into her nostrils and up, through its
appropriate pathways and transformations, into her mind, entwining
the whole of her being, ravishing. The moon shone its whiteness
down on the flowering lawnscape with an exquisite sensation
ameliorating the night's heat for her. Yes, it almost seemed as
though it were for herself alone these things shone-flowered-dewed
themselves. But also it seemed, as she ducked her head to yet
another great rose (and then looked up again across the pale
flowering moonshiny summer garden), that she was herself *only
made for* and *only given to* these lovely things.

They must want us to love them.

She would never have thought this before.

How wonderful. How wonderful.

She would never have tried telling *how* wonderful. Surely
words would not do it. Words could scarcely do anything! Tell
anything! Show anything! And she had worked with them all her
adult life....

"My dear," said a light yet rich voice behind her. "Some
people believe these things were brought into being by words alone."

Still on her knees, Mrs. Havard looked round on the Great
Man standing hugely, mountainous, there in the pathway amongst
low, flowering roses. Were it any other voice, she would have
jumped up immediately, vainly endeavoring not to be seen so

199

worshiping. *Yes,* she thought shyly, *I have been worshiping. Absolutely adoring the night, moon, flowers, roses, creation.*

Kneeling still, she beamed. "Oh! Isn't it wonderful?"

How he filled her gaze. Greatly. *So big!* He seemed to fill her sight much as the garden and moon had a moment ago. In gazing at him she almost forgot the garden, the night, the pocked white moon and her worship of these wonders... and yet... he was not unlike any of these. Not unlike these, either, in their tonal visibility and verve. *So alive!* He looked moon-glorious, loving, and wise. He *felt* so in his quiet look upon her, smiling. Her heart, disposed toward him, was become lovingly worshipful.

Suddenly she bethought he had spoken. She found she wanted very much to talk with him. Mrs. Havard had heard various accounts of his streetcorner juggling (in the afternoon before the first riot), but had not much credited them. Now, gazing at him in this garden, in this night, she felt sure it was all true.

Still smiling, still exuding all friendship and calm, he held out his massive hand to help her rise.

She stood. Still now, holding unto his big fingers, saying with delight, "But this is amazing. You with your perfect refinement of enunciation and diction—you are my countryman! I should not have told this when we saw you onstage—from the performance at the Opera House... the way you told us the stories of each act."

"I know many inflections, dialects, tongues—dialogues, analogues ... numerologues, my dear." Eyes twinkling, he smiled bigger. "Prologues and epilogues."

She laughed with delight, the whole of her features involved. Like a child's. He was the only one. The only human being. The only earth-mild air-cloud-sun-moon-stars-planets-galaxies swirling and spinning; and ponderously, yet lightly it seemed, pirouetting. Yet, she saw, he stood stone still like a mountain. He did not move a mite. Like a great tree planted, as rooted and branching, immovable. Nothing might move him. She felt sure of it.

She gazed at him. How long did she gaze?

She said, "But just now you said—What was it you said?"

"Some people believe everything—all this—was brought into being by words."

"And ourselves, too," she answered. Truly at this moment believing.

"Yes."

"Do mere words have such... such energy and power?"

"They do if we have faith in them."

"... Do you mean also in who is speaking them?"

"I do."

"But how can mere words do all this?" She glanced round. And now she did see the gardens stretching out, and embroidering, the bedecked moon-silvered lawn. She gazed back up into his great gentle face—filled with hope and love of him. "And yourself—so made... as well?"

"As you see me at this moment, yes."

The strength in his big fingers flowed into her with gentle loving force.

She looked a wondering question up at him, gazing her fill.

He answered it. "Otherwise? No. I am all the words, but all the words might not contain me. Rather, I overflow with these words I am making...." And here he gestured with slow half-rotation, showing everything visible at *Stonehewn*: gardens, glimmering pools, fireflies, the very stones and mullioned panes and half-timbered design of their veritable castling. "They, too, overflow with me."

She did not look perplexed, but may have felt—just a bit— that sensation. She could not be tormented in his loving presence. His free spirit upheld hers. She said, "There are so many confusing, disappointing, distressing, horrible, violent ... frightening words... as well."

"Yes." The sadness of his gaze rushing in, nearly collapsing her: Still, his fingers flowed life and health to hers, upholding her. Only his look communicated the sadness, but it was more than she could bear as streams flowed down her face. And he said, "Can you stand the self-dismantling in making I have endured? It is the cost of speaking, of making all from words. In your experience of them it is a cost that—a bit at a time, and sometimes with Great Force Born in Being—is the residue, or offscouring, of creation loosed among us. I would not have it do lasting harm ... though at times it shall seem so."

"But why?" she asked. "You feel it, too?"

"Oh more. And *much more* have I felt it, my dear."

"But not now? You sound in these words as though painful suffering has passed from you."

"It has. All but the residue I endure, as I suffer with you."

"But why then? Why do we suffer? Why not take it away?"

"You mean, *Seeing that I have passed with all things through the crucible of great making-and-remaking.*"

Mutely she nodded her lovely brow, ducking it just a bit, reverently.

"This suffering, and even violence, is how you know it was not easy for me. This is how you know, proportionally, the totality of doubt and difficulty, the evil I endured. A small, very small measure I have given you. You experience small measure by the grace meeting you, and in uplift such as this—from time to time. The whole of your life is not that concentration of evil endured by me in getting the Light and Word to shine."

She gazed at his great moon-bright face. It was brim full of light in its large enduring and endearing features. She was silent, looking, still holding his fingers.

"Should you like to love me?"

He asked it.

"I should," she answered.

"...Very much, indeed." She said it, her gaze falling. She closed her eyelids and whispered. "Very, very much indeed."

After some moments, in which softly she lingered still holding his fingertips, she looked up at him again. What she saw, instead, was the white moon shining. The great white face of the moon. And her fingers felt only the memory of his touch.

Because of this interview there would be two years less at the end of her life. And never a word of it, without being somehow transmuted, would get into print. And, richer or poorer in memory (as it came to her from time to time), she would keep that night always with an up-filling heart.

She walked slowly through the gardens, half-circling the mansion. She met the big and bony Daphnes coming toward her on the path, dressing grown streaming out. Daphnes strode from the direction of the carriage house. There a great shadowy *Something* passed near the estate stone wall and drive. Miss Priam was exhilarated.

"I met the Grandmaster! It was grand!!" She guffawed at her pun. "He said to tell you he was sorry he had to hurry away. It seems there may be a late show tonight despite the riot."

She then exclaimed, "He must be something more than the Grandmaster. He has to be. I believe he is!" The two women hugged one another. Mrs. Havard pulled back, smiling, aglow.

I hugged Daphnes Priam!

Miss Priam, broadly smiling, thought, *The Anglish woman hugged me!*

Together they walked arm in arm toward the carriage house speaking of him. It was such a night!

At the stair beneath the archway leading to Miss Priam's apartments, they said good night. Mrs. Havard had explained that it was such a night!—And she would be walking back toward the hotel.

Miss Priam, however, determined that she would soon send a gig to her on the way.

Five Points Akropolis

The End of the Beginning

Meanwhile upstairs in the mansion-house, in the quaint little room of his sister Ann Gladys, Brant was reclining on her little canopied bed. The canopy was partial, extending only over the head of the little bed, and it was trimmed with lace that was changed for fresh, then washed, starched and ironed each week by one of the maids. Brant was recuperating in his sister's room, in her bed, because it was cunningly made either to recline or lie flat, depending on the position of a peg-and-hole mechanism in back. It was a design of the great Morris Williams. The wallpaper on the walls of the room were also from a design of his, with regard to both pattern and texture if not color. With the exception of the flocked texture, which gave a certain density or loft, it was dainty and refined.

Ann Gladys and her brother James Horatio were in the little bedroom with Brant—who, at the moment, was scribbling on the tablet of paper using Ann Gladys's lap desk. This desk was of fine teakwood, with a hinged lid beneath which were kept the ink bottles (blue, black, and red ink) and some exquisite ink pens of silver and white-gold. One these ink bottles was in the well of the little desk above the hinge, where it was flat. Otherwise the desk slanted for easy writing. The scribbling of Brant was his end of the conversation they were having about the riots and the police... and, now, about Argus.

"The people at Five Points all say he did not do it," James was saying.

Brant's face and head were bandaged. He had been told that he would look different and hardly recognize himself when the bandages came off. He was preparing himself for that, daily. James, on the other hand, was tremendously apprehensive, and was even scared each time he looked at his brother. Ann Gladys knew that it had been very brave of him to be so often by his brother since this happened. Neither she nor James were allowed in the room whenever the bandages were changed.

"Is that so?" said Ann Gladys, her voice high and light. Whose golden ringlets were down and lying on her shoulders in preparation for bed. She wore her nightdress and silk robe but would still be going into the other rooms to romp a bit with her brothers and sisters before bed. And she would be sleeping in Brant's room till he was better. "I didn't think he would hurt anybody."

Brant, who alone knew the exact nature of the harm done the little mute girl, showed them the writing:

Of course Argus did not do it. We must get father to help him.

Brant was too old to call his father papa any longer. Someday, perhaps, he would be helping Mr. Priam run the rubber works and he did not want to sound immature, but would say, "Father wishes it so," or "Father thinks it better to...."

"Wasn't it Papa who got them to move Argus?" said James.

Scribble scribble, tap tap, scribble, went the dainty pen. The tap came when he was knocking excess ink off the nib.

That may be, but he needs to do more.

It is doubtful whether Brant—who was a classy scholar boy-about-town-&-country-club—would have taken much interest in Argus's trouble if he had not been shot—owing to his brother's excitement and ignorant bravado, as Mr. Priam had said. But now he was thinking (almost) of nothing else. He did not even think as much about Priam's riots, although that, too, now occupied some of his thought. He had just now been writing of it... and evolving his thoughts on the subject of the rubber workers. Some of these he regarded as great loyal diligent workers, almost heroes so manly and jocular were they (a few of them). ...But of course some of the workers were children, too. A boy was badly injured while splitting para biscuits a few weeks back.

"But how else can Papa help him?" said Ann Gladys. "Can he just make them let him go?"

Scribble scribble scribble.

Yet James was saying, "I think that's what the lawyer was here for earlier."

Brant crossed out his scribbles. He wrote, *That's it! Why didn't you to tell me?*

James cocked his head to look at the note. "But you were sleeping! Was I supposed to wake you and say the lawyer is here, why is the lawyer here?"

Scribble scribble.

Grant turned the tablet.

Let's hope that's why. But mention it all the same.

Five Points Akropolis

Inside smoky lamplit Paddy's amid the knocking of the balls, FivePoints 2017 stood staring out the plateglass onto Sharon Road where the gasman, with an igniter sparking on a long pole, was lighting lamps. He moved beyond sight of the windows. They had seen the man in the bowler and checkered suit move from lamp to lamp with him, twice, before turning away to head back down Stock Exchange Street. That is, Pomala saw them. The others were watching the game just beginning outside in the road. And more of the 1900 clientele were now moving into the bar again.

"What are they doing?" asked Jayrai, pitching her voice to be heard over the fiddle player (just starting up). Later there'd be a banjo playing, very rousing.

"Playing some game," said HB. Distracted.

She flung a leg at him, knocking some beer from both glasses. "I knew that, yo?"

"I think it's kick-the-can," said Fabian.

Quadri thought, *Wish I could play.*

Even Tu, though he was considering the arrangement they'd need on the cemetery wall at 11 o'clock, had put away the pod and was watching, taking cautious sips of the bitter brew in the heavy glass mug. He was, after all, thirsty—he told himself making a face over it.

Behind them the table—pool balls knocking—was surrounded with onlookers, game ensuing. Someone had out a violin and was solemnly sawing away at *The Bowowery*. Some of the men sang lustily along; swaying, swinging time with their thick, foaming, mugs. *We'll never go there any more.*

"My grandma told me about that. You could make a pretty good mash-up of the things she says about being a kid. PreInternet and all that. Plus, she's got a handle on stuff going on before that from stories of *her* great aunts and uncles, grandparents. I think they were North Reginans like that kid out there." Fabian was getting interested. He pointed at Glacas who was just bringing the can back to the center of the road. The other kids had vanished in all directions like particles in some supercollider game. Or like the pool balls on breaking away from initial formation.

"You mean like in politics?" said Jayrai. "Where the mayor kicks the whatever down the road so she won't have to deal with it?"

"Looks like *McGuffin PlaneTTesimals*" piped Quadri. They looked at him. He seemed a little chuffier than he had been.

"I think he's right, only maybe more like *McGuffin BigBanging*," said Tu. And he went on to describe parallels between the real game here and the virtual on the PopPad or other device. He had to speak up more than he liked to make himself heard over the din.

Fabian said, "You could never play can-kick now. I mean 2017—too much of the wrong kind of traffic, too steady and fast-flowing at night.

"Looks like fun," said Pomala, tipping back her *Akropolis Pop*. She took the empty bottle Quadri handed up to her. "Want another?"

Gazing out onto the empty street, he shook his head, wondering. *Where'd he go*? The *It* (Glacas) had been there a moment ago.

Tu was a bit concerned over Fabian's new nonchalance. It almost seemed like the *Time Change* no longer disturbed him.

Pomala was wondering where the girl in long skirts went. None of the women in this town wore sLegGings or even trousers or cargo pants, it seemed. Then she thought: This town! It's Akropolis! It's FivePoints, the Zettler soup kitchen!! She had seen Gwendolyn outside with the others as they gathered round what turned out to be a can. But now the pretty-dressed girl seems to have gone off like the others. Oh, there was the kid in torn stockings and CapriPants come back. He seemed to be guarding the can. And had only one suspender and no shoes. *He might as well go barefoot*, she thought.

"Think they'd let us play?" Fabian was starting to settle in, it seemed.

This was Tu's big fear. Cats are never easy and, without a superior draw—the big motivator—you could count on exactly nothing.

But Fabian was already out the door. Tu brushed past the others who were also now headed that way.

"Mugs!!" called the bartender. He eyed them.

"Mugs!!" The others chorused and went to set them, bottles included, on the bar.

"I'll get theirs," said HB, looking him in the eye, gesturing out the door.

"We agreed!" Tu was yelling, stomping the boardwalk. Not like Tu. Tu yelling? Not like Tu!

HB came out and took away the thick, ridged glasses. Tu's had beer in the bottom, which HB immediately downed. He went back into the saloon.

The fiddle player had switched to *The Raspberry Blonde* and the singing had turned to shouting. *Casey would dance....* Banjo plinking, the pool hall was jumping.

HB leaned in, wanting to snag a few words with the barkeep, as they called him. But the man was too busy turning the taps, filling mugs, and pouring out Eriemen whiskey. Looked to HB like he needed help. Briefly he thought maybe he'd volunteer. Maybe find something out, or at least take his mind off what had just happened. So-called in the game, this *Twinkle-in-Time* (as he could only think it) had not seemed to bother the others ... and that was more disturbing than anything. He looked again at his outstretched arms, his torso. He felt his face. His tooth had been hanging, now it was rock solid. He moved his tongue around inside his mouth, feeling each tooth, the stony ridges of them, the bump down the middle of his pallet; the soft tissue of his lips, licking them. Maybe it has to do with my new head? (Meaning the software implemented by CossycSystems on his entering puberty.) But it had never happened before. ... Maybe he had been supplanted—like some Jacob in that SF story. *Maybe I'm not me? Maybe I'm somebody else?*

Oh man! Got-to-stop-this!

If only they'd said something. Why don't the others know it too? He looked around. To think he might not get born was nothing to this.... *This was so much worse.* Being isolated like this... in 1900 CE. At least they were with me in it before.

He saw now that being with them had made bearable the first wrinkle—wrinkle!—these are *chasms*!...

He stopped. Took a calming breath, the way Pomala had told him.

Yes. It was being with them made the first one OK. Look how they helped me get over the grandfather paradox. Tu actually offered to hold my hand!... Maybe... if I just axe'em...? Would this give him good results? He feared not. HB wandered slowly out the door. On the boardwalk he turned back to glance in again. There was the barman working away like nothing had happened.

Can you dream without going to sleep?... Like about a Fatman riding horse while fixing things?

"Tu!" called HB approaching him. Jayrai and Pomala were there, too, a bit apart, talking about the dressed up girl. All here but Fabian and Quadri, who was with Fabe in the street.

Tu stood on the boardwalk glaring at Fabian, who was in the lamp-made dusk with the can; with the kid they called Glock or Glacas. HB saw Tu's glare but was too intent to notice it. The glare was not registering. But when Tu turned and said, "What!" HB saw the mirror image of his own disastrous state reflecting off his friend's features. Instantly he grabbed Tu and hugged him.

"We'll be all right, Tu! We'll get back! I'll help you. We'll get'em back."

And, *oh, by the way, what is consciousness*? he was about to ask, but thought better of it for the time being.

Tu leaned briefly against him, shivering. Then he straightened up and pulled back, mumbling his thanks. But he was thinking, *So glad to hear you say that.* So so so.

"Wait here," said HB. He stepped down into the street. The saloon behind him was thundering, raucous, the blinkered horses at their hitching rails patient through it all. In the stinking street, as he approached, he heard Fabian offering something to Glock without quite understanding. "What's going on?" said HB.

The other FivePoints 2017 stood on the boardwalk, watching.

Fabian shrugged his shoulders, dusted his buzz cut with his fingers, and let the happy-light show in his eye. "I'm gonna help him find the others."

"I don't think that's a good idea."

Quadri looked up at each in turn.

"Cussit is!" said Glacas looking at him, thinking, *Outlandish nagger. Outlandish.* "You moon-men kin all hep me kitch'em. More fun that way. You'll see. More fun."

Quadri nodded and jigged up and down on his toes.

Blake Griffin thought: *Wasn't this the guy socked Tu?*

HB had been getting his ribs kicked yet he'd been aware, even so, of that! Of the barman high above him vaulting the counter of what used to be or was going to be Zettler's Gospel Mission. HB thought of wrapping his arms around Fabian and carrying him back to Tu. But Fabian wasn't that small. He might get his back up and resist. They had fought—real, physical—before now. It was not pretty.

"C'mon, HB. We've got time yet. It's only about nine. Check the phone!" Fabian felt his own pockets, cammo cargo pants, up and down. *Where's the phone?*

HB said, "I don't want to check the phone, man; this is serious. Besides, the UT on it might not be right. Tu said it, you did. We got to get our butts—." To Glacas HB said, "We got a show, late show. Got to earn our bread and all that, you dig?" He turned his high-topping broom-cut head sidelong, earrings dangling.

Amazingly Glacas did. The bread part he understood clearly... if not the digging. What did that have to do with it? And he *hated* the casual way it was said. He thought it bold (to him meaning presumed equality). He scowled at HB and spat tobacco juice into the dust.

HB looked away, frowning, considering. His hands balled reflexively. *Better not go there* — remembering the casual bigotry of the saloon. And that other dimension.

Fabian saw the troubled frown and clenched fists. He said, "He's right, we've got to go to the show." He turned back toward the boardwalk, talking low to HB.

Five Points Akropolis

"I think this is an evil place, know that? Thought it was gonna be fun. I wanted to let'er rip, you know?"

"Fabe, you got to stick with us, not them, man. We gonna be daid, you don't. Tu said don't mess with things, and said we got a date—time-date—with November 2017 and don't want to miss it. Please."

Fabian looked quickly at him on hearing that *please*. It was contrite but almost, not quite, desperate. HB was no doubt from time to time intense, but this was *too* intense. The others were with them now, having overheard much of the exchange; and, beer notwithstanding, were greatly sobered.

The fiddle was bowing and banjo plucking. Others came unto the boardwalk entering Paddy's, filtering in from other nighttime venues and activities. (And when Paddy's was closed, in a few hours down the road of time, some underground illegal places would be opening in local houses—called *After Hours Bars* in the Akropolis parlance.)

And among these gathering folk slipped Parry and "the girl." Heirolynn. Still holding hands. He saw that his friend Gregoff the Grak had already been caught and now he wanted to make a play for the can. While 2017 were conferring in a huddle, he hopped down and ran, dragging the girl by the hand. A few of the 2017 heads popped up as he brushed past.

But Glacas was too quick for the little boy. He scrambled to tag Parry, and then the girl—for good measure. Crowing. Strutting in the road cock-a-doodle-doo-ing, hands in his armpits, arms folded like wings flapping. Smiling gap-toothed in his triumph.

"Like that's a big deal," said Jayrai to 2017. Parry came back to the boardwalk drooping, girl in hand. "Don't worry too much about that kid getting you," she said to Parry. He seemed so deflated—like he had actually expected a great victory. "He crows but he's just a rabbit. Bet you!" She was smiling.

Parry perked up a bit.

"Hey," said Jayrai, looking at the girl. "Bet she plays a mean pinball!" Jay was no longer listening to the Z-pod of course—the earbuds had been stuffed into the pocket of her cargo pants along with the pod—but the tune was going through her head as she watched the girl. "A regular pinball wizard," she said to his inquiring look. Parry did not pick up on the first part of that—though one of the game's precursors was on a sideboard in Paddy's. And Parry was never to go in there on any account. But that word *wizard* stuck out.

"Don't you mean witch?" He asked, wide-eyed, wondering. "Girls can't be wizards can they?" The moon-girl was giving him the prickles again. Well, not her so much as *the girl*. He turned to look at her, seeing her for the first time since this afternoon in the doorway when he had run away from 2017. She was staring, not seeing anything—(as he had sometimes till this moment supposed). Was she really a witch? Was she really seeing stuff? And casting spells? She had on the scarf the sisters of St. Invincible's had first put there, but, as usual, it was askew over her thick patch of hair (sticking every-which-way). The lamplight shone down on her stare.

Parry considered. *This is imagining us.*

"Sure," said Jay. "It depends on the gender and there's more than two."

"Oh," said Parry, considering this also. Yes, he had heard something about different genders if you wanted to speak Fronche. James, he thought, had said something about it. "Well, then, what *do* they say in Franche?"

"Franche?"

"What do they call wizards or witches in Franche?"

"Zombies," piped Quadri. "They say zombies."

"Zombies!? *Zommm-bees.*" Parry spit the word around in his mouth awhile, repeating it.

"You know. —Ghouls," said Quadri.

"Oh. Yes. That's what Willie says, too." Parry looked at Heirolynn again. "Willie thinks she's one." Then he looked around for Willie. Quadri nodded vigorously.

There were Willie's knees in knickerbockers, sticking out from the entryway steps to the clasp-locker shop and rooms upstairs. Either he hadn't started playing, or he'd let Glacas catch him. Parry felt a brief compunction. Willie worked so hard. He knew his brother was resting, watching goings on instead of playing or going to bed. But that feeling passed almost at once and he started over, girl in hand. "C'mon," he said to Jayrai and Quadri.

"Hey!" yelled Glacas from the middle of the street. "I thought you had a show!"

"Jay!" called HB. "Don't be doin' that."

"Just take a sec!" She yelled over her shoulder. The girl, and what they thought of her, was intriguing.

Now Pomala was going too! —HB waved Fabian and Tu to follow with him. There might be a better chance if they stuck together—if he did not try to command.

Fabian turned back to Glacas with something nasty—but then thought, *Maybe not. What if*—? And he was again thinking of the Capital of North Regina, and his ancestors. "Just drumming up business!" he called. "—Later. See you at the show!" He walked on. When he caught up he heard Willie saying,

"There's no such thing as ghouls—or ghosts, either, Parry. This is the 20th-century." Hearing it, Fabian got the creeps.

Five Points Akropolis

Willie was smoking what looked like a joint—a home-rolled tobacco cigarette by the smell of it.

There was another kid there now, one with a very faint Churman accent. He was saying, "It has to do with the mutations. She is behind, that is all."

"Does that mean she can catch up?" Parry was asking.

"No. She can not. It is too late for her. All her ancestors were not so fit; and she turned out just so." He indicated her silent, unhearing unseeing, stare. "If her mother and father are not found you will have to take care of her for the rest of her life.... My father will help, I think. He takes an interest in such things." It was a lot for Johan to say, proud taciturn boy that he was.

"Not fit like the coloreds," said Glacas, coming near.

There was silence.

Then HB took a breath and said, "Yeah, that's right. Black *is* Black after all."

Tu could not help being relieved. He shot HB an apologetic look.

Glacas saw it and said, "Chonks, too! And whatever else you moon-men are."

Willie, though exhausted, said, "You've never heard of this stuff in your life, Glacas." He did not look apologetic at 2017, but fierce. "He doesn't know any better," he said. Smoke from his dangling cigarette drifted up into the night.

Pomala said, "Gene therapy. That's what she needs. It may not be too late. He's a geneticist?" She asked Johan.

"A eugenics engineer of some kind?" Johan answered, shaking his head.

"Not that, exactly," said Tu. "It's not based particularly on race."

Pomala said, "Race is bigotry."

"Big-gamy?" Parry was asking.

"A medical man," said Johan Zettler in answer to Pomala's question about his father. He had been leaning against the entry frame where the two doors stood at right angles to one another. He tipped his slouch cap back, looking at her blueness in the glow of lamplight. It even showed through the light of her corset cover, or whatever that was. She was certainly not wearing a corset. *It is hard to tell what she looks like without that.* (The tattooing.) He looked at Jayrai, at her bionic arm. "He would be interested in her, I think." He moved onto the boardwalk.

"Are you through with them?" HB was asking Parry.

"In a minute. But what about Franche?" said Parry to his brother. "Is it the 20th-century there? Have they got witches and wizards, or ghouls and zommbees?"

"No," said Willie.

"No to the 20th-century, or no to zommbees?"

"Yes and no," said Willie, looking at him from under exhausted and weary brows.

"I don't think that's it then, you see," said Parry turning to Jayrai.

"No, you don't understand," said Jay.

"If he doesn't understand it's because you didn't explain it right," said Willie, frowning, abstracted. *Why are they here?*

Blake Griffin suggested, "Maybe we should go to the show now, Jay?" He was walking with great care all around this.

2017 looked at him. HB? Merely suggesting?

All except Tu. Tu was already deep in conversation with Johan. They had moved a little apart and were standing before the darkened (but lamplight reflecting) plateglass of the clasp-locker repair shop. HB looked over at them.

Oh MAN?!

He heard the boy with faint Churman accent saying, "That is not easy to believe. These mutations are random. Why do you think evolution could have a mind of its own, such as you suggest with these words? That would make it God, not evolution. Do not things evolve without, as this suggests, 'thinking about it'? How can anything but humans think?"

HB now stood very close to Tu, almost leaning against him. And still Tu did not notice. Tu, who was normally very conscious of his space ... and of his dignity.

"Take the question of blue—or of green—or any colors, silver and gold," said Tu. "Or of pleasure and pain. Here are examples of it at work in the consciousness: Natural selection knows these sensations, as they rise through the brain it is also knowing—its physical foundation—and preferring it. Consciousness is itself preferred to the inferior unconscious—so that means it's better. Better means planning because planning is better."

"But that would be the same as God," said Johan, contending but in monotone.

"... Not exactly."

"It *must* be mindless."

"Look at the DNA (—I know this means nothing to you but think theoretically then). The DNA molecule is a code manual for building and operating the human being. Genes aren't always alike, so copies vary—with conflicting alleles, I'm saying." He saw the perplexity in Johan's face, who had taken off his cap to see Tu better. "These can be random copies—but maybe not."

Johan stared at him. He said, "Is it like pi? The ratio of the circumference to the diameter. If they can just build a machine—

maybe Cabbage's machine and with a lot of ability—they may find a pattern—I think anyway—"

"We have those now," said Tu. "—on *Gliese 581d*, I mean."

"Oh no, we are back to the vaudeville now." Johan shook his head, did not smile.

"—No, and they've gone out to septillion places and still no overall numerical pattern. The quintessential irrational number where the ratio—"

He elbowed HB. Who was breathing on his neck.

Who stepped back just a bit but said, "—Just please don't get him started on quantum jumps or multiverses, or we'll be here all night!"

"No," said Tu, "that's not the analogy at all."

"Look, I didn't mean it to be—just—" here HB stuck his face right next to Tu's and looked into his eyes real hard.

Tu moved away, eluding interruption, continuing nonstop. "If you don't stick to the math, or you try to grasp it in words instead, you don't get anywhere. I don't. Words can be quantified for statistical analysis for inventing games like BabBle and CritTerRati or for producing a pattern to make, say, old bits of texts fit together, but you can't use words to reduce the math comprehensively. Even we might be summed up mathematically, and turn out to be a line of zeros and ones. So at least with pi you are discovering a *non*-pattern, whereas with the alleles you've got a chance to get it." Without stopping he made another leap: "Comparing the measured and unmeasured particles will get you a different answer every time."

"Oh *man*!" said HB, his face contorting in distaste. "Get outta here with that sht! You're driving me crazy! I should've known better than to think you could explain—everything—*anything* to me."

He kicked fiercely at nothing with his foot. And then again. "You think my consciousness is going to evolve so I can understand this stuff?!"

He looked at Jayrai and Pomala—who nodded vigorously—as if saying, *Tell him!*

"Needs gene therapy," said Pomala.

"I need therapy all right," muttered HB.

They heard pairs of feet running, and then a metallic rattle of the can tumbling across dust and cinders. They all looked that way. Cheenie was flashing that handsome white smile of his, victoriously. Glacas was stomping the cinders in stocking feet. 1900 A.D. all cheered and ran off, even Parry and the girl. All but Johan, who looked at Tu. Willie sat smoking, thinking.

But soon he'd be nodding.

S. Dorman

When Willie came into the dim parlor he saw the dark bulk of Ma lying bunched on her side in the sagging sofa, asleep. So this was how Parry had managed it. He was relieved to see his younger brother had presence of mind to turn low the gas. In his own bare room, he had just mind enough of his own to stop himself falling into bed with his clothes on. But then he remembered how he had left the mower by the iron gate at the cemetery, intending to come back after supper and put it away. That had been forgotten in helping Ma with the clasp-lockers for the Bennett Bros. account due tomorrow. Sixteen boots had needed the finish stitching. He almost teared up. Willie turned abruptly and went back out and down the short hall to the parlor, past Ma gently snoring beneath the window, and out through the kitchen darkness now lit to full gloom by faint lampglow from the street below.

Out on Sharon Road the strangers were gone. He saw that Johan was *It* all by his lonesome; and doing a lackluster job of It. They had a few words together, Willie asking about Parry and the girl. "We don't want it to happen again," he said, meaning, as Johan well knew, that Gwen's father was still on the job. They, too, had soaked up the gossip.

"Maybe the man will be wary of it now," Johan suggested.

"I don't know. Just, if you see him say I said get home with her. Say why. —He doesn't know it was Partum, I guess. So say it if you want." Like James and Ann Gladys, Parry also did not know exactly what had happened—only that, except for bruising, she was hurt in a way that was very very bad but somehow invisible.

Willie went on down toward Stock Exchange past Paddy's Saloon, more subdued now that the fiddler had gone home.

Once inside Akropolis Rural Cemetery, pulling the heavy mower behind him, Willie felt done in. He was grateful he did not now have to push it mowing grass, and that, flipping it over, was easy towing. *Wicker wicker wicker wicker*, it sounded behind him. Crickets were chirruping, bats swooping past unheeded. He did not see 2017 huddled in the summer shadows against the stone wall, deeper in the shade than they had been earlier in the golden evening when the outlander colored kid had asked about Argus.

Willie, though unconscious of their presence ... and tired as he was ... let his thoughts drift in speculations of the outlander strangers. He was wishing Parry had not filled his mind with all that weird stuff, the strange and amazing stories he had been reading. Some of that alien stuff could actually be true, he saw, now that the 20th-century was upon them. He remembered hearing that people in the middle of last century had actually thought of flying—and now here they were: Some people were trying to make it happen. So that was the great thing, and good. What a boon to mankind. Then his mind drifted back to what he knew about the past, as he trundled the mower down the dark path lit only by lampglow from cracks between buildings, and some faintly lit windows, on Bechtel above.

Think how we're progressing. How hard our ancestors worked and endured. Suffered. Making life better a piece at a time. So we could be here now making these machines, marvels. He had looked the other way up toward his father's grave, but now he glanced up past the tomb knoll, hidden by another knoll, some mausoleums and trees, toward where the mansion stood high in which the man who had invented the electric light got married. *That was a lot of work with only a little inspiration.* They are damming the river for power generation. We are going to get rid of the germ-infested sewage water with the aqueduct. The automobile will get rid of horses pooping up and down the street. People won't get as sick anymore. Better paving, no blocks popping out after frost, no mud. Streets and real sidewalks that won't need much repair anytime soon. Bridges everywhere over the A'ndian River made out of steel, connecting all the hills of Akropolis. They can do it all, he thought (ever the forward thinker). And future generations will have jobs maintaining it. Brant sees it, too, James said the other day.

And on his thoughts ran, hectic, as he went down toward the tomb where groundskeeping tools were kept. He had worked himself into that state of exhaustion which knows greater strength and feels no bounds.

Someday there will be small machines to dig graves.... Maybe I'll invent one. I know we are building better and better. Then he thought of the A'ndians seen at *Stonehewn* the other night—almost naked they were. *Of course that was for the show.* They didn't dress like that now. Then he thought—but they *did* not long ago. And that's how we all lived. All our ancestors knew no more than the A'ndians. Everybody had to get better and better. *James and Brant thought it was capital....*

...But Willie thought it was work. *Think of all the hard work it took* to make everything, *takes* to make everything. Think how it's all built, building on that effort—all because everyone works hard like Ma. Once there were great rows of buttons needing buttoned. It took hours to button all those buttons with a buttonhook. Now people can, if they want, have clasp-lockers with teeth and rings to close... and someday soon we'll improve on that so all you need to do is *zip*—pull two pieces of clothes together. How much easier for Ma then.

There are all kinds of math to measure all kinds of stuff. How can there be irrational numbers? Parry said ratio is in rational and irrational. Why can't the ratio of the circle to its diameter be a rational number? Then, abruptly, he muttered, "*Why are they here?*

Who are they? Not the vaudeville, that's sure."

Huddled by the stone wall of the dark Akropolis Rural Cemetery, HBBBAH muttered with extreme distaste. "A line of 0's and 1's."

Pomala said, smiling into the z-pod lit dark, "Or, x's and o's."

Tu had again worked out the calculations—just as the battery now gave out. The display was suddenly and disconcertingly dark. And the cemetery around them, which they had not been attending to while gathered around the lit z-pod, was like a pit surrounded by hidden fire—streetlamps and some household electric glow thrown down from beyond the wall; on the west side where the monoliths of high school and church hunkered as black shadows. Five Points was outside the Cemetery, still with rhythmic nightlife of pool halls, bars, and neighborhood sociability—including kick-the-can—in ebbing and flowing frequency; with its remote fiddling and the tinkling of an upright piano somewhere. They were thinking of wearing their jackets again, ready for the fresh twinkle in time.

As the pod flicked off, Tu felt a great elation and would have jumped in the air and floated, hovering, gently crowing the fact. But he was Tu, so instead he said only, "Got it. And just in time."

They all looked at him, eyes goggling. "You mean," said Jayrai, "the battery *is*—really gone?..."

"You mean we're stuck here without games, apps, anime—anything?" Quadri was bewildered.

"This is it," said Fabian, affirming Tu. "No more anything if we don't get back to FivePoints."

"FivePoints 2017," said HBBBAH. "How I miss the Prez." This was said with fervent affection for all things 2017 CE.

"The Prez!" exclaimed Jayrai. "What about chocolate cinnamon cappuccino? What about my upcoming baristaHood. My hoped-for job! What about Real-Life—*WorldCraft*, *Hadesthon*—Hadesthon—!! This. Better. Be. Right!"

Tu looked blank, but for him it was apologetic. "It's all we've got. Experimental, yes, be glad of that: At least it's not *gedankenexperiment*, it's probably not Schrödinger's cat I hope, but it may be an entanglement—the changing face of Pluto influencing throughout the entire solar system and on out toward the abyss at the center of the galaxy."

"Oh please," said Pomala. "Can we just get back on the wall?" She did not like the eerie feeling of the dark peopled with gravestones and the great shades of scattered mausoleums... though it was far emptier of monuments than she remembered from her escapades there in 2017. Maybe it was that, or the gaslight, or the shadows—so different from the artificial day-glow of the Akropolis light pollution that made FivePoints seem so much friendlier.

Five Points Akropolis

They crept through shadows toward gaslit Stock Exchange Street, climbed up and settled on the wall to await the return of 2017.

From beneath the overhanging boughs, in tree-shadows, they watched the activity down at the corner. So different from what had been the boring traffic, with its homogenized lack of interest—but this morning!? Before, when it was what they knew. So hoping to see that great library again in a moment. In November ... would the sun be shining?

"Let's hold hands," suggested Tu.

They looked at him. *Tu*?! He picked up Pomala's hand and held it. Tu. They groped shyly and held hands, Tu at the FivePoints end, Pomala next to him. Then Jayrai, Fabian, HBBBAH, and Quadri.

"Can I be in the middle?" asked Quadri. He wanted, especially, next to Pomala.

Could the configuration make a difference? A scrambled consultation. They did not recall their exact positions from 2017 at the precise moment of the trans-chronic twinkle. Quad was the youngest. It was a BIG moment: Time to be merciful. Merciful, not teasing. He climbed over HBBBAH and Fabian, sat between Pomala and Jayrai, holding hands. They waited. The churchtower clock, they had agreed, was all they had to go on. The UT clock was no longer streaming, automatically syncing in the pod. As soon as Time twinkled the striking would stop, because clockworks were no more in 2017. The UTC in the pods would start, and the game pick up where they left off.

The hour was about to be sounded. This was *It*. Had. To. Be.

Oh. Please. (Pomala)

Jayrai was thinking, *It's only a game.*

Tu remembered, *It's a game based on science.*

Quadri was hopeful, looking at them.

HBBBAH thought, *We're toast.*

"Look," said Pomala, pointing. "Here comes the autism girl and her keeper."

The small couple was passing on its way to the gate to find Willie. Pomala jumped off the wall and grabbed the girl's hand away.

Willie had put the mower and other tools back into the tomb against the rock, then headed over to the wrought-iron gate, not expecting to meet his brother and the girl. But now—approaching the gate—he heard yelling, tussling. He passed on through. And saw down the boardwalk: a tug-of-war, girl in the middle. Parry on one hand, blue girl on the other tugging with all her might.

"Willie, Willie!! The moon men!"

"What are you doing?!" screamed Fabian. "We've got ONE chance Pomala!"

"She's got to come back with us, it's her only chance! She can get help at the clinic!" Surprise had been her advantage, and now with the clock sounding out toward 11 p.m., she made the wrench, folded the slight unresisting girl to her and backed up the wall. "Oh please, Jayrai! Give me your hand!" She could scarcely clasp the girl and hold hands. "Tu hold my leg! Grab hold my pocket!!"

Willie thudded over the boardwalk toward them seemingly out of nowhere; and Parry, screeching, his hand on the girl's leg where they hung over the mossy wall was not giving up. "Let go of her! Let go!"

Fabian: "Out of here! To the deep." The FivePoints gang had scrambled over the wall into the cemetery, Pomala—wrenching — pulling the passive girl with her. All were holding hands as the clock tolled the fourth hour, and the fifth, and they ran, Willie and Parry only now just tumbling over the wall and after them through shadows.

"In here," gasped Fabian, ever (nominally) the leader. And they rushed toward the greater dark of the mausoleum, unaware that their hiding place of opportunity was already familiar to Willie as the tool shed for grounds-keeping implements. Having been razed in 2010 to make way for the new digital tech mausoleum to assist mourning, this particular vault was unknown to them. They flew into its dark like a flock of homing pigeons and lighted there, closing the door. Here was a deep smell of must, the clanking of shovels and rakes.

Gasping, giggling (some of them), jabbering in hushed tones, they waited for the two 1900 kids to pass. "I thought it was a crypt!" Someone else said, "I thought a dead body'd be in here!"

"Why'd you do that!?" whispered Fabian to Pomala. Remotely they heard the clock gonging 9.

And the doors came open. Willie stepped close to their faces, Parry with him.

"What do you think you're doing, space aliens?" Willie demanded an answer. "Are you going to abduct and take her back with you to Glees planet 5-8 or what-you-call-it?"

From the rear dark where the musk smell was deepest came a movement, quiet, several, firm. The whole group was swept, on the gust of 11, into the night. The mausoleum was not. And, the Akropolis ambient light gone, the night sky twinkled above them.

The girl, still wearing the scarf and Ma's cutdown frock, looked up, recognizing and fascinated by star designs, if not actively remembering. There was the thick Milky Way dividing the lustrous sky in two. Night noises she heard, rapid repetitive clickings, distant howling, slow rhythmic knocking, *coos*. All going into the new design.

Behind *1900* and *2017* was the rock ledge, glistening, dripping with spring moisture. But between it and them stood a wall of brave warriors, fierce as the moon, stolid and gleaming in full panoply of feathers, paint and cat-tailed cloaks—with weapons to hand. *True People* stood there, and one with scar shining across his face—one, namely Quick Claws—had hold of the girl's hand. Another held one of their smaller fellows limp in his arms.

Night shone above them all; twinkling richly in woven, faintly budding, towering high branches of massive chestnuts and oaks.

2017 started back in surprise and thrilling horror. They watched as the scouts led the corn-girl, captive, away.

The A'ndians would walk a league, following downstream through deep high woodland, down toward the river where their canoes were banked. It had taken longer than any one of these scouts had thought: In the morning they'd send up the smoke saying that the girl was found.

The others stood and looked after as these A'ndians, feathers a'glimmer, disappeared along the small brook in shadows. 2017 CE looked around then, bewildered, still holding hands. They saw that the great former rubber capital, former medical laboratory capital of the world—the industrious City of Akropolis—was gone. Just gone. And in its place was a woodland, high, earthy, damp and mysterious. They felt as though shot into deep space, spinning away from the planet and life they knew. And alone could survive in. There was no gravity here to stop them, pull them into the orbit of something welcoming, comforting, pleasurable. Pluto with His sun-changing surface had, ripping, flung them into the outer Kuiper Belt. It would be generations before Neptune, rising, might fling them back again.

At least that's how it felt to FivePoints 2017 CE.

To Five Points 1900 A.D. it was the vaudeville entertainments. The minstrel show had kidnapped the two loving brothers. They were going to be an attraction on the opera house circuit. And there was nothing they could do about it. Except to hold hands and learn to live off the land. Willie, especially, would work on it.

S. Dorman

Epilogue

Ma supposed that the boys, along with the girl, were kidnapped by the aliens to work for the minstrel show. This fate was not known for a certainty. The vaudeville, of course, was gone from the Opera House the day after Willie, his brother Parry, and the girl disappeared. Detective officers Phillips and Levinson were sent on the circuit, in different directions, to see what they might find out. It was not lost on the police that the neighborhood suspected Partum of the girl's rape, as had one or two of the station-house force.

However the Grandmaster did provide for many happy beginnings. Mr. Priam's lawyers cleared Argus in court. Witnesses testified that he was seen walking down the hill, toward Five Points and on to Third St., but there is no crime in walking home. Because it was "well-known" who did it, and because "the girl" was gone, it was no matter to anyone anymore.

Partum became an entrenched drunk and so lost his job lighting lamps. Gwen's catastrophically drunken household could no longer restrict her, making it ideal for her to escape Partum when needed. She went to live with Mrs. Wilusa when the woman bought a small farmstead in Sharon, but this came after Ma gave up the clasp-locker repair shop on Sharon Road. Thirty-five years later, at Five Points Akropolis, one of Partum's female descendants initiated the helpful *Alcoholics Humblus*—a real and continuing appeal to the Grandmaster in another guise.

Ma sold the shop to Gregoff's parents. Later it evolved into the *Zipper Hospital*, which Pomala's great great grandmother owned and operated. Ma went to work at *Stonehewn* mending tack, living in tiny rooms in the carriage house below Miss Priam's, her rooms next to Gilbert's. She did tack repair at *Stonehewn* Farm Tuesdays and Fridays. On Sunday she visited Pop's grave at the newly named Glimmer Dale Burial Park. She and Gilbert were married and got the farmstead and had foster kids, teaching them to labor. Glacas's son (after Glacas got a bit older and had one), went to live there for many years before returning to Five Points. Ma also had more

220

children with Gilbert. She kept a vigil for Willie, Parry and the girl, hoping—with passing time—for their return as grown-ups.

The labor union—United Latex Workers of Ehio—was eventually established, so that safety, wages and health-care, in due course, were also instituted. Justly compensated for their labors, their lives and that of their families stabilized, improving considerably. Children no longer worked at Priam's and other rubber works. Many great gains for Americle's humanity were established.

Mrs. Havard did not marry Mr. Priam. She covered all sides of the trade union question in an unbiased way because her work, and its craft, meant more to her than ideologies or a fight. On finishing the articles on Akropolis industry she moved westward to report on Lac'Lcadill Mishigamaa's nursling auto industry.

Two weeks after the conversation in Brant's room, Argus ate his first meal in the *Leg Bone*, amid a swift and noisy jubilation—full of church folks, friends, kinfolk, and many children. He was in the garden and scullery at *Stonehewn*, happily working again, almost before he knew it. He had no words of condemnation over his treatment in the Groverland Municipal Jail, in part because some of his jailers were Nagros, and in part because Levinson and Phillips got out the word among them of his innocence.

Starlight shone in—there being but scant lamplight on Third St.—on that first night in bed with his Mabel. ...It is left to the reader's imagination of the sweet sounds and sweet words passing, during the sweet sweet lovemaking. Let it be said that Blake Griffin did not get born for no reason. (Nor, we have seen, did Pomala or Fabian; nor, by inference, others of the FivePoints 2017 gang.) Meanwhile, Choco, looked up from his crib, giggling at the sweet noises and shadows over in the dark corner. From that time more people of color were able to move to the neighborhood of Five Points.

Meanwhile, in *Anno Domine* 1769, the A'ndians sometimes spied on the 1900 A.D. brothers to see how they fared. Not too too badly; on account of past reputation (it will again be inferred). Things—articles of bone or flint or deerskin or dried meat of the wapiti—were sometimes left for them ... by way of instruction.

Not long afterward, the clan moved on up to the High Lake, to be called (formally) *Acme Lake and Amusement Park* in 1900 A.D.. The girl had been a tremendous assist to the Grandmaster. Red Fox was given a fine reward because he came close in discerning, and most believed in the corn-girl's worth. She, too, was rewarded: When grown, Heirolynn, now called Rabbit-Foot-Woman-of-Grandmaster, became the squau of Red Fox, assisting him in his capacity of tribal shaman, seer, medicine man, and storyteller. She learned to speak (twice or thrice when spoken to) and, to outward appearance, was not quite so clumsy and stupid: She was a hard worker and gained on it every year.

Five Points Akropolis

SiXPointz HiTopOLis

DuOPolis

S. Dorman

Five Points Akropolis

S. Dorman

Five Points Akropolis